Wild Mystic

OTHER TITLES BY SANDI AULT

NOVELS

WILD INDIGO
WILD INFERNO
WILD SORROW
WILD PENANCE

SHORT STORIES

WILD JUSTICE

A **WILD** MYSTERY

Wild Mystic

SANDI AULT

HandInPaw

HANDINPAW PUBLISHING
Published by HandInPaw Publishing ©2018 Sandi Ault
In the Rocky Mountains of Colorado, USA

WILD MYSTIC ©2018 by Sandi Ault all rights reserved
Published in the United States of America by HandInPaw Publishing
www.sandiault.com

ISBN-13: 978-1-7335099-1-6

PRAISE FOR
THE WILD MYSTERY SERIES

"Scenes of the high, dry, glittering landscape are as clean as a sun-bleached bone, and there are thrills galore…"
— *New York Times Book Review* (WILD INDIGO)

"Ault uses her knowledge of the high, dry West to give us a look at Pueblo Indian culture."
— *Tony Hillerman* (WILD INDIGO)

"Crackles with life and novelty."
— *The Washington Post* (WILD INDIGO)

"Smashing."
— *C. J. Box* (WILD INDIGO)

"Simply put, a page-turner of the highest order."
— *The Barnes and Nobel Review* (WILD INDIGO)

"Ault has another page turner…"
— *Richmond Times Dispatch* (WILD INFERNO)

"Ault is such a good writer that crime fiction buffs who enjoy a good mystery with plenty of action and great background detail will put this on their hold lists. Highly recommended."
— *Library Journal* STARRED REVIEW (WILD INFERNO)

"The vivacious Ault knows whereof she writes in Wild Inferno…Where Ault excels is in developing a suspenseful, action-filled mystery on rugged Southwest terrain."
— *New Mexico Magazine* (WILD INFERNO)

"She's a master at describing nature."
— *Albuquerque Journal* (WILD SORROW)

"Ault is often compared to the late Tony Hillerman. While it's an honorable and helpful comparison, it's also a bit unfair. Ault's novels are unique and original, and they deserve to stand on their own. ...Ault's WILD INFERNO was recognized by Publishers Weekly as one of the Best Books of [the year]. ...Ault, like many a great storyteller of the American West, understands the richness of 'deep time.' And we are fortunate she has once again given us a glimpse into the great heritage of a great people."
   —*Estes Park Trail Gazette*

"Ault has the background to write this outdoor series, and it shows on every page. ...You might as well turn off the phone and lock the door, you are in it until the very last page releases its hold on you. About the book: The suspense is one thing — and there is plenty of it — but you will feel like you're reading a literary work at the same time. Ault uses the language in unique ways."
   —*The Coloradoan*

"Ault's portrait of Pueblo life and the conflict of cultures she dramatizes are integral to her rousing debut."
   —*Kirkus Reviews*

"Tinged with mysticism, this artfully told story should appeal to fans of Nevada Barr...Tony Hillerman... and Margaret Coel."
   —*Publishers Weekly*

"Read this for outdoor adventure and take a walk on the Wild side."
   —*Rocky Mountain News*

FOR TIWA

In loving memory of my great teacher, my dear friend,
my beautiful wolf companion.
You are now and will always be in my heart.

ACKNOWLEDGEMENTS

I would like to thank all my readers, who waited so long and patiently for this book, and who repeatedly clamored for another episode in the WILD Mystery Series.

I would also like to thank my Puebloan family. Whatever my soul is, it is nourished by the practices you have taught me and by the gift of your presence.

AUTHOR'S NOTE

As we all know, truth can sometimes be stranger than fiction. Most of this story is not true. But some of it is based loosely on rumors and legends that may or may not have been drawn from true events.

The characters herein are entirely fictional and not representative of anyone living now or previously—any similarities to persons living or dead are entirely coincidental.

If you, dear reader, see any synchronicities with stories you've heard, they are no doubt due to the great pool of common knowing in the collective unconscious...which anyone can absorb while dancing in or around the edges of the Mystic.

Let your soul and spirit fly into the mystic.

—Van Morrison

Wild Mystic

0

In the exquisite freedom of another world
They wait for me—
Invisible, luminescent.
They are the awakened dreamers
And also the dream,
The formless flying ones,
Who are flight itself,
The masters of unbeing and power.

They wait for me, their betrayer.

Once, I was awake in dreaming
But I have forgotten how to dream.
Long ago, I soared beside them
But I no longer know how to fly.
Now, I yearn to be amorphous
But I am afraid not to exist.
In this small poem
Lives my only power.

—Adoria Ximena Abasolo
United States Poet Laureate

1: INTRUDER

The door of my cabin crashed back against the wall and the silhouette of a man backlit by moonlight filled the opening. I roused instantly from my dream, rolled off the far side of my bed and crouched behind it as I grabbed the shotgun propped in the corner against the wall.

"Jamaica Wild?" the man shouted.

I stayed low, cocked the pump-action with a hard pull, the telltale *Ch-Ch* sounding a warning. "I'm a federal agent," I screeched, my throat dry. "Drop your weapon and put your hands up high, where I can see them." My mind was groggy with sleep. *Am I still dreaming or is this really happening?*

The intruder raised his palms above his head, one of them holding an automatic pointed skyward. "Secret Service," he said, "don't shoot! I'll put it down right here." He squatted low and I heard the *thunk* of the heavy pistol on the wood floor. He stood again, palms raised. "Ma'am, I'm sorry to startle you. I knocked several times, but there was no answer. If you'll allow me to reach into my pocket, I'll show you some identification."

I kept the barrel of the Remington fixed on the man's chest. "You move nice and slow, and if you so much as look like you're going for a gun, I'm going to make hamburger out of you."

He lowered a hand into the deep shadow his body created in the doorway. I could barely make out what he was doing, and I held my breath until he produced what seemed to be a thin, rectangular ID folder high over his right shoulder. He deftly flipped it open, a dark patch against the moonlit sky behind him. "Keep holding that right there. Reach your left hand along the wall inside the door, slow and easy, and then flip that switch," I said.

A shock of light stunned my eyes, but I kept the shotgun trained on my target. In the newly illuminated scene, I saw Mountain poised in a low crouch right in front of the man, ears back, teeth bared, a ridge of hair standing high along the back of his neck and between his shoulder blades. I wondered how long he had been there. He emitted a low, barely-audible growl.

The man saw him, too. "Whoa!"

"Now," I said, ignoring the man's reaction to my wolf companion, "tell your buddy—or buddies—to stay back."

"I assure you, ma'am..."

"Do it," I said, flatly.

He tipped his head slightly to one side. "Stand down," he said, "she's going to look at my ID and then we'll be fine."

"We'll see about that. Toss it on the bed." I tipped my chin toward the mattress in front of me. "Throw it underhanded."

He flipped the folder in a gentle arc onto my down comforter. I held the butt of the shotgun tight to my chest with my right hand, my finger alongside the trigger, as I reached out with my left to get the badge holder. I held it up high, in line with his face, barely glancing at it, keeping my eyes on the trespasser. His credentials looked real enough, but I didn't lower the gun barrel.

"Agent...Harold Coronel," I read. "What are you doing here?"

"I have orders to collect you and escort you to Kirtland Air Force Base in Albuquerque."

"Collect me?" I snorted. "Why?"

"It's a matter of national security. Ma'am, could I ask you to put that gun down and call off your dog?"

"What do I have to do with national security?" I stood up and lowered the shotgun barrel, half-thinking this had to be a dream—even though it felt as real as the throbbing in my head. "I'm a resource protection agent for the Bureau of Land Management. This must be some mistake."

"I assure you, there's no mistake. The data I have says that you work for the BLM. I didn't know for sure if you were here, but since your Jeep was parked outside, I figured you might be, so I knocked. But I was also told that you work in the wilderness, and on a horse half the time, so when you didn't answer the door, I was going to come inside and wait." The man still held his palms up as he nodded toward Mountain. "The dog?"

"Not a dog. He's a wolf. And why did you have to kick the door halfway off its jamb? Couldn't you come back in the morning when you didn't get an answer in the middle of the night?"

"I'm afraid not. This matter is extremely time-sensitive. I couldn't tell if you were here, or if you were, if you were all right. Your dog didn't even bark."

"I told you, he's a wolf. A wolf is a stealth predator. He doesn't bark and give his whereabouts away."

"Could you call him off, please?"

Mountain remained in a menacing pose, low and ready to spring, his teeth still bared. I moved around the bed and went to him, feeling exposed in my boxer-shorts-and-tank-top jammies, Agent Coronel still standing in the doorway just a few feet from me, the cold air from outside hitting the bare skin on my legs and arms. "It's okay, Buddy," I said to Mountain. Gently, I placed my hand against his back, just below the shoulders. I felt him relax a little, and his ears twitched and then stood upright. "It's okay," I said again, soothing him with a soft stroke down his spine. He pulled back, still eyeing the stranger warily, then circled behind me and stood at my side, fixing his eyes once again on the man.

Agent Coronel slowly lowered his hands. "I had no idea you would be so combative."

"You don't know much about me, then. I have my reasons. Besides, when you crashed through my door, I was fast asleep, dreaming."

"That must have been some dream. Most people don't spring for cover and then rack a shotgun the moment they wake up."

"Most people don't break in the home of someone they haven't met."

"I only meant to temporarily disable the lock," Agent Coronel said, as he bent down and picked up his weapon, then straightened and holstered it. He began to examine the damage. "That door doesn't fit well in the frame, so the bolt doesn't extend as far as it should into the box. The receiver came right off when I put my shoulder into it." He started re-attaching the screws that held the dead bolt receiver with the tip of a pocket knife. He looked up from what he was doing and frowned at me. "I'll make sure your door is all right, and that will give you a few minutes to get dressed, and to do whatever you need to do to secure the wolf."

"Secure him? I'm not leaving him."

"I'm afraid you'll have to in this instance."

"Look, I'll come with you, even though you haven't explained to me why I should. But he goes with me. So you do whatever you have to do to prepare yourself, because I'm not leaving him."

"Ma'am, there's no place for an animal like that in the car."

"I'm not going without him."

"We don't have room. He's pretty good-sized."

"Then I'll drive and follow you. My Jeep is all set up for traveling with him."

"That's not our protocol," Coronel said.

"Well, figure it out." Still clutching the shotgun in my right hand, I went through the narrow pass-through closet and into my tiny bathroom with the wolf on my heels—and once Mountain and I were inside, I closed the door.

2: THE MISSING

The two agents rode in the front of the black Chevy Tahoe, and Mountain shared the backseat with me because the rear cargo area was fitted with a locked-top weapons cache. I'd had to work to get the wolf into a strange vehicle, luring him in by tugging on his lead and climbing in first, gradually persuading him to follow me. When the agents tried to assist, Mountain had turned and snarled.

"Stay back!" I told them. "He's not aggressive, but he will defend himself if he feels threatened—you saw that when you came through my door." I managed to coax Mountain into the car, but he wasn't accustomed to riding in a passenger seat, so he didn't know how to comport himself. I pulled him partway onto my lap and the rest of his big body sprawled across the vacant stretch of seat—but his legs hung off the front of it awkwardly, and his feet twitched until he finally pushed them into the back of the driver's seat for leverage. He remained like that for the first half-hour, panting and drooling out of fear. Because he was nervous, he began shedding profusely, and strands of his mane began to come off in my hand when I petted him. I knew the previously-pristine interior of the car would soon sport a layer of wolf hair. I had brought his favorite toy, a long braided rope tug made of cotton cord, tied in the center and at each end. The thing weighed three or four pounds depending on how much wolf slobber it contained, and was too thick for my hand to close around completely. I wagged this in front of Mountain, thinking he might want to chew on it, but he paid no attention. So I stroked his neck and hummed softly into his ear, and finally he lowered his head into my lap and began to relax. A few minutes later, I saw his legs droop and I knew he was asleep.

When we first started out from my cabin in rural northern New Mexico, I had queried the two agents in the front about why they had come for me and where we were going. "You'll be briefed when we get to Kirtland," was all Coronel would say.

As we sped through the black landscape that flashed by outside, the blue-lit interior of the car with its big navigation screen made me think of a small ship traveling through deep space. I tried to sleep away what I knew would be a long, silent drive—wishing I could return to the dream I had been enjoying when these two bozos had so rudely interrupted me. Once, I almost dropped back into that dream, the smell of my lover's neck, the warmth of his chest as I lay against it, listening to his heartbeat...*his heartbeat!* That was what had awakened me when I had been fast asleep in my bed, dreaming—when Kerry's heartbeat suddenly sped up and got so loud that I feared his chest would burst open...and then the door flew back against the cabin wall. Now I realized that the sound of his pounding heart must have been Agent Coronel knocking.

I slumped against the cold glass of the car window, missing Kerry. He had left only two days ago to resume his forest supervisor assignment in Washington State, a job which had separated us for a year. Even though I knew he was gone, that dream had felt as real to me as the precious time we'd just spent together in my cabin with Mountain. I could have stayed in that dream forever. And so, as I huddled in the back of the car with my four-legged best friend, trying not to give into fear and confusion, I calmed myself with the memory of those wonderful days with Kerry.

☽

When we drew to a stop on the tarmac of the airfield that Kirtland Air Force Base shared with the Albuquerque Sunport, the clock on the dash read 3:05 a.m. I peered out the window and saw two large metal buildings, brightly lit and marked with the distinctive star-and-stripes symbol used by the Air Force. Coronel got out and opened the car door for me, and I unfolded myself and stood upright. Mountain scrambled out after me and I grabbed for the lead I had snapped onto his collar before we left home. I looked across the top of the car toward the runway and saw a big blue and white plane; the lettering that ran nearly the whole length of its side read: UNITED STATES OF AMERICA. "Is that what I think it is?" I asked.

Two men stood guard at the bottom of the airstairs. Coronel and his pal went to meet them. They gestured at me and then at Mountain. There was an animated discussion, and then one of the sentries darted up the stairs and was gone for only a few seconds before he came back, wearing a stern frown but nodding his head. Coronel came back toward me. "I had a tough time convincing those guys that you weren't going anywhere without your wolf. Come on. Bring him."

I stared at the plane. My feet had turned to concrete. "Agent Coronel, what am I doing here?"

"You're about to meet the president-elect of the United States," he said. "You and Mountain." He waved a hand forward. "Follow me."

The ordeal of getting a wolf to climb the airstairs would have made great comedy if we hadn't been repeatedly reminded of the urgency of the timeline. I'd had to sweet-talk and near-drag Mountain while two clearly nervous Secret Service agents formed a wall behind him so he couldn't retreat. Unsure of what he might do, they had reluctantly followed my directions and moved steadily upward behind him, funneling him into the door of the plane. Once onboard, I loosened the grip I held on his lead, and Mountain suddenly broke away, making a mad dash down the wide aisle. He bolted into the nearest open door, where he proceeded to rush behind the desk and then huddle beneath the surprised occupant of the office chair.

"Well, hello there!" President-elect Maria Clarissa Vargas looked down at this unruly visitor. She reached out her hands and picked up Mountain's muzzle and looked directly into his face as she spoke to him. "Was that scary for you, to board this big plane?" Her voice took on the tenderness one might use when speaking to a small child, and she ruffled his mane and stroked his neck vigorously. "Well, you're very brave, and I want you to know that everyone is excited about having you as our guest."

Mountain trembled, his ears back, eyes wide. He turned his head, still in her grip, and peered over the top of the desk to find me, and when he did, he looked relieved, but only slightly.

"I'm so sorry," I said. "I've never seen him go up to a stranger like that, much less allow one to pet him! He'll shed all over you. Mountain, come over here, baby. It's okay." I said, patting my thigh. The wolf didn't move.

"I'm sorry, too, to have to summon you here in the middle of the night." The president-elect released her hold on Mountain and he half-scrambled around the desk. "They told me that you refused to come without your wolf. He seems tame enough. I really like him." She stood up. "As you might imagine, my every move is scrutinized and we had to do some maneuvering to keep this meeting off the press's radar. I'm due in Los Angeles later this morning, so I'm going to have to be brief." She nodded at Mountain. "What can we do to help put him at ease?"

"Believe it or not, it's better if we just ignore him. He's not like a dog, so a lot of affection and attention keeps him worked up.

If I could sit, he might relax a little. And while we talk, it will be best if we don't make any sudden moves."

"I'll ignore him, then. But I think it's safe to say that the crew will be disappointed that we can't make a big fuss and let everyone meet him. I'm pretty sure this is the first time we've had a wolf onboard a plane in the presidential fleet." She gestured toward one of the chairs opposite her desk. "Have a seat. Can we get you anything—you or Mountain?"

"I'd love a cup of coffee." I lowered myself into the chair and then patted the floor in front of me, hoping the wolf would take the hint and come lie down. "Mountain probably needs a drink of water."

Vargas picked up a phone. "Coffee and a bowl of water, please."

Mountain stood in front of me while I continued to pat the floor but he did not lie down; he was too afraid for that. Instead, he maneuvered around and took a position standing on his front legs while he pressed his haunches onto my knees until he was virtually sitting on my lap. I shook my head. We must have looked ridiculous.

Maria Vargas moved slowly around in front of her desk, as Mountain tried to settle himself into this ludicrous position. A young man came in with a tray of coffee with cream and sugar, a small plate of biscotti, a white china bowl with a blue and gold presidential seal imprinted in the bottom of it, and a carafe of water. I poured Mountain a drink and he moved from my lap and stood again as he slurped from the bowl. I poured him some more and lowered the dish to the carpeted floor, and the wolf obliged me by lying down to finish his drink.

When Mountain had settled, I sat upright again.

Vargas held out a cup of coffee that she had poured for me. "Do you take anything in it? Cream? Sugar?"

"A little cream, please," I said, and reached to accept the proffered cup. "Thank you so much."

"I would love to ask you a thousand questions about him, but let's get down to brass tacks, shall we?" Vargas took a perch on the front of her desk, lowered her head and stroked one eyebrow repeatedly. "I had a roommate in college," she began. "She was my best friend, and also my maid of honor when I married my late husband. Do you know who it is that I'm talking about?"

I shook my head. "No. I'm sorry."

"Well, she is very well known in certain circles. She is the current Poet Laureate of the United States of America. Her name is Adoria Ximena Abasolo. Now do you know who I'm talking about?"

"Yes. She won the Nobel Prize."

"She did. And a Pulitzer and many other awards. And she was commissioned to write the traditional poetry offering for my upcoming inauguration. She and I had discussed the elements of this poem in some detail, first on the phone, and then in a series of emails. And last week, she sent me a draft to review, but what she sent was incomplete—a little crazy, to tell the truth—and it bore no relevance to the ceremony it was supposedly written for." She got up and walked around to the working side of her desk and opened a drawer.

The moment she moved, Mountain jumped up. I hastily threw my left arm around his neck and soothed him, holding tight to his lead with my right hand. "Shhhh…" I whispered into his neck. "It's okay."

Ms. Vargas drew a pack of cigarettes and a lighter from the drawer and set them on the desk. She took a deep breath and then took her hand away. She walked around to the front of the desk and resumed her perch. I noticed dark circles under her eyes. "I quit smoking five years ago," she said. "Now I find myself struggling with it as if I had never stopped."

I waited for her to go on, still stroking Mountain gently on one side. He sat his rump down on top of my left boot and pressed into the front of my leg.

"You see, we think something has happened to Adoria Abasolo. Her participation in the inauguration ceremony was very important to me. Not only is she my oldest and dearest friend, she is the first Latina Poet Laureate. And I will be the first Latina president, a single woman now, a progressive woman with ideas of my own. It has been a long and difficult battle to arrive at this milestone.

"I ran for the presidency on a platform of real change— changes that will end practices that are harmful to the environment, that will bring equality to women and minorities. There are very powerful people who don't want these kinds of changes. Some are making a lot of money off of fossil fuels, many more benefit from keeping minorities from prospering; they don't want to see a woman—especially a Latina—in a position of this much power. They would love to see me embarrassed—or better, defeated in some way. I won the election, but I have no illusions about having the support of congress or their controlling allies." She stopped and looked at me, clasping her hands together tightly. President-elect Vargas looked tired, as tired as I felt. "I want to know what has happened to Adoria because I fear she may have been harmed."

I widened my eyes and waited, intrigued.

She did not go on but instead looked at me expectantly.

"I guess I don't understand what all this has to do with me."

"You have ties to Tanoah Pueblo. You're the liaison to the tribe for the BLM. The last time Adoria wrote to me with that partial draft I mentioned, she said she was going to some kind of ceremony at the pueblo and would finish the poem the next day. No one has seen her since. We tried to find out about the event, but the reservation is observing some kind of silence..."

"Quiet time—kind of like a spiritual retreat from the modern world. It's not literally a time of silence, it's more about honoring the old ways. They have a lot of kiva doings going on right now."

"Kiva doings?" She wrinkled her brow. "I won't ask, only because we don't have the time. An agent in my detail tried to investigate discreetly, and the tribe started a ruckus that threatened to bring the media in. We don't want the press...well, we want to keep them out of this as long as we can. So I want you to make some inquiries. Will you do that?"

I shook my head no. "I can't...it's considered rude to ask questions."

"I beg your pardon?"

"The Tanoah people consider it rude to ask a direct question. I can't make inquiries. Even if I tried, it would not be successful. It would shut down all conversation."

Maria Vargas's face reddened. Clearly agitated by my refusal, she went back around the desk, placed a cigarette between her lips, and struck the lighter. It flared as she held it in front of her, but she did not light up. Instead, she returned both items to the desk top, and sat down in the high-backed chair behind her. "I have no way of knowing what has happened to Adoria, but there are more reasons to be concerned that she is missing than simply because she is my friend. Here's one example: she is an American citizen, but she was born in Brazil, and the United States is in the middle of some important negotiations with Brazil's government right now regarding reducing their reliance on fossil fuels. I don't know if her disappearance has something to do with that. I just don't know what has happened to her or why."

"But surely the Secret Service or the FBI...I mean, you have all the means at your disposal..."

"No, I don't—not yet. Right now, all I have is my Secret Service Security Detail, just a handful of people. Two of them who are loyal to me and were with me through the campaign are working on this. But that reservation is evidently some kind of a black hole for them. Even if I were already in office, Tanoah Pueblo is a sovereign nation, so we have no authority. If Adoria is there, we have no way of finding out quietly. I need someone on the inside. Miss Wild, I am asking you to do this as a personal favor to me. Will you help me find my longtime friend?"

I realized my mouth was open and my head was still shaking ever-so-slightly back and forth. My body was saying a firm *no, there is no way, I can't do it, I shouldn't even try,* but I could not find a way to voice it to the woman who was about to become president of the United States of America.

Vargas did not wait for me to answer. "You seem pretty capable to me. You found a way to get a wolf onboard a presidential plane in the Air Force's Special Air Mission fleet. You can find a way to get onto Tanoah Pueblo and find out what happened to Adoria Abasolo." She picked up a folder from the desk and looked me directly in the eye. "One more thing, Miss Wild. I need you to keep this conversation strictly between us. An agent with my Secret Service detail will get you started. No one else is to know that I asked you to do this." She handed the folder across the desk. "This is all we have: there's some background, the latest intelligence reports we have on Adoria, and copies of the most recent emails between her and me. There's also copies of some things they found on her desk, and a few poems she was working on. You'll see, as time goes on, that her writing became strange, almost cryptic. We discovered that she was scrawling odd notes on everything, on the side of a utility invoice, on store receipts and even on a twenty dollar bill."

I took the folder and began to page through it. I read a few lines of a poem:

I turn my body inside out
and from the bottom of my belly the moon
speaks.
I empty myself in continuous conversation with
the world
that is no longer a world
and I am no longer in it.
"Merge with me," the moon whispers,
and I vanish!

"Wow," I said.

"I know," Vargas replied, nodding her head. "She sounds like she's become some kind of a wild mystic."

3: THE ANCIENTS

It was around eight in the morning when I arrived at the home of my medicine teacher at Tanoah Pueblo. When I got out of my Jeep in front of her house, I smelled smoke from Momma Anna's woodstove, the sweet-sharp, sap-rich scent of burning *piñon* wood. As I walked up the path, I bent low to avoid the bare limbs of the sprawling apple tree that guarded her entry, then pounded with the butt of my fist on the wood door. Mountain waited anxiously beside me as a small filament of drool escaped his lip and stretched impossibly long, almost reaching the packed dirt beneath the brush arbor that shaded the front of the old adobe home. The wolf salivated because he knew he was in for a treat: our hostess would almost certainly give him a chunk of venison or bison out of a stew she might have cooking on the stove. This was the way she welcomed everyone—she fed them the moment they arrived.

My medicine teacher opened the door wrapped in a Pendleton blanket. Beneath her long dress and apron, she wore her traditional white deerskin moccasins billowed in soft folds from knee to ankle. This handmade footwear was kept for ceremony and for Quiet Time, in keeping with the old ways, when no one wore a heeled shoe in the Pueblo. "Come in, I feed them." She nodded her head toward the only bedroom in her small house. "You talk them now. I give this wolf breakfast."

By *them,* Momma Anna was referring to her ancestors. During Quiet Time, the ancient ones were said to gather and move about the village as if they had never left. They would appear behind you when you were cutting firewood, or even join you in the outhouse when you were emptying your bladder. They expected to be fed, to be referred to as if they were present, and to be included in all your activities. Some stories shared at winter's Quiet Time gatherings told of incidents when a grandparent or great uncle would join a man in bed with his wife and try to participate in their lovemaking. These tales brought shouts of laughter and also instilled a little fear in the youth who might be considering a secret assignation.

Under the window in Momma Anna's bedroom stood a makeshift altar. A spread of filled plates lined up before tokens representing the departed, a framed photograph or ceremonial object from each ancestor. On the floor a folded horse blanket waited, and I knelt on this and dipped my chin in a perfunctory show of respect. "Hi. How are you guys?" All the candles flickered at once, with a *whoosh*, and the curtains rustled. A few years ago, I might have assumed that Momma Anna's old adobe house was just drafty. But by now, I had witnessed enough strange events at the pueblo, and in the company of Momma Anna elsewhere, that I had come to believe that things weren't always as black and white as they seemed. I assumed a more reverent attitude. "Greetings, grandparents, aunties and uncles," I said, "and blessings to all of you." It was the custom not to invoke the names of the dead, so I was careful not to directly address those members of the family I had known— Grandma Bird and Grandpa Nazario, who were Anna's parents, and Yellow Hawk, her brother, whose tragic suicide I had witnessed firsthand. "I am honored to be in your presence," I said, looking across the plates of buttery fried eggs atop *posole* in red chile, thick wedges of pueblo bread, slices of fried apples, and venison stew. "I am so happy we will be seeing one another again during this time. Enjoy your meal." I stood and bowed my head again, then went into the kitchen where Momma Anna was adding wood to her cook stove and Mountain was furiously licking at an empty plastic bowl that he held between his paws.

"*Tst-tst.* You not stay long, keep them company," Anna said.

I widened my hands in a sort of half shrug, half surrender, then untied the scarf I had draped over my hair, which I had been instructed to wear during sacred times at the Pueblo. I also removed my coat and hung it on the hook behind the door.

Momma Anna had taken off her blanket wrap and folded it over the back of her chair. "Wash hands. You sit there," she said, pointing to another chair at the table. "You eat." She carefully flipped an egg in a cast iron skillet and then dished this up atop some *posole*.

I went to the sink and dipped my hands into the water in the blue speckled enamel pan. I washed with the big wedge of goat's milk soap kept in a dish in the window sill beside the peyote plant. Momma Anna used to make soap herself, but lately she had been buying it from the Hispanic women who lived in the villages in the mountains, one of many small signs that consumerism was beginning to infiltrate the total self-sufficiency that had for centuries sustained this ancient pueblo. I took my place at the table and my medicine teacher set a plate before me.

"Eat." She sat in the chair opposite me.

"You're not having any?"

"I wait for my parents, my brother. They leave me bite, I maybe eat that."

"Oh. If you want me to wait, too, I can eat the leftovers…that is, if there are enough."

"There be plenty. You eat now. I already fix you plate."

With a chunk of the bread, I broke the soft, intensely yellow yoke of the egg which had probably been laid by one of Momma Anna's chickens less than an hour before. I took a bite. "Thank you so much, Momma Anna. This is delicious. I was really hungry. I was up most of the night and didn't have time to eat before I got here."

"You skinny, look like stick. You little bit round that next other time, look more nice, pretty. Not this time. You need eat."

I thought about Kerry telling me I was too thin, asking me why I'd lost weight. My clothes were too big lately; I had to cinch in my belt to keep my jeans up.

"You get full belly, maybe you sleep good when it dark."

I spooned *posole* into my mouth and nodded. "This is so good."

When I had finished my meal, I got up to wash my plate, and Momma Anna watched me. "Your boy go away," she said.

"Yes. He went back to his job in the northwest." I looked at her and tried to smile, but felt my eyes grow moist.

"You got sad heart."

"I do. I dreamed about him last night. It was as real as if he was right here." I held my fist to my chest.

"You put food out, that one. Him maybe come visit in nighttime. Might put a baby in that belly so you get round, next time."

I opened my mouth, but didn't speak. I didn't know how to respond to her suggesting that Kerry might impregnate me from a distance in my dreams. I waited a few seconds, and then decided to take a stab at getting some information I could use. "Momma Anna, I am trying to find someone."

She gave me a guarded look.

"This woman I am looking for was said to have come to the pueblo, but now, no one can find her. I thought maybe you might know her."

"This Quiet Time. You not insult old ones."

"I won't. I'm not. I'm not asking questions. I'm just telling you what I'm doing."

Anna Santana stood up, as if she might want to be ready in case she needed to flee the room.

"I'm going to say the woman's name to see if you might know her. If you might have seen her. If you might be able to give me some ideas about how to find her."

She didn't move.

"The name of this woman is Adoria Abasolo. This is who I'm looking for."

"Spanish." She gestured vaguely toward the south wall of her kitchen. "You maybe ask you friend up there. I not know that one, that name you say."

"Adoria," I said again. "Her name is Adoria."

"You ask that healer."

"Tecolote? You know that she lives in the mountains a long way from here. They say Adoria came to the Pueblo the last time anyone saw her. Now she's missing. I think I need to be talking to people here."

Momma Anna considered this for a few moments. "You maybe got some money."

I reached in my pocket. "A few bucks." I gave her a questioning look.

She jutted her chin upward in the direction of the window. "You maybe feed him, talk him."

I wrinkled my brow, wondering if she meant one of her ancestors. Then I remembered the time she referred to her peyote plant as *him*, and said we had to feed him coins because we had *talked about him.* "Oh. Oh, I get it." I fished around in my pocket some more and came up with a couple quarters. "All right. Just feed him, right? Like before?"

"You feed him. You talk him."

I went to the windowsill and put the quarters on the dry dirt in the pot next to the peyote plant. "I'm looking for Adoria Abasolo." I felt utterly ridiculous, but no less determined. "Please give me any information that might help me find her."

"Now, you go," Momma Anna said, picking up her blanket and putting it around her shoulders before escorting me to the door. She pressed against my back to hurry me along. I grabbed my coat and scarf off of the hook, but she gave me no time to put them on before she had opened the door and was ushering me through. "You cover that yellow hair," she scolded, and she closed the door almost on top of me. A moment later, the door opened just slightly, and I didn't see Momma Anna, but Mountain barely squeezed through, and the door shut behind him.

4: THE BOSS

When I got in my Jeep, a gust of wind blew up out of nowhere and brushed past me, hurrying to get into the car and see what it could stir up. I had left the folder of papers President-elect Garza had given me on the passenger seat and—animated by this stiff blast of air—the blue cardboard file sprang open and the sheaf inside shuddered with a sound that reminded me of a deck of cards being shuffled. Several white sheets flew out of the stack and hurriedly smacked hard against the passenger side window, flattened and trembling, as if they were desperately hoping for someone outside to see them and help them escape. I managed to pull the door shut behind me before any more pages took flight. As I gathered them back into the folder, I noticed a photocopy of a receipt from a chain store in Española. The printout of itemized purchases was so faded that I could only make out a few things on the list:

> SANTA FE TORTILLAS
> COLBY CHEESE
> BLUE SKY ALMOND MILK
> NATURAL AMERICAN SPIRIT LOOSE TOBACCO

On the bottom of the receipt, a poem had been written in small letters so neat and even, they might have been rendered by an architect:

I won't sleep tonight.
Tonight, they are coming again,
I feel it.
One more time, they will show me
the glowing root
That connects them
A beautiful new race of beings.
I am the missing stalk.

I returned this to the folder and then reached into the back for my backpack. I set it on top of the folder in the seat to prevent the file's contents from fleeing again. As I drove the narrow dirt road that led west out of the pueblo, my BLM-issued cell phone rang, startling me. It had such a loud and unpleasant tone that I had dubbed the device *the Screech Owl.* I punched the hands-free button on the wheel of my Jeep. "Wild, Resource Protection."

My boss Roy asked, "You're back from vacation today, right?"

"I am."

"You anywhere close to the office? Where are you?"

"Just minutes from you, Boss. I'll be right there."

"I'll be waiting."

When I entered Roy's office, he was on the phone. I sat in one of the chairs in front of his desk while Mountain ran around behind it to greet Roy. The Boss absent-mindedly patted the wolf, then groused at the party on the other end of the phone line: "What do you mean you can't find him? He's got to get those cows out of that meadow." He paused a moment. "Well, tell you what: you go down to that little café there and you get yourself a big old cup of coffee and then you hang around there while people come in and out for *sopapillas* and breakfast burritos, and you watch for him. And if you don't see him, you spread the word that we're going to confiscate his cattle if he doesn't get them off of that meadow right away, and we're going to have us a big ol' barbecue right here between the offices of the Forest Service and the BLM and cook us some beef. See if that doesn't get him up there to get those cows." He slammed down the phone receiver.

"Lemme guess," I said. "Somebody didn't renew their grazing permit."

"Worse than that. It's that Eddiejoe Ibanez. He does this every year—brings his cows down in winter and leaves them someplace without a permit. This time, he's put them right outside the ranger station in Peñasco, behind that meadow where they graze the stabled horses. He's either cut or beat down the fence back by the tree line so his cows can just wander out into the horse pasture. So now, when the rangers put out extra bales of hay when it snows, his cattle just mosey on over and get them some of the high-priced chow, too. That Ibanez is a real piece of work."

"Why is that our problem? That's Forest Service land, right?"

"Aw, it's one of those gawdang grey areas. That meadow is Forest Service land, but on two sides, it abuts BLM land, and the cows have wandered from our land through the fence onto theirs. So we get the ball. Ain't we lucky?"

"Well, hopefully your idea will work, and Ibanez will come get his steers. You wanted to see me?"

"Not me. None other than his royal highness, the Deputy State Director from Santa Fe is in the conference room waiting to talk to you."

I rose from my chair.

"Wait, before you go, I got a little news. Remember last month when you were riding fence lines down around Rinconada and you reported that dog that was bit by a bat?"

"Yes. I took the bat to the lab and called animal control about the incident. I'm hoping the dog didn't test positive."

"Well it did. Thought you'd want to know."

"Oh, no. I hope they can save the dog."

"They got it quarantined. I'm sure they'll do whatever they can."

"If you hear any more, keep me posted. So, what does the director want with me? And why'd you let me sit here and listen to you for so long with him waiting?"

"I just like you, I guess. And I don't mind keeping his majesty on ice for a bit, seeing as how he hasn't set foot in this office for years, and now all of a sudden, he comes by in person to pilfer one of my people even though he darn well knows we work on a skeleton crew around here all winter long. Didn't come to see me, no. Instead, he says he's on his way to Farmington and thought he'd just stop in and brief you on the way. Now you know as well as I do that Taos is not on the way to Farmington from Santa Fe." He raised his eyebrows at me, looking for a reaction.

I realized this must be about my new covert task to find the missing poet, so I tried to act nonchalant. "Well, I better not keep him waiting." I reached down to touch Mountain, who was already standing up. "C'mon, Mountain."

Roy stood, too, but he wasn't quite ready to let me leave. "The director says you'll be on assignment out of the Santa Fe office for a few days. I figured since he was here to purloin one of my crew, I'd guilt him into signing off on those new vehicle decals with the BLM seal. We'll try to get your Jeep into the shop in Santa Fe to have them put on in the next day or two while you're down that way."

"Okay. Just give me a shout."

Roy stalled me again. "Evidently some archaeologist surveying up around Picuris Pueblo doesn't know how to get along with the Indians and needs your help. So when you finish staving off the next Indian war, let me know. I might have a problem with a bear up where you're going."

"A bear? Now? Usually they're hibernating this time of year."

"I know. I figured it could wait a few days for that reason—I can't tell what's really going on. Over the New Year's holiday, an emergency crew for a cellular company was working on a tower up that way, and reported that a bear had broken into one of those caves at the mica mine. Said it was all boarded up one day, then the lumber had all been tore through and it was open the next, and that scared them half to death."

I wrinkled my brow. "That doesn't sound right. If it warms up enough for black bears to come out at all this time of year, they're half asleep—and if they don't find an easy food source, they go back in their dens until spring."

"Yeah, could be they were smoking a little too much Bob Marley, it being a holiday weekend and all. Anyway, that road into the mine is supposed to be closed with a gate across it so folks can't go in there and get into trouble. But the cell tech said the gate wasn't locked. They were able to go through without a key. Wouldn't hurt to check it out when you're done."

"Wouldn't this be something for the mine's people to look into?"

"Mine's been closed for months now. They boarded it all up and went out of business. It's on BLM land, which used to be reservation land before some bureaucrat took a payoff decades ago and issued the mining company a permit. We still manage the mining lease. Anyway, don't worry about this now. You go take care of whatever it is the higher-ups want, and I'll have you check out the bear report when you get done with that."

"All right, but if it was a bear, she's probably back in her cave fast asleep now." I headed down the hallway toward the conference room with the wolf scampering behind me.

5: OFF BOOK

The Deputy State Director was sitting in the conference room when I came in. He got to his feet. "Miss Wild?"

I was a little nervous about how this was going to unfold. I extended my hand and walked toward the director, Mountain behind me. "Please, call me Jamaica."

"I'm Wade Nichols. I stopped by to give you a temporary change of assignment." As he held out a copy of orders transferring me to the Santa Fe office as a loaned asset, he glanced down at the wolf. After his face registered initial surprise, he did exactly what I preferred for people to do when they first encountered Mountain—he ignored him completely. "For the next few days, your assignment states that you will be assisting a field archaeologist named Prescott who is dealing with a land boundary issue between the BLM and Picuris Pueblo. He's there in the field. Just stop by and see him, if you have a chance, so long as it doesn't interfere with what you're already doing."

"So do I check in at the Santa Fe Public Lands headquarters, or do I go directly to Picuris?"

"You are not required to report to anyone. Just stop by and say hello to Prescott if you have a chance. Roy will be looking for you to come back to work here by Friday, but until then, you will be on your own schedule. You're off book, as far as the BLM is concerned."

☽

After I settled Mountain into the back of my Jeep, I pulled out of the BLM parking lot and drove to the nearest gas station. I parked on the side and retrieved a small black pouch from my backpack. Agent Coronel had given it to me after I met with the president-elect and told me to open it when I got my new assignment. I used my pocket knife to break the seal. Inside was a smart phone and a car charger. It startled me when it began vibrating in my hand, making a buzzing sound. I pressed the screen with my finger, and before I could speak, I heard the faint sound of a woman's voice: "Good morning, Miss Wild."

I held the phone to my ear.

"You will see a GPS position of interest when you open the maps application. Should you need to contact me, dial zero. Have a safe and productive day." She hung up.

I pressed the *Map* icon and a rendering of northern New Mexico filled the screen. I pinched and spread my fingers to zoom in, and recognized the area immediately. A red dot hovered southeast of Picuris Pueblo, between the tiny villages of Ojito and Peñasco. "Hey Buddy," I said to Mountain, "We're going up the High Road."

The dot on the map led me into the heavily-forested mountains of northern New Mexico, via a stretch of high-altitude two-lane highway rolling through switchbacks and S-curves and small villages still living partly as they did when the Spaniards first came to settle this land. Because these mountain enclaves were so remote, this part of New Mexico had been slow to modernize. In the tiniest hamlets, a solitary dirt and gravel road led to a church and a few surrounding homes that constituted the community, and these rustic routes closed with snow through the winter and became too muddy from the melt-off in the spring to travel except by foot or horseback. Even ATVs bogged down in deep snow or in the thick, slick mud known as

La Mugre to the locals. Villagers here still spoke an ancient dialect of Castilian Spanish as their first language and carried on religious rituals from the time before the Vatican ruled against self-flagellation and other means of mortification of the flesh. Although time had begun to march forward here in the past few years, its progress was slow and uneven along the High Road.

The map led me to a short stretch of gravel road that was the sole access to two parallel plots adjoining a large tract belonging to the Mountain Mission, a monastery populated by a dwindling order of Trappist monks. One of the lots was undeveloped, a meadow with a gated, grown-over two-lane dirt track. A low necklace of fog hung over the trees at the end of the trail, and beyond it I could see the Picuris mountains, their peaks white with snow. In contrast, the drive to the southern parcel looked well-used and the steel gate had been pushed back to the edge of the lane and left open. I could see a structure on a low ridge, set back into the tree line. I turned onto the drive and took it toward the house. At the end of the lane, a cleared parking area had been spread with pea gravel and lined with young trees planted in neat rows. Beyond this, an adobe wall, with an arched wooden gate that stood slightly ajar. Through the narrow opening, I could see a hacienda-style adobe house, shadowed by the trees. It was cold here in the mountains, and I felt a chill creep under my clothes and settle next to my skin.

"Stay here," I told Mountain as I got out of the Jeep. I went to the gate and peered through the gap. The bones of what had been a lush summer garden still showed beneath broad swaths of snow. A flagstone walkway to the rustic ramada over the entry had been shoveled and swept. Elegant double doors of hand-carved wood beckoned. I approached them and knocked. The right door swung inward with the first strike of my fist, and it creaked softly on its hinges and yawned into the room. Inside the open central lobby area, a woodstove stood on a wide square of tiles with a small stack of firewood nearby. I called out, "Hello?"

There was no answer.

"Anyone home?"

My voice rang in the air, met only by silence.

I stepped inside and went to the stove to feel the iron top: barely warm. The fire had gone out, but it had been used recently, perhaps early last evening. I returned to the entry door and it gave a creak of complaint as I closed it; in this cold, what little heat remained in the house wouldn't last long. I moved around the dwelling, taking an inventory of its layout. The east-facing main entry lobby served as a hub, with all the other rooms leading off in the other three directions. To the south a wing of public rooms—a large living room with a tiled fireplace. Beyond that, a long dining table big enough to seat twelve or fourteen people. I noticed that two chairs had been pulled out, as if a couple had recently breakfasted there. In the big kitchen, pots hung from a rack above the stove, and all was clean and neat except for two small dishes and a fork in the copper sink, waiting to be washed.

I thought I heard a noise, as if someone had bumped against a wall. "Hello?" I called, and I heard one of the pots ring with the sound...then the faintest squeak telling me the door had opened. I hurried back to the entry and found the door ajar. I stepped out onto the *portal* and looked around. No one in sight. I waited, quietly, listening. A cold draft of air swept across the courtyard and stung my cheeks. *Must have been the wind,* I thought. After a few moments, I stepped back inside and pushed the door closed again, this time making sure the latch caught. I resumed looking around.

To the west of the front entry, a hallway led to the sleeping quarters. First, a pair of small bedrooms, one on either side, each with an adjoining bath. The beds in both rooms were unmade, their sheets and blankets rumpled and pushed to one side. On a nightstand in one of the rooms, an empty beer bottle suggested a lonely nightcap. At the end of the hallway, the master bedroom. I passed through its sitting area, and at the far end, a canopy bed dominated the space, draped overhead with swaths of soft fabric and sheer lace. Adjacent this room was a closet and a large private bath. The master suite, unlike the other two bedrooms, looked as if it had not been used since it was last cleaned and appointed with fresh linens.

The third wing off the entry lobby led directly through double doors into a large office that looked out into the trees, some of which stood so close that their branches touched the roof and made a rasping sound as the wind stirred them across it. Here, a desk sat heaped with papers attended by a well-used office chair with a shawl draped over the back.

Bookshelves lined the walls from floor to ceiling on either side. I studied the books: Latin American poetry, twentieth century literature, a sizeable collection of novels by women writers. I noticed a group of books by Videl Quintana, a controversial author who had created a tremendous stir with his purportedly non-fiction anthropological accounts of encounters with an Indian shaman in Central America. Some say he had invented these adventures, but hundreds of thousands had become devout followers of his exploits into primitive religions, animalism, and magic; his books became bestsellers. Adoria Abasolo must have been keenly interested, because she had collected sixteen of his books. I noticed a bit of fluff protruding between two of them. I grasped it between pinched fingers and pulled out a small black feather, likely a fledgling raven's, downy with a relatively stout quill. I felt it vibrate in my hand. *A draft?* I shook my head.

Still holding the feather, I stepped close to the desk and glanced across the piles of notes, bills, magazines, notebooks, and more, but I didn't disturb anything. A book of love poems by Pablo Neruda lay unopened on one corner, several bookmarks protruding from the top of its pages. A computer sat at an angle in front of the chair. I pressed down on the space bar, and the screen came alive. Lines of poetry spread across the white field of a working document:

I am going tonight
And I will become nothing
No trace will exist
Of the me that I am now
But the promise
Of what was meant to be
I pray...

I heard a commotion outside the entry, a rattle of metal and a thump against the exterior wall near the front door. I started to move away from the desk when I heard the door creak as it had when I had first arrived. A woman's voice called out: "Adoria? It's me. Is someone here with you?"

6: *LA VECINA*
(THE NEIGHBOR)

Before I could get back around the desk and across the room, a woman appeared in the front lobby, looking at me through the open office doors. She demanded, "Who are you?"

"I'm here to see Adoria," I lied. "And you?"

"I'm a neighbor. I live up there," she pointed, "off the county road." The woman studied me with mistrust. She was auburn-haired, olive-skinned, slender, and small—the size of a girl half her age, which was perhaps mid-thirties. She wore jeans, heavy boots, a down jacket and knit cap, and a leather bag which hung crosswise from one shoulder. "Where is Adoria?"

"I don't know." This much, at least, was the truth. "I was hoping I'd find her here."

"That big dog you have in your car scared me when I was walking my bicycle up to the house."

"Sorry," I said. "He's actually fairly friendly."

"Where's the housekeeper?" She turned and went back toward the woodstove in the entry. "It's cold in here; she's let the fire go out. I better get one going." She squatted, then began scooping ashes out of the firebox and into an ash bucket.

I asked, "Was Adoria supposed to meet you here?"

"I always come on Mondays. Except for last week; I was away for the holidays."

"Oh," I shook my head, as if this made all the sense in the world.

She glanced at me, then back at what she was doing. "You never said what you're doing here."

"Oh, sorry." I walked toward her, moving into the entry. "I'm working with an archaeologist with the Santa Fe Public Lands office doing some boundary work. Ms. Abasolo's land borders the Mountain Mission's property, and we just wanted to let her know that we will be surveying the fence lines while we're up here during the next few weeks. We always notify the land owners before we do that, if we can." I silently congratulated myself for my story.

The neighbor glanced up at me for a moment between shoving logs into the stove. "And did you think you'd find her behind her desk?"

I bit my lip for an instant trying to think what to say. "I knocked on her door and it just swung open. I called out, but no one answered. I felt the top of the woodstove, and I was concerned— like you—that the fire from last night had gone out. No one leaves their house open with no heat in the winter. I began looking around to see if she might have fallen or fainted or something."

The neighbor stood up and dusted off her hands by brushing them back and forth together. She drew a wooden match from a tin, struck it and lit the wadded paper beneath the pile of firewood. A flare filled the fire box with an orange glow. She watched it until she was satisfied and then tossed the matchstick into the flames.

"You said you always come on Mondays. So Adoria is normally here at this time?"

"Yes, for my lessons."

"You know, I didn't introduce myself." I slipped the feather I was still holding into my jacket pocket and then held out my hand. "My name is Jamaica Wild."

"I'm Susan Lacy."

"So what kind of lessons is Ms. Abasolo giving you?"

"Don't you know? Adoria won the Nobel Prize for poetry."

"You're studying writing with her."

"Yes. I can't imagine why she's not here. Her car isn't out front, so maybe she just went out for a quick errand and was delayed getting back. She usually has a book of poetry out and ready for me."

"I saw a book on the desk," I said, and I went to get it. I came back and held it out to her: "Pablo Neruda."

"I'll bet that's it," the woman said, taking the book from me. "He's Chilean. She likes Latin American poetry best. I'll go ahead and get started, now that I have a fire lit. I'm surprised her housekeeper hasn't been here and done that already. I'm sure Adoria will be back any minute. Before I start to work, I'll walk you out. Did you want to leave a card? I'll make sure she gets it."

I handed the neighbor my card, and she walked with me onto the *portal* where she'd parked her bike. She stood watching as I went to my car. As I passed it, I noticed that the bicycle that leaned against the house had expensive, hand-tooled leather panniers on a rack on the back, and they were splattered with dried red mud. It was a nice new hybrid street/mountain bike with hardly any wear on the tires, tricked out with a wide, cushioned leather seat, lights front and back, a horn, and custom pedals. I guessed that Susan Lacy was probably from California, or possibly someplace like Denver, where she could ride mostly on paved streets. No one from northern New Mexico would ride a nice bike like that on these awful mountain roads in winter.

I drove away from Abasolo's house and onto the gravel road that led to the paved two-lane county throughway. At the intersection of gravel and asphalt, a figure sat on a stump, huddled against the cold—as if waiting for a bus or a promised ride. Mountain stood up in the back of my Jeep, intently focused on the bent-over shape. I pulled over, rolled down the passenger door window, and looked at the slumped contours of a woman in a long dress, her head and shoulders covered with a thick black woolen shawl. "Is someone coming to give you a ride, Auntie?" I asked, using a term commonly used in these parts to show respect for an elder woman.

The *mujer* slid the shawl back from her face and she grinned at me with a near-toothless mouth and two beady black eyes. *"Mirasol,"* she said, jumping up and moving toward me as fast as a spry youngster. She leaned down to look in the window. "I was thinking I might have to come remove you out of that *bruja's* nest!"

My mouth fell open. "Tecolote!"

She grasped the door handle. *"¡Abrir la puerta!"*

I unlocked the car door.

7: FRIENDS IN SILENCE

Once Tecolote was seated in the car, she pulled a worn elk hide bag from beneath her shawl and set it on the floor between her feet. She pointed a crooked finger out the windshield. *"¡Vamos! Take me over here to los hermanos monjes. One of them needs a cura."*

Esperanza de Tecolote (a name loosely translated to mean *Spirit of the Owl)* was an old *curandera* who lived in the high country above a tiny hamlet named Agua Azuela, not far from where I had just found her huddled in the cold. The people from her village and beyond came to her for healing when the powers of modern medicine held by the doctors and nurses at the clinic down in Embudo failed to cure their sickness, wounds, depression, nightmares, or whatever malaise they suffered. She capably splinted broken bones, wrapped and soothed sprains, and made her patients salves, poultices, and teas from the herbs and other wild plants she collected, as well as from the parts of animals and insects she dried and stored in her little one room adobe *casita.* To cure some clients, she might assign a task—something that must be done to conquer fear or cause a wart to desiccate and drop off, or to entice someone to fall in love, or someone else to leave.

I first met Esperanza several years ago when she approached me in the yard of the ancient church near her home and insisted I come to her place for tea. When I visited her, as requested, she warned me that I was being pursued by a dark element she called *Lo Negro,* or *the black thing,* and she gave me a concoction that led to an unforgettable hallucinogenic experience. At that meeting and a later one, she helped me to solve the mystery of a friend's murder, and to evade being harmed myself. As a result of that, and another subsequent life-or-death experience where Tecolote's advice saved me, I had learned to respect the old crone and to listen when she spoke, whether or not what she was saying made sense to me in the moment.

I drove down the county road several miles, and then turned onto the dirt track that led to the monastery. We passed under an enormous log archway with a sign that read:

MOUNTAIN MISSION MONASTERY
MASS SUNDAYS 8 A.M. AND 11 A.M.
VESPERS DAILY AT 5 P.M.
CONFESSION THIRD SATURDAYS 4—7 P.M. (HOLIDAYS
EXCEPTED)
VISITORS AT OTHER TIMES BY APPOINTMENT ONLY

The road was deeply rutted, and bordered on one side by a crumbling edge that rimmed a precipice of sheer rock dropping straight down into a narrow ravine. I had to concentrate to keep the Jeep from straying from rut to rut and too close to the edge. Tecolote turned in her seat and stared at Mountain, then reached an arm back and patted his head and neck. The wolf seemed to regard Esperanza as I did—with affection and a dose of caution.

It took almost a half-hour to drive that four-mile-long road. As we went, Tecolote chattered about how cold the nights were growing and how much time she had to spend gathering kindling and firewood every week to keep her house warm. At one point, she asked me to stop, and when I did, she got out and walked back a few yards and picked up what looked like a raven feather. She held it up to show me and smiled, then hiked up her dress and squatted down to pee. I got Mountain out of the back of the Jeep and let him romp a little as I looked over the side of the cliff at what might await a car that slid off the track. I was grateful we had come when the road was somewhat dry. When Tecolote was done with her comfort break, she returned and rummaged through her leather bag. She pulled out a length of dried tendon, perhaps from a deer, brandished it above her head and called, *"Montaña,"* and the wolf ran toward her. She held it out, the wolf jumped in the back, and she gave the treat to him and patted his head. Mountain dropped down with his prize between his front paws onto his pile of blankets in the back, and Tecolote settled again into the passenger seat, carefully straddling the hide pouch on the floor between her feet. I got behind the wheel and resumed driving, wondering to myself why Tecolote carried a dried tendon in her "medical" bag unless she somehow knew she was going to meet Mountain today.

Like most of the adobe churches built by the Spaniards who settled here in the late Middle Ages, the monastery was enclosed within an adobe wall. Beyond a pair of thick, time-worn wooden gates in the front of the wall, a buttressed building stood two stories tall with a bell tower rising from the roof. Another vehicle huddled in the dirt lot, an old wood-sided Grand Wagoneer, encased halfway up the sides in dried mud.

We walked through the half-open gate and down the gravel walk. At the main entrance, Tecolote grasped the leather pull on the bell and tugged hard. The loud clang echoed in the covered recess. The door opened, and a robed friar recognized my companion and smiled. *"Doña Esperanza,* thank you so much for coming. Your patient awaits you." He gestured with his arm for us to come in. "I'm Brother Tobias," he said to me.

"Hi. I'm Jamaica."

"Are you her assistant?"

"No, I just drove the car. She's the healer."

"Well, thank you for bringing *la curandera* to us. One of the brothers has a persistent cough. She always has just the thing." We moved into a dark hallway, where the only light came from two dimly glowing sconces high on the wall. "I will escort our physician to her patient. Would you like to wait in our library?"

"That would be lovely, thank you. But first, could I take some water to my wolf? He's in the car."

"I'll have a novice bring you tea and some water for your animal. The young man is observing silence, just to let you know."

In the library, a comfy reading area in the center of the room was surrounded by high walls shelved and filled with books. Long study tables were piled with books, as were the end tables on either side of the couches. I wandered over to the shelves and browsed titles on psychology, self-help, gardening, cooking, philosophy, and religion. I heard a shuffle, and looked up to see a young man standing in the doorway with a tray. I didn't know if I should greet him verbally, so I simply smiled and nodded my head. He set a pitcher of water, a pottery mug, and a small teapot on the coffee table and left the room. I took the pitcher and went out to the car to give Mountain a drink.

The wolf was standing in the cargo area of the Jeep, looking around, probably wondering where I was. I gave him a drink. "I'll be right back," I assured him. I said it again and saw him visibly relax. I had used this phrase, Pavlovian style, to painstakingly train him to stay alone for short periods of time, despite his intense abandonment anxiety. I began with just five minute increments and gradually increased the duration, always rewarding him with a treat after a successful practice. It hadn't always gone smoothly. He chewed through a lot of my stuff initially, but Mountain finally got to the point where he would wait contentedly for up to two hours if he was someplace where he felt safe. As I was closing the hatch to go back inside,

I noticed that the mud-encrusted Grand Wagoneer had left the parking lot.

I returned to the library, poured myself a cup of tea, and went back to the shelves and continued browsing. A name on the spine of a new-looking book caught my eye: Adoria Abasolo. I bent down and turned my head to read the adjacent titles. There were more than twenty books of poetry by her. I chose one and examined the first few pages. The title page read: <u>Songs from My Heart,</u> <u>Adoria</u> <u>Abasolo.</u> It was personalized: *To my friends in silence,* and autographed with her name scrawled in large, flowery handwriting.

Just then, Brother Tobias came in the room. "Miss Jamaica? How do you like our library?"

"It's wonderful," I said. "I noticed that you have a lot of books by Adoria Abasolo. Did you know she was your neighbor?"

"Oh, yes, we have all of her work. She sends over an autographed copy of every book she publishes."

"Does she ever come here—for mass or vespers or anything?"

He wrinkled his brow. "Why do you ask?"

"I'm a fan of her work. I just wondered."

Right then, Tecolote approached and stood beside the monk, looking at me. "She is full of questions, that one," she said, pointing her bony finger my way. *"¡Venga, Vamonos!* I left a nice soup over the fire *en mi casa.* It waits for me now, but if we keep on like this, it will all bubble away."

8: IN FOR A DISAPPOINTMENT

In Tecolote's tiny casita, a simmering pot of soup hung from a hook over the low fire, emitting the rich, gamey aroma of *carne de cabra*—or goat meat—stewing with garlic and the Mexican oregano that the locals called *oreja Indio.* The *bruja* went to the hearth, lit one of her charred punks and used the flame to ignite the wicks in five or six tall cylinder jar candles. These flared and flickered, casting golden light on a host of *santos,* the rustic carved wooden statues of saints displayed in the large inset *nicho* in the back wall of her adobe hut. On the other side of the hearth and above it was a thick slab of adobe upon which a straw-filled cotton bag served as a mattress. In centuries past, this was known as a shepherd's bed; the thick base of the bed retained and transferred heat from the fire and kept a sleeper warm long after the flames died down to a smolder in the night. Atop Esperanza's high bed and its mattress, a neatly folded red wool blanket sat crowned with the small deerskin pillow stuffed with wolf hair that I had made for her one Christmas.

I brought in an armload of firewood and a handful of kindling, and Esperanza used this to stoke up the fire. She offered Mountain another tendon, and he dropped to the dirt floor and went to work on it. *"Siéntese!"* She squeaked at me, telling me to sit, and she stuck a cast iron griddle onto some smoldering coals on the edge of the fire. "We will make tortillas. But first, tea."

The only furniture in the one-room abode was a crude cottonwood table and two rough-hewn wooden chairs. Tecolote placed two cups on the table, added a pinch of intensely green herbs to each, and topped this with hot water to make tea. Then she set about making *masa* using fine ground corn, a little lime, water, and a lump of goat butter. She took a wooden spoon to the bowl containing the mixture and proceeded to whir it all together as vigorously as if her arm were motorized. Once the dough was smooth and elastic, I pinched off small balls and pressed them one at a time between a cast iron skillet and a large stoneware plate, flattening them into nice round tortillas. Each time I finished one, Tecolote cooked it on the hot griddle, turning it over once with her fingers, and then placing it between layers of cotton sack cloth to stay warm. This was a ritual we had repeated many times when I visited.

I sipped my tea. "I am looking for someone," I told Esperanza. "Anna Santana thought you might know her. Her name is Adoria Abasolo."

The *bruja* turned her head from the griddle to face me, eyeing me over the large hump of her shoulder. She made a grimace with her mouth. *"Este no es tu sueño, mi hija."*

My Spanish was getting better the longer I lived in this area, but sometimes it was still woefully inadequate. The older she got, the less Tecolote wanted to use English, and the less tolerant she was with me about not learning what she called *el lenguaje de la gente*—the language of the people. *"¿Sueño?"* I said. "What does that mean?"

"Sueños can mean two things. One is...eh...hopes, *Mirasol.* You know how when you are hoping things will turn out a certain way?" Tecolote ladled some soup into a bowl and set it down in front of me along with a spoon. She brought over the cotton towels filled with the warm tortillas and placed them in the center of the table.

"And the other meaning?"

"Like when you sleep."

"Dreams. So what you said is: *this is not my dream.* Is that right?"

"I can always tell when you are trying to make someone else happy."

This puzzled me, and I held my spoon in mid-air, thinking about it.

"And now you are hoping *la sopa* will come to your spoon? You are in for a disappointment."

"Very funny," I said, putting the spoon down on the table. "Just be straight with me for a minute, would you? Do you know Adoria Abasolo?"

"No." She brought her own bowl of soup to the table and sat down with her spoon in hand.

"Do you know something about her?"

The *mujer* began making short work of the bowl of soup. She shoved one spoonful after another into her mouth, then grabbed a tortilla from the stack and soaked up some broth in the bottom of her bowl. "I know *una bruja* was living in that place where I came to get you."

I laughed to myself. *"You* came to get *me?* Okay, now when you say *una bruja,* do you mean a witch, or do you mean a healer like you?"

"Yo soy una curandera. Pero, sometimes *las brujas* can be healers, too."

"Are you saying that Adoria Abasolo is a witch? Or a healer?"

Tecolote looked at me with coal black eyes. "You did not eat your soup."

"I'm not hungry."

"You are hungry, but this matter has made your hunger invisible to you." She reached across the table and confiscated my bowl and spoon and pulled them to her side. "It already has you under its power."

I grimaced. "I'm just focused on finding Adoria Abasolo, that's all. That's what…"

But Tecolote did not wait for me to finish my sentence. She knocked hard on the table three times, and the bowls and teacups jumped and the spoons rattled. "You better come back and be here where you are right now, *Mirasol.* Wake up! Those *brujas* have you asleep already, and they are the dreamers, not you."

I was so stunned by this that I sat in silence for a moment. "You said 'those *brujas'.* Adoria is not the only witch?"

Esperanza took the bowls to the hearth and busied herself with the dishes. She worked with her back to me, but she spoke loudly: *"El cuervo* tells me you have the means to fly with one of those *brujas.* It is right there in your pocket!"

Now I was really confused. I shook my head. *"El cuervo?* Like the tequila?"

Tecolote scowled, obviously frustrated with my lack of comprehension. *"El cuervo*—the big black bird."

"A raven told you…" I recalled when Esperanza had asked me to stop the Jeep on the way to the monastery and she had held up a feather that she found. Then I remembered the raven chick's feather I'd slipped into my pocket when Adoria Abasolo's neighbor had surprised me in the act of looking through the poet's papers. I reached into my pocket and retrieved the downy black plume. Again, I felt it vibrate slightly between my fingers; it was so light that it trembled in the currents of heat wafting upward from the hearth.

"If I were going to try to find somebody—anybody—I would start looking for *el dinero."* Tecolote handed me a jar with a piece of cloth tied over the top.

I took it from her and felt the warmth of the soup inside.

"When you go to *su casa,* eat some of this *buena sopa* I made for you, okay? And take these." She rolled up the top few cotton towels with the tortillas tucked inside and pushed this across the table toward me.

I got up from the chair. Mountain took notice and jumped up at my side. I knew the gift signified my dismissal, but I tried again. "Wait. You mentioned looking for *el dinero*. What money?"

"How do I know what money? *Esta no es mi sueño.* This is not my dream, *Mirasol,* and neither is it yours."

9: BOUNDARY ISSUE

It was midafternoon by the time I drove up the graded road that led from the highway toward San Lorenzo de Picuris, the old mission on the northeast side of the pueblo. I figured I might find Prescott, the archaeologist from the Santa Fe district, someplace in that area. I spotted a white truck with the BLM logo on the door like the decals I would soon be getting on my Jeep. Down the road a little farther, two men were waving their arms and shouting at one another.

I pulled over. "Guys, guys, guys," I called as I got out of my Jeep. "Wait a minute, both of you. Let's calm down here a second. Why don't you each take a step back."

The Anglo man wearing a BLM coat like mine stepped back. The Indian he'd been arguing with lowered his arms, but his jaw remained set.

"Now, would one of you tell me what this is about?"

They both started speaking at once.

"Hold it! Let's share a talking stick." I looked around, but all I saw in the immediate vicinity was a pathetic little twig. I picked it up. "Okay, what year were you born?" I pointed at the Indian.

"1970," he said.

"And you?" I looked at the man I presumed to be Prescott, my new temporary pseudo-boss.

He threw up his hands. "Let him have it. I'm younger than him."

The Indian took the stick and smiled. "Thank you. We are observing Quiet Time. This man was photographing our mission without a permit."

I was glad that he was young enough to speak English well. So many of the elder Puebloans did not—or even if they did, they often chose not to when it would benefit them.

"I was n..." Prescott began, but the Picuris man and I glared at him with such intensity that he stopped.

The Indian continued, "We don't allow photography during Quiet Time anyway, so there would be no way to get a permit." Finished, he held up the stick.

Prescott reached for it, but the Picuris pulled it away and gave it to me. "This woman has made the peace we have at this time. She will decide who gets the talking stick next."

I took it from him and handed the twig to the archaeologist.

"That is not a camera," he said, pointing to the device on the tripod. "It's a theodolite. It measures angles."

The Indian was quiet, his jaw set.

I looked from one to the other. Prescott realized the stick was still in his hands, so he started to pass it to me, but I gestured for him to give it to the Indian man.

The Puebloan asked, "This light, it captures angles?"

"No," Prescott said, but then remembered and reached for the stick. "No, it just measures them. It's all numbers. Nothing is recorded but numbers. I'm measuring boundary lines for the BLM. The land here at the edge of Picuris abuts public land."

The brown-skinned man considered this.

I reached for the stick. "If I could say something? I think I recognize you," I said to the Picuris man. "Weren't you one of the uncles who spoke the night before Frank and Lupé Santana's son married at Tanoah Pueblo?"

The man smiled. "I remember you now, too. They let you come in after they talked for quite a while about whether to allow it."

We were referring to an occasion several years before where a young couple, Momma Anna's grandson and his bride-to-be, were counseled before their wedding by elders of Tanoah and their sister pueblo, Picuris. I was honored to be allowed to observe this, and to help the women in the family bake and cook for the occasion. "You must have given good advice. Those two are still happily married. I have forgotten your name," I said. "My name is Jamaica."

"I am Paul Deherrera. Frank Santana is my cousin."

"I am so happy to see you again," I said, smiling.

As the conversation went on, another Picuris man who had been crossing the dirt plaza saw us and came over. He stood on one side of Paul and squinted his eyes, examining these two white people who were having a discussion with one of his tribe. He looked to be about the same age as Paul, but he was wearing a Pendleton blanket, the traditional robe worn during holy times in the pueblo.

No sooner had this man joined the group than a boy of about fourteen tooled up on a dirt bike and came to stand on the other side of Paul—the three Picuris demonstrating a diverse range of appearances. Herrera was dressed in jeans and a down jacket. His friend wore the wool blanket in accordance with the old ways. This young man's hair was cut in a Mohawk on the top with a long black braid in back, and he wore a black leather jacket over torn jeans. The one thing all three had in common was their footwear—they all wore soft, boot-like, flat-heeled moccasins.

Deherrera nodded to the newcomers, and then gestured to me. "This woman, Jamaica, is learning from Anna Santana."

The two smiled and took turns shaking my hand. The young boy glanced into my eyes as our palms touched, but then he lowered his head shyly.

Paul returned to the matter at hand: "I do not know what the war council would have to say about recording numbers and angles. But as long as this man is not in the village with the device..."

"I am sure he understands," I said, and I looked at Prescott questioningly.

The archaeologist nodded. "Sure. No theodolite in the village."

There was a moment of quiet. Seeing there was no trouble after all, the two newcomers to the gathering nodded politely, and took their leave. The younger one held a hand up in a static wave and gave me a beguiling smile as he got back on the dirt bike and roared off down a side road that led away from the plaza. *That one's going to be trouble for the girls,* I thought, *if he's not already.*

"Paul, I will tell Anna Santana that I saw you," I said. "I just came from her house this morning."

"Please tell Grandmother that I will be seeing her at the feast of Saint Paul later this month."

"Your name tells me it will be a celebration of your birthday, too," I said.

"Yes. I hope you will come and join us. There is always plenty to eat, and we have dances."

"I'd like that very much. Perhaps I can drive Momma Anna. I will ask her about it."

The Indian man reached out his hand to me, and he held mine for a second or two. "Good-bye for now, Jamaica." He walked away toward the mission church. I turned to look at Prescott, who had been silent for a while.

He pretended to mop his brow and whispered, "Whew!"

"Situation under control," I said.

"So you're Jamaica Wild. I've heard about you."

"What have you heard?"

"A few tall tales."

I wondered which of my adventures he was referring to. My boss Roy accused me of being a magnet for trouble, and there was beginning to be a fair amount of evidence to support his theory.

"I tell you what, they're right about one thing," Prescott continued, "you're supposed to be good with Puebloans, and I can attest to that. Hey, is that the famous wolf Mountain in the back of your Jeep there?"

"Yes, that's him. I'll get him out and you can meet him." I walked over and lifted the hatch.

Mountain jumped right out, ran over, and began sniffing where the Indians had stood, concerned that he might have missed something. Next, he trotted up to Prescott and began to smell his boots and pant legs.

"Best thing to do is just ignore him. Let him warm up to you when he's ready."

Prescott stood still until the wolf moved on to the grass alongside the road. "He's beautiful. Listen, I'm glad you came along when you did."

"I'm just lucky I had met that guy Deherrera before. It might not have gone so well if I hadn't. Anyway, I came to check in with you. I'm currently working on another project, but I was told you might need help in dealing with the war council at Picuris. I think we narrowly escaped that once already. Do you have something else you need to discuss with them?"

"I might. A ruin was discovered last fall on a ledge on the east side of the reservation, in Picuris Canyon. It's on BLM land, but it's close enough to them that they may dispute the boundary, or even launch a legal case to reclaim the area where it sits."

"Would that be a bad thing?"

"It could be. If we don't protect that ruin, it will be decimated by hikers, climbers, and curiosity-seekers. Picuris Pueblo has a dwindling population—only 92 folks live here at last count. They don't have the people power to safeguard that ruin. It's outside their boundary, no one lives near there. And yet, they are a litigious tribe, sometimes for good reasons. They just took the mining company to court and put them out of business when they won back rights to their ancestral clay-gathering sites. And that's the reason a BLM crew has been up here doing surveys—because the court restored those lands to them. We've got to figure out where the lines are now, after that ruling." He turned off his theodolite and removed its foot from the tripod. "Now this cliff ruin I'm talking about is not in the mine area where the boundaries have changed—it's just beyond it, in the canyon, very clearly on BLM land. But it's something that I thought we should address while we're re-mapping—to save any further disagreement and to initiate a joint plan to protect the site. If we could convince the tribal government that we mean to either cover it up or close off and protect that ruin from further damage, then they might not turn around and take *us* to court, contesting whether the location of the site should be restored to them, too."

"Why don't you just ask if you can talk to the tribal council about it then? I can be there with you when you do."

"I need to assess the ruin before we start any negotiations, or none of us will even know what we're talking about."

"Then let's go *see* what we're talking about."

"That's where it gets tricky. There's three possible ways to get to it, and they all have problems. One way is to go the mine road, and from there, hike deeper into the canyon and climb. I'd need to bring in some equipment and ideally a small team. It wouldn't be easy getting to it, and I think that it would be likely to attract the attention of the tribe, so that's not getting it done quietly. Plus, now that Picuris won back some of what was formerly the mine's land, we could easily be crossing their lands before we got to public wilderness."

"My boss was just talking with me about some possible vandalism in the mine area—one of the caves that had been boarded up. He told me it was on BLM land."

"At the moment, it's a legal quagmire. The BLM manages all the subsurface rights of nearly all the land around here. Doesn't matter who actually owns it, we still manage what's under it. Except for reservation lands. With this recent legal decision, the tribe is watching our survey in the mine area carefully right now. There's no way we can go in from that direction without attracting a lot of attention."

"Okay, so the mine road is out; what are the other ways to get there? Picuris Canyon is a big drainage. Can you get to it from another direction?"

"Well, the closest other way *was* down Indian Service Route 210. Public access is allowed on it, even though it crosses the rez, because it's technically a through-road. It just skirts across the north edge of the pueblo before it drops down into the canyon. It's a four-wheel track and it's pretty rough. I'd try it anyway, but it's currently impassable. After that heavy snow we had last week, and the warm-up right after, the surface turned to pure mud. Some numbskull decided to drive it in a big vehicle and half buried their wheels all the way down it when they did. That trail is no more than one car wide, not an inch to spare on either side, and a lot of it runs right along the rim of the ravine. You can't go around those ruts, and only a fool would risk trying to drive in them. So now that way is no good."

"So what's the third option?"

"There's a road that comes in from the south and leads to the cliff rim where we could rappel down to the ruin from above. But that way has a problem as well—it crosses right through the most populated area of the pueblo. It's closed to non-Indians for Quiet Time. I think that's where they thought you might be able to help."

"Well, they were wrong. At least for now. Nobody drives a motorized vehicle in the village during Quiet Time, unless there's a special dispensation. After this dust-up today, I don't think the tribe will cut you any slack. The Indians get very protective when they observe the old ways. That ruin will have to wait."

"There's a problem with waiting," Prescott said as he started walking toward his truck with the tripod. "Someone or something has uncovered part of the ruin, and now winter snows could damage it. The walls and interiors are fragile, once exposed. The crew that discovered the site says there's a ceremonial cave in the cliff face above the dwelling area that has some extraordinary pictographs on the walls. Those could be extremely delicate, and as you probably already know, rock art panels are a magnet for vandals. They use them for target practice, carve their initials and graffiti on them, paint over them, scar them with sanders, and even try to chisel whole slabs of them off the cliff walls to take them home. Assuming we were going to conserve the site, we would want to get in and document those—photograph them and measure them, even if we're going to cover it all up without any further study. So waiting leaves the ruin at risk, but no matter how we try to get there now, it's going to set off red flags when we do it."

"Look, I know you're already up here doing this survey, but it's the wrong time. You need to wait, no matter whether there's damage to the ruin from snow or not. The ancestors walk among the people right now, and you don't want to disturb their dwellings when they are present."

Prescott screwed up his face at me. "You don't need to lecture me. I'm not ignorant." He pulled his keys from his jeans pocket, ready to go. "My supervisor told me not to rely on you because you had another project. But you showed up, and I'm glad, so thank you for helping me out. Now, I have briefed you on the situation, and you've told me you can't help further. Is there anything else you wanted to say?"

I hesitated, watching Mountain as he methodically moved along the fence line examining every post and peeing as high as he could on each one to leave his mark. "If you need me to go with you to talk to the war council about the ruin, I will. But I won't deceive them about why you are asking to use the road during Quiet Time. You'll just have to risk telling them about the ruin if you can't wait. And given that you said you'd need equipment and a team, and you don't have them here right now, do you think it's worth disturbing their sacred time today?"

Mountain, noticing the strained tenor in our voices, perked up his ears and came toward me. He sniffed again at Prescott's boots.

I went on: "And I apologize. I didn't mean to pontificate about the Picuris and their traditions. Everything I said, you probably already knew."

"I know that Quiet Time is about the worst time to be doing this work. And it's funny that they just suddenly decided to have it now, when usually at this time of year, they're holding dances that are open to the public."

"I know. It's the same way at Tanoah. Since they're sister pueblos, I wonder if something happened that caused both of them to cancel their usual ceremonies."

"This is when they get the heaviest snows up here. If I can, I'd like to assess that ruin soon. I just don't know when or how right now. Have you got a number where I can call you when I do figure it out?"

"Can you even get a signal up here? Didn't use to be able to. You might have to leave a message; cell phones still don't work a lot of places where I have to go."

"Tell me about it," Prescott said. "But Picuris got a grant and put up a cell tower. Works pretty good in the high places. Still nothing in the canyons or the valleys. Just the same, here's my card. Give me yours and I'll call once I've made up my mind how to proceed."

10: STANDOFF

BLM range tech Dominic Gomez had taken his post as Roy had instructed. I found him near a window not far from the front door of the Bear's Paw, an artisan restaurant on the side of the two-lane state highway that passed through Peñasco. The place had seating for about twenty, and most of the tables and chairs were full, but the main business today—as it was every day—was their carry-out trade in gourmet coffee drinks, wild berry scones baked fresh daily, and homemade green chili and venison burritos.

Gomez nursed a gigantic plastic mug of coffee and made chit-chat with the locals as they came and went. I watched him talking to a pair of tourists.

The woman pointed to a map she held, asking about a location. A knit scarf adorned her neck while a matching cap set off her long brown hair. Mittens dangled from clips attached to the sleeves of her new-looking red down parka. The male of this pair was only slightly taller and wore a spotless red parka as well, topped with a quilted ball cap with ear flaps. The two looked like they had stepped out of a catalogue for winter outdoor wear.

Dominic wore an expression like an animal in a trap.

I stepped in to rescue him. "Hey, Gomez." I looked from one to another in the group. "Sorry to interrupt,"

Dominic looked at me with surprise. "Hi, Jamaica. No, no, you're not interrupting."

"We had to be going anyway," the two fashion plates said. They muttered farewells to Gomez and went to the cash register to pay for their meal.

"You looked like you were in a bind. Thought I'd help out," I said.

"Yeah, thanks. I don't know why Roy made me do this. I'm not that great at small talk." Gomez set his coffee mug down on the wide adobe window sill. "I'm just wasting my time here. That Ibanez guy hasn't shown up, and nobody seems interested in whether or not he loses his cows and we make barbecue out of them."

"The day's not over yet," I said. "You'd be surprised how word travels in a place like this."

"I know. I live in a small village not too far from here. But I feel like I'm fishing and nobody's biting. I've had to listen to an old man go on for a half hour about his gout, and a woman from Texas started telling me her whole life story; I couldn't get rid of her. Just one person after another, *gab-gab-gab.* I thought I maybe had a nibble with one guy. When I asked about Ibanez, he just turned around and left, but that was quite a while ago."

"Still, that's a good sign. I bet he gets the word to your guy."

"Could be. But so far, all I'm doing is drinking coffee and standing around shooting the breeze. I have to mend that fence and get those cows out of that horse meadow. What are you doing up here, anyway?"

"I'm working for a few days as a loaner to the Santa Fe office, helping a BLM archaeologist over by Picuris."

As we stood by the window, we saw two pickups converge on the parking lot, each of them carrying a crew of Hispanos in their cargo beds. These ready riders jumped out like a platoon on the move, the trucks' doors flew open in unison, and the occupants of the cabs spilled forth and joined the march to the door of the Bear's Paw.

"I think your new pal Ibanez has come to talk grazing rights with you," I said, "and he brought his negotiating team."

The door of the restaurant swung open and slammed into a wooden rack filled with tourist pamphlets on the wall behind it. A short, broad-shouldered, angry-looking man led the pack. He made straight for Gomez, his chest thrust out. "You the *pendejo* who's saying you are going to make *barbacoa* out of my steers?"

Gomez seemed to puff up in his uniform jacket and jeans. "You the guy whose steers are grazing in the meadow where the Forest Service keeps their horses over winter?"

A line of Ibanez' backups moved in on both sides of their buddy, creating a wall of northern New Mexico back-country vigilantes, effectively blocking us in with the window at our backs. The vigilantes seemed to pay little notice to me. All eyes were on Dominic.

"I didn't put my cows in that meadow," Ibanez said. "The fence maybe came down if they got in."

Gomez countered: "Probably so. Do you have a grazing permit for the land behind that meadow?"

"Yeah, I got one."

"We don't have a record of it at the BLM, and neither does the Forest Service."

"Well, I got it. I talked to somebody at the ranger station and they told me I could graze my cows back there."

"May I see your permit?" Dominic spoke in a civil tone, but I noticed that the fingers of his left hand were trembling beneath the cuff of his coat sleeve.

"I don't got it with me."

"I'll wait here if you want to go get it."

"I ain't going to go get it, I told you I have it, and that oughta' be enough." Ibanez pushed his chin forward and his upper lip curled into a sneer.

"You can either produce that permit," Gomez said, "or you can remove your cows from that meadow before 5 p.m. today. Otherwise, the BLM will confiscate the animals. Those are your options."

At this, his posse began to grumble loudly and wave their hands, urging Ibanez to stand up to this ultimatum.

The customers in the restaurant, who had been creating a low din of noise before, had all gone quiet, every eye on this new development.

Ibanez gave me a lewd grin. *"Esta chica flaca,* this skinny girl here, she your posse? That all you got?" He wrinkled his nose and flicked his fingers in front of it, as if to get rid of a bad smell.

I eyed him back, my face deliberately blank.

"Look, we don't want any trouble," Gomez offered. "We're just looking to get your cows someplace where they're properly permitted to graze. But we can call the sheriff's office for backup if you think I might need some."

Through the window, I saw a white BLM truck pull up in front of the café. I made eye contact with Prescott as he was getting out of the cab and raised my eyebrows. I turned to face Gomez as if I were speaking confidentially to him, but so that Prescott could see me through the window. "I'm sure someone already dialed 911," I said, pronouncing the number slowly and distinctly, and making a gesture with my thumb and pinky as if to put a telephone to my ear. "That couple you were just talking to? They were watching when these guys came in the door. I saw the guy through the window and he held up his cell phone to let me know he was calling 911." Again, I made the hand gesture and said the number slowly and deliberately.

Eddiejoe Ibanez furrowed his brows, then looked to either side at his buddies, grinning, and making the thumb-pinky-phone gesture himself. "Is she for real?" His crew laughed heartily.

I tried to stall a few seconds longer: "And the cashier took a phone into the back room when you fellas came in, so I think she had the same idea. I would imagine the nearest deputy is on the way right now."

Ibanez and company turned to look at the cash register. There was no one behind the counter.

As if on cue, Prescott walked through the open front door and announced, "There's a sheriff's deputy on the way from the ranger station. Be here in less than a minute."

Eddiejoe looked from me to Dominic, and chewed on his lip. Then he looked at one of his buddies and said, *"Sabes, yo tenía un lugar para pastar las vacas antes de que la wetback puta se puso en el centro de las cosas."*

His gang laughed at this, and I made a mental note to ask Gomez for a translation when this was over.

Ibanez moved close to Dominic, only an inch from his face. "I'll make you a deal. I can maybe get my cows out tomorrow, but there's no way I can do it by tonight."

"Tomorrow by noon then," Gomez said.

Ibanez shook his head ever so slightly up and down, his mouth in a half sneer. And slowly, the knot of angry men began to untangle and to shuffle back out of the café. On the way out the door, Ibanez grabbed a scone from the tiered plate on the front of the counter by the register. He held it up defiantly as if counting coups. And he walked out the door.

"What was that he said in Spanish?" I asked.

"Something about how he had a place to put his cows until some wetback bitch got in the way of it."

"Yeah, right. Blame it on a woman. Hey, you did great," I said to Dominic. "And you did great, too," I said to Prescott.

"I'm glad I showed up when I did. I figure this makes you and me even for the thing earlier today. I'll call and cancel the deputy. She wasn't coming from the ranger station, but I thought it would help if they thought so, since that's just right down the road." Prescott dialed his phone and put it to his ear, going back out the door as he did so.

"I don't mean to be rude, Jamaica," Dominic said, his shoulders slumping now, his hands still trembling. "I really appreciate what you did. But I have to use the restroom right now. And I may need to go over to the ranger station to get a change of pants."

11: THE SHADOW

When I got back to my car, Mountain was standing up in the back, moving to look out first one window and then another. I opened my Jeep's hatch and poured some of the water from the bottle I'd just purchased into Mountain's dish. But he wouldn't drink. He emitted a series of sharp pinging whines, like a radar SOS.

"What's the matter, Buddy?" I glanced around. "We got rid of those bad guys, if that's what you're worried about." I trusted Mountain. Like Tecolote, I didn't always understand what he was saying, but he, too, had saved my life, and I knew his behavior intimately. The way he was acting now told me that whether or not I could see it, he sensed danger of some kind. After the standoff with Eddiejoe Ibanez and his gang, my adrenalin was pumping, too, and I had no doubt that the wolf was reading his cues from me.

"Come on," I said, as I poured the untouched water from his dish out onto the asphalt and reached up for the lid to the hatch. "We'll go the scenic route. That will help us unwind."

I turned north onto Highway 75 and doubled back to State Road 518 and headed for Taos. Although the distance I would be driving was less than 20 miles, I would pass through the wild and rugged Sangre de Cristos and Carson National Forest by going this way. It would take some time to make the journey, especially if there was snow on the road. But I wanted to think, and I knew that I would be less distracted taking this route than going the more-traveled road down into Dixon and then up the busy main highway into Taos.

Mountain eventually tired of the effort of balancing on all fours in the back and reluctantly sank into a sitting position. But he did not lie down. Instead, straining his neck down and forward, he watched avidly out the windshield, his head just a few inches over my right shoulder.

"It's okay, Buddy," I said in a soothing tone. "Let's enjoy this pretty drive." I focused on the road for a while and then I began to let my mind wander over the events of this already-long day. The Secret Service had returned me to my cabin at dawn and I'd been going ever since. I reviewed the key people I had encountered since I'd received this strange assignment. All of them showed signs of suspicion, some even acted threatened. Roy, for example, didn't seem to buy the cover the Secret Service had created for me to be off book with the Taos BLM, though it could have been because he felt insulted that the Deputy Director had made his first visit to our offices to see me instead of him. And the moment I had mentioned Adoria's name to Momma Anna, she had reacted as if I were about to offend the ancestors. This might have been one of her usual attempts to reign in my curiosity for fear I would transgress polite custom, as I unknowingly had many times. But after she suggested I talk to Tecolote, when I pressed further, Momma Anna had told me to consult the peyote plant and make an offering of money. What did she think I would learn from doing that? Tecolote had talked about dreams and witches and ravens before she finally told me to look for the money. What did all that mean?

I began a mental review of any ceremonies I knew of at Tanoah Pueblo that Abasolo might have attended. The tribe did the *Matachines* dance on Christmas Day, and the pueblo was open through the New Year's holiday, during daylight hours. On New Year's Day they did the turtle dance, and the next public dance would normally be tomorrow, on King's Day, for which they usually did the deer or buffalo dance. But this year, the *cacique* had ruled that there would be no public dances on the Christian holiday marking the arrival of the three kings at the crèche. Instead, the pueblo would be observing their ancient traditions in Quiet Time for ten days. After that, they would re-open and remain so through the beginning of March, when Tanoah Pueblo would once again observe the old ways during the nearly seven-week-long Spring closure.

I shook my head, unable to see even a thread to follow in all of this. Before I wasted more time looking in every direction, I needed to know the facts at hand. I knew I had to do more research on Adoria Abasolo.

"Mountain, let's go to the Taos Library," I said to my companion. "Those librarians adore you, and we haven't been there in a while. I've got some reading to do."

As I said this, I looked in the rear view mirror to make eye contact with the wolf, whose head blocked my view of the road behind me. He responded by reaching over and licking me on the cheek, and as he did so, in the mirror I saw a black Hummer a quarter-mile or so behind us on the two-lane road. I hadn't remembered seeing it before. I wondered how it had come up on us so unexpectedly—especially since this trail led through twists and curves and there was a chill wind occasionally blowing snow and limiting visibility, which had forced me to drive more slowly than I might otherwise have. I decided to perform a test. I slowed my speed by ten miles per hour, well below the speed limit. This should have caused the Hummer to overtake me in a few minutes.

But the follower slowed, too, and the slight tingling in the back of my neck turned into a tense rigidity. I noticed I was clenching my teeth. This wasn't the first time I'd been followed in high country, and when it had happened before, I'd nearly been run off the road and then forced to defend myself in a shootout. I chastised myself: *Why didn't I take the more heavily traveled road through Dixon?* Here I was again, alone and miles from anywhere with someone tailing me.

I sped up. The Hummer matched my speed. My mind ticked off a list of possible perps, starting with Eddiejoe Ibanez, or one of his goons. I thought of gaining cover on one of the switchbacks, then taking one of the forest road turnoffs and trying to hide in the trees so I could reverse positions with my shadow. But that's how the shootout happened the last time, and I didn't want to find myself on the defensive and trapped down a primitive Forest Service road without backup, especially when I didn't know how many people were in that car. My cell phone had no signal here, and I couldn't use the radio to hail dispatch because there was no line-of-sight in these mountains. I figured it was best to keep driving straight ahead and hope they didn't try to overtake me and force an altercation. I reached between the folded-down backseat that Mountain was perched on and the back of the front passenger seat, my eyes still on the road. When I got my hand on my rifle, I pushed the butt all the way until it pressed against the back door behind my seat. I was a crack shot with a rifle. If I had to get out and fight, I wanted to be able to grab it in an instant.

12: NEVER JUDGE A BOOK

By the time I got on the Paseo del Pueblo in Taos, my shadow had dropped out of sight. I turned off the road and waited for a while in the parking lot of the grocery store, but I did not see the black Hummer go by. I began to think I'd been too quick to assume the car was following me—it could have been anyone coming from Peñasco or Mora traveling to Ranchos de Taos or one of the small villages around the Taos area. I was sleep-deprived; maybe that was making me twitchy.

I headed directly to the Taos Library. As usual, the staff flocked to the wolf, emitting squeals of delight—and if he hadn't known them, he might have turned tail and run. But Mountain had been coming to the library with me since he was a tiny cub, so he forgave his fans their inability to contain their enthusiasm. Besides, both here and at the bank, he generally received several dog cookies, and there was no better way to a wolf's heart than through his stomach.

I enlisted the help of Carla, my favorite research librarian, who directed me to the shelf where Abasolo's books were kept. I picked up several of these and headed for an upholstered reading chair, where Mountain joined me and made himself comfy on the carpet at my feet. I began with her first published collection of poems, and as I thumbed through and read one or two, I knew why President-elect Vargas had become alarmed by the mystical nature of Adoria's latest efforts. Her early work was grounded, rustic, earthy and more like a still life in words than a trip to another dimension. I particularly liked the imagery of one poem at the end of her first book:

A Woman's Worth

A woman's body is her great gift.
In its strength, she finds herself a warrior
Even if it is only a battle
With a stain on a white shirt
Or a skirmish with the cupboard's contents
To make them last until the end of the month.
In her body's womb, she finds herself a creator;
Her children will always be her greatest work of art
But she may also find a moment to paint
Or sew, or draw, or to form up a little figure out of the clay
While she is hanging out the wash in her bare feet.
She may dance, or write love songs,
Or tell fortunes while the children are napping,
Or imagine a way to design a dress
On the way home from work, or as she starts supper—
So great is her ability to create.
In her body's health, she may find the tenacity
To live long enough for things to get better,
To outlast an unkind husband…
Or retire happily with a loving one,
To witness the descent of the uncle who shamed her
To outlive the nun who beat her,
To see an unfaithful boyfriend grow bald and fat,
Or better—to nurse her sick grandchildren
And make them well again,
To run and play with them
On the soft grass under the shade trees by the river.

But in her body's beauty,

Which only lasts for a moment,
She can trade at high market
For all the stars in the sky.
And there, the timing of the deal is everything.
Her beauty peaks when she knows nothing of her worth
And begins to diminish as soon as
she starts to value herself.

I perused other collections of Abasolo's work and all of it was similarly hard-edged and down-to-earth, beautifully poignant while made up of everyday imagery. I opened my backpack and took out the blue folder I'd placed in it. Scanning through the file's contents, I read some of Adoria's recent poems. By comparison to the larger body of her work, her last twenty or so poems seemed like they'd been written under the influence of a powerful hallucinogenic.

And here I began to make a series of associative leaps in reasoning. I remembered Momma Anna telling me to ask "him" for help in finding Abasolo, and to feed the peyote plant. Peyote was a hallucinogenic, and somewhere at Tanoah Pueblo or on their reservation lands, there were regular meetings of the American Indian Church, which was a group of peyote dreamers. Further, I remembered seeing those books by Videl Quintana in Adoria's study. And I knew just enough about Quintana to know that he had made his name and fame publishing purportedly true accounts of learning the ways of a Central American shaman who made the pupil ingest peyote to begin instruction. I got up and looked for Quintana's books, but the library only had copies of two of them. I decided to check them out and peruse them later.

Had the peyote church conducted any meetings recently?
Could that be where Abasolo had gone when she disappeared?
Vargas had said she had gone to Tanoah Pueblo for a ceremony of some kind, and from what I knew, the peyote

rituals were ceremonies conducted by elders, medicine men and women. But why at Tanoah Pueblo when Adoria lived practically right next door to their sister pueblo, Picuris? Because of their much smaller population, it could be that the Picuris who practiced the religion went to Tanoah for this ceremony. Or maybe Abasolo preferred the anonymity of going a distance to avoid running into her neighbors. Perhaps I could find out more about the poet's routines from her neighbor, Susan Lacy. By now, she surely would have realized that her writing teacher had gone missing.

I took a selection of volumes to the check-out desk, where Carla gazed at a computer screen. She scanned my card and the books, and as she picked up the two by Quintana, she said, "You're lucky. We can't keep these on the shelves. And the circumstances surrounding his death! They've never solved all those mysteries!"

"What mysteries?"

"Oh, there are so many. His death was kept secret until months afterward. And I don't think they've settled his estate yet—it's been more than ten years since he died. Some of the people who were named in his will just disappeared. Quintana's followers who believed all that woo-woo stuff he wrote said that those closest to him went with him into the next dimension! It was quite a stew for a long time. And it sure spiked his book sales!"

"How about Adoria Abasolo's books? I saw you had most all of them on the shelf."

"Well, poetry doesn't make it to the bestsellers lists like Quintana's books did—his read like fantasy novels, and some say that's what they were—not anthropological studies, as he claimed. But there's not much demand for poetry. We did see interest in Abasolo pick up some when she won the Nobel prize a few years ago, and then a flurry of checkouts again when she was named the US Poet Laureate this past year. Most of our poetry has a slow rate of use, but Abasolo is local, so we keep a copy of everything she does."

"It's a shame more people don't read her. I was just reading some of her early poems, and they're really good."

"Most people don't even know about her around here. She might have more of a following if she did some events when her books came out. But she doesn't do public appearances."

"I didn't know that."

"Yes, we asked her to do an event for local authors here at the library last summer—and this was right after she'd been named poet laureate. I sent an email to her publisher and they forwarded my request to her agent who replied and said Abasolo didn't do public appearances."

"Do you happen to have that agent's name and contact information?"

"Not handy, but I might be able to find it. Are you thinking of asking her to do an appearance?"

"Something like that."

"If I find it, do you want me to use the email address associated with your library card—like we've done before when you requested research information?"

"That would be great, thanks. And Carla, would you do a small research project for me as well?"

"Sure thing. What do you need?"

"Any information you can find for me on peyote and the American Indian Church. And before I leave, will you give me the log-on password for today? I want to use one of the public computers."

13: A GOOD TRAP

The mountains of northern New Mexico were wild and beautiful, but in many ways they created a barrier against so-called human progress. Here, as in other high places, the terrain was rough and rugged, and the weather made the roads unpredictable. The lack of line-of-sight connections to the high mesas nearby prevented cellular and Wi-Fi from working. But more than that, the sparse human population that these mountains sustained—a number held in check by the lack of water—meant that the spread of advanced technologies into rural areas was not cost-worthy. And unlike so many other beautiful spots on the map, rich developments did not spring up in the loveliest areas precisely because of these difficulties, especially the fact that one might have to drill halfway to China to get a drop of water. So, while some locals celebrated these protective landforms, saying *las montañas del norte* were sleeping giants who kept the region pristine, others found it difficult to settle for a life without modern amenities, no matter how beautiful their surroundings.

I was happy without technology at my cabin in the pines, where I lived practically off-grid. I got my electricity from the rural electric coop, I paid to have water hauled to my cistern every few months, and I heated my home with firewood burned in a small, centrally-located woodstove. When the power went out, which it frequently did—especially in winter—I cooked on that woodstove, too, because the range was electric. For years, I had lived and worked without a mobile device, but when I got into some trouble last winter, Roy had insisted I begin carrying one, even though there was no service in half the places I was assigned to protect.

Lately, I was grateful to have the Screech Owl, and to be able to check my email on the computer at the BLM or a public computer, because it allowed me to stay in touch with my faraway boyfriend, Kerry. And so, before leaving the library, I logged into my email to see if there might be a note from him. There was!

> *Babe,*
> *Now that I'm back in the northwest,*
> *I feel lost, like I left half of me with you.*
> *I can't go on being separated, living so far apart.*
> *We belong together.*
> *Kiss Mountain on the head for me,*
> *and feel my arms around you.*
> *Love, Kerry*

He included a few photos: a breathtaking view of a turquoise lake surrounded by pine-forested peaks, a "selfie" that he'd taken of the two of us laughing while we were on a hike just days ago, and one of Kerry, me, and Mountain with heads touching—lying on the big rock in the woods near my cabin where I always went to talk to the stars.

I sat unmoving, running my fingers back and forth across my lips, tears welling in my eyes. I heard a woman clear her throat behind me. I turned and looked.

"I'm sorry to bother you," Carla said, "but there's an old man in the front lobby—he told one of the librarians he wanted to know if you were here."

I closed the screen, stood, and followed Carla to the front entry. The man who stood wrapped in his blanket just inside the big glass doors was an old friend of mine. "Sevenguns, I am so happy to see you. It's such a surprise that you found me here." This seemed like a very curious circumstance. I had never seen the old man away from Tanoah Pueblo before.

"I saw that Jeep. Easy to know that's you. Got wolf hair all over in there," he said.

I laughed. "Yes, that's true." I was quiet for a few moments. "I don't think you have come here to use the library."

His chin dipped down. "No, I do not read so good. Remember, I tell you at that school when I am small, I make the trap, catch a lot of rabbit for stew. They like to have that meat, so they let me out of class. I never learn much read or write, but I get by."

Sevenguns referred to the Indian boarding school that he had been forced to attend as a child, when government workers forcibly took children of school age from their families at the pueblos and attempted to convert them from their native ways, beliefs, and languages. That school had long since been shuttered, but not before it had caused irrevocable harm to most of the children who attended, and to their families and their tribal legacy.

I smiled at my friend. "Well, I am glad to see you." Careful not to ask a direct question, I said, "I am thinking that if you will not be staying here for a time that perhaps you are on your way somewhere."

"I have friend over at this church." He hitched a thumb back in the direction of Our Lady of Guadalupe, two blocks away. "I come see him, hope he will give me a ride home. But he is not there. I see you drive by with that wolf of yours."

"So I am thinking that you might like a ride back to the pueblo."

He lowered his head. The Tanoah not only frowned on asking questions, but especially asking for things from others, because this would nearly always create an imposition. There wasn't a word for *no* in the Tanoah language, hence it was difficult to refuse any request without being rude. Instead of inventing a way to express the negative, this peaceful tribe had long ago developed a tradition of avoiding queries and requests, and this had worked well for them for many centuries. Sevenguns spoke in the general direction of the floor. "I can walk. I come by to say hello."

"Well, I was just going out by the pueblo. I would love it if you would ride with me. You could keep me company."

"I could do that for you." He smiled shyly.

On our drive north and west of Taos, I decided to see if I could get any information from Sevenguns. "I have a friend who went to a ceremony in your village recently."

"We have only turtle dance this month," he said. "Christmas, we do *Matachines...*"

"I don't think she went to the dances. I am thinking it was a religious ceremony."

"Women not go in kiva."

"Not in the kiva. I think it was someplace else."

"No place where white woman can do ceremony there."

"She's not white, she has brown skin."

"Other tribe maybe can come, maybe a relative."

"I am looking for this woman and this is the last place I know that she went. To the ceremony."

"Maybe talk women. You know some those aunties."

"I will. But I am hoping someone can tell me if there has been a recent ceremony, so I could know which auntie to talk to."

Sevenguns looked out the window and did not reply. I wished I could take back what I'd just said. Whether or not I'd asked a question, it was a request, and now he had to either ignore it or figure out a way to politely refuse it, and feel as if he'd been rude to me either way. A thing like this could sour a relationship forever.

The old man shifted in his seat and pulled a section of his blanket up across his chest. "I think they have that one for them women maybe New Year Day, before we go Quiet Time."

I gently bit my lower lip lest I say anything and spoil the gift I'd just been given. Sevenguns had overlooked my transgression and told me what little he could. I wanted to hug and kiss the old man!

By this time, we were approaching the pueblo gate. "Since it's Quiet Time, I can go in the back way, but not to your house in the main village. I know that it's forbidden to drive in the old part right now."

"Right here, I am good," he said.

"Then I will leave you here, my friend. Thank you for keeping me company on the drive."

He smiled at me as he unlatched his seatbelt. "That other time you catch that big cat and those little ones, help them get free." He was referring to the previous winter, when I asked for his permission to put a trap on pueblo lands to capture a wounded mountain lion and her cubs, all of them badly in need of rescue. The old man got out of the car, but leaned in before closing the passenger door. "You maybe can set good trap like that, this time, find that one you are looking for."

14: EVENING

The sun was starting to set by the time I made it back to the highway. Mountain was making noises in the backseat about wanting to get out and romp. And I had a lot of reading to do. It was time to go home. As I drove, I passed through a long stretch of open mesa and then crossed the Rio Grande at the Gorge Bridge. Just on the other side, in the visitor parking area, I saw a black Hummer waiting to turn onto the road. I could not make out the driver, as the windshield was tinted, and it was almost dark. I drove past and then checked my rear-view mirror. The SUV turned west, the same direction I was headed, and stayed well behind me all the way to the junction at Tres Piedras. *How could this be a coincidence?* Though Hummers were no longer being manufactured, there were still a lot of these extra-rugged sport vehicles on the road, especially here, where so many outdoor enthusiasts lived and vacationed. But what were the odds of being followed in two different remote areas by the same kind of vehicle twice in one day? I was trying to decide whether to stop and try to use my radio or cell phone in Tres Piedras when the black car turned north and then pulled in to the Three Rocks diner, leaving me to travel south alone.

My cabin sat in a heavily forested area in the foothills, my nearest neighbor three miles away. No networks other than the rumors the ravens told from the trees, passing news in a cacophonous relay along great distances, or the yipping of the coyotes, their forlorn choruses a common lullaby for me as I was dropping off to sleep. Once in a while a fox would keep me up half the night with its eerie cry, a long harsh shriek crossed with the strangled sound that a cat makes in heat. And even more rarely, a mountain lion might call out from his isolation to see if there was a mate within hearing. These were the only channels I received, but I felt all the richer for them.

I worked alone in the wild for the most part, so I was used to spending long periods of time with no one but the wolf, and sometimes a horse, to talk to. My cabin consisted of one large room, plus a small shed-style add-on with a pass-through closet and the little bathroom that the landlord had constructed years ago to make the place rentable. It wasn't much, but it was home, and Mountain and I were comfortable there. After such a long day and almost no sleep the night before, I was ready to read a little and then get to bed early.

I pulled down my long drive, turned the Jeep around so that it pointed nose-out facing the road, and got out and raised the hatch. Mountain scampered out the back and headed straight into the woods, and I reached into the floor of the backseat and took out my rifle. I stood watching the road that ran in front of the property for several seconds. Things seemed like they always did: quiet and lovely. I followed the path Mountain and I usually took into the woods, knowing it was his habit to go first to the little stream that ran behind my place, the one called *La Petaca.* Sure enough, he was snorting around on the banks to see who'd come to drink from the place near one edge where the ice melted and the slow-moving water was cold and fresh. I watched him for a few minutes while he marked every tree within a twenty-yard radius. "Come on, Mountain," I said, as I turned and headed back toward the cabin. "It's getting too dark for us to see what we're doing out here." The wolf moved in my direction but stopped to sniff something on the ground and then continued to trail after me, lingering here and there to *read the news,* as I called it. He was enjoying his freedom for the first time that day, but I knew he would be right behind me, wanting his dinner.

On the way past my Jeep, I picked up my backpack filled with the library books and the folder president-elect Vargas had given me, and I stuffed the jar of soup and the roll of cloth with the tortillas from Tecolote's kitchen carefully inside it, then headed up onto the porch. I reached to open the door and found it barely ajar, a slim sliver of light from inside lining one edge of the frame.

"Don't shoot, it's me," a man's voice said from within my cabin.

I set my pack down to one side of the entry, shielding my body behind the jamb, readied the rifle, and pushed the door open with my boot, pointing the barrel into the cabin as I peeked around the door frame. I blew out the breath I'd been holding. "Agent Coronel. What are you doing here?"

"Christ," he said, standing behind my table in the kitchen area, his palms in the air. "You're so ready to draw down. I tried to call you a dozen times today on that phone we gave you, but you must have been out of range. I wanted a debrief on what you've discovered."

I lowered the rifle. "It's getting to be a habit with you—barging your way into my home. Where's your car?"

He put his hands down. "I parked down at the intersection and walked up."

"I didn't see a car when I turned onto my road."

"That's because I was behind you."

"In the Hummer?"

He looked confused. "Hummer? I drove the same SUV we used to transport you and the wolf to Albuquerque."

"Oh. There was a Hummer behind me as I was driving home. And it's the second time one has followed me today."

"Well, they don't make them anymore, but there are still plenty of them on the road. I would guess that a lot of people have them in a place like this. Do you want me to…"?

"No …it could be a coincidence, I guess. Just seems odd. Why did you park down at the intersection?"

"We have a protocol about keeping the cars spotless. Your road and drive…"

"I see. Anyway, why couldn't you reach me earlier? I was in Taos for almost two hours."

"I was tied up in the late afternoon."

"Well, I don't have anything for you yet." I picked up the backpack and stepped inside, and the wolf followed me in. He stopped and whiffed at the air, looked at Coronel and rounded the table to sniff his boots.

"He's not going to bite or anything, is he?" The agent stood rigid as a post.

"I kind of doubt it, or he would have attacked by now." I grinned and set my pack on the table.

"Very funny." He continued to watch Mountain. "Have you got anything to drink?"

"Why don't you sit down? It will put him at ease. You want a glass of water? Or I could make you a cup of tea."

He pulled out a chair and sat in it. "Anything else?"

"No, sorry."

I went to start a fire in the woodstove. "Hey, would you bring in an armload or two of firewood? I have enough here to start the fire, but I'm going to need more to keep it going."

Coronel got up from his chair and went to the door.

"Wait—see that metal bowl on the counter? Fill that up with water and set it by the woodpile, would you? Put it on the south end so it gets sun in the morning."

"Sure. Who's that for, your wolf?"

"No, there's a fox living under my shed this winter and she's got a couple of kits. With the pond frozen up in the woods, she will appreciate being able to get a drink close by. It will freeze overnight, but when the sun hits it during the day tomorrow, it will thaw."

Coronel stood at the sink and filled the bowl, but I felt his eyes on me. When I looked up, he smiled. He took the water with him and went out the door. Mountain started to go after Coronel but I stepped in front of him. "Not you, Buddy. I don't trust you not to run off if I'm not there." I tipped the door shut after Coronel went out, but the wolf didn't look too disappointed. He eyed his food dish and then looked at me.

"First, the fire," I said.

After the flames devoured the tiny sticks of kindling and began to work on the logs, I left the door to the woodstove open just a quarter-inch to keep the blaze going. I removed my jacket and hung it on the coatrack behind the door, then took the jar of soup and the bundle of towels with the fresh-made tortillas out of my backpack.

The agent came through the door then with a huge armload of firewood and went to the tiled hearth area, where he stacked the logs with the few others left there.

"Are you hungry?"

He straightened. "I could eat. What you got there?"

"It's goat-meat soup. I imagine it's really tasty." I held it up and looked at the contents through the glass. "It has potatoes and carrots in it, and I could smell the garlic when it was cooking. Probably has wild herbs and sheep sorrel."

"What's wrapped in those rags?"

"Tortillas. Have you ever had them fresh-made?"

"I don't believe I've had the pleasure."

"Well, you're in for a treat. But Mountain eats first." At this, the wolf pricked up his ears and came to sit beside the kitchen counter, right where he always did when I was preparing a meal for him.

"So what do you feed a wolf?"

"Elk. Venison. Sometimes we'll get a fresh trout from the Rio Grande or some bison remnants from the pueblo."

"And you cook those for him?"

"No, he eats the meat raw, just as he would in the wild. I take a package out of the freezer at night and put it in the fridge for the next day. It may not be totally defrosted, but it doesn't seem to bother him." I picked up the wolf's dish and took it to the fridge, where I filled it half full with chunks of meat for tonight's meal. I walked up to Mountain and held two fingers up to my eyes, indicating he should meet my gaze.

He looked at me, and a bubble of drool formed on the side of his lip.

"Now, wait," I said as I carefully lowered the bowl.

Mountain made a false start and I raised up with the bowl still in my hand. "No, you wait. I pushed one palm out. "Wa-a-ait," I said again. I set the bowl on the floor and returned to a standing position. "Okay!"

He launched his muzzle into the dish, selected one of the chunks, and raised his jaws up as he snapped and gnashed, biting into it several times, then swallowing it only partly-chewed.

"I guess that's where they get the expression 'wolfing it down,'" Coronel said.

I laughed. "Yeah, that's right. He's an efficient eating machine." I put the kettle on and lit the burner under it, then poured the jar of soup into a pan and started it heating, too.

"It's nice of you to share your dinner with me."

"To tell the truth, it will be good to have the company as well as a hot meal. Normally, I might have a bowl of cereal, if that."

"You like living alone like this?"

"I'm not alone, I have Mountain. And all the wildlife—and the only reason I have so much of them is because there aren't any more people."

"Still, you kind of talked like you don't enjoy eating by yourself."

I looked away. "I think it's because my boyfriend was just here for a while and then he left. We had a lot of fun making supper together every night and then telling stories while we ate here at the table."

"A breakup is never fun."

"No, we didn't break up. He works in Washington State. We both saved up and took three weeks of vacation and he drove down and stayed with me. But he had to go back to work just a couple days ago."

"Oh, I see. I thought when you said he left…"

"Anyway, I'll make us some tea. What kind do you like?"

"If tea is all they got at the bar, give me what you're having."

"You can set the table. There're spoons in that drawer over there. And we'll have to use paper towels for napkins."

He got the items and focused intently on folding the paper towels.

I brought cups of tea and went back to the stove and started warming the tortillas one at a time and putting them back between the layers of cotton cloth.

Coronel was still folding. After a minute, he placed his creation beside the spoon at the place where I would sit, and said, "ta-dah!" It was a perfect origami bird, a raven with a thick neck, a Bowie knife of a beak, and tiny folded tips of paper extending at the throat like the ruffled neck feathers for which the big birds are known.

"Wow," I said, leaving the stove to examine the small winged figure on the table. "Where'd you learn to do that?"

"You think of things to do with your time when you're in my line of work. A lot of it is spent waiting."

"It's a raven, right?"

"Exactly. As in: *Quoth the raven, nevermore!*" He grinned. "A lot of people guess that it's a crow…"

"No, the throat feathers are the giveaway, and the larger body relative to its feet."

"You know your birds. I guess I shouldn't be surprised. I wanted to learn some of the less common ones. Everyone who does origami can do a crane. But very few can do a raven."

"It's wonderful. I'm not going to use it for a napkin, though, because it's a work of art." I picked it up and set it on the counter. "I seem to be getting a lot of raven messages today."

"Raven messages?"

"Never mind." I returned to the stove and ladled the soup into two cereal bowls and brought them to the table. "There's not a lot here, but I bet the soup is rich. And we can fill up on the tortillas."

"I'm sure it will be wonderful. So, you went to Abasolo's house. Did you get to look around any?"

I sat down. "Not too much. A nosy neighbor stopped in, and she was really suspicious of me."

"A neighbor? But that place isn't close to any other houses."

"In rural New Mexico, people within a twenty or even thirty-mile radius of you are your neighbors. This woman was a writing student of Adoria's. I'm going to make some notes tonight and I have things I need to read. I've only had a chance to glance at the file President-elect Vargas gave me."

"Let's not refer to that person by name."

"The neighbor?"

"No."

"Oh."

"From now on, we'll refer to that person as... *The Bartender.*" He held up his tea mug and smiled.

"But there's no one here but you and me...and Mountain." I noticed the wolf had ceased licking his bowl and was trying to find the comfiest spot on his lambskin rug in front of the fire, his tug toy dangling from either side of his mouth.

"Let's establish a protocol and keep to that. No more mention of *The Bartender* by name or specifying the gender, please."

"Okay."

Coronel slurped a mouthful of his soup. "Oh, man! That's amazing!"

"It's just rustic mountain cuisine, but it's so fresh and everything in it grew right here—the goat was raised right in Teco—...I mean...right on the land by the cook."

Harold Coronel looked at me and smiled. The sharp angles of his face seemed to soften. "Not everyone is included in our protocol. Just *The Bartender.*"

But I hadn't stopped because of the protocol. For some reason, I did not want to tell the agent the *curandera's* name.

We finished our meal over small talk. He had never been to this part of the country and was amazed by how different it seemed from the world he knew. I gave him a brief cultural digest. While we talked, we gobbled down all the tortillas, dipping them in the soup as we went, until we polished our bowls clean with the last ones.

"What did you learn at the pueblo? Do you know which ceremony Abasolo went to?"

"No, but I have a line of thinking on that, and I want to do a little research. I'll do some reading tonight, and then I'll make inquiries in the morning."

"So you have nothing to report at all?"

"Not really. I just got started."

"Okay." He rubbed his forehead with his hand. "I probably don't need to tell you that time is of the essence."

"No, you don't. The other ceremony, the one with *The Bartender*, is not that far away."

"Well, yes. But even more importantly, when someone goes missing, there's a window of time when there is some likelihood of finding them. And that likelihood dwindles with every passing hour. Generally, after the first few days, the chances are next to nil. There are exceptions, but they are few."

"I don't even know when the clock started ticking," I said.

He looked at his watch: "About 70 hours ago—that's our best guess."

I felt the pressure of this bearing down on me. And I felt tired. "I better get busy studying that folder, then. And the other things I brought to read."

"If you like, I'll keep the fire going, make more tea."

My eyes met his. I realized that I wasn't the only one feeling lonely right then. "No, but thank you. I am really tired. I want to get in my jammies and read in bed, and hopefully get some sleep after that."

He got up from the table and took his bowl and spoon to the sink. "Can I help with the dishes?"

"No, that's all right. I'll just rinse them tonight."

He went back to the chair for his jacket. "I'm sorry I intruded this evening. Maybe I should get you a sat phone since I can't always reach you on a cell when I need to."

"Sat phones are a little more reliable, but they don't always work here either, especially in winter when a snowstorm blows in."

He opened the door, and turned. "Have a nice night and get some rest."

"Am I supposed to check in periodically or anything?"

"I'll contact you for now. If you get anything of importance, get to someplace where the device I gave you works and dial zero."

"Okay. So I guess I'll see you when I see you, then. And I'll use Buzz if I need you before that."

"Buzz?"

"It makes a buzzing sound. I have to carry two phones now. I can tell which one is ringing by the sound it makes."

"I never heard of anyone naming a phone before. Except something like 'John's cell' for the purposes of backing it up to a computer."

"I name all sorts of stuff. You can actually increase your recall by doing that."

"Good to know." He walked through the open door. "Good night."

I pushed the door shut and locked it the best I could, given the state of it after the events of the wee hours of that day. I turned and looked at Mountain, who hadn't even bothered to get up from where he was sprawled on his lambie in front of the fire. "That guy isn't so bad once you get past him breaking in all the time."

15: UNDER COVERS

The intelligence report on Adoria Abasolo contained a vast amount of data: she kept at least $10,000 in the bank, had donated her Nobel Prize money to several charities, had type O blood, and size 5 feet. She had graduated with honors with a Bachelor of Arts degree from Stephens Women's College in Columbia, Missouri, in 1976, gone on to receive an MFA from Sarah Lawrence just three years later, and received her PhD in creative writing at the University of Illinois at Chicago just three years after that. Her publishing career began in journals and periodicals while she was still an undergraduate, but Abasolo's first book of poetry was released the year she completed her doctoral studies. Her second book of poems won a Pulitzer Prize. After this, she retired to northern New Mexico to devote herself to her writing, and the report stated that there were few photos of her and no interviews.

After skimming through financial data, utility bills, and more, I set the intel report aside. "Talk to me, Adoria," I said, as I fluffed up the pillow behind my back and then opened one of the volumes of her poetry.

In Search of Pablo *(a Tribute to Neruda)*

I long for your lips, your smile.
Alone and aching,
I wander over the hills.
I want no other nourishment
Beyond your kiss, your warmth,
Your musk.
I search for the shadow
Of your footprints
Or the hint of your feet dancing
In the pool of ivory light that streams
Between the branches of the trees.
I want to feast on the radiance
That erupts from within you.
I want to swallow the angle of your brow
And devour your eyes, too,
Your jaw,
Your muscled shoulders,
Your lean legs.
I travel these mountains
Starving for your scent,
Your strength,
Smelling around for you,
And your maleness
Like a wild cat
In the black night.

I swallowed hard. "Wow," I said to no one but Mountain, fanning my face with my hand. I looked on through the books of Abasolo's work. With passionate eloquence, she skillfully crafted words to create multi-dimensional pictures of migrant workers harvesting grain in Texas, the hope people feel for a young couple at their wedding, sunlight coming through a stained glass window, a child watching her parents fight. I was becoming a huge fan.

But I was also getting sleepy. I started to stack up the books on my nightstand, and something on the cover of Videl Quintana's Traveling Between Worlds caught my eye. It was a picture of a large black cat, perhaps a puma, silhouetted against a white light streaming between tall trees. I studied the artwork for a few moments, and then I opened the book and began to read. After I'd flown through three riveting chapters, I stopped and checked the time. Midnight. I closed the book and looked at the cover once more, then turned off the light.

I woke in the morning with my clothes drenched in sweat and an insatiable ache between my legs. I had been dreaming of Kerry again.

16: TALK TO THE BONES

There was an expression around Taos: *Scratch someone in nice clothes and you'll find a hippie underneath.* This was never more true than in the case of Riley Franklin. In a previous incarnation, a mere two or three years ago, he'd gone by the name of Bone Man and lived in a commune off the grid on the west mesa, on the other side of the Rio Grande Gorge. Filthy and unkempt, he hitchhiked and panhandled, brazenly opened and sampled foods from the shelves of the local market without paying for them, traded crude taxidermy for psychedelic drugs, and—until they shut the place down—sold animal skulls, bones, and faces to tourists on the highway between Taos and Española. Among the locals, he had earned a reputation as something of a psychic. Recently, however, in a true Renaissance, Bone Man improbably became Riley Franklin, and his signature chicken bone totem necklace was either gone or hidden under his spiffy après-ski sweater. The greasy dreadlocks had disappeared, and his now-fashionably-highlighted hair cascaded almost to his chin on one side in contrast to the short, neatly clipped locks on the other—this asymmetrical design no doubt the brainchild of a high-priced stylist in Santa Fe. Wearing expensive sheepskin boots, with his soft pants bloused over the tops of them, a thin shimmering gold chain at his neck and one diamond earring, the metamorphic gonzo waited on customers in Joseph Jacquez's gallery.

Jacquez was a Tanoah sculptor who had briefly lived in the same commune as Riley before he left to apprentice at a foundry near Corrales. His bronze renderings of romanticized Puebloan figures brought him renown when he won the best in show at the Heard Museum and the Santa Fe Indian Market. Prices for his work soared, and he soon became inundated with orders. He opened the showroom on Harwood Street near the plaza in Taos and hired his old friend Riley to curate it while he focused solely on his art.

I studied the new persona Bone Man had created, but I still remembered the old one— especially the stench of his clothes and body, which made it easy for him to pilfer goods at the markets, because no one wanted to confront him for fear they would have to spend time in his vicinity.

Riley spoke to a couple about Jacquez's maquette of a bison bull charging. "You can see the energy in the animal's muscled thighs. And look at the detail of the dust rising around his hooves, and the hair of his mane."

I perused the artwork—most of it studies of Indians captured in the deeds of a life that was now extinct—but I kept one eye on Riley. At one point, he looked away from the customers and saw me, and the change in his expression made me think of a stage when the curtain drops. He returned to his pitch and rotated the bronze on its swivel base so his potential buyers could view it from all sides.

Within minutes, the couple left and Riley sauntered across the gallery to me. "Jamaica!" He held out his arms as if hugging was something we did.

I pulled back. "Well, look at you."

"I know, right? I'm like a phoenix rising from the ashes of my former self."

"I heard about your conversion to a socialized grown-up, but I had to see it to believe it."

He spun slowly around, like the bronze on the swivel base. "Do you like my new look? Joseph insisted on a makeover when he gave me the job."

"I don't know, Bone Man. You don't smell as bad, but you don't seem quite yourself. Not even a cleaned-up version of yourself."

"Jamaica," he cocked his head to one side and almost whispered. "No one calls me Bone Man now. I'm Riley. That's my real name, Riley Franklin. Remember when you used to give me a few bucks now and then so I could pay to shower at the north side gym? Well, now I have a membership there! I work out three times a week. You should feel my biceps," he raised his arm and flexed the muscle, but I didn't take him up on the offer.

"That's great. You do look like you're in better health."

"So!" He scrubbed his palms back and forth on each other. "Enough about me; how have *you* been, Jamaica? You look as thin as a supermodel. What kind of a diet are you doing?"

"Riley, I don't even know who you are when you say things like that. But more importantly, I don't have time to chit-chat. I came here to ask you a few questions."

He frowned. "Fine."

"A few years back, you told me that you were a member of the American Indian church, and that you went to meetings at Tanoah pueblo. I want to ask about that."

"Why? It's legal, it's a church, a private religious thing. There is nothing wrong with it."

"I know. How often do the members meet? And where?"

"There's no schedule."

"Well, how do you know when there's a meeting so you can plan to attend?"

"It's all word of mouth. Someone tells someone, and they tell someone else, and the word gets around. If you see a guy who comes now and then, you let him know about the next meeting."

"Well if, for example, they were going to meet next Sunday, how would you know?"

"It probably wouldn't be on a Sunday. Usually, it's on a Saturday. Except once. Once it was the night of a feast day in the middle of the week."

"Okay, if they were going to meet next Saturday..."

"Someone might tell me."

"But how, exactly?"

"Why do you want to know?"

"Let's just say I'm curious."

"I don't want to get anybody in trouble. Besides, I don't go anymore. You have to be in the right place at the right time to hear about the meetings, and I'm in here six days a week. I don't know when the next one is. So I can't tell you anything."

"I'm not looking to bust anybody. This isn't about the use of peyote. I'm looking for someone."

"One of the tribal elders?"

"No, why did you ask?"

"They're the ones who administer the sacrament. And there's the peyote chief who oversees most of it. He's the only one who can dispense the jimson weed."

"Do women come to the church and take the peyote?"

"A couple of old grandmothers in the tribe."

"Any outsiders?"

"Like me, you mean?"

"Yes."

"There used to be a dozen or so of us. Now there might be half that many, if that."

"I'm looking for a woman. She would have been an outsider."

He shook his head. "I don't think there's ever been a woman outsider at the meetings. Not when I went. Last fall they were talking about banning non-Indians. They are one of the few fireplaces that allowed non-Indians, but I don't know if they still do."

"What do you mean by fireplaces?"

"It's like we say church, only they say *fireplace* for a peyote group."

"Okay, thanks." I started to go, then turned back. "Do you still do that thing with the chicken bones?"

He put a hand to his chest. "I still have the medicine, but the circles I travel in now... there's not a lot of use for it."

"The woman I'm looking for is not from Taos. The last time anyone heard from her, she was going to Tanoah Pueblo for a ceremony. At her age, she would be considered an elder."

Bone Man grimaced. "Only for you, and only because you were always good to me." He looked in one direction and then the other, making sure we were alone, then reached a hand under the wool top and pulled out the necklace. Dozens of chicken bones were laced together side by side, small and white. He began to strum his fingers up and down the bones from one side to another like he was playing a marimba, tapping here and there, jumping from bone to bone with his fingertips. After a minute or so, he began rolling his head atop his neck and he breathed loudly in and out of his nose. Abruptly, as if someone had snapped their fingers to bring him out of his trance, he stopped moving, drew up straight, blinked his eyes, and once again hid the string of bones back beneath his garment. "Do you still have that wolf?"

"Yep. He's in the back of my Jeep right now, waiting on me. Do you still have your dog—wasn't his name Bob Marley?"

"No. Marley's still among us, but he fell in love with a girl I met and followed her when she left for Vegas. It was the right thing to do, to let them have each other."

I nodded my head. "Okay, well, I'm going to head out now. It was nice talking with you." I knew that if Bone Man had seen a vision, he would tell me about it as soon as he could assimilate it into speech. Right now, I doubted he was even aware that he'd gone into one of his trances, and it might take him a while to get himself grounded again.

Riley Franklin walked with me to the door, and a *di-ding* sound rang from the bell when I opened it. He stood in the doorway after I'd walked through. "It was really good to see you, Jamaica."

"Take care," I said. I crossed the street to my Jeep, opened the driver's side door and started to get in.

I heard footsteps coming fast behind me and I turned and saw Bone Man just before his feet slid on a patch of ice and he slammed into my car, still upright.

"You okay?"

"Oh, yeah. The bones…I just got something."

"What is it?"

"I'm not sure what this means, but for some reason, she really wanted to be able to go to another time. I'm kinda out of practice. That's all I got."

"Thanks, Bone Man."

"No problem." He moved back as I got in the car and then— still standing in the middle of the narrow street—smiled and waved as I drove away.

17: MAD ABOUT A DOG

I was headed out to Tanoah Pueblo when the Screech Owl sounded. "Jamaica?" Something in Roy's voice sent up a red flag. "I know you're working for Santa Fe right now, but I thought I ought to warn you."

"What's up, Boss?"

"Lor Talgren was just in here about that dog of his, and he was looking for you. He was so worked up, I had to call the town police, but he left before they got here."

"Oh, no." I pulled over on the side of the road.

"He talked like he was out for blood. I filed a complaint with the cops. But you need to watch your back."

"Great. Well, hopefully Talgren will simmer down before I get back."

"I don't think so. The man was a ball of fury. If you ask me, he's as rabid right now as that dog of his was. I was afraid this might happen; they couldn't save it, euthanized it yesterday. Lor threatened to make you pay, and I don't think he was talking about the vet's tab."

I wish he would have vaccinated his animals. This could have all been prevented."

"I don't like having to call you like this, but the guy is a nut case. He was in here yelling about how he'd find you, that he knew your Jeep. Said he was going to take it out on your wolf and make him suffer like his dog did, and make you watch. It was downright grisly. Way he was acting, I didn't hesitate to call 911."

"What did the police do?"

"What they did was take their sweet time getting here. Talgren was already gone."

"Well, are they going to do anything now?"

"I suppose if they see him in town they might arrest him on the complaint I filed. But Talgren doesn't live in town. And seeing as you're up on the High Road; Lor's place is closer to where you're at now, so it's more likely he'd run into you up there."

I wasn't "up there" at the moment but I decided it was better not to mention where I was, given that I'd be back in the High Road area soon enough.

"I want you to take extra precautions."

"Okay, I will, Boss, thanks."

"Why don't you give me a call before you head home tonight."

"I don't think you need to worry..."

"It might have sounded like I was asking, Jamaica, but I wasn't. You're loaned to the Santa Fe district at the moment, but you still work for me."

"All right, I'll call you. It might be late."

Just do it." He hung up.

Lor Talgren owned what had formerly been a winery in a wide, winding canyon that led from the Rio Grande valley up into the mountains and connected to the High Road. The winery had gone under, the property had been foreclosed on, and Talgren probably bought it for pennies on the dollar at auction. It was in need of a lot of work when he did, and it had only gone downhill since then. The rows of grapevines were strangled with brush and weeds, the fences in need of mending, the metal roof on the vat room was now held down by an unsightly collection of used tires, its corners alternately curled and sagged where they had been hammered by wind. The three buildings on the property cried out for upkeep and care.

Talgren's acreage abutted BLM land on two sides, and when I was range riding that area in December, I saw three dogs running after what I thought was a wounded raven. When I got closer, I discovered that it was a bat. Before I could intervene, the lead dog—a pit bull—had the mammal under his muzzle, but then he yelped and jumped away. The bat spread its wings wide, then drew them around its body and keeled over dead. The other two dogs sniffed around, but I got off my horse, yelling and waving my arms, and all three dogs began to growl aggressively. The one that had likely been bitten by the bat lunged at me as the other two barked and snapped—ready to join in. Before they got to me, I drew my handgun and fired it into the air. The dogs ran off. Wearing gloves, I bagged the bat to take to the wildlife center for a biopsy, but I was certain it was rabid. No healthy chiroptera would be so active in daylight.

Before I left that day, I went down to Lor's winery to talk to him. He was all but violent with me then, when I mentioned that one of his dogs had surely been bitten. I told him that if it had, it would need to be quarantined. Talgren threatened me then, waving his arms and yelling for me to get off his property.

I got a report right before Christmas that the test of the bat's brain tissue was positive, and an animal control officer from the county was dispatched to get Lor's dog for quarantine and testing to see if the disease had been transmitted by a bite. And then Roy had informed me just yesterday that the dog had gotten rabies from its quarry. Now this.

Before I got back on the road, I dialed Roy back. "You didn't happen to see what Lor was driving, did you?"

"No, why?"

"I just wondered. I want to be on the lookout."

"I'll call Deputy Padilla at the Sheriff's Office. He'll find out what he drives."

"Thanks, Boss." I hung up. I tried to remember any vehicles I might have seen when I was at Talgren's place. The only thing I could recall about that incident was how big, how tall, and how inflammable Lor Talgren was—and how even his own dogs, who were vicious themselves, ran and hid when he raised his voice.

☽

I rumbled down the back road into Tanoah Pueblo, the Jeep jostling over the ruts, Mountain and I bouncing uncontrollably. The dried clay rose up in monster ridges and collapsed into deep tire traps, and in between it drummed under the wheels like a zydeco *froittoir*. The only thing I could do was focus my eyes through the windshield and hold on as I struggled to navigate the rough road. By the time I pulled up in front of Momma Anna's house, my knuckles were white from gripping the wheel.

As I shifted into park, Anna came out her door.

I got out to greet her. "Good morning."

"I go see Yohe," she said. "I walk."

"It's cold out; I could give you a ride."

She headed for the passenger side. "You maybe drive."

I backed out of the spot in front of her house and turned down the road by the buffalo pasture. "I know it's Kings Day, but I was hoping I could talk with you. If you're cooking for the feasts, I could do something to help while we talk."

"No feast today. New War Council vote extra Quiet Time, no dance, no feast. We go see Yohe."

"No feast? On Kings Day?"

"Tst," she made the sharp sound with her tongue against her teeth as she held up her hand, reminding me not to ask questions. "You drive. We go see Yohe."

Yohe invited us in and brought a pot of coffee and a paper plate of cookies to the table where we sat. She delighted Mountain with a length of her homemade elk jerky. As soon as our hostess sat down to join us, my medicine teacher pointed at the cookies. "Eat. You look like stick."

I ate four or five of them, and the two elders ate as many, too, all of us dunking the crisp, sugary pastries in our coffee.

Then Anna suddenly said, "White girl need help."

Yohe looked from her to me.

I hoped I understood what Momma Anna was doing. "I'm trying to find someone. It's a woman who might have come to a ceremony here. Her name is Adoria Abasolo."

"Spanish," Yohe said.

"Spanish," Anna uttered, almost under her breath.

I remained quiet. Clearly my mentor had brought me to Yohe because she might have either knowledge or ideas about this. If I spoke too soon, they might not continue the conversation.

They both began to laugh.

"What?" I glanced from one to the other.

They laughed some more, and covered their mouths, smiling at one another.

Yohe said, "That how baby who drink mama milk start eat food!"

I was perplexed.

"Baby drink milk, then maybe have some that cookie, too." Momma Anna pointed to my shirt.

I looked down. The tops of my breasts were sprinkled with cookie crumbs. I chuckled, too, and brushed the crumbs off my shirt.

The cookies had disappeared and we finished our coffee. Yohe put both her palms flat on the table and sat up tall. Round, brown, and with her greying dark hair pulled tightly and tied in the traditional knot on the back on her head, she reminded me of a wise-looking beaver. "Very quiet here this day. First time, no feast, no dance today. They talk at Carry Water Clan. Say because that one boy steal medicine."

"Unh!" Anna made a low, percussive grunt to release the unwanted energy of a theft from the tribe. The women often made this sound after something unpleasant was talked about, as if the sound itself cleansed the atmosphere and their spirits.

Yohe added: "I cannot talk them now. Maybe next time."

Momma Anna stood and pulled her blanket from the back of her chair and began to wrap it around her. "Oh-h-h," she said in a sing-song voice, "Them cookies so good. You bake them just right, crispy. Thank you that coffee, too."

I followed suit, grabbing my jacket. "Thank you so much, Auntie. You are so kind." The wolf got up and came after me. "And thanks for giving Mountain some of your jerky."

As we drove back to Anna's house, I attempted to start a conversation. "So Yohe must be a part of the Carry Water Clan."

The old woman barked: "You not speak that."

We rode the rest of the way in silence. When we arrived, I got out to help her with the door, and Momma Anna looked at me, this time less sternly. "You got answer this time."

I waited, but she didn't continue. "If I have the answer, I don't know what it is."

"You wait," Anna said. "Like corn. You plant this time, you eat next other time. Corn there all time."

18: BACKWARD

It was getting close to noon by the time I drove through Ranchos de Taos and headed toward the High Road. I heard a thrumming sound and realized it was the mobile device Coronel had given me, buzzing and vibrating in the backpack like a trapped hummingbird. I pulled over on the side of the road. "Okay, okay," I said, reaching into the pouch on the front of my backpack. "Wild, Resource Protection," I said, out of habit; the only time I answered a phone, it was one of the BLM's.

Once again, a woman's voice said, "Good morning, Miss Wild. You will see a GPS position of interest when you open the maps application. Should you need to contact me, dial zero. Have a safe and productive day."

I pressed the maps application, and the blinking dot seemed to be at the same location given before. "I was headed there anyway," I said. "You see, Mountain? We're already one step ahead of the Secret Service on this." I felt a tinge of concern, though, as I put the Jeep back in gear and nosed out onto the road. In that area, the likelihood of crossing paths with Lor Talgren would be much greater. From what Roy had said, I definitely wanted to avoid Talgren until he'd had plenty of time to cool down.

The blinking dot on the map led me toward Adoria Abasolo's and I assumed the intended location was as before. I had planned to try to sneak back into Abasolo's house anyway and search around some more. There was one thing in particular that I wanted to examine more closely.

But that was not meant to be. As I approached the place, I could see that the gate to the long drive was still open but a car occupied the spot at the end where I'd parked my Jeep yesterday. I navigated a wide turn on the road and backed the Jeep in, parking nose-out at the edge of the road, ready in case I needed to make a quick getaway. I reached into the glove box and took out my Sig Sauer P229 and holstered it beneath my jacket. "Stay here, Buddy," I told Mountain, as I exited the Jeep. As I walked the long drive, a Hispanic woman came and went from the house twice with what looked like baskets of laundry and bags of trash. As I came close, I called out. *"¡Hola, Señora!"*

The *mujer* set a bag beside her car and straightened, looking at me. *"¿Hay algo que pueda hacer por ti?"* Was there something she could do for me?

"¿Habla usted Inglés?"

"No, Señorita."

"Okay. ¿Está la señora Abasolo aquí?"

"No." She looked at me expectantly. Then she asked, *"¿Qué estás haciendo aquí?"* What was I doing there?

I proceeded in halting Spanish, telling her I was just visiting and asking when Abasolo would return.

The woman shook her head at me. *"No lo sé."* (She didn't know.)

I asked if she knew the neighbor, Susan Lacy.

She assured me she didn't, and that she knew everyone around there.

I gave up at that point and said good-bye.

When I got back to the Jeep, I took the device I'd dubbed *Buzz* out of the pouch, and looked again at the map. I'd misread my destination. The little dot was still blinking, but on the land next door, the vacant parcel next to Abasolo's that also backed to the Mountain Mission property.

I drove a quarter of a mile down the road to its gate, broken down and grown over with buffalo grass and small juniper starts. I continued a little ways past it until I was sure my Jeep couldn't be seen from Abasolo's drive. At a wide place where the dirt shoulder looked solid enough, I pulled over and parked, and set the backpack that had been on the passenger seat in the floor where it was less visible. "Come on, Mountain," I said as I opened the back door on the driver's side, and reached under the backseat and pulled out my rifle. "Let's take a romp."

Like Abasolo's place, this plot of land had a long trail-like drive that led to the back. However, here there was no house sitting at the end of it. At the fence beside the gate, the barbwire sagged low—probably bent by hunters stepping over it—so I held the top two wires down with my boot while the wolf jumped over, and the two of us meandered down the trail. I noticed narrow tire tracks here and there on those few patches of dirt where the drive hadn't been completely obscured by overgrowth, probably made by a small motorcycle or one of those fat-tire dirt bikes.

As we walked, I scanned my surroundings constantly, including behind me. Mountain meandered with his nose near the ground, reading the news. We walked about halfway down the drive into a sparse grove of old-growth junipers, which told me that the land here had never been cleared. I lost sight of Abasolo's house but I kept eyeing the road behind us, and even spent some time walking backward and keeping my eyes peeled for cars on the road. I saw no one. At the back of the parcel, I discovered an *acequia,* an ancient irrigation ditch like those in the lower-lying farming communities. It had been well maintained and was relatively clear of brush and trees, and was likely the dividing line between the brothers' land and this piece. I had been so concerned about someone coming up behind us that I hadn't noticed until we stopped here that there was an immense arbor-like structure on the monastery's land, at least ten or twelve feet tall, with some withered vines on top. I'd never seen grapes grown on anything as enormous as this. It had to be something else. The high country growing season was too short for anything that wasn't frost-tolerant. *What could it be?*

Mountain stopped and sniffed the air. I inhaled deeply, too, but I caught no scent beyond that of the junipers and the dry grass—with a hint of sweetness that might have been from the water in the *acequia.* But as we walked back toward the road, Mountain stopped and stood erect, his head up and his ears turning as if he were trying to locate the source of a far-off sound.

As we returned the way we had come, I decided I would drive into Peñasco next to see if I could find anybody who might know where Susan Lacy lived or even what kind of car she drove. But that wasn't meant to be, because as we approached the Jeep, I realized what the wolf's keen ears had alerted on earlier. A vehicle was parked behind the Jeep, and two men stood alongside it, watching intently as Mountain and I approached.

19: GROWING REALIZATION

My companion had been padding along beside me, running his nose along the ground; he hadn't yet spotted the strange car and the men ahead. "Come here, Mountain," I said, and I vaulted two big steps to reach him. Unlike a dog, he had about as much interest in minding me as he had in getting a job. I caught hold of his collar with my left hand, but kept my rifle in my right. When we were about twenty yards from the cars, I called out. "Can I help you fellas?"

One of them answered, "We're from the monastery. Could we speak with you?"

By this time I recognized the Jeep Wagoneer I'd seen when I took Tecolote there yesterday. I kept Mountain's collar under my fingers and proceeded forward. "What can I do for you?"

The same man spoke again. "I am Brother Odin, and this is Brother Gregor. We wondered if you would come with us to the monastery."

On closer inspection, I could see that they probably constituted a low threat, if any. Brother Odin was lean and tall but didn't have much meat on his bones. And Brother Gregor had the opposite body type—short, plump, not at all muscular. They were both dressed in jeans with heavy shirts and down vests. "Thanks for the invitation, but I'm working."

"I wish you would reconsider. Our abbot, Father Anthony would like to talk to you. It won't take long."

I followed the Wagoneer down the same cliff-edge rutted road. It was already almost one in the afternoon, and considering how long it would take to get back and forth, I worried that I would be losing as much as an hour with this detour to see the abbot. But the brothers ahead of me whizzed along. I figured if they could do it, I could, too, and so I sped up, and Mountain and I bounced and banged from bottom to top of the Jeep, but we got there all right.

Once inside the entry hall, I was asked to wait near the door—not in the library as before—and both monks disappeared. After a few minutes, a man came toward me wearing jeans, a pullover sweater and a large silver pectoral cross suspended from an ornate silver chain over his chest. "Miss Wild? I am Father Anthony. Welcome to the Mountain Mission Monastery."

"Hello, Father." Not knowing if it was proper to extend my palm in introduction, I kept my hands at my sides, and as I did this, I felt my pistol in my holster beneath my jacket on my right side and realized it was probably bad form for a guest to wear a gun into an abbey.

"Let's go into the library and have some tea, shall we? Brother Tobias is setting up a tray for us."

I followed him into the library, and Tobias, the monk who had greeted me when I brought Tecolote, was pouring tea when we went in. He nodded at me, and I returned the gesture.

"Tobias will take your coat."

"No thanks. I'll keep it on."

"I assure you, you'll be warm enough. The brothers have laid a nice fire in the fireplace."

"I'm sure I'll be fine. I prefer to leave my jacket on, though."

"Please, have a seat."

"Thank you," I said, but I remained standing. When Father Anthony had seated himself, I went to the chair opposite him and took a seat. Brother Tobias gave me a slight smile and an approving nod.

"I understand you were asking about Adoria Abasolo when you were here yesterday," the abbot said.

I glanced at Tobias again, but he was looking at the floor. I didn't speak.

The father continued: "And it has come to our attention that you were talking to her housekeeper today, asking about her."

I didn't want to lie to an abbot, so I said the most truthful thing I could muster. "I'm looking for Ms. Abasolo in a matter related to my work."

"Could you tell me what that matter might be?"

I examined the room, noting all possible exits. "With the greatest respect, Father, I am not sure that would be appropriate for me to do."

Father Anthony turned and looked up and behind him at his attendant. Brother Tobias promptly left the room. Then the father turned back to me. "I understand. Would you like some tea?" He picked up a cup and offered it to me.

"No, thank you. I'm working, you see, and I need to get back on the job."

"I'm sure your superiors won't mind if you talk to the abbot in the area where you are working. I understand that you work for the Bureau of Land Management?"

"Yes, sir."

"Is there a land management problem that concerns Ms. Abasolo or her property?"

I furrowed my brow. I didn't want to tell Father Anthony the same lie I'd uttered to Susan Lacy the day before. And I was beginning to wonder what all this was about. "Pardon me, Father, if this seems disrespectful, but I am wondering why it is of concern to you that I am wanting to talk to Adoria Abasolo. Is she here?"

He smiled stiffly. "Women are only allowed as guests in the abbey at certain times—for mass, or vespers, or confession. Or by appointment."

"And yet, I'm here," I said.

"By my request." Father Anthony's voice seemed cooler. "Ms. Abasolo is our neighbor. We look out for our neighbors when we can."

"So you know her."

"Yes, I know her. And I'll kindly ask you again to tell me why you are looking for her."

"As I said, Father, it's a work-related matter." I wanted to stand to signal that I was through being interrogated, but I wasn't sure that it was appropriate for me to do that unless he stood first. Instead, I changed the subject. "Could I ask you something? What is that enormous structure you have on the northwest side of your property? It looks like you grow some kind of vining plant there, but I know it can't be grapes."

"That was our bold experiment this past summer." He smiled. "We grew hops there. We had great success with our first harvest."

"So did you sell the hops?"

"No, in fact, we have renovated the old stables to create our own state-of-the-art brewery and we intend to manufacture a boutique line of beers. Of course, this endeavor is just in the beginning stages, but we hope to launch our debut beverage with our brand next fall: Mountain Mission Beer. Would you like a tasting sample?" He stood.

I stood, too. "No thanks. As I said, I'm working. And I'd better go."

If you learn anything we might need to know or can help with regarding Ms. Abasolo, I hope you will let us know."

I pulled at my earlobe. "I definitely will. And, given that you look out for your neighbors, I wonder if you are also acquainted with Susan Lacy?"

He shook his head. "I'm afraid I don't know her. She may be new in the area." Just then, Brother Tobias came in and whispered something in the father's ear. "Well, I'm sure you will let us know if there is any need to worry about Ms. Abasolo. Now, if you'll excuse me, Miss Wild?"

Certainly, Father. It was nice to meet you."

"Likewise. Brother Tobias will see you out now." He turned and left the room.

20: IT TAKES A VILLAGE

Peñasco was little more than a wide place in the road, but still the largest of several nearby communities, each no more than a cluster of a dozen or two homes that barely showed up as freckles at the outer edges of the Picuris reservation on the map. This burg boasted a rural clinic, the Bear's Paw Café, a small general store that was seldom open, a gas station with limited hours and no pay-at-the-pump, four in-home roadside art galleries, and a summer-only potato store which ran out of a 1960-s double-wide trailer set on concrete blocks. It felt less like a town than a long stretch of disconnected, struggling enterprises scattered along the two-lane state highway. There was no visible town center. The largest structure one could see without leaving the pavement was the ranger station. Traveling through on a Sunday or after 4 p.m. on any winter day, one might think it a ghost town. But somewhere back of the main road the homes of several hundred villagers nestled in the surrounding hills, plus a school, the cemetery, a Catholic church, and its accompanying Penitente *morada*—the gathering place for the brotherhood in the community who discreetly practiced ancient rituals of self-flagellation and crucifixion re-enactment.

The easiest way to talk to people in Peñasco, as Dominic had learned, was to go to the Bear's Paw. I parked out front, went inside, and stepped to the register, ready to get some grub. I'd missed lunch and it was almost three in the afternoon, so I'd probably have to take whatever they had left.

The woman behind the counter interrupted me before I could place my order. "You're not going to cause trouble in here again like you did yesterday with Eddiejoe and his brutes, are you?"

"I think that's settled now," I said. "I just wanted to get some coffee..."

"You think it's settled, huh? Let me tell you something: nothing is ever settled around here."

"What do you mean?"

"Listen, honey, people here are still angry about things that happened hundreds of years ago. The Indians are mad at the Spanish for coming and taking their land five-hundred years ago. The Spanish are mad at the Indians for the Pueblo Revolt a hundred years after that. They both resent the Anglos for settling here over a century ago. And if somebody did something that you didn't like twenty years ago, it's still good cause for payback."

I had heard this story about northern New Mexico before, and saw some truth in it. "I just meant that I think the grazing permit issue..."

"You don't get it, sweetie. It's not over. You and your buddy might have backed Eddiejoe and his goons down yesterday, but they'll be looking for you now. Besides, this grazing thing is a double-grudge for him."

"I don't know what double-grudge means."

"He's already good and mad about the land deal that cut him out of a place to graze the cows. Now, he got his macho bruised by you guys for trying to graze them someplace else."

"Wait a minute," I said. "What land deal cut him out of a place to graze?"

She cocked her head to one side. Two long grey braids hung from beneath a ball cap that said *Talk to the Paw* across a graphic bear paw print. "That poet lady. She bought the land when she found out Eddiejoe was about to lease it for grazing."

"What land are we talking about?"

"Over by her place, that piece that belonged to old Bota Romero. He was going to lease it to Eddiejoe to graze his cows, but that writer gal got wind of it and came over to Romero's with a cash deal too sweet for him to pass up. Eddiejoe was furious."

"Are you talking about Adoria Abasolo? The US Poet Laureate?"

"Yes, her. This was a few years ago. She seemed nice enough, but after the land deal, everyone from Chimayo to Dixon and beyond shut their doors to her. She couldn't even buy a gallon of gas as far away as Velarde or a taco at the road-side stand down in Rinconada. Everyone with a drop of Hispanic blood around here took Eddiejoe's side, and that meant that author woman had to go all the way to Española for anything. One time, someone broke into her car at night, right outside the wall by her house. They put sugar in the gas tank— completely ruined the engine; she had to get a new car. She put a lock on the gate where her drive meets the road, so someone left about fifty bags of trash blocking her driveway so she couldn't get in and out. Then, they hauled a mattress up there and set it on fire at the end of her drive. For a while, it was so bad that she hired a security guard to watch her house around the clock. She really started keeping to herself after that, although she was never all that social to begin with. She used to come in here to breakfast sometimes and she came to a lot of the kids' little theater performances, even gave some money to the camp they started for the latch-key children. But after the whole thing with Eddiejoe, she didn't come around anymore."

"Could you tell me where I might find Bota Romero, the old man who sold her the land?"

"For that, you gotta go to the cemetery next to the church. He died about a month after the land deal was made. Why are you so fascinated with our persecuted poet?"

"I'm more concerned about getting some coffee and something to eat," I said, smiling.

"I'm out of burritos, but I got one scone left. You'll have to pay for it and the coffee, but the chit-chat was on the house." When she placed the coffee and a bag with the scone in it across the counter, she added: "You're about the fourth person in the past couple weeks asking about that gal. Must be because she's got that thing coming up at the inauguration."

"Who's been asking?"

"Strangers. That's all I know."

"Could you describe them?"

"Listen, I'd love to keep chatting with you, but I gotta sweep up, and then I got pies to bake and get ready for tomorrow. You need anything else?"

"No, thanks."

She held up a finger and then lowered it at me, as if it were loaded. "I wasn't kidding about Eddiejoe, doll. I'd keep one eye on my rear-view mirror if I were you."

21: PARKING VIOLATION

As Prescott had mentioned, thanks to a technology grant and the labor-intensive retrofit of a former radio tower, Picuris Pueblo had managed to guarantee cellular coverage for the reservation and nearly all of the surrounding area, except for in the low mountain passes. This achievement not only demonstrated the super-sized power of such an undersized indigenous population (Picuris was the smallest of the nine northern Indian pueblos in New Mexico), but it also endeared the Indians to many in the neighboring community. This was especially true for the Anglos and the few business owners, who benefited by this technology most—because no connectivity of any consequence had been present before the tribe moved to gain a foothold in the new millennium.

I was happy to take advantage of this relatively new development, too, when I got back in my Jeep outside the Bear's Paw. I checked the Screech Owl for messages, hoping that perhaps Kerry had left one for me. Nothing from him, but my favorite librarian Carla had called to let me know that she had a stack of research materials for me, so I should come by the library at my earliest convenience. And there was a voice mail from Roy, as well, but I cut it off before listening to it when darkness suddenly came over my vehicle. A sound like a jackhammer and a shadow in my rearview mirror told me something big had pulled in right behind me. I looked through the rear window and saw Eddiejoe Ibanez glaring down at me as he hung out of the passenger-side window of an ungodly huge exhaust-oozing monster idling less than a foot from my bumper.

If a truck could have a personality, this big, butch, super-pimped diesel dooly truck would have been Darth Vader— painted a flat stealth black (even to the wheel covers), with windows like obsidian mirrors, tricked out with a custom locomotive-style cow-catcher grille, and towering high on six oversized, heavy duty, all-terrain tires. The engine revved louder and louder, dominating everything in range with its near-deafening din.

The wolf rose up on all fours in the back cargo area and began to pant nervously and stare out the rear window. "It's going to be all right, Mountain," I said as I leaned as unnoticeably as I could to open the glove box. I carefully pulled out my pistol in its clip-on holster and then brought it across toward me, keeping it low and behind the cover of the seats. As I turned to open the driver's side door and stepped out, I used the motion to deflect attention from what I was doing simultaneously—reaching behind me to clip the holster on my belt in back.

Eddiejoe jumped out of the demon truck, went to the back of it and hoisted a plastic bag of considerable size and weight out of the bed. He came around the side of the vehicle and heaved it toward me. It landed right at my feet, just hitting the toe of one of my boots, bursting open and splattering the side of the car. "Just a little present, Chiquita," he yelled over the persistent pounding of the truck's engine. I'll give you something even better next time I see you." And then he turned and went back to the passenger side of the truck, stepped onto the running board, gripped the handle on the cab, and slid back inside. The Vader-mobile backed out onto the highway, and Eddiejoe rolled down the window and extended a leather-jacketed arm in my direction. A middle finger stood erect from his upside-down fist as the truck peeled away to the south.

From the smell, I already knew the nature of my "gift." It was at least twenty-five pounds of cow manure, and when the bag had cracked open, it splattered my boots as well as the Jeep and all around where I stood. I shouted after the truck. "Oh yeah? Well, I've had worse threats from much bigger containers of shit than this," remembering the time a couple years back when my brake lines had been cut and Mountain and I nearly collided with a septic pumper on a steep and winding gravel road. Since no one was around to appreciate my remark, I drug the offending parcel by its still-intact corners up next to the trash can beside the entrance to the café. I got back in my Jeep again, cursing myself for varying from my usual routine of parking my car nose-out, ready to get away. I also cursed the fact that since Eddiejoe wasn't driving that truck, I couldn't be sure what kind of a vehicle he would be in next time he came bearing gifts.

Within seconds, the smell of the manure on my boots and the bottom of my jeans began to pervade the atmosphere inside the car. I punched the voicemail icon on the Screech Owl and listened to Roy's message: "Jamaica, I just got a call from the monsignor, or whatever the hell you call him at that mission up there, and he was up in arms about you conducting some sort of top secret investigation into one of his neighbors. He said you're upsetting everyone in the community. Before I call Santa Fe—or he does, and gets us all in trouble—what the hell is going on? I assured the man that we worked as caretakers of public lands, and nothing we did was secret, but he said you had said otherwise. This fella was really steamed. I told him I'd get to the bottom of things and call him back, so how 'bout you call *me* and tell me what *is* at the bottom of this so I'll know what to say."

I put my forehead in my hand and sighed, then realized that my hand smelled foul, too—evidently handling that gift bag had left some of its goodies on my hands as well. "Wait here, Mountain," I said, and I went back into the café to wash my hands.

The same woman was sweeping the floor behind the counter, and the place was quiet. In the ladies' room, I used a damp paper towel to brush off the bottoms of my jeans and wipe off my boots. I washed my hands, then stopped back by to ask another question: "Do you happen to know what kind of a car Adoria Abasolo drives?"

She stopped and gripped the broom handle high up with both hands, leaning slightly on it. "I think it's a Mercedes, an SUV. Silver."

"And Ibanez? What does he drive?"

"Lord, that guy has about two dozen rides. He shows up in all kinds of things from big Harley hawgs in the summer to trucks like that one he was just riding shotgun in."

"So, you saw that? I'm sorry, I put that bag of manure up by your trash can. I didn't know what to do with it."

"Manure? That figures. Don't worry, we can use it. Makes a great winter dressing for the kitchen garden out back. I worried more that it might have been a dead animal, just by the look of it."

"He wouldn't do anything like that, would he?"

"Baby, I wouldn't put anything past him."

I got back in my Jeep and dialed the BLM. When I got Roy on the line, I felt acid begin to bubble in the middle of my chest. I hated having to lie to him. "Boss, it's me. I'm sorry you got taken to task by the abbot. I don't know why he's so upset."

"Well, what the hell are you doing asking a friar—or whatever you call him—a bunch of questions about his neighbor? I thought you were working with an archaeologist at the pueblo up there."

"I am. I'm working with a man named Prescott on some boundary issues at Picuris."

"So, what has all this got to do with the monastery and some woman neighbor of theirs? And did you tell them that what you're doing is top secret?"

"No, I...*we* wanted to ask this woman's permission to access the back of her property, and it borders the monastery. She isn't home and her housekeeper doesn't speak much English. The abbot sent some brothers to summon me to come talk to him. It was already well into the afternoon, and I still had a lot of work to do. I really didn't mean to involve him at all, but I went, out of respect, and while I was there, I asked if he knew when I might find his neighbor at home, or where she might be."

"Well, hell, that don't even sound like the same conversation that he told me about."

I hesitated a moment. "I don't know why I did it, but he seemed overly inquisitive about why I wanted to talk to her, and I just told him I wasn't at liberty to say."

"Why in hell did you say that? You know as well as I do that the church leaders in these small villages are the *de facto* government in nearly every case. Man's just trying to watch after his community. Why didn't you tell him the same thing you just told me?"

"I tried to, but he kept pressing, and it got my back up a little. I finally told him it was a matter between us and the landowner."

"Well, according to the father, he *is* the landowner. So he has every right to know what's going on."

"He's the landowner?"

"Yes, that's what he said, that lot where the neighbor that you were asking about lives—it belongs to the Mountain Mission. I don't hardly think a man of the cloth would lie about something like that when you can look it up in the public records."

"But...he led me to believe that he barely knew who I was asking about."

"Maybe he doesn't know this woman very well. Just because he's the landlord don't mean he's on a first name basis with her."

There had been nothing about this in the Secret Service file, nor the information I'd just learned about Abasolo buying her neighbor's land. The abbot hadn't told me he owned the property either. "Well, I can't think why he didn't tell me that when he had me there for a command appearance. I'm sorry this landed on you, Boss. What can I do to make it right?"

"Keep your nose out of things is what you can do. I already hear you taking exception to this guy and it can't do any good, given he's who he is, so leave it alone. Nobody can sniff up a bunch of trouble out of nothing like you, Jamaica. Why is that?"

"I don't know." The Boss had said this same thing to me more than a few times before, and I used to argue with him until too much evidence had mounted on his side for me to have a chance to win.

"I guess I'll call the guy back tomorrow and tell him what you told me. In the meantime, please try to steer clear of him. But if he happens to talk to you again and wants to know what you're doing, tell him, for chrissakes! I'll let you know if there's anything else we need to do to smooth things over."

"Thanks, Boss. Oh, and did you happen to get with Jerry Padilla about what kind of car Lor Talgren drives? I'd like to be on the lookout and try to avoid him."

"I did. In fact, I forwarded you an email Jerry sent me with the tag numbers and everything. Talgren has several vehicles currently registered and a few more with tags that aren't up to date, but Jerry says he's the type who would still drive them, regardless. So he could be in any of as many as 6 trucks and cars, most of 'em old clunkers, but a couple recent models, too. There's no way to tell which one he's going to be driving."

I was quiet.

"You haven't seen him, have you?"

"No."

"I hope to hell you don't. I think he must have been hepped up on something when he was in here. He was clean out of his mind. Remember, you call me when you head home tonight."

"Like I said, it might be late."

"I can get back to sleep if you wake me."

"Okay, Boss."

Once again, as I headed back to Taos, I took the High Road instead of driving west and down the mountains into Dixon. Partly, that was because I didn't want to go anywhere near Lor Talgren's place, and I would have had to go right past the turnoff to it if I'd gone the highway along the Rio Grande. But it was also because I needed to think, and the beauty of the scenic drive through the mountains and Carson National Forest was just the kind of thing that would quiet my addled brain and let my intuition go to work.

22: WILD TEMPLE

At this time of the day, in the late afternoon, the bright winter sun was still shining bright out on the flats of the high mesas. Yet as I drove through the mountains between Peñasco and Taos, I traveled deep into hollow valleys brimming like bowls of black tea with the shadows of the tall peaks around them. The ponderosas and junipers stood out black-green against the white snow, as if gathering for some solemn occasion— perhaps a ceremony for oncoming night, or a procession to mark the crisp cold of winter, or a memorial for one among them who finally succumbed to wounds from a summer lightning strike.

At the base of a steep slope, a turnoff to a trailhead was masked by snow, but I made out a gate—twenty or so yards in—that stretched across a cattle guard over a culvert. The narrow track leading to that gate offered just enough room for me to park the Jeep next to a stand of thick junipers, well off the highway. I backed the Jeep in, snug up against the trees, reached into the glove box and retrieved my leather medicine pouch, grabbed my rifle from behind the seat, and then opened the hatch to let Mountain jump out and savor some freedom. I knew that I would enjoy the liberty, too. As I climbed through the wide opening between the bars of the gate and headed up a gradual incline that led into the wildwood, I knew that I would soon feel my mind let go and my intuition kick in. I had journeyed enough in nature to know that any problem I needed to solve, any truth I longed to know, would be unraveled and made evident there—sooner, and more certainly than anywhere else.

Mountain glided noiselessly through the snow and deftly wound through the trees, his long, beautiful tail slightly elevated. His ears stood erect, pivoting, even when he lowered his muzzle to drink in the scents on the ground. At one point, he dropped to a low crouch, his nose pointed straight ahead, his haunches trembling. I followed the trajectory of his gaze and saw three bull elk foraging in the woods just beyond us. "They're too big for you to take, Buddy," I said softly, but even so, the sound of my voice split the silence.

The elk raised their heads high and looked for the source of this unusual disturbance. The youngest of the three turned and took a low hop and disappeared upslope. Another of the trio followed him. But the largest, with a massive rack of antlers and a full, thick throat covered with a dark brown mane, pushed his head higher and turned it to the side, eyeing us menacingly. Mountain made a false start to measure the bull's confidence, but the elk did not move. And now, neither did the wolf. The standoff continued for almost a minute, and then the bull seemed to lose interest. He turned and ambled off in the direction his pals had fled.

We continued on, and within a few minutes, my four-legged companion sped off like a bullet after a rabbit who had been grazing in a clearing. The hare took evasive action but found his adversary too clever to be fooled. It was all over in a minute, and I heard the bunny squeak as Mountain seized it in his jaws. I looked for a fallen tree or a rock outcropping to use as a seat while I waited. I wasn't going to get the wolf to surrender that rabbit, and I wasn't going to allow him to bring his prize home in the Jeep, so I might as well let him eat it here. I dusted the snow off of a wrinkled slab of lichen-laced stone and sat down, propping my rifle against the rock beside me.

At first, while I tried to appreciate the beauty of the spot, I was distracted by the sounds of ripping flesh, smacking lips, and an occasional crunch of bone. But in time, my senses began to train on other stimuli: the singing of the long-fingered pine needles in the breeze, the soft *pflump* of a mass of snow falling from a branch, the musty smell of bark, and the intense cold of the ancient stone against my backside. I felt the strength of this rock mass, which had been blasted here from the boiling center of the planet and left to cool and gather life around it so long ago. I sensed the ardor of the trees coursing upward with stoic determination. I knew that if ever there were a house of God, I was in it now.

I took a pinch of cornmeal from my medicine pouch and sprinkled it as an offering. I had brought these questions to the altar of this living sanctuary: Where was Adoria Abasolo and what had happened to her? And who was following me, and why?

As I studied the descent of confetti-like dust motes in a shaft of faint light, I tried to follow first one speck and then another, my eyes drifting with the slow, aimless free-fall of matter so light that it couldn't even interest gravity. Those dots of dust were like the particles of information I had gathered—non-cohesive, undefined, insignificant in and of themselves. Adoria Abasolo had disappeared more than three days ago, after writing what appeared to be drug-inspired poems marked by paranoia of people coming for her. She was living on land owned by the monastery and was somehow linked to that institution; however, she had bought the vacant parcel next to hers to prevent having cattle grazed there. In doing this, she had made enemies in the high mountain villages sufficient to make her unwelcome among nearly all her neighbors. But one local, a writing student, came regularly to the poet's home. And Adoria also employed a housekeeper who was a near-constant presence. Houseguests stayed at the residence when their hostess was not there. Abasolo had told the president-elect that she was going to a ceremony at Tanoah Pueblo, despite the fact that the neighboring pueblo, just a few miles from her house, had an almost identical schedule of public dances and events to commemorate sacred days. And where was her car? It wasn't at her home, and if it hadn't been found wrecked or abandoned, then it was likely that she was still with it.

More motes: Tecolote had told me to follow the money; Abasolo gave her prize winnings from both the Pulitzer and the Nobel Prize to charities. But which ones? I would need to investigate that, or ask Coronel if he could find out. Momma Anna had advised me to talk to the peyote plant, and Yohe had let on that a young man had stolen some of the medicine from the tribe. But Bone Man had said that there were never any women outside of the tribe at peyote ceremonies, and perhaps no outsiders at all any more. And besides, the fireplaces—as he called them—were almost always on Saturdays at sundown, according to him, and that didn't fit with the time when Adoria disappeared.

And what about the black Hummer that was following me? Could it be Lor Talgren? Roy said his dog had been euthanized yesterday morning, which seemed to fit—the first time I'd noticed it following me was yesterday afternoon. But how would Lor have known to find me on the High Road? It didn't make sense.

I sat alert in the silence for a few minutes, waiting for inspiration. And then I realized that silence meant that Mountain had finished the rabbit. I looked around, and my wolf companion was nowhere in sight. I stood and periscoped my head from side to side. No wolf. I hurriedly reached into the medicine pouch, pinched some loose tobacco, held it toward the sky and then the earth, and sprinkled it on the ground as an offering in thanks for the rabbit's life energy. I grabbed my rifle, studied the snow for tracks, then sprinted away in the direction they led, whispering, "Mountain? Mountain!"

The wolf was posed as still as a statue in a grove of trees, less than fifty yards from the Jeep. His eyes were fixed on the two-legged walking toward my vehicle. The man cupped his hands around his face and peered into the passenger window. I touched Mountain's back gently but he didn't react—meaning he had heard me approach. I ducked to a kneeling position beside him, under the cover of some low-reaching fir branches. I could smell the rabbit's blood, and I saw red stains in the fur around my companion's mouth and on his neck, making him look fearsome. Snow began to fall.

The man was tall, dressed all in black. He wore boots with the kind of tactical pants that military and law enforcement wore. His heavy jacket didn't disguise a muscular build. And the black stocking cap made it impossible for me to tell his hair color, but the fair skin on his face told me he was Anglo. He studied the ground and our footprints there, and his eyes followed the route we had taken up into the trees.

Fortunately, Mountain had come back well to the north of the way we had walked earlier, so the man's gaze angled away to one side of us. All the same, I ducked lower behind the arms of the tree. Mountain didn't move, alert, ready.

The man's head moved from side to side as he scanned the forest. The snow was falling faster now.

I carefully brought the rifle up with my right hand and laid the bottom of the stock into my left. I pulled the butt to my shoulder, careful not to stir the skirts of our sheltering fir as I did so.

The man looked up at the sky, perhaps noting the rapidly-increasing rate of snowfall. He turned and walked back to the highway, then headed northeast along the shoulder in the direction from which I had come—toward Peñasco.

Mountain started to move, but I reached my left arm out like a gate and held it in front of his throat. "Shhhh. Wait," I whispered. I noticed the accumulation of white flakes atop his forehead and along the ridge of his nose.

In less than a minute, I heard the sound of a vehicle on the road. The black Hummer, frosted with snow across its top and hood, drove past the turnout where my Jeep was parked and on toward Taos, a small storm of tiny white crystals taking flight in a fine spray behind it.

23: CLOSED TO THE PUBLIC

In Taos, I stopped by the library, where Carla waited at the research desk with a stack of books and papers for me. "Some of this would have taken too long to scan and email," she said, "so I just copied a page or two from a number of different sources. You can get more information if you want by requesting the original. And because we were talking about him yesterday, I put some things in there about that author Videl Quintana—the one whose book you checked out. Remember, I told you about his mysterious death, and the details still weren't sorted out yet? Among other things, he was big into peyote, and that's what you wanted me to research."

I used the computer at the library to check my email. Nothing from Kerry. But the list of vehicles that Roy had forwarded was there, and I printed it off. I wrote a quick message to my lover:

> *Dear Kerry,*
>
> *I miss you, my love. I hate having to write emails all the time. I wish I could hear your voice. Maybe we can talk soon. For the next day or so, I'm working where there's cell coverage, at least some of the time. So if you are anyplace where a phone works, try to call!*
>
> *I have little to add here beyond a small list of complaints: the bed is too cold and too empty*

*when you're not in it. And I'm so hungry for
another of your famous Forest Ranger Flapjacks.
Beyond that, there is only this one little matter of
housekeeping: I found one short brown hair on
the edge of the bathroom sink. I might chide you
for not policing it up properly...except that it made
me smile. I taped it to the nightstand so part of
you is near me at night.*

I miss your face.

Mountain misses you, too.

Love,

Jamaica

As I left, snow was falling gently. I held Mountain's leash in my left arm and with my right, I wedged the library materials against my body. A lump in my pocket dug painfully into the side of my hip. I loaded Mountain and the books into the car and reached into my pocket to find the offender. It was my bag of offering medicine I'd used in the forest, the small leather pouch I always kept in my glove box and regularly filled with sage, corn meal and loose tobacco. Suddenly I remembered something I'd seen in the folder *The Bartender* had given me. It had been one of the few items still legible on the receipt from a grocery store in Española—*Native American Spirit Tobacco, loose.* Tobacco—especially loose tobacco, and even more specifically Native American Spirit Tobacco, was traditionally offered to a medicine teacher or healer to show respect, and was also used as an offering to the Earth Mother in one's own medicine journey. Adoria was either seeing a shaman for healing or taking instruction in the medicine way.

"Okay, Buddy," I said to the wolf as I slipped behind the wheel and started the car, "I hope you're not too full from your rabbit snack. Because we're going to visit Momma Anna again." As I headed toward the north end of town, under a low grey cloud deck and softly falling snow, I noticed that many of the luminarias along the roadsides and the adobe walls lining the homes and businesses had already been lit in honor of Kings Day. The soft yellow light from the candles in the paper bags glimmered against the fresh white blanket surrounding them.

Because it was snowing and beginning to get dark, I decided to take the paved main road into Tanoah Pueblo from which I could veer off onto the narrow dirt lane called Rattlesnake Road right before entering the old part of the village. That way I could get to Momma Anna's place with less risk and rattle than going the back way. But when I got to the Rattlesnake turnoff, I saw a confrontation taking place between three people. As I pulled closer to the scene, I made out two Anglos—a man and a woman—arguing and waving their arms as a stoic Tanoah tribal policeman stood with his legs spread wide, unyielding, his arms crossed over his chest. I could tell by their perfect red parkas that this was the same couple who had been asking questions of Dominic Gomez in the Bear Paw yesterday in Peñasco.

I had no choice but to stop. If I'd veered around them and onto Rattlesnake Road, the tribal policeman would have eventually tracked me to Momma Anna's to question why a BLM vehicle was on the reservation during Quiet Time, and after business hours, to boot. And it might make trouble for my medicine teacher if she had to defend me as a family member or even just a family friend. So I stopped, got out, and approached the trio.

"It said in the *Nine Northern Indian Pueblos* brochure that there were dances today," the Anglo man argued loudly.

Nodding her head in agreement, the woman added: "The flyer said the public was welcome at the dances. You had no right to tow our car!"

"The War Council voted not to have the dances this Kings Day," the officer said. "That leaflet you got there says all events are subject to change and to call ahead to make sure."

"But we didn't know the pueblo was closed."

"You can't read?" The officer turned and pointed to the sign on the tripod in the middle of the road behind him. It read:

TANOAH PUEBLO IS CLOSED TO THE PUBLIC
NO TOURISTS OR VISITORS ALLOWED
THE PUEBLO WILL RE-OPEN ON JANUARY 12

He looked at me. "You can read that, right?"

"Crystal clear," I said. "Even in twilight with snow falling."

The two redcoats spun to see who had spoken.

I smiled. "Anything I can do to help?"

"Yeah, you can get this goon to give us our car back," the man barked.

I winced at the *goon* thing. "This officer is just doing his duty."

"And you were trespassing," the tribal policeman said. He pushed his chin high and looked down his nose at the two agitated pale-faces.

"We were not trespassing," the woman retorted.

"You parked here in an empty lot, which should have given you a clue, and you went right past this sign, and you were wandering around inside the wall of the village, in an area where there is nothing but residences, and where there are about a dozen *No Trespassing* signs."

"We got lost," she replied.

I cut in. "Look, I wonder if I can do anything to help resolve this situation. Can I give you two a lift back into Taos and you can plead your case to the War Council tomorrow?"

"A lift?" Parka-Man shouted, "we have a lift, it's our car. And this guy towed it off someplace."

I knew this cop. He was a good man. I gave him a pleading glance.

He picked up the mic on his lapel and held the talk button. He spoke in Tiwa to someone, turning away to keep the conversation private. He turned back and looked from one redcoat to the other. "You'll go peaceably and stay off the reservation while it's closed if I give you back your car?"

The male redcoat bit his lip, but the female nodded in silence.

"You two wait over there," the officer pointed at the side of the road near a cleared gravel parking area.

They shuffled away, grumbling to one another.

The Pueblo man took off his glove and extended a broad brown palm to me. "Agent Wild, how you doing?" His hand was warm as he shook mine.

"Officer Rainwater. Thanks for your leniency. It's Kings Day, so I think you did a good thing. Now everybody can go home happy tonight, having kept the peace."

"I wish I didn't believe there would be a next time," he said, "but things like this happen here almost every day. Tourists treat the pueblo like it's Six Flags, like we ought to be open 24/7 so they can tramp around our sacred places and gawk at us Indians and take pictures with their phones."

This was a common complaint. Unfortunately, a small portion of the tourists who flocked to the Taos area behaved as if all the riches of its tri-cultural heritage, all the beauty of its surrounding wilderness and wildlife, and all the events that were held in the villages, towns, and pueblos were simply entertainment for their benefit.

"I imagine that gets frustrating," I agreed. "I know how trying tourists can be, especially when they are ignorant of tribal customs and rights. I saw those two up on the High Road yesterday, asking a million questions of one of our field technicians. They're probably just trying to see all the sights in the area. I only stopped to see if I could do anything to assist. I didn't mean to interfere."

He grinned. "Well, you probably saved me some grief by butting in. I was about done with their belligerence. So what caused you to happen by right about now?"

"I'm not here on business," I admitted, "I'm visiting."

He narrowed his eyes.

"I was going to see a friend, an elder. But she doesn't live in the old part of the village, so I'll be outside the walls."

He put his glove back on and took his time adjusting his fingers into it, then looked up at me. "Tell you what. You take care of those two in them red marshmallow coats over there, and I didn't see you." As he said this, an oversized pickup approached, towing a green Subaru behind it.

I headed for the couple on the side of the road. "Hey, you guys, I know you're upset, but I think it's best if you don't say anything more to the officer. He's got your car here, so why don't we all calm down now, and you guys drive on. What do you say?"

The man's face was full of fury. "Excuse me, but just who are you?"

His partner squeezed his arm and then patted him, clearly trying to calm him down.

"I work for the BLM, and I'm the liaison to Tanoah Pueblo." I pointed to the patch on my jacket sleeve. "You can call me Agent Wild." I took out my badge and showed them the brass shield. "I'm a federal agent."

At this, they glanced quickly at one another. "Well, we didn't mean any harm," the woman said.

"I'm sure of that," I said. "It is unusual for the pueblo to be on Quiet Time right now. The new War Council came into power on the 1st of the month, and normally the Kings Day dances celebrate and symbolically give power to them from the tribe. There must be some important reason why they've cancelled the dances and closed the pueblo. Are you two visiting this area on vacation?"

The man answered, "Yes. We're here for the first time, just trying to see all the sights."

"Did you go to the dances over at Taos Pueblo today?"

This time the woman spoke. "No, we missed them. I guess we prefer things a little more off-the-beaten-path."

"Well, Taos Pueblo is a much larger tribe, and their dances are all the more magnificent because of their numbers. Next time around, try them first, and try during daylight. Dances usually start in the early morning hours."

"We came in daylight," the man grumbled. "It just got dark earlier than we expected."

"What are your names?" I asked.

They both hesitated. The female spoke. "I'm Uma. And this is Kyle."

"Hey, you two, your car is ready over here now," Officer Rainwater called from a few yards down the road where he and the driver stood next to the big truck that had towed the Subaru.

"We better get going," Uma said with a pinched smile, and the two promptly made for their car.

When I opened the door to my Jeep to get back in, a stench rose from the back of it that would have rivaled any cesspool. I waved my arms and screwed up my face. "Aw, Mountain! That rabbit is coming back to haunt us both!"

When I got to Momma Anna's place, her house was dark. I approached the door and knocked softly just in case, but I already guessed she wasn't home. There was no smoke puffing out of the woodstove and no tracks in the soft white powder that coated her walk. She'd been gone since before the snow began falling.

When I got back to the highway I called Roy while I had cellular coverage. "You told me to call before I headed home," I said.

"I wish to hell you had phone service out there," Roy said. "I got a bad feeling about this deal with Talgren. I don't think the man's going to let it go."

"I know what you mean. He's disturbed."

"You got that right."

"Well, I'll keep my sidearm with me, and I sleep with a shotgun by the bed," I said.

24: OUTFOXED

When I opened the hatch on the Jeep, Mountain scrambled out and fled into the darkness behind the cabin, so urgent was his need to relieve himself from the rabbit's revenge. But even as he bolted, he hesitated for just an instant to sniff at several small white mounds on the ground near the propane tank. I went to see what he had discovered and found the bodies of the mother fox and her two kits frozen and coated with snow next to the bowl I'd asked Coronel to set there the night before. I knelt and touched the stiffened body of the mama fox and saw that her lips were curled back and a frozen glob of gel extended from the corner of her mouth. "Oh no!" I gasped. Someone had put poison in the water. I stood and looked around, the message clear, the threat of it overwhelming the sadness I felt for the fox family.

I worked quickly to get in enough firewood to last the night. Coronel had only barely repaired the lock on my door by screwing the receiver for the slide bolt back into the same holes he'd busted it out of when he first arrived. As soon as I got a fire going, I pulled the screw gun out from under the sink and removed the slide bolt altogether so I could place it elsewhere on a new section of wood. But the battery on the drill went dead before I could reattach it. I plugged the battery into its charger and went outside with a flashlight to the shed. The power often went out on nights like this when sudden cold came and there was heavy moisture in the air, and I couldn't know for sure if the electricity would stay on long enough for the battery to charge. After rummaging around among the fence-building materials I had left from when we built an enclosure for Mountain, I found a two-by-four long enough to span the door, and I thought that if I had to, I could nail it across the jamb before I went to bed and pry it back off in the morning. A hammer didn't need a battery, but nailing a board across the door would not just keep an intruder from coming through it, it would also block me and Mountain in, which carried its own risks. I stopped by the Jeep and retrieved my handgun from the glove box. With Mountain and me back inside, I decided to wait for the battery to charge until bedtime, and hoped I didn't have to resort to the two-by-four.

I had no appetite after discovering the poor little foxes, and Mountain's bunny binge had pre-empted his evening meal, so once the fire was going well, I spread the things I'd picked up from the library across my kitchen table. I needed to distract myself from the tightness in my chest and the anxiety that came from the knowledge that I could be attacked at any moment. I was certain the foxes were the victims of Lor Talgren's rage, and I didn't know how far his desire for revenge over the loss of his dog would take the man. He could have poisoned the water thinking it was for Mountain and gone home satisfied that the matter was finished. Or he could be outside my cabin now, waiting for the right moment to come after me. It was an unfortunate fact that a considerable number of dogs were killed by poisoning every year in Taos County. But the people who poisoned their neighbors' dogs were generally among the less-educated population living in the small rural villages where folks had been handling their own affairs for centuries. And their actions were usually done subversively—with no announcement or threat—as a means to settle a score, without public ado. Lor Talgren, on the other hand, had pronounced his intention loudly and publicly, and seemed to care little that it was now a matter of record. Because he went looking for me at the BLM's offices, it seemed to me that Talgren had declared his own war and was not likely to consider putting some poison in a bowl enough to match all that noise and bravado. He meant to cause some suffering.

I flashed a look at my shotgun, still in the corner next to my bed. I pulled my Sig Sauer P229 out of its holster and laid it on the table beside me and took my seat in the chair facing the door. Mountain stretched out on the lambskin in front of the woodstove, his head on the knot of his tug like it was a pillow, his tummy making intermittent squeaks and snarls. I started sifting through the papers Carla had given me at the library. I glanced at a few of the articles and began separating them into three stacks as I went. One stack contained information about the American Indian Church. Another was the more generalized information about peyote. And finally, there were the things Carla thought I might be interested in regarding the notorious author, Videl Quintana.

I took a pen and a legal pad and began to scribble. I wrote: *Peyote,* and underlined it twice. I drew an arrow pointing downward and wrote: *Fireplaces at Tanoah Pueblo,* another arrow down from it, where I wrote: *Carries Water Clan? Boy stole peyote*

Beneath this, without a connecting arrow, I jotted two notes: *Quintana* and *Abasolo's recent poetry.*

On a fresh page, I scribbled the word *Monastery* and underlined it. Beneath this, I wrote: *Brewing beer, Beneficiary of Abasolo's prize-winnings? When did they last see Abasolo? Owns Abasolo's house/land.* Next to the note about Abasolo's land, I drew two lines leading to two other ideas: *Grazing land Ibanez wanted to use?* And: *When did Abasolo move into her house? Did monastery own it then?*

Finally, on a third page, I listed all the people I had encountered who might have anything to do with Adoria Abasolo: *Neighbor—Susan Lacy, Landlord—Father Anthony, Housekeeper, Eddiejoe Ibanez...*After that, I drew a blank.

I looked across the table and saw the information Carla had printed for me about Quintana. I made a wild leap and scribbled his name on the People list, too.

Shuffling through the pages Carla had provided, I noticed a reprinted article from the front page of *The Los Angeles Times* from November, 1998, carrying a big, bold headline: *Videl Quintana's Secret Death Leaves More Mysteries.* The article revealed that the author had died of liver cancer a few months before, but that the matter had been kept from the public. The journalist who discovered this had also learned that Quintana left an enormous estate, and a will that was being contested at the time of the story's publication. In fact, claims filed in contest of the will were how Quintana's death eventually came to light.

In recapping the author's life, the paper had few proven facts. Quintana professed to have been born in 1935 in Argentina, but the newspaper was unable to find records to substantiate this. In fact, most of what would normally be cited as life statistics in an obituary were questioned in the article. What the newspaper could verify was that Quintana and a woman named Rachelle Helena were married in 1981, and that Helena bore a daughter less than two weeks later. The couple named her Nona Dodd. But *The Times* said that Quintana also kept what the author and his cult of followers referred to as "a coven of witches," and Helena was but one of them. Only a month after daughter Nona Dodd was born, Quintana legally adopted an adult woman as his daughter, which was allowable under California law; and this newly-adopted adult woman was said to also be one of the "witches" in the coven. The paper went on to say that all four of the women who were reputed to be members of Quintana's coven disappeared soon after Quintana died. The reporter promised that the story would be continued as investigations into the whereabouts of the "witches" proceeded. Since Quintana was not merely an author of books that were questioned as to whether they were fact or fiction, but was also the leader of a cult and of this so-called coven of witches, the speculation among his followers was that the witches had "gone into the beyond" with Quintana when he passed.

I shook my head. *What craziness!* None of this had anything to do with Adoria Abasolo's disappearance. I drew a line through Quintana's name on my list of people. *What was I thinking? She has his books on her bookshelf—so what? He writes about peyote—so what?* I hesitated. I went back to the page titled: *Peyote* and saw Quintana's name on that list, too.

I got up and fished the blue cardboard file that President-elect Vargas had given me out of my backpack and brought it back to the table. I read through the stats on Abasolo's life: born 11/30/1954 in São Paulo, Brazil, took advanced classes at the University of São Paulo while still attending high school in her home city, then just shy of the age of eighteen became Maria Vargas' roommate at Stephens Women's College in Columbia, Missouri, via a scholarship in literature. So while Quintana—who was perhaps thirty years older than Abasolo and already published—was marrying, fathering, adopting, and maintaining women in a coven as witches, Abasolo was studying literature, earning an undergraduate and two advanced degrees, publishing her own books of poetry, and earning the Pulitzer Prize. There was nothing there.

I stretched my arms above my head and yawned. I began gathering the three stacks of papers into one when Mountain suddenly awakened and sat upright. I listened, and then I heard it, too: the sound of a car engine. Someone was coming up my long drive.

I raced to the switch by the door and shut off the light, then grabbed the heavy government-issue flashlight that could easily double as a club. I crouched behind the table and slid the handgun off the top and grasped it, ready to fire. I didn't need to rack the slide to chamber a round. After the events of the prior winter, when a greedy local landowner had sent goons to trap, beat and try to rape me and had later left me out on the mesa tied to a post as food for a family of mountain lions, I had begun carrying my sidearm with a round in the chamber, ready to go.

The sound of the car grew closer and then stopped, just off the side of the porch. I heard a car door open and then shut softly. *One guy,* I thought. *At least it's only one guy.* I strategized how I could fire the first shot and then hurdle across the bed and into the corner behind it and use the shotgun if I needed to do more. Mountain had risen to all fours but had not moved from in front of the woodstove. He sensed the danger, and at least at this moment, he acknowledged my leadership in our small pack.

Footsteps crossed the wood plank porch, and there was a soft knock on the door, which promptly sprung open because of the missing slide bolt. With my left hand, I turned on the flashlight, aimed it directly at the intruder's face and raised my right hand with the Sig Sauer pointed in the same direction. I yelled: "Stop right there or I'll blow a hole right through your head!"

"Dammit, Wild!" Agent Coronel's hands flew up into the air over his head and he dropped something heavy, which hit the porch with a dull thud. "What the hell is the matter with you? Why do you pull a gun on me every time I come to see you?"

I raised up from my crouch and set the flashlight on the table, shouting back at him, "Why do you always come sneaking around my cabin after dark?"

"I wasn't sneaking around!" His voice thundered, bouncing off the corners of the cabin walls. "I drove right up the drive this time, didn't park down at the intersection, I knocked on the door, the damn thing just swung open when I knocked, I didn't do anything to make that happen."

By then, I had hurried to the doorway and flipped the switch beside the frame, allowing light to fill the room. My heart felt like a speeding train in my chest. "I was going to put the slide bolt on in a different place." I noticed I was practically screaming this, as if there were a contest to see which of us could be louder. I reined my voice in but it was still uncontrolled as I added, "The wood is splintered where it came off the other night when you broke in."

Coronel lowered his hands. He bent and picked up the bag he had dropped. "I can help with that," he said, and he pushed the fingers of one hand through his hair as if to unruffle his feathers. "I brought you a new locking doorknob and a heavy-duty slide bolt." He looked at me, and I noticed that his face was red—either from the cold or from adrenalin.

"That's kind of you," I said, feeling a little foolish. "But my drill battery went dead when I tried to fix the lock before. I don't know if it's charged up again yet." I looked at the receiver on the kitchen counter, hoping to see the green light that indicated the battery's energy was restored. But it wasn't even blinking amber, as it usually did when it was charging. "Shit," I said. "It looks like the whole thing has died."

Coronel went to take a look. "Could be your charger was the problem all along. Let me see if I have anything in the car." He went out the door and I heard his footsteps cross the porch toward the drive.

I looked at Mountain. He was still peering out the door to see what was going to happen next. I took a few deep breaths, trying to calm my nerves. I slid my handgun back into the holster and pushed the stack of papers on the table to one side.

When Coronel came back through the door with his tool kit, he said, "We gotta stop meeting like this."

Later, I was getting up to refresh my cup, but I noticed he'd only drunk a sip or two of his. "You don't like tea much, do you Harold? May I call you Harold?"

"Call me Hank," he said. "And, no, I don't much like tea. It tastes like boiled twigs and grass clippings or something close to that."

I laughed. "Well, don't hold back! Tell me how you really feel about it!"

He laughed, too. Then he sobered and pressed his chin forward, thinking for a moment. "So basically, all you have is some questions about who owns what land. Did Abasolo give the land she lives on to the monastery, or did she rent from them? And did she buy the land that guy—what's his name—wanted to graze his cattle on just to prevent that from happening, or was she going to build on it or whatever? And you want me to try to find out if the monastery is one of the charities she gave her prize winnings to. Am I right?"

"I also think there could be something to the peyote thing," I said.

"You don't have anything there, from what you told me."

"I know, but I think I should follow it."

"We don't have time. We need something solid. Now."

"I know," I said, "but things don't move fast in this part of the world."

He got up from the table and pressed his fists into the small of his back, arching his abdomen forward and stretching. "I haven't got much to share either, but there are a couple of things I'm looking into. Abasolo had a cell phone and made frequent calls to one number in the past few weeks. We're trying to track that number down. And I have a friend looking into something peculiar I noticed on her birth certificate."

"Her birth certificate? What about it?"

"I'm not sure. I will get back to you when I have something real, but I thought it looked phony. Of course, I don't look at a lot of birth certificates from Brazil. I have a guy checking it for me."

"Why would she have a phony birth certificate? I mean, isn't she already vetted since she's doing the inaugural poem? Wouldn't she have to be who she says she is to get the Pulitzer Prize and the Nobel Prize for literature in poetry? Even to get the scholarships she did to go to all those high-dollar schools?"

"It could be nothing," Coronel admitted. "But we have to turn over every stone, and we don't have much else besides our instincts to follow at this point." He put his hand on top of the jacket he'd hung over the back of the chair. "You think you can relax and get some rest with the door like it is?"

I raised my eyebrows. "Sure. That slide bolt you put on will hold for now, I think. Thank you."

"I'll bring a screw gun and put the new doorknob on tomorrow. Sorry I didn't have what I needed for that."

"Well, I appreciate it. I guess I need to buy a new drill anyway, so I can get it."

"It's no trouble. I'll come back tomorrow and bring what I need. You want me to put some water out for the foxes?"

"No," I said, and without notice, I felt tears well up in my eyes. I fought to hold them back, but one escaped and fled down my left cheek. "I'm sorry. This is so not like me," I said, and I grabbed a square of paper towel off the roll and dabbed at my eyes.

"What is it?"

"The foxes are gone."

Hank Coronel wrinkled his brow at me. "You mean they moved away?"

I drew in a long breath. "No, I mean they're dead. Someone poisoned the water."

His face went blank for a moment. "What kind of a sonofabitch does that?" He crossed the room toward me, and before I knew it, he had gathered me into his chest, one hand patting my back. "No wonder you're so twitchy. I'm sorry about your little fox family."

I didn't move. Coronel hugged me tightly and his patting evolved into a small circular rubbing between my shoulder blades. I felt the warmth of him, and I smelled a faint hint of cologne on his sweater that reminded me of the woods in autumn. I remained as still as I could, part of me wanting to collapse into that warmth and that earthy scent and be consoled, and part of me uncomfortably aware of how awkward this all was. He pulled back slightly, looking down at me from the closeness of his loose, but still-present embrace. "So, is this personal, this poisoning your foxes? Is it a message from someone?"

"I think so," I said, and I recapped the story of Lor Talgren and his rabid dog as briefly as I could.

"Jesus," Hank said, one arm still around me, as he gestured with the other. "It's like a third world country here! You sure you don't want me to stay so you can get some rest?"

I turned and slid out of the warm shelter of his chest, away from his enveloping arm, and I stepped across the kitchen and threw the square of paper towel in the trash, as if I couldn't wait any longer to unburden myself of it. "No," I said. "Mountain and I will be all right."

"If I had the manpower, I'd put a detail on you," he said.

"Hey, no worries. You know how I am," I smiled, bravely. "I draw first and ask questions after."

As I propped myself up on my pillows in bed later, I read more of Adoria Abasolo's poetry. A few lines in a poem titled *What Is Left Behind* intrigued me:

The waning flower's petals drop.
Her radiance fades.
Another blossom already waits
To take her place,
A vigorous bloom of radiant promise
That burst into the garden
And without warning,
Forced the world to change

25: FREAKBOY

The next morning, I headed out early for Tanoah Pueblo. The top of Taos Mountain and the bowl of the ski valley were frosted with fresh snow, and a pink light to the east of Wheeler Peak illuminated a giant blooming cloud with the first blush of sunrise. The tribe's herd of bison grazed in the pasture close to the highway, their breath steaming around their faces. I drove down Rattlesnake Road toward Momma Anna's house and saw the small adobe homes huddled in the rural fields outside the main pueblo walls begin to glow in the yellow light of the morning sun. Beyond the thin skeins of gray smoke curling from the chimneys, there was no sign that the residents of Tanoah Pueblo were awake.

But Momma Anna already had the coffee on and was feeding the ancestors when she invited Mountain and me into her home. To my surprise, Yohe was sitting at the kitchen table kneading a mound of bread dough, indicating she'd been there a while. "You're just the person I wanted to see," I said. "Well, actually, both of you."

I started to remove my jacket, but Yohe said, "Keep that. You go stir fire out there." She tipped her head toward the back door, indicating the direction of the *horno,* the outdoor adobe oven where Momma Anna, like all the Pueblo women, baked bread, cookies, pies, and other delights. I went to the back of the house and took the poker to the ash-covered logs in the base of the big oven, shoving the wood to expose the red glow of fire within the thick coat of ash. I picked up the rubber dish draining mat that Momma Anna kept nearby to fan air across the smoldering embers. Yohe came out with three pans of bread dough lined up along one long, muscular arm, and she placed these, one at a time, on the oven floor above the fire, then used the poker to push them back into the dark recess of the *horno*. We both worked to secure the heavy door, and then I adjusted the smaller door on the fire box so it was barely drawing in air. I had been taught to bake this way by Momma Anna and the aunties in her clan. The fire only needed to be ablaze for the time the oven was open, to counteract any cooling that might occur. Otherwise, only a small, low flame was required to bake the bread loaves up plump and brown and to make crisp cookies and prune pies.

Yohe looked to the east and checked the position of the sun. This was her way of setting a timer so she would be ready to retrieve the loaves when they were done.

A few minutes later, as we enjoyed plates of venison stew, I told Momma Anna and Yohe why I had come. "I am still looking for the Spanish woman," I said.

They looked at one another, then down at their plates.

"I am worried about this person's safety," I said. "She is an important woman to people holding an upcoming ceremony in this country, and I am concerned that she may be in danger. I would not bother you with this if it weren't an urgent matter."

The two women looked up at me, and Yohe spoke. "She maybe go fireplace, that Spanish. That time, some Picuris come. They not have fireplace Picuris, come here in winter."

I waited for more, and after a long silence, I spoke: "I wonder if the Spanish woman came with a man or a woman."

They ignored my comment.

Anna got up and started clearing our plates and I thought our chat had ended. But after a moment, Yohe said, "Women, not too many go fireplace. But this time, some women Carry Water Clan hold fireplace, invite women, invite relative from Picuris. Maybe the Spanish come that time."

I said, "I wonder if anyone knows what happened to the Spanish woman."

Again, the two women looked at one another. Yohe shook her head. "Nobody talk, that. Boy take medicine, so no more fireplace, that what they talk about. Make that Freak-Boy go stay relative, away from here. *Unh!*"

Freak-boy? I wondered.

Momma Anna brought a rag from the sink and began picking up items and wiping under them, then nudged my elbow aside and cleaned in front of me. She seemed to read my thoughts. "Federico Yazza, that boy, his mom call him Rico, but them guys he hang around, they call him Freako, some his friends just say Freak. He belong Glorianna Reyos, Sky Runner clan. She much shame, they send him away."

"So, the boy's from here, not Picuris," I said.

Yohe nodded. "Him Tanoah. But now go Picuris, stay with uncle."

"I wouldn't keep pressing like this if it weren't that a woman is possibly in danger," I said, "but I have one more thing I am wondering about. I am thinking perhaps there is a shaman or teacher in the Carry Water Clan whom this Spanish woman, Adoria Abasolo, might have come to see. I believe she was bringing tobacco to someone."

They both laughed. "Maybe Rico bribe one them old men," Yohe said, and the giggling continued. "Get Spanish in village, that way."

Momma Anna clutched the lower corner of her apron and pulled it in front of her mouth, having a good chuckle at the idea of putting one over on one of the elder men who sat at the gate to Tanoah Pueblo to authorize whoever entered.

26: THE SWITCH

As I was leaving Tanoah Pueblo, Roy called me on the Screech Owl. I talked to him via the Jeep's hands-free system while I drove.

"Before you get too deep into whatever trouble you got planned for today, I need you to stop by the ranger station in Peñasco and leave your Jeep. The detailer in Santa Fe will pick it up from there and put the new decals on it. Gomez is off today; you can drive his rig. It's parked there at the station. It shouldn't take that long to hose off the doors and stick a couple of BLM emblems on them, but just because this is New Mexico, you might as well plan on them having your Jeep the whole day. You can switch vehicles back out when you get ready to head home."

When I got to the ranger station, I moved the things I thought I would need for the day from my Jeep into Gomez's Blazer and put the backseat down to enlarge the cargo area for the wolf, spreading one of his blankets over the carpeting. I made sure to transfer my rifle and the backpack containing the documents I'd been studying to the car as well. Gomez's rig had a sheath for a rifle and another for a shotgun on the back of the front passenger seat, so I stowed my Remington there. I clipped my handgun on my belt rather than put it in the glove box like I normally did.

I headed for Picuris Pueblo, taking the turnoff from the county road and following the graded dirt lane about a half-mile. I parked the Blazer well off the side with the right two wheels in a shallow culvert and lowered all the windows halfway so Mountain would have some air. Since it was Quiet Time at Picuris, not only was I forbidden to drive on the reservation, but I wasn't even supposed to be there at all. I was hoping that I would see someone at the main gate leading into the village so I could ask them to have Paul Deherrera come out to talk to me. Unfortunately, the scarf I normally kept for covering my hair was still in my Jeep, so I pulled my long locks pony-tail-style through the opening in the back of a BLM ball cap that Gomez had left in the car, tucking up my bangs on either side.

I was in luck. I'd only gone about a hundred yards when I saw a youngster coming down the road on a low-slung, fat-tired bicycle. I could make out more details as he got closer—the black leather jacket and torn jeans, the Mohawk. It was the same teenaged boy who had come to see what all the ruckus was about two days ago during the talking stick incident.

"I thought that might be you," the young man said as he came in fast and then braked, twisting his front tire and spitting rocks and grit. "I couldn't tell at first with your hair up in that hat."

I smiled. "What's your name?"

"Why?"

"I just wondered. If we're going to have a conversation, we ought to know one another's names. Mine is Jamaica Wild."

"I know who you are," he said. "I asked around about you. Call me Ray."

"Okay, Ray." *Not Rico, Freak, or Federico,* I thought. It also occurred to me that if he knew this Freakboy—and as small as Picuris Pueblo was, he surely did—he might warn him if I let on that I was I was looking for him. "Hey, I need a favor," I said. "Could you have Paul Deherrera come out to talk with me? Obviously, I can't go in the village now; it's Quiet Time."

The young man tipped his chin up. "Why do you need Paul? I can tell you whatever you want to know."

"Thanks, but I just need to talk to Paul."

"Okay, I'll see if I can find him. If I can't, I'll come back and let you know so you won't be left waiting." He spun his back tire as he made a quick turnaround on his bike and returned to the village.

I lingered for nearly a half hour before Deherrera approached. The sun had climbed up above the trees and was busy creating that signature New Mexico mild winter day that made you forget that the thermometer had read fourteen below zero just four or five hours ago. I was almost too warm in my heavy BLM jacket, but I kept it on because it covered the sidearm on my belt. Paul Deherrera approached in his shirt sleeves with a down vest that was open in front.

He gave me a smile and a gentle handshake. "I did not expect to see you again so soon."

"I know, and I'm sorry to bother you during Quiet Time, but I need your help. I'm…"

BOOM! A thunderous blast shook the air around us and then echoed across the nearby peaks in cannonades. I turned to look behind me, toward the source of this barrage. A thick column of black smoke surged into the sky from down the road, right where I'd parked the car. "Mountain!" I screamed. "MOUNTAIN!" I tore off running as fast as I could toward the smoldering Blazer. As I ran, I saw a tongue of orange flame emerge from under the hood, then another and another, licking at the sky like great snakes rising out of a nest. "Mountain," I cried, gasping for air as I forced my legs to run faster toward the smoke and fire.

As I approached the burning vehicle, I smelled scorching metal and felt a wall of intense heat. I made for the back hatch but to my surprise, it was already open. The car was filled with a thick smog of dark smoke and I couldn't see inside.

"Miss Jamaica!" A voice shouted emphatically over and over, barely audible above the cracking and popping. "Miss Jamaica! Miss Jamaica! Over here!"

I turned in the direction of the shouting and saw the young boy called Ray huddled on the ground a few yards away, his bike down in a heap beyond him. His face bore dark smudges on the cheeks and forehead, his behind was up in the air and he was bent over, as if he were protecting something. I saw Mountain's head peeking out from under Ray's chest. "Mountain!" I sobbed as I ran toward the pair.

"I got him out," Ray said. "I got your backpack, too, and your rifle." He pointed at a pile of smudged items on the side of the road. "I saw smoke coming out of your car, and I got what I could. Then, I think the carburetor must have blown." He stood up, but Mountain remained prone on the ground.

"Oh, God. Are you okay?"

"I'm okay," Ray said. "I tried to put that dog blanket over him but he was too afraid so I just threw myself on top of him right when that explosion happened."

I knelt to examine Mountain, and he licked my face, but his ears were down and he was trembling. "Oh, Mountain," I cried. "Are you all right?"

The wolf gave the slightest wag of his tail.

I turned to look at the Pueblo boy more closely. "Are you sure you're not hurt?" Behind him, the Blazer was living up to its name as flames had fully involved the engine now. "Let's get back," I said. "Hurry, before the gas tank goes."

As we moved away from the noise and the smoke of the burning vehicle, I heard the faint sound of sirens coming from far away down the county road.

☾

The big blowup had drawn an assemblage of firefighting vehicles and personnel, including six members of the Peñasco Volunteer Fire Department, two technicians from the Peñasco ranger station, and a little later, six hotshots from the Type 1 Carson National Forest Team who had been working mitigation between Rinconada and Pilar during the winter off-months.

One of the firefighters from Peñasco was also an EMT, and he immediately pulled me aside for a rudimentary examination. I was more concerned about Mountain, who had been in the smoking vehicle and close by when whatever exploded in the engine blasted smoke and flames. "I'm okay," I told the EMT. "I wasn't even close when the fire started. But that Pueblo boy was right here, and he saved my wolf. You should check him to make sure he's all right." I turned around to point to Ray, but he was nowhere in sight.

The firefighter looked around, too. "I don't see him. There's a lot going on, he might be somewhere nearby. If you see him, bring him to me, and I'll check him out. I'm just looking at your wolf, and he seemed like he followed you over here okay, no limping or anything. But he does look scared. Just to be sure, you might want to have your vet check him out." He turned to look down the road as a car approached. "Oh, there's Chief Salas coming now."

The chief of the volunteer fire department pulled up in a tricked-out red Humvee which had been outfitted as a fire attack vehicle with a winch on the front plus a pump motor and 300-gallon tank. He stopped and looked over the scene. The crew had hosed the blackened Blazer with water from the two tanker trucks until it stopped emitting steam. The hotshots had already cleared weeds and dry grass on both sides of the road, creating a narrow circular track of dirt which would serve as a fire break to prevent any sparks which might have flown into the surrounding fields from turning a one-car fire into a major wildland event. The chief got out of his truck and walked over to a group of the attending crew and began talking with them. After a few minutes, they turned to look at me, and one man pointed in my direction.

The EMT and I had been standing in the shade of one of the tankers, but now he put his stethoscope and other items back in the medical bag and left to put it back in the truck.

The chief approached me. "I'm José Salas. I'm the fire chief. You the one whose car blew up?"

"I'm afraid so," I said. "Actually, it's the BLM's, but I was driving it. I picked that rig up at the ranger station just a little while ago. I only drove it a few miles, from the station to where I parked it there. I turned off the engine and walked down the road since it's Quiet Time in the pueblo, and I'd been gone about a half-hour when we heard a big *bang* and saw smoke churning into the sky."

"They're gonna pry the hood up as soon as it's cool enough," he said. "Since you're BLM, I guess the ranger called for a fire investigator from Santa Fe. They'll be here any time now to determine the cause."

"Do I wait here, or can I go and maybe leave my phone number so the inspector can contact me?"

"I think you better stay here. Shouldn't be too long now."

"I'll stand by, then. So, I was checking out your Humvee. That's the first one I've seen outfitted like that."

"Yeah, you know our district covers about 90-square miles of rough mountainous terrain. We gotta use some innovative ideas to provide fire protection. One of our guys got us a grant, and we purchased that and equipped it so we can reach some of the more difficult areas."

"Not too many Hummers on the road these days. They were all the rage when they first came out."

"Well, that extra-wide base and the heavy frame makes it perfect for what we need it to do. Plus you can pack a lot of gear in the rack on top. Military still uses them for the same reason."

"I've seen a black Humvee up here on the High Road around Peñasco several times in the past few days," I said. "You wouldn't know who else owns one around here, would you?"

The chief chuckled. "Nobody owns one around here. We're just a poor little village, mostly unemployed. If we didn't get that grant, the fire department wouldn't have one either. That pumper and that tanker over there, those are the newest equipment we have, and they're ten years old. Everything else is mid-1990's or older. This Hummer is our prize, and it was a lot easier to get a grant for it than for the quarter of a million dollars we would need to buy a new fire truck."

Now that the fire threat was past and the Blazer sat blackened on the side of the road, the crews began to disperse. I found Deherrera talking to some of the Picuris who had come out to see the scene. "I wonder if you might know where that boy on the bike went."

He shrugged his shoulders. "He could be anywhere. He rides that bike of his up and down every game trail and all through the woods."

I sighed. Already, it had been a long day, and it wasn't quite eleven in the morning. I took one of my cards from my shirt pocket and scribbled the number for the Screech Owl a second time on the back of it, so he wouldn't call the BLM office in Taos, which was the first number listed on the front. "Will you please make sure he gets this and ask him to call me?"

Paul's brow furrowed. "I can tell him any message you have."

I shuffled my feet in the dirt of the culvert, trying to figure out what to say. *The Bartender* had instructed me to keep my investigation secret. I had already let on to two aunties at Tanoah Pueblo that a woman was missing and I was looking for her, plus the abbot at the Mountain Mission was suspicious. There was no way I could keep this under wraps if I kept on asking questions. I was thinking of ways I might glean the information I wanted from Paul Deherrera when one of the firefighters waved at me and shouted: "Fire investigator wants to talk to you."

"Be right there," I called back, and then I turned to Deherrera again. I spoke the truth when I said, "I want to thank the boy for getting my wolf out of the car. I'd like to tell him personally. He saved Mountain's life."

27: IN DEED

After I'd spoken with the fire inspector, I arranged a ride for Mountain and me to the ranger station in the back of a Forest Service truck. I went to pick up my backpack and heard Buzz thrumming in the front pocket of the pack. I punched the green button and before I could answer, a woman's voice said: "Good afternoon, Miss Wild. You will see a document of interest when you press on the link in your messages application. Should you need to contact me, dial zero. Have a safe and productive day." She hung up.

"Have a safe and productive day, my behind," I muttered. I shoved the phone into my jacket pocket, threw the backpack on the bed of the pickup, carefully placed my rifle along the raised side of the tray, and was startled when Mountain jumped up and laid down on the truck bed beside it. Once we were hunkered down in the back, the rangers headed toward the state highway. I pulled Mountain to me and held him tightly around the neck. I tried to sing to him, as I often did when he was anxious, but I couldn't hear my own voice over the truck's engine and the clatter of the tires rattling along on the gravel road. I felt my racing pulse slow a little, and my adrenalin level begin to subside. *Who torched the Blazer?* I wondered, certain that it was no accident. *Was it Lor? Did he see me get in it at the ranger station and then follow me to where I parked it?* It made perfect sense. He'd sworn to get even over his dog, and killing

Mountain would be his objective in that case. *Or was it Eddiejoe Ibanez?* The gal at the Bear's Paw seemed adamant that he was a vigilante and would seek any means to settle scores. In addition to these two possibilities, I thought of the man dressed in quasi-military style who had followed me in the Hummer and peered into the windows of my Jeep when I stopped on the High Road yesterday afternoon. *Who was that guy?*

I pulled out Buzz and found the link to the document mentioned in the call earlier. It was a recent filing in Taos County regarding Abasolo's property, transferring its ownership to the Mountain Mission Monastery, with the stipulation that Abasolo could continue to live on the property for the duration of her life. I glanced over it briefly but didn't take the time to read every detail on the tiny screen of the device. "I know where we're going next, Buddy," I said to Mountain, and I tousled his ears. "I could be wrong, but I think it's a fairly safe place…for a change."

When I got to the ranger station, my Jeep was still there, still spattered with dried mud, no decals on the doors. Obviously, the detailer hadn't come for it yet. I went to load my backpack, my rifle, and Mountain into the car, when I saw a doubled-over sheet of paper wedged between the wiper blade and the windshield. I unfolded it and read the big letters scrawled in thick red marker: *Roy says you are to call him NOW!*

It was only then that I realized that I had left the Screech Owl in the cup holder of the Blazer and it had no doubt been obliterated in the fire. That meant that if Roy had tried to call me—or if anyone else who had the number had tried—their attempts had been in vain. So the number I'd just scribbled on my card and given to Deherrera to give to Ray wouldn't work, and I'd have to figure out another way to try to find Freakboy.

Mountain and I were already inside the door of the ranger station when I realized that the scorching of the Screech Owl also meant that when Kerry tried to call or text, he, too, would not be able to get through. I had done a pretty good job of disguising how rattled I was at the scene of the car fire. But now, I felt a huge weight descending onto my shoulders, and I almost couldn't move. I closed my eyes and breathed deeply, in and out, a few times.

"You okay, Agent Wild?" A woman behind the high reception desk with a name tag that identified her as *Vicky Kasza* was leaning forward, studying me with a wrinkled brow, as if she wasn't sure whether to call an ambulance or offer solace. I must have looked terrible, because before I could think how to answer, she and the two field techs who had just given me a ride hastened over in unison, arms extended, as if they thought I might collapse. The woman gestured to a chair.

I didn't sit, but instead asked, "Could I get a drink of water for me and my wolf? And I need to use your phone."

It felt reassuring to hear Roy's voice on the other end of the line, barking and cussing like he always did when he was concerned about me, which was a fair amount of the time. "I just got off the line with the fire inspector. He's not done looking at the evidence yet, but he seems to think that someone tampered with the Blazer."

I told him about the dead foxes, and that I was concerned it had been Lor Talgren who poisoned them.

"Dammit," The Boss said. "Did you call the sheriff about it?"

"It's no use talking to them about someone killing wildlife, believe me. They didn't care when a lunatic was decimating the only wolf pack in this part of the state, remember? So they're not going to care about a few foxes. Besides, I couldn't prove it was Lor."

"Well, now we got something that goes way beyond poisoning a few foxes, Jamaica. You're still off-book with me, but I say you get off-book with that other deal, too, and take some personal time. We'll get you a paid leave order."

"It's not going to help if it was Lor Talgren. If he's the one who tampered with the car, then he must have seen me switch vehicles and followed me. How else could it have happened? And even if I took some leave time, he knows where I live. We can be sure of that because of the foxes."

"Well then, first off, we gotta get you someplace else to stay."

I was quiet a moment. "I think you might be right about that."

"Have you got someplace? Be better if you weren't alone."

"I have a place in mind. I'll let you know for sure. And I'm not alone. I have Mountain."

☽

The treacherous, cliff-edge road to the monastery had been freshly graded, and although that still didn't eliminate the washboard-effect, it made the drive considerably smoother. I drove in silence, trying not to think of anything but the stretch of dirt and gravel ahead of me.

But when I arrived, the mission seemed anything but calm and serene. Looking through the gates, I could see a dozen or so of the brothers scurrying around between the two buildings on either side of the main chapel. Another pair of monks worked with brushes and paint to touch up the window frames and wood trim around the doors. I rolled down the windows to leave Mountain some air, and I worried whether he might be unwilling to stay in the Jeep after what had happened earlier, but he stretched out in his familiar cargo area and looked like he was ready to nap, so I left him to sleep off some of the stress.

The two great entry doors stood open, and I was wondering whether or not I should pull the rope and ring the bell. Before I could make up my mind, I saw Brother Tobias walking in my direction, though he hadn't noticed me yet. He was holding two large iron candlesticks and had been about to cross into the library when he glimpsed me standing there. "Hello," he said, and when he hesitated a moment after that, I guessed that he'd forgotten my name.

"It's Jamaica Wild, Brother Tobias," I said. "How are you?"

"Oh, yes, yes, Miss Wild, of course. I'm sorry...were we expecting you?"

"No, I'm pretty sure you weren't," I said, "but it looks like you're expecting somebody. Everybody seems to be rushing around like the Pope is coming or something."

"Well, we're not expecting His Holiness the Pope, but His Excellency the Archbishop of Santa Fe has decided to come for a visit."

"Is Father Anthony here? I need to talk with him."

Brother Tobias gave a slight frown. "I'm afraid we only allow women at the monastery by appointment, Miss Wild."

I thought about this for a moment. "Well, tell him it's about his neighbor, Adoria Abasolo and I have some information I think we should discuss."

The monk straightened. "Please wait in the library, and I will see if Father Anthony can spare a moment for you." He set the candlesticks down on a table and hurried away.

I took advantage of the time alone to cross to the shelf with Adoria Abasolo's books. I chose the newest-looking one based on its pristine and unwrinkled jacket. It was titled <u>Taking Flight</u>, and the copyright was dated last year. I turned to the title page and read the inscription: *For Father Anthony, in gratitude for your listening ear and wise counsel.* "Aha!" I spoke aloud as I snapped the book shut.

"Have you gained a small measure of enlightenment?" Father Anthony stood in the doorway.

"As a matter of fact, I think I have," I said. I put the book back on the shelf.

"We're quite busy today, Miss Wild," the father said. He sat down in one of the overstuffed chairs and gestured for me to sit.

I took a seat on the loveseat opposite him. "I just discovered that Adoria Abasolo transferred the ownership of her property to you only three days before she disappeared."

The abbot frowned. "Why do you insist that she disappeared? I don't see how you are qualified to make that determination. I talked with your superior in the Taos office…"

"You told me when I spoke with you yesterday that her land adjoined yours. You didn't mention that she had donated the land to the monastery, and it was in fact yours."

"I don't see how this has anything to do with you, Miss Wild." He stood as if to dismiss me. "I have important work to do. The Archbishop is coming from Santa Fe to inspect our new micro-brewery, and we have been working around the clock to get everything ready."

"I think you summoned me here yesterday because you don't want me to talk about the fact that Adoria Abasolo has gone missing. Maybe it has something to do with the Archbish…"

He interrupted: "She might have just gone somewhere, on a trip, or to visit someone. She's under no obligation to tell me of her comings and goings. It's possible she went early to the east coast. You know she is scheduled to appear soon at the presidential inauguration. Besides, your superior told me that…"

I held up my palm to stop him from going any further. "I mean no disrespect, Father, but you must have a reason for trying to silence me. I think you know that Abasolo has been missing, and you're covering it up. I just haven't figured out why yet."

"Well!" He clenched his jaw. "That's quite an accusation!"

"I read the inscription in her latest book, there in the bookshelf. She thanked you for listening and for your advice. You obviously know Ms. Abasolo quite well, and I need to know anything that you can tell me. I believe she is in grave danger."

Father Anthony sunk back to a sitting position. "This isn't just about surveying property lines, is it?"

"No."

"But your boss…"

"My boss doesn't even know…I need you to keep this conversation in confidence before I tell you anything more."

"And you will do the same with anything I tell you?"

"If I possibly can. But if it will help me or others to find Ms. Abasolo, I need to share the information."

"Well, first let me say that I cannot tell you anything that has been said in the sanctity of confession."

"So you were her confessor?"

"Yes."

"When did you last see her?"

"It was on New Year's Eve. She came here to evening vespers."

"Did you talk with her then?"

"Yes. Among other things, we discussed some upcoming arrangements…you see, from time to time, Ms. Abasolo generously allowed certain guests of ours to stay in her home— both vendors and visitors who required an overnight stay, but who were not on spiritual retreat, thus not prepared to experience the austerity of a Trappist monastery for lodgings. It has been the custom over several years. We had scheduled some houseguests for two nights right after the first of the year, men from the company who installed the tanks for the brewery. We were having some service issues and they were coming to make repairs. We chatted about the arrangements for this."

"And what were the arrangements? Was Adoria supposed to be there to host the visitors?"

"No, not really. You see, in these cases, we paid for her housekeeper, Mrs. Munoz, to do the extra work to make the beds and launder the bed linens and for meal preparations for the guests. Mrs. Munoz would usually greet the visitors when they arrived, especially if Ms. Abasolo wasn't home or didn't wish to be disturbed."

"So, she just let you have people come and stay in her house from time to time? It seems like it would be inconvenient, not to mention an invasion of privacy. What did she get out of it?"

"It was simple generosity on her part, another way of giving to the Mountain Mission. You see, the visitors would typically pay a bed-and-breakfast rental fee to the monastery, and Ms. Abasolo kindly allowed us to pocket the funds—after we paid her housekeeper, of course—for some of our daily needs. She said she had a big house and didn't mind. This has occurred more than a few times, and it began long before she deeded the property to us."

"So when she was here for New Year's Eve vespers, you told her that some visitors were coming who needed to stay at her house?"

"Yes. They arrived here to begin work on a Friday…let's see, that would have been the second of January, and they worked through the next day, Saturday. They stayed both of those nights, leaving on Sunday morning, the fourth. On their first night there, the housekeeper went to open the house and see to the guests' needs. She told me afterwards that Ms. Abasolo was not home at that time, and it did not look like she had been there the night before. Mrs. Munoz had already been instructed to do whatever was necessary to take care of the visitors; as I said, that's our customary arrangement when visitors to the monastery stay there."

"Did Adoria say where she might be going the evening before the brewery people arrived?"

He looked down at his lap. "Not exactly."

"What? Do you have some idea about where she went?"

"It was some time previous to that conversation that she told me she was planning to go to a ceremony at Tanoah Pueblo. But I don't know when that ceremony was to be held. I can't be sure if this was where she went at the first of the year."

"And do you know if the housekeeper saw her after the visitors left?"

"Mrs. Munoz did not see her. She was concerned when Ms. Abasolo's bed was still made the next morning after the visitors arrived. And our guests were there for two nights. Ms. Abasolo did not return after I saw her here at vespers on New Year's Eve."

"And you didn't think to tell someone?"

"I told you, she could have just taken a trip. She often went away for several days at a time when she was writing. It is even possible she left early to be ready for the inauguration ceremonies."

"Three weeks early? I don't think you really believe that. I think you didn't want to stir up any controversy when the Archbishop was coming."

He frowned. "Our very survival as a monastery is at stake, and I know that Ms. Abasolo would want us to do anything we can to remain here in service to God and to the people in this area. You see, the Mountain Mission has been struggling to remain afloat for some years now. Two years ago, we received notice that we were in danger of losing our status as a monastery because we were not demonstrating enough economic viability. When Ms. Abasolo learned about this, she expressed a desire to help us. She offered to give us quite a lot of money, or to start an endowment. But our financial strength cannot simply come from one generous donor. We have to be able to prove that we are not beholden to any individual and can create revenue sufficient to stay afloat. After some consideration, we made the decision to launch a program to raise hops and brew an artisan beer, but we needed more water to do that. She helped us to obtain a piece of land behind and to one side of hers, along with its water rights. We believe that producing this beer will allow us to remain open."

"That piece of land, did it originally belong to Bata Romero?"

"Yes. It was undeveloped land—a portion of it runs along the rim of Picuris Canyon and abuts with ours and the Pueblo lands there at the canyon rim. It had been leased seasonally for cattle grazing."

I paused a moment to take all this in. "And Abasolo's own property?"

"That was never a part of the original plan. The bed and breakfast charges for the visitors generated a little extra cash for us, but nothing regular. A little more money now and then to buy groceries or gas for the car."

"So, once she bought that piece of land for you and you had a practical economic plan in place, why did she also sign over her own property to the mission?"

"That was so that we could have her water rights as well. We learned as we went forward with our plan that we needed more water not just to grow the crops, but also for the brewing process. Originally, we leased her water rights. But then, she came to me in early December and suggested that we could secure those rights in perpetuity if she deeded her house and land to us, with a provision that allowed her to live there as long as she wished. This ensured that no one could ever divert or block off the water from the acequia that fed the plot between her land and the vacant lot she had already donated to us. She has always been very generous, but I actually tried to dissuade her from doing this because I was concerned about her emotional state at the time."

"What do you mean?"

"I can't go into that, I really can't. It violates the sanc…"

"But how could you accept a deed to her land if you didn't think she was in a healthy state of mind?"

"I didn't say she wasn't in a healthy state of mind. I think she always intended to give us her property. But she was dealing with…an emotional issue…toward the end of the year."

I considered this. "Was she in good health?"

"I couldn't say, really. She seemed all right to me. I have no information that would lead me to believe otherwise."

"Then what do you think drove her to do this while she was dealing with the emotional issue you mentioned?"

He shook his head. "I don't know for sure. What little I do know, I cannot share with you, and it does not shed any light on the question anyway."

We both sat quietly for a few moments. Then I spoke. "So when did you first know she was missing? Exactly when did the housekeeper talk to you?"

He cleared his throat. "I didn't truly know that she was missing, as I said. The housekeeper talked to me when she came for her pay on the day the guests left." He ticked off the days on his fingers. "That would have been on the fourth, and today's the seventh, so three days ago. But I did not begin to surmise that she might really be missing until after you were here yesterday. We began a constant prayer vigil for Ms. Abasolo immediately after you left. There are novices in the chapel praying for her safe return now, as we speak."

"And her car?"

"We have not seen her car either, which is what made me think she had gone on a trip."

"She drives a Mercedes, right?"

"Yes, a silver one, rather large, new model."

"If she took a trip...do you have any idea where she might have gone?"

He shook his head. Then he stood up. "I'm sorry to interrupt our conversation, Miss Wild. I know this is important, but I feel I've told you everything. I need to get back to our preparations for the Archbishop."

"You might be able to help in another way, Father." I stood, too. "You said you frequently used Ms. Abasolo's house for visitors. Is it booked for tonight?"

"No, why?"

"I would like to stay there with my wolf, Mountain. He's very well behaved and doesn't get on the furniture." This was only stretching the truth a little. He didn't get on the furniture, but he was only well behaved when he wanted to be.

"Is this to do with your inquiries about Ms. Abasolo?"

"Yes." This was, at least, partly true.

"I think that could be arranged," he said.

28: THE KEY TO THE PLACE

As I drove back down the long road from the monastery, I mulled over the few details I knew that might help me to find Adoria Abasolo. Unfortunately, I couldn't name many people who knew her. She wasn't a regular at Tanoah Pueblo or Momma Anna or Yohe would have known who she was. The abbot and at least a few of the monks at the monastery knew her, but given that many of them were under vows of silence, there wasn't much more to be gleaned there than I had just learned from Father Anthony. The woman at the Bear's Paw knew who she was, but since Adoria had been ostracized by the locals after buying Bata Romero's land, she didn't trade with the few area businesses. Peñasco was a small, tight-knit community of folks, many of whom traced a common heritage back to the settling of New Mexico by the Spanish *conquistadores;* no surprise the villagers had sided with Eddiejoe in his dispute with Abasolo. Had she known any of the Picuris? Was that how she had learned about the peyote ceremony at Tanoah Pueblo? I tapped my chin, wondering how to proceed. I decided I would try to encounter Mrs. Munoz when I stayed at Abasolo's house and see if I could get any further than I did the first time I tried to talk with her. Beyond her, the only person left who seemed to see Abasolo with any regularity was the neighbor, her writing student Susan Lacy.

There was something about Lacy. In a place that was so often sharply divided along ethnic lines, I couldn't tell which group she belonged to. With her coloring, she might have been Hispanic, or partly so. Her facial features were delicate, unlike those of the local Indians. I supposed that she could have been Anglo, but her complexion was swarthy enough that she might not be entirely so. She had no discernible accent—if I had to guess, she was probably raised somewhere in the west, but not New Mexico. And that bike of hers! Definitely not from around here.

When I reached the end of the Monastery's road, I decided to return to the ranger station to use one of their computers. As soon as I turned south onto State Road 75, a black Humvee sped past me going the other direction, almost certainly the same car that had been tailing me. With its tinted black windows, I couldn't make out the driver. I looked for a place to make a U-turn so I could get behind it to see the plates, but there was not even a wide place in the road that was safe enough to try it for well more than two miles. The Hummer was long gone by that time. I struck the steering wheel with my palm and swore aloud. "Damn!"

Mountain raised his head from his nap in the back.

"It's okay, Buddy," I said. "I'm not upset with you."

At the ranger station, I let Mountain out to run in the pasture with the horses. I noticed that the fence on the far side had been repaired, and Ibanez's cows were gone. When I went inside, I asked receptionist Vicky Kasza if I could use one of the computers.

"Let me check," she said, dialing a number she obviously knew by heart.

I walked to the window that looked out onto the pasture and saw Mountain sniffing along the fence line.

Vicky must have gotten a green light. "Okay, Jamaica. Right over here," she said, and led me into one of the small cubicles behind her. She stood over the desk and typed in a password. "You're all set."

"Do you know when Ibanez moved his cows out of your meadow?"

"Well, in spite of what he promised Gomez, he didn't move them yesterday. It must have been sometime this morning before daylight, because the cows were here when the sheriff's deputy did a routine check of the premises just after midnight. And they were gone when I opened the office at seven."

"Do you have security cameras on the exterior?"

She laughed. "The inspector for your car fire asked me that, too. Remember this is the *Peñasco* ranger station," she said. "We barely have staff to cover the day shift half the time, and less than that in the winter. There's no budget for anything like that. That computer you're using is practically an antique. It will be a cold day in a very warm place before we get security cams."

First, I checked my email to see if there was a message from Kerry, but my inbox was empty. I wrote him a note:

> *Dear Kerry,*
> *In case you've tried to reach me, I wanted to let you know that my phone got damaged. I'm not working out of the Taos field office right now, so I won't get another one until I get back there, and that might be a few days. I'll try to check my email whenever I can. Please send me a note when you get a chance!*
> *I miss you. Mountain misses you, too.*
> *Love, Jamaica*

I pushed *send* and sat motionless. I could feel the seconds passing, but I didn't move. I wanted so badly to talk to Kerry. We'd spent a year trying to maintain our relationship over the long distance between here and the northwest. Then our too-brief reunion, then him leaving again...

I reigned in my thoughts and typed Adoria Abasolo's name into a search field. Her Nobel Prize win topped the list of links, followed by another few regarding her recent naming as United States Poet Laureate, a link to her publisher's website for selling her books, and more for other bookselling sites. Below that, I saw a tag from a story published by *The L.A. Times* just a few months previous: *Reclusive US Poet Laureate Declines Interview.* I clicked on the link and saw a fuzzy photo taken many years ago; Abasolo looked to be in her twenties or early thirties. Another, in which she looked considerably more mature, was taken when she accepted her Pulitzer Prize. The article said that she hadn't appeared in Stockholm to accept the Nobel Prize, and hadn't done public appearances with the release of her last several books. The *L.A. Times* reporter had contacted her editor for an interview and reported the same thing that my librarian Carla had recounted to me: that Adoria Abasolo did not do public appearances, signings, or interviews. There was much more to the article.

"Can I print a few things off?" I called out to Vicky, who was back at the reception desk.

"Just hit *print.* The copier is out here," she called back.

I printed two items: the story I'd just read from *The L.A. Times,* and a biography on her publisher's web page. I cleared the history on the browser and closed the application, then went out to the printer behind the reception desk where the pages were whooshing and clacking as they shuffled out. I grabbed them up, eager to get them before Vicky Kasza saw them. I had to talk to anyone I thought might have information about Abasolo, but I didn't want to reveal anything to those who were not involved. "This will do me for now," I said to Vicky. "Thanks."

I went out to check on Mountain and found him wet and muddy, lying contentedly in the shade next to the stock tank that watered the horses. I retrieved an old dirty towel from under the mat in the back of my Jeep, kept there for just such occasions. As soon as he saw me at the gate, the wolf ran toward me. I grabbed him by the collar and wrestled with him to towel off his feet and lower legs, getting most of the moisture and mud off. "Come on, Buddy," I said. "Let's go check into our digs for tonight."

The housekeeper was standing in the entry door when Mountain and I arrived at Abasolo's house. "You going to bring that dirty *lobo in esta casa?*" Her hands were balled into tight fists planted on top of her ample hips and her face wore a stern expression.

"Hello, again, Mrs. Munoz. I'm glad we can understand one another today, since we had so much trouble with the language barrier yesterday. Yes, Mountain and I will be staying here together, with the abbot's permission. We'll try not to make a mess."

"Aye!" she said. "Can you at least wipe his paws?"

"I did the best I could with a towel from my car. I'll clean up after him if he leaves any dirt on the floor."

She wheeled on one foot and went inside. "Let's get you a place to sleep in here." She led the way down the hall to the first bedroom.

The bed that had been left rumpled the day before was now made, and a stack of clean towels rested on the folded blanket at the foot of it. The beer bottle was gone from the nightstand and a carafe of water with a glass had replaced it. "This will be perfect," I said. "Thank you."

"I put some tamales in the refrigerator. There's some rice and beans, too. You just have to heat them up in the *microhorno. Aye!* You know what I mean, the...." She wagged her hand in frustration, and before I could let her know that I understood, she snapped her fingers loudly and exclaimed, "the microwave."

"That will be great. Thank you so much. I just have…"

"For guests, I do the breakfast at seven. Otherwise, if that is not good, you will find it in the kitchen whenever you want it, okay?"

"Okay, that's great, but I just…"

"I don't have the dog food for that one," she pointed a finger at Mountain, "but *El Padre* told me to take some hamburger out for him, so that is thawing now in the sink. This should be all you need." Without waiting for me to respond, she turned and started back down the hall toward the entry lobby.

I hurried to catch up with her. "There is one more thing I need."

She spun and looked at me. "And what can that be, *Señorita?*"

"I was wondering if you could tell me anything about the young woman, the neighbor, Susan Lacy. The one who comes here every Monday to study with *Señora Abasolo?*"

"I don't know anything. I just bring the food and clean the house and make sure the guests are taken care of."

"How about where Ms. Lacy lives?"

"She lives not too far, I think. She comes on a bike."

"From where, exactly?"

"Over that way." The housekeeper pointed south. "She comes down the highway. Not from Peñasco, the other way. I think maybe she rents a room. Maybe a *casita.*"

"But you have no idea which house…"

"I don't know anything more." She went to the coatrack in the corner and lifted a heavy wool coat and a black scarf from one of its arms and put them on. "I have to go now, so I hope you have everything?" Without waiting, she opened the door and stepped through.

"One more thing," I said. "A key?"

She turned around and shook her head. "No, this is not how we do it. The guests come in the evening, sometimes I make the dinner for them or maybe this is not required. I make up the fire, I show them the rooms, and then I come back in the morning to make up the fire again and to serve the breakfast. Then they leave." She said this last emphatically, as if she could hardly wait for me and Mountain to go.

"But I might be here for more than one night."

"I will come back tomorrow evening and let you in. What time, *Señorita?*"

"I'd prefer to come and go as needed. Is there a spare key?"

"Eee a lah!" She said as she bustled back in the door and into the kitchen. Before I could follow her, I heard a cupboard door slam and she came back holding up a key by an attached bit of cord as if it was a dead mouse.

I offered my palm and she dropped the key into it. "Thank you," I said to her back as she shut the door behind her.

I turned to look at Mountain, who was sniffing around the place, trying to figure out where we were and who had been here before us. "We have one more errand to run before we settle in here," I said to the wolf. "And when we come back, we'll find someplace to park the Jeep where it can't be seen. Come on, buddy, let's go for one more ride."

29: EL CUERVO (THE RAVEN)

It wasn't that far a drive to the village of Agua Azuela, where Esperanza de Tecolote lived. I figured if we were in luck, Mountain and I could get to her small *casita* before sundown and we wouldn't have to climb the steep slope to her place in the dark. That much went as planned, but when I topped the knoll that offered a view of the *curandera's* place, I was startled to see Tecolote standing on the *portal* with a raven's talons clutched in her fist—the big black bird violently flapping its wings in an attempt to escape. A flurry of conflicts flitted through my mind at once: *did she trap it, and was she going to eat it or make medicine of the bird? Was she planning to keep it captive, or intending to try to train it?* Ravens are a protected species under a federal migratory bird treaty, and it was illegal to hunt or trap them; I was a resource protection agent, sworn to defend all wildlife, including ravens. Even if Esperanza was only training it, the capture of a raven was still an issue. As I hurried closer, the creature began to calm and the old woman began to speak to it, gesturing with her open hand emphatically. By the time I got to the pair, the situation had become less strained but even more strange. The *bruja* uttered a string of words that I couldn't make out and the raven replied with a series of clucking noises. Tecolote spoke again, still so softly I couldn't tell what she was saying, and the bird huffed, expanding its shaggy neck feathers and then answered with a muffled *ka-ka* and a throaty half grumble. The two were talking!

Mountain stopped, sat, and looked from the *mujer* to the bird and back again as if he, too, were trying to discern the details of their discourse.

After a few back-and-forth exchanges, Esperanza released her hold on the raven's talons and her feathered companion lifted gently off of her fist and swooped away. The *bruja* looked at me but didn't speak. Instead, she stumbled across the *portal* and through the door of her *casita,* which she left standing open.

I hastened after her.

Tecolote started lighting candles against the darkness that had already begun to overtake her cottage interior in the late winter afternoon. She coughed raggedly several times, as if something had lodged in her throat. *"Siéntese aquí,"* she rasped, pointing to the chairs. Her voice sounded exactly like the raven's.

I was so flummoxed that I couldn't think what to do or say, so I simply took a seat.

Mountain slunk in the door with his ears down and sat beside me, staring at me with pleading eyes, telegraphing: *let's go, let's get away from here!*

The *bruja* turned from her candle-lighting to regard me. "It will soon be night. *Estoy muy cansado. El intercambiar* just now with *El Cuervo,* this has cost me my strength. I am weak now, very weak. *Espero recuperar, pero soy una mujer vieja, después de todo."*

I struggled with all this Spanish. It took me a few moments to translate some of what she had just said: *I am very tired, the exchange with the raven...I hope to recover, but I am an old woman after all.* I opened my mouth, about to decry this last...

"Listen only now, do not speak. I know why you came. What you want to ask." She turned her head and spat a gob of phlegm into the fire, then tried repeatedly to clear her throat but it sounded like sandpaper on dry wood when she spoke again. "You may not enjoy the answer." She teetered and grabbed the table to get her balance, then dropped her head, swallowed hard, and gave another dry cough.

I was already halfway out of my chair to help her, but the *curandera* raised her palm, signaling me to stop. "That good friend of mine sees much from the sky. She tells me things, I listen. Now you listen to me, *Mirasol.*" Again, she coughed and spat into the fire. "You need to look for *los gemelos*. You will need to fly to find them, perhaps you will fly many times. You will be flying tonight, just like *mi amiga el cuervo,* that beautiful raven. You will see from above what you cannot see from over here where you walk on two legs. You will be able to see much more." She turned away from me and back to the statues of saints in the *nicho* where she had lit the candles. She coughed and coughed and then cleared her throat again. This time, her voice came back as a hoarse whisper: *"Ahora, eso es todo."*

I stood up. "What do you mean, *now, that is all?* That is not all! Let me take you to the clinic in Embudo."

"No. Go now."

"I'm not going to leave you when you are so weak. I can help you. I'll make some tea for you and you can rest."

She didn't turn around, but waved me off with her hand, shaking her head.

"I'm too worried about you to go."

She barely managed to rasp: "You must go. Go! Leave me now. You know what to do."

"But I don't know what to do! And I don't know what *los gemelos* means. I don't know what anything you said means. I didn't understand one word of it, much less what I just saw happen!"

Again, the *bruja* huffed and spat something into the fire, regaining a little voice from this effort. "*Mirasol,* you must go now and prepare. You will not sleep well tonight. I am very tired.

I need to rest." She wagged the back of her palm to one side, as if to brush me out the door.

I bit my lip in frustration, and turned to leave. Mountain had been ready and bolted out before me. When I looked back as I pulled the door shut behind us, I saw Tecolote struggle to lower herself into a kneeling position before the host of *santos* and flickering candles and then fold her hands in front of her chest, muttering what must have been a prayer.

30: A REAL DICK

I drove up Lower Llano Road toward Rio Chiquito, a route which would take me to Highway 75 and through Peñasco. It was getting dark and I wanted to get to Abasolo's house while I could still see well enough outside to find a hiding place for the Jeep nearby. I didn't know who or what had caused the Blazer to explode, but I didn't want the same thing to happen to the Jeep. I figured if I could park it behind the house or in some thick brush or trees, that would be one less worry for me during the night. I was still feeling a mix of concern and confusion about the old *bruja* and the incident with the raven when I glanced in my rear view mirror and saw a car behind me driving with headlights off. I slowed to let it come closer so I could make out what kind of vehicle it was, but the driver echoed my movements and slowed, too. It was a big vehicle, dark-colored. It could have been Eddiejoe Ibanez in his pal's oversized dooly diesel pickup, or more likely, it was the Hummer that had tailed me before, given the way it matched its pace with mine to stay out of clear view. I was trying to think what to do, but I still felt rattled from the episode with Tecolote. I took a slow, deep breath. Suddenly, my conversation with Sevenguns from the day before came to mind, and it was as if I could hear the old man's voice in my head: *You maybe can set a good trap...*

I knew from traveling this road before that just ahead, where it turned east, there was an old, deteriorating barn right beside the road, sheltered by giant cottonwoods that drank from the nearby *acequia*. As I approached the curve, I cut the Jeep's lights, sped up suddenly, torqued the wheel to the left and pulled off onto the side of the road. "Hurry up," I told Mountain as I urged him out of the back, grabbing my rifle from under the seat. I led the wolf by the collar to a place out of sight behind the barn and settled into a squat to watch the car I'd left as bait. "Lie down," I told the wolf.

For once, he did as I said.

"Okay, buddy," I whispered. "Let's see what we catch with this trap." I had brought my rifle with me so it couldn't be pulled from the Jeep and used against me, but it was not the weapon of choice for close range. I set it down carefully alongside me on the ground, unsnapped my holster, and drew out my SigSauer P229 semiautomatic pistol.

Within a matter of seconds, the Hummer came around the curve and slowed, idled at a snail's pace past my Jeep, and then drove on.

"Shhhh, wait," I said, holding up a hand as Mountain started to get up again. "Stay right here."

The wolf peered intently in the direction of the Jeep and seemed to sense that we were in hunting mode. Once he realized this, I knew he would remain stealthy and not give away our position.

We didn't have to wait long. The black Humvee returned, heading in the opposite direction from which it had just come. It slowed, passed by my vehicle again, and drove on past, still not using headlights in spite of the deepening dusk.

Mountain and I held our position and waited.

A few minutes went by, and I was thinking of giving up, until I spotted a dark silhouette on the roadside, someone on foot moving toward the Jeep. As he came closer, I made out the shape of a large man, certainly the same one who had peered into the windows of my car yesterday when I had parked it by the Forest Service gate while Mountain and I took a romp in the snow. I held up my left hand again, signaling Mountain to hold, and I carefully balanced the fat grip of the handgun in my right, finger alongside the trigger, and prepared myself for what would come next.

The tall man drew close to the Jeep, and I saw his head swivel from side to side. After surveying the surroundings, he fixed his attention on the barn. I pointed the SigSauer at him. "Federal agent," I yelled. "Put your hands up!"

His shoulders dropped for an instant, and then he slowly raised both hands into the air. I moved out from the cover of the barn and walked toward him. Mountain kept apace along my left flank, nose down, eyes fixed forward on the target.

When we were a few yards from the man, I stopped, the pistol pointed squarely at his center mass. "Are you armed?"

"I am," his voice was deep and flat, no emotion. "I have a permit. I'm a private investigator."

"Why are you tailing me?"

"You're not the one I'm investigating, if that's what you want to know."

"That's not what I asked you. Keep one hand in the air and carefully take out your wallet. I want to see your permit and your I.D. And while you're doing that, answer the question I just asked you."

"My wallet's in the back pocket of my pants." He reached behind his back and I watched carefully as he brought the wallet forward, in front of him, then said, "I'm going to need to use two hands to get my license and permit out of here. And to answer your question, I tailed you because I'm looking for someone, and I think you are looking for her, too."

"Drop it on the ground," I said. "Now, where's your weapon?"

"I have a handgun in a shoulder holster. It's inside my jacket on the left side."

"Unzip the jacket and slowly take it out, only the tips of your fingers on the butt, and then drop the gun, too."

He did as he was told.

I moved forward and kicked the weapon to the side. "Hands up," I reminded him.

He raised his hands again and put them on the back of his head.

"Who are you looking for?"

"Adoria Abasolo. Isn't that who you're looking for, too?"

I came toward him, keeping the pistol pointed at the center of his chest and used my left hand to reach around the back of his waist and pat the middle of his back to be sure he didn't have a second pistol. I squatted down in front of him and brushed my hand down the sides of his ankles, and then picked up the wallet from the ground as I stood up and handed it to the man. "Let me see your license."

He reached fingers into the folds of the wallet and retrieved a laminated photo I.D. and a business card and handed both to me. It was too dark for me to read it without a flashlight. "The permit is issued by the State of California," he said. "And that's my card. My name is Zeke Mitchell. I'm investigating for a client, and Ms. Abasolo is someone who figures large in my research."

I pocketed the business card and handed back the license. "Who hired you?"

"I'm not obligated to tell you that. Aren't you with the BLM? Do you even have any jurisdiction right here?"

I frowned. "I definitely had jurisdiction where I parked my car yesterday when you were looking in it. And I have jurisdiction wherever I am if it involves any criminal activity on public lands."

"So you don't actually have any authority to be holding me at gunpoint here, am I right?"

"I am a federal agent and I have a right to protect myself from anyone I deem is a threat. You're stalking; that's a threat. What do you want with me? Why have you been tailing me?"

"I told you that." He started toward his handgun, then stopped, faced me, opened his palms and made a questioning face, as if to ask permission.

I waved my hand to signal it was okay. "Go ahead. When did you start investigating Abasolo?"

"I'm not required to tell you that either," he said, "but as you probably guessed, she seems to have disappeared."

"I know," I said. "You don't have any idea...?"

"Not the slightest. I was doing records work on her in L.A. before I came out to do surveillance, and by the time I got here, she had evidently already taken off."

"Taken off?"

"I'm assuming. Her car is gone."

"Has she committed a crime or something? Why would she take off? Why would you be surveilling her anyway?"

"I've been hired to solve a case, and she's part of it. Why are you looking for her?"

"I can't tell you that," I said.

"See? Likewise. You don't share, I don't share. So if we're done here, I'm going to stroll back to my car and go find some dinner."

"We're done," I said, begrudgingly. "I trust you will stop tailing me now?"

"No promises," he said, and started walking back in the direction from which he had come.

"I'll file a complaint if you don't. I work with everyone in law enforcement here, you know."

He called over his shoulder as he continued walking away, "I doubt there's a law against someone just driving around in these beautiful mountains," he said. "I'll be seeing you."

31: LOOKING TO GIVE BACK

There was no way to hide my Jeep behind Adoria's house. Her dirt lane dead-ended at the small gravel parking area, and that was lined by closely-placed trees. A wall shielded the front of the house and I couldn't access the sides or back by vehicle because of the vegetation on either side of the parking space. I could have gone off-road across her land and not taken the driveway at all, but in the night in winter, after snow thaws had created deep mud in many areas, I worried that I might mire the vehicle up to the wheel wells in an unseen bog of still-wet ground. Instead, I drove back out the lane and onto the drive leading through the property next door that abutted the monastery's hops field, just pulling far enough down the track to make sure the Jeep wasn't visible from the county road. The thickets of brush and scrub on either side helped to conceal the Jeep, but it meant that Mountain and I had to cross a wide, overgrown meadow in the dark to get back to the door of our night's lodgings.

That was okay by me. I figured the wolf would get his business done, sniff around, and work off some of the anxious energy he'd exhibited ever since we'd encountered Esperanza and the raven. And I didn't mind a chance to clear my head, too, so I ambled slowly along and looked up at the stars, which appeared so large here—away from any city's lights—that they looked like bright, plum-sized gemstones, close enough that I could reach up and pluck them from the dark dome of the heavens. I breathed in the cold air, listened to the *shushing* sound of the brush against my boots and the soft fall of my footsteps, and I noted how otherwise silent the surroundings were. I slowed my steps even more to allow myself to absorb all this and to shift gears from the strange, busy day I had experienced. Mountain darted in circles around me as we crossed the open field, and then fell in on my left flank as my boots crunched across the gravel parking area and we approached the wall in front of the house and walked through the gate.

A dim amber light had been left on in the *portal* over the front door, so I easily managed the key in the lock and pushed open the big entry door. Mountain scurried in and then immediately pressed his nose to the tile floor and moved down the long hallway that led to the sleeping rooms. I paid no attention to this at first, and instead hung my jacket and backpack on the coat rack in the lobby. But my companion exhibited the telltale signs of an alert as he neared the end of the hall, at the doorway to Adoria's bedroom: a ridge of fur stood up on the back of his neck, his ears lowered, and he stopped, silent. I crept down the long, narrow passage as quietly as I could, and as I got closer, I heard bottles clinking and doors and drawers opening and closing. For the second time that evening, I pulled my P229 from my holster. I gripped the gun with both hands and pushed with my boot on one of the two French doors, which was already partway open, pressing it wider so I could see into the room. I trained the pistol from left to right. The bedroom lamps were not lit, but light escaped from the doorway beyond and partially illuminated the room. The noises and the light were coming from the bathroom.

I stepped toward the open door of the bathroom and stood to one side of the jamb, tilting my head slightly to look around it and inside. I lowered my pistol but I didn't holster it. "Ray," I said, in a loud voice. "Come out of there."

The clinking and clattering sounds stopped, and the room fell silent. For an instant I thought I might have to go in and retrieve the boy, but he stepped into the bathroom doorway, his face in shadow, his slender shape framed by the light behind him. "Busted," he said.

I turned the switch on a bedside lamp and studied the young man. He looked frightened but he tried to mask it with a smile. "This is not what you think, Miss Jamaica."

"What are you doing in here?"

"I'm looking for something."

"Looking for what?"

"Something I gave Auntie Adoria. I mean, Mrs. Abasolo."

I cocked my head to one side. "I think we need to talk. I'm going to put my gun back in the holster because I don't intend to use it, but if you try to run off before I get a chance to find out what you're up to, I will chase you down, and if necessary, I will get the sheriff and bring a warrant for breaking and entering. Do you understand me?"

"I understand." His eyes were as big as an owl's and he suddenly looked much younger and more fragile than he tried to let on.

"Now, go back in there and close that window you came through, and then let's go to the kitchen," I said. "Mountain is hungry. So am I. Have you eaten dinner?"

In the brightly lit *cocina* with its colorful hand-painted tiles and hanging copper pots, I let the boy calm down while I broke up some of the block of defrosting hamburger into a bowl for Mountain, then took the tamales, rice, and beans from the refrigerator and heated them, one by one, in the microwave. I set two places at the kitchen table and told the teenager to get us each a glass of water. He did so in silence, then sat in a chair, looking small and a little desperate.

I brought the food to the table and put some of everything on a plate for him, then served myself. I sat down and picked up a fork. "Now, tell me. Tell me everything."

The boy didn't touch his food. He sat with his hands gripping the chair, working his lips back and forth as if he were trying to find his own tongue. Finally, he tried: "I've got nothing to say."

I set the fork down. "You want to play it that way? Fine. I'll call the sheriff's office and you'll be living in a juvenile jail down in Española before you know it. Is that what you want?"

He glanced at my face and saw the stern look on it. "Okay. I gave something to Auntie Adoria. I was trying to find it. I need to get it back. I've been waiting for her to come home, but she hasn't been here for days. I need it back. I wanted to ask her to return it to me, but she's never here when I come. I think she has gone someplace for a while."

"Your name's not Ray, is it?"

He dropped his head. "No, Miss."

"It's Federico, am I right? Federico Yazza?"

He didn't lift his face. "Yes, Miss Jamaica. They call me Rico. Or sometimes Freako."

"So why did you tell me it was Ray?"

He didn't answer.

"Look at me. What do you like to be called?"

He raised his head. "Rico. I like Rico. My mom calls me that."

"Okay, Rico, did you give *Señora* Abasolo some peyote buttons that you took from the Carry Water Clan at Tanoah Pueblo?"

He let out an almost imperceptible whimper and dropped his forehead into his hand. "I want to make everything right. I want to give the medicine back. I don't want to live up here with my uncle. I want to go home!"

I drew in a long, slow breath, and let it out. "Let's eat our dinner while it's hot," I said. "And then I want you to tell me the whole story. But first, eat some of this good food Mrs. Munoz has left for us."

We were doing up the dishes when I started questioning Rico again. "You're from Tanoah Pueblo. That's a little ways from here. How do you know Adoria Abasolo?"

"She taught some writing workshops last summer in our village, at Tanoah. It was part of an artists in residence thing. We also had a glassblower come and some people who taught dance. We got to choose which workshop we went to every week. I like to write. I really liked Auntie…Mrs. Abasolo. She encouraged me whenever I wrote a poem. I went to every one of her classes."

"And so you became friends?"

"Yes. Nobody ever told me I could write before. She made me feel like maybe I can do that, you know, when I grow up. For a job. Like she does."

"So that was last summer. And you kept in touch?"

"Not really. I didn't see her any more after school started again. The workshops were just for the summer. They were supposed to keep us pueblo kids from getting into trouble. I didn't see her until we did the Deer Dance a few weeks before Christmas. She was there. My uncle brought her."

"And who is your uncle?"

"Paul Deherrera. You were just talking with him the other day. And remember, you told him to tell me thank you for saving your wolf?"

How had I missed that? I knew Paul had ties to Tanoah Pueblo, but I hadn't thought to ask him about Abasolo. "So you saw your teacher at the Deer Dance. What happened then?"

"She came to my mother's house with Uncle Paul for the feast after the dances. She asked me about my writing and even helped me put wood on the bonfire outside and we talked and kept warm by the fire for a while. After that, she left with my uncle. I heard some people talking in the kitchen after they left.

My mother told the other women that Mrs. Abasolo had asked Paul to bring her to the fireplace, and he spoke for her to the elders in the Carry Water Clan. They allowed her to come because he is an important member of the clan and he sponsored her."

I dried the last dish and put it back in the cupboard. "But how…"

"You're so impatient! I wasn't going to stop," he grinned, giving my shoulder a light shove. "I'm going to tell you."

I twisted the dishtowel and swatted him on the back with it. "Well, go on then!"

"Maybe we should sit down again. This could take a little while."

We moved into the living room, where Mrs. Munoz had laid a fire, complete with crumpled paper and kindling. I struck a match and lit the paper.

"There was another feast two days after that at Picuris," Rico said. "My mother and some other family, we all came up for it together. Uncle Paul was dancing, and I saw Mrs. Abasolo on the plaza while the dances were going on. I went to talk to her, and she told me that she had seen a vision when she went to the fireplace at Tanoah Pueblo, and she needed to see more. She said she was looking for something important and the peyote would help her find it. She asked me if I could get some peyote for her. I told her that they would have another fireplace soon, but she said she couldn't wait. I didn't want to do it. I tried to tell her I couldn't do it, that it was wrong to take the medicine. She said it was urgent, and she gave me some money. I still have it. I didn't ask her to pay me. I didn't want to do it, but Auntie Adoria…" He stopped in mid-sentence and looked down into his lap.

"What? Adoria…what?"

"She saved me," he blurted, and then began to cry.

I waited, lest I interrupt this boy's delicate confession.

"You know, before, I was hanging around with some guys. They were doing drugs and stealing and doing a lot of bad things. When Auntie Adoria came to Tanoah Pueblo and gave those workshops, she made me see that I don't want to be like that. She gave me hope....hope of getting out...hope that I could be someone...that there is something good inside of me... I don't know how to say it. She just saved me. I think I would already be in that juvy jail you talked about if it wasn't for Auntie Adoria. Or maybe worse."

"I see."

"It seemed like she needed the medicine pretty bad. I just couldn't say no to her when she kept pleading with me. She was crying and practically begging. I just wanted to help her."

"Did she tell you what she was looking for that she could only see in the vision?"

"No," he said, shaking his head. He wiped his tears from his face and regained his composure. "I just wanted to help her, that's all. Now, I don't think I can go on unless I do something to get back home. It's even worse here at Picuris. There's no one my age. The place is like a ghost town. I have to get back home. I miss my mom. I want to go back to school. It starts again next week, and I won't be there. I'll fall behind if I don't get back. I just want to go home, but I can't go back until I make it right again. I thought if I returned the medicine, the tribe would let me come home. I wanted to ask Auntie Adoria to give it back to me, but she is gone. So I decided to find it myself and take it to the clan leaders and ask them to forgive me."

I fluffed up a pillow and wedged it behind me and put my feet up on the coffee table. Mountain had chosen to lie underneath Rico's already-propped-up legs and was stretched out on his back, upside down against the edge of the base of the couch with his hind legs spread wide, looking absurdly comical and even slightly obscene. "So where is your uncle now? Does he know you're out running around like a bandit in the dark of night?"

"Uncle Paul is at kiva doings at Tanoah Pueblo. They only have two clans left at Picuris, so my uncle has to go to Tanoah for his clan rituals. He doesn't know I'm out, and he won't be home until daybreak. He'll be tired then and need to sleep."

"Okay. Well, no matter, I think you ought to get home—I mean back to your uncle's house. Get some rest. Don't get your internal clock all switched around and start becoming a night owl." I swung my feet off the side of the coffee table and stood up. The wolf twisted and then leapt to his feet as nimbly as a cat.

"You never told me why you are here," Rico said, standing now, too.

I tussled the Mohawk on the top of his head. "That's for me to know and you to find out." I smiled.

"Is Auntie Adoria coming back?" He asked as we walked toward the big front door in the entry lobby.

"I don't know when she will be back," I said, truthfully. But as I spoke, I also knew that as time passed and I grew no closer to finding her that answer could ultimately be *no.* I opened the big door wide and saw that a fog had settled in while we were eating and talking, the stars no longer visible. "How did you get here, by the way?"

"I rode my bike," he said. "It's around the side of the house. There's a trail across this open land right here that leads back into the forest." He pointed toward the land to the south side of the house where I'd parked my Jeep—the land Abasolo had bought from Bota Romero and given to the brothers. "It's just a game trail, but it goes clear over behind the mission. It cuts through onto Pueblo land along the rim of the canyon and onto an old road that nobody ever uses much. I chase rabbits on that trail sometimes with my bike."

"Well, you be careful riding that thing in this fog, especially on the canyon rim road. I can barely see the wall around the garden out there, and it's only a few yards away."

"I will, Miss Jamaica," he said, trying for a smile but not completely succeeding. I could tell he was still feeling unsettled about what he had done and how to make it right.

"Listen, keep your chin up. We'll see what we can do about getting you back home to Tanoah Pueblo."

He had started to cross the *portal* when I said that, but he spun around, his eyes wide in the porch light. "Are you going to help me?"

"I know some people," I said. "I'll see what I can do."

32: VISION

I pulled Buzz from the backpack, and when I raised the device in my hand, the screen lit up. I found the keypad symbol, enlarged it to fill the screen, and pressed the image marked zero.

"Good evening, Miss Wild," the woman's voice said. "How may I assist you?"

"I need to speak with Agent…"

She cut me off. "Certainly. Stand by for your device to sound. Should you need anything further, dial zero. Have a safe and productive day."

A minute later, Buzz began to rasp and dance in my hand. I pressed the talk icon on the screen. "I need to speak with you," I said.

"Where are you?"

"I'm at Ab…I'm at the poet's house."

"I am unable to get there tonight. Can it wait until morning?"

"I suppose. I have a little info to share. And I wanted to ask a couple things as well."

"This is a secure line. Go ahead."

"It's nothing urgent. I'll wait to brief you until tomorrow. How thoroughly have you looked through this house?"

"Bare minimum. We were interrupted."

"Have you gone through her computer files?"

"Affirmative. We copied her hard drive, looked through her desk. That's about all."

"Okay. Hey, can I use her computer? Or is that going to screw something up?"

"If necessary, you may search only. Clear your search history when you're finished. Do not create, modify, or destroy files."

"Is it okay if I send an email?"

"Negative. That creates a file. You can use the device you're using now to communicate, to send and receive emails and text messages, and you can also use it to search and print. You can create files to store directly to the device like photographs of physical files or evidence. I would prefer you used it in lieu of the computer at that residence."

"Okay. I just wanted to send a personal email."

"That is permitted on the device."

"But it's monitored. I mean, there's no privacy…"

"That is correct," he said. "It is monitored and reviewed. Anything else?"

"No. I'll make a list and look to hear from you in the morning."

"Assume I will find you at some point; do not wait. Just proceed with the business of your day. Good night."

I held the phone away from my face and frowned at it. "Boy are you a different guy when you're not breaking in to my house."

I made a mug of black tea in the kitchen, figuring I'd be up most of the night searching Abasolo's personal effects for clues. I decided to start in her office, as I had begun to do when I had been interrupted by the neighbor, Susan Lacy. I took my cup and went to the desk and shuffled through the stack of papers on one corner. She had a file drawer, but all the most recent paperwork—going back several months from the look of things—was amassed in a heap in the in-basket or piled up on the two corners of her workspace.

It became apparent after about twenty minutes of sifting and speed-reading that most of this was not creative work but rather receipts and mail. Utility bills. Royalty accountings for her book sales. Statements for repairs and maintenance on her house and keeping her drive cleared of snow. Maintenance and service tickets for her Mercedes from the dealership in Albuquerque. Invitations to speak or appear at events. Even a few pieces of fan mail and several old magazines with post-it notes stuck to the pages marking articles that must have interested her. One of these struck me as curious.

A dog-eared, four-month-old issue of *Outside Magazine* sported a blank sticky-note in the fold at a feature titled: *Mystery Solved: A Witch's Bones in Canyonlands.* After scanning this to get the gist of the story, I was intrigued. The article detailed a true life mystery about a woman who was said to be a witch among several in the coven kept by the now-deceased author Videl Quintana, and the tale went back to a time right after Quintana's death, years before the article was written. The piece began with the same information I had read previously— that immediately after Quintana died, his coven dispersed and the women disappeared, never to be seen again. And then it focused on an event some years after that occurrence, when a woman's bones were discovered by hikers at the base of a steep cliff in a narrow slot canyon in Canyonlands. A forensic autopsy of the bones estimated that at the time of discovery the remains had been there for at least four years—and possibly more—before being found, and that perhaps the woman had jumped or fallen off the cliff edge into the canyon far below. I stopped reading there, thinking I had much more looking around to do.

But because I had registered the reference to Quintana, this grisly tale continued to pique my curiosity. I finished a perfunctory sweep of the remaining items on the desk, then picked up my empty mug and the magazine and started for the door to get more tea and a comfier spot to sit and read the article in depth. As I swung around the side of the desk, I noticed again all the books by Quintana on Abasolo's bookshelf. I bent down to review the titles and detected a slim sheaf of folded papers in between two of the tomes. I pulled at them and extracted a folded stack of about twenty sheets of letter-sized paper. I looked at the first few lines of the poem on one of these pages and decided to take this bunch with me to peruse further.

In the kitchen, I made another cup of tea, then took it and the items from the study into the living room, where the fire I had started earlier while talking to Rico had died down to ash-coated coals. I stirred them up with the poker and threw a couple logs on top, then sat down with the tea and my reading and put my feet up. Mountain curled up in front of the fire, having already slept a fair amount of time nearby me on the floor of the study while I was hunting for clues on Adoria's desk. My nighttime sleuthing was not interfering much with his beauty sleep.

I began with the story in the magazine, which held my rapt attention. I read every word, then doubled back to study the dates because it contained a complex and somewhat confusing correlation of events that took place in approximately four-to-five-year increments. As the story recounted, the bones of a woman were found more than five years after Quintana died, and the forensic pathologist estimated her death had occurred at least four years prior, or possibly more, which would have been roughly around the same time as Quintana died. The cause of the woman's death appeared to be a leap or a fall from a cliff edge into a deep slot canyon. Once discovered, the bones were interred in Utah as a Jane Doe.

More than four years after the interment of the bones, an investigator sought to have them exhumed relative to an ongoing case regarding the contesting of Quintana's will. The significance of the bones in relation to Quintana figured into both the settlement of the will and a cult legend that had yet to be proven as fact.

In laying out background for this legend, the article echoed much of what I had read previously: that Quintana was not only world famous as an author, but also worshipped as a sorcerer and teacher by a cult of followers. That he was known to keep what he referred to as a coven of witches, also known as his sorcerer's apprentices—anywhere from four to five women at any given time. And it detailed how they lived with Quintana, served in many cases as his sexual companions, taught classes in sorcery and a strange form of exercise called *Powerform* at his foundation, and managed the vast Quintana compound on the outskirts of Los Angeles, where dozens of people lived and worked, including several children thought to be either Quintana's or the witches', or both. The cult followers knew the "witches" by esoteric aliases, identities the women had assumed when they joined forces with their mystic master, Quintana. Because of this, the women could not be traced by their coven names to any real person, living or dead. When Quintana began to rapidly decline in health, the four apprentices in the coven at that time told a handful of friends and cult members outside the compound, and all those within it, that they intended to go with their leader "into the beyond." After Quintana died, the four witches who had been living with him at the time—known as Rachelle Helena (a/k/a *The Nonbeing),* Qual (a/k/a *The Wingless Bird),* Salma Esteban, and Yini—suddenly and mysteriously disappeared.

The story skipped ahead to the current time, ten years after the death of Quintana and the disappearance of the witches, and back to the Canyonlands bones, now exhumed: DNA tests were run just before the *Outside Magazine* article was published, and the results showed the bones found in Canyonlands to be those of Ursula Lindstrom, who had abandoned her former identity when she joined the coven, and assumed the name of Qual, also known to Quintana and his cult-like followers as *The Wingless Bird.* The conclusion the journalist drew was that soon (if not immediately) after Quintana's death, Qual had leapt from the cliff "into the beyond," as the witches were said to have pledged to do.

Quintana's books told of his own leap from a cliff decades before, as he was striving to become a powerful sorcerer through his apprenticeship with a Yaqui Indian capable of superhuman feats of witchcraft. The first few of his bestselling books, discounted by scholars and experts as pure fable, detailed Quintana's schooling in the use of psychedelic drugs to reach altered states of reality at the hands of this teacher who claimed to be a Toltec. Later books in the series told tales of Quintana emerging as a sorcerer in his own right, and eventually becoming so powerful that he, too, became a master who trained apprentices not unlike the women he lived with and referred to as his coven of witches. The magazine article concluded that in the case of the bones, if Qual did try to leap into the beyond like the sorcerer had purportedly taught Quintana to do, she did not take her bones, nor likely her body, with her, notwithstanding her nickname of *Wingless Bird.*

I wondered if this article and Abasolo's obvious interest in Quintana as a writer—given that she owned every one of his books—had sparked her quest for hallucinogenic experiences and using peyote. I felt an uncomfortable sense of dread, much like I had felt when Rico had asked me earlier if Abasolo was coming back.

In one sense, I completely related to Abasolo's interest in Quintana's work. Like hundreds of thousands of other Americans who had read his bestselling first book, I found his early writings fascinating. I could also relate because of two very strange and powerful characters in my own life story. Both Momma Anna and Tecolote knew things and were capable of doing things that I myself might disbelieve if I hadn't witnessed their powers. Tecolote had referred to herself as a *bruja,* which meant that she knew herself to be a witch or sorcerer. And she had also given me a powerful hallucinogenic the very first time I went to see her which gave me a glimpse into an altered state of reality. In contrast, though, I had never learned these skills nor practiced them myself. Momma Anna had years ago agreed to teach me the ways of the traditional Puebloans, and cited her reason for doing so: the youth of the dwindling population of Tanoah Pueblo had shown little interest in maintaining their culture. From her, I had learned to bake bread, to make a few small bits of pottery, to cook and observe a few feast day rituals, but I had also witnessed unexplainable things in her presence and by her hands. Rather than training me in any secret or dark arts, what both of these amazing women had taught me by encouragement and example was to trust my own intuition, to honor my hunches, to look deeper than others and to be present for whatever I observed or sensed. In particular, Momma Anna had taught me to see life in everything, even things I might have previously considered inanimate or without intention—like stones, trees, the wind—and to read the messages coming to me from everything I experienced. She had shown me the sacred in life, something I had never been taught as a child. Tecolote, on the other hand, was an immensely powerful seer and healer, and her cryptic cautions, potions, foods, and teas had often had a potent effect on my thinking and/or my consciousness. It was no accident that, even now in the 21st century, the mountain people surrounding her village still looked to her for healing that they could not otherwise find.

Calling Tecolote to mind now worried me about how tired and weak she had been after the incident with the raven. Until now, I had only thought of her as a force of nature—strong and formidable. She had never complained of anything before in my presence, except being hungry, which she usually rapidly remedied.

I looked at the clock over the fireplace. It was three a.m. I was tired. I determined to scan through the papers I'd found wedged between the books by Quintana and then try to get a little rest before I had to begin another day. I quickly glanced over their contents. One contained a poem that gave me pause, and I read it three times to make sure I wasn't imagining its meaning:

The Smallest Star

I swallowed the smallest star
In the earliest times,
When we were naked and clean
Against one another,
Radiant,
Filled with fire and dreams with wings.

Within me it grew, luminous,
Round and smoldering,
Churning with shame and promise,
Consuming me,
Until I could no longer contain it.

Walking under dark sweeping trees,
Full of smoke and decay,
One night, I decided to vanish,
Eclipse,
Belly full of my heart's shadow.

Half past three and foaming,
I felt its slithering escape,
A pain that has never stopped hurting,
Comet!
Wails of sorrow and dark honey followed.

Now, every night, I look for you,
O, smallest star in the wide black heavens,
Do you talk to God, do you dream?
I search the sky
And feel the wound flare again in my heart.

The back of my neck tingled. Had Abasolo lost a baby when she was young? Perhaps a miscarriage, or an abortion? When she spoke in the poem of searching the sky, looking every night for someone, I thought of how she had expressed an urgent need to Rico for more peyote so she could find something she had lost. What could she find in a hallucination that she couldn't locate by searching in full consciousness on the mundane plane? Could she be trying to have a shamanic vision that would connect her with her lost child?

I pried myself out of the sofa's soft cushions and stood and stretched. "Come on, buddy," I said to Mountain. "I'm going in circles with this. I've got to get some sleep. Let's go to bed."

On the way to the guest bedroom, I stopped at the coat rack and picked up my jacket and my backpack. I put the pack on the floor beside the nightstand and threw the jacket over a nearby chair. As Mountain flopped down at the foot of the bed, I pushed the door closed, then pulled back the bedspread and folded it over the foot of the bed. Unclipping the holster from my belt, I unsnapped the stay so I could quickly draw the pistol from it if needed, and pushed it under the pillow. Next, I grabbed my jacket by the collar and plunged my hand into the pocket, feeling for my keys. I wanted them on the nightstand in easy reach, just in case. I grasped the fob, drew it out, and a bit of fluff followed, dangling from my hand. It was the raven feather from Abasolo's desk that I had shoved into my pocket when I was interrupted by the neighbor. Pulling the plume by the quill tip, I separated it from the bands of the stainless steel ring, and again felt the smallest flutter vibrate through my fingers as whatever draft or air currents in the room set it in motion. I carefully placed it with the keys on the nightstand beside the bed, stripped down to my undershirt and panties, and crawled under the covers. I looked down at Mountain and saw his nose tucked under his tail. He was curled into a perfect wolf donut. "Good night, buddy," I said and turned off the lamp.

"Can you see me?" A voice whispered.
"Can you see me?"
I lifted my eyelids and peered into the darkness.
A large black eye appeared, right in front of mine, then withdrew to a few inches away. The raven stood atop me, examining me closely, its face turned to the side so it looked directly at me, the long ebony beak pointed toward the door of the room.

I felt the bird's weight on my chest. It stepped backward and onto my abdomen, then lifted its wings and settled them down again, all its blackness gathered about it, darker even then the unlit room. "Can you see me now?"
"Yes."
"See nothing I do not. See only what I see." The raven lifted its wings again, and I felt my own body lift with it, and then felt the exhilaration of rising…high, higher, higher…up through the field of fog that blanketed the house below. Here, the sky was clear, the stars shimmering.

"Who sees with my eyes?" the bird's voice whispered. Then a loud cry: "Ka-ka. Ka-ka."

As the raven called out, I felt the night sky surrounding my body, first caressing, and then enveloping it like a silk cocoon. I looked down and saw the earth passing below me, the clouds of fog clearing, then gathering, then clearing again.

"Who sees with my eyes?" the bird said again.

"I see. But I don't know who I am."

A long, flat mesa stretched across the land in the darkness below, and the raven and I suddenly made a swooping dissent to its rim. I felt a strange desire to spread my reach wide. My chest expanded and flattened like a sail, but my arms were so heavy that I could not raise them.

A seed pearl, the tiniest moon, rose over the edge of the landscape and hung suspended, bobbing ever so slightly, as if it were trying, but could not gain any more height. "I promise," it sang, with a voice like a bell softly rung, "there will be more light to come."

The illumination from this miniscule orb made just enough difference that I could now make out a group of people by a river below. They were women, naked and blue as sapphires, their bodies young and beautiful, every one of them round in the belly. One woman nursed an infant at her breast. Another of the maids fell to the ground at the edge of the river and opened her legs wide into the current. She gave out a wail and two ice-blue bubbles burst on top of the water, and I heard babies crying. Several of those attending plunged into the river to retrieve the pair of newborns, and when they came out with the babes in their arms, all of the women gathered in a circle and began to sing, rejoicing and then handing the newly birthed twins from one to the other, all of them but one. The woman who had been nursing her child slipped quietly away with her charge, into the trees, and out of sight.

"Spread your wings," my companion whispered, and I realized we were perched on the edge of a cliff.

My torso trembled as a loft of air whooshed over the edge of the precipice. But, hard as I tried, I could not open my arms.

"Jump."

A stabbing fear overwhelmed me. The ground dissolved beneath my feet and I violently forced my arms outward, feeling them rip at the web of night fibers that had been holding them down. I flailed at the sky, to no avail. I felt myself falling, faster and faster.

"You may think of looking back," the raven called, "but there will be nothing there. You must fly."

I woke gasping for air, my heart pounding in my chest. I sat up, and for a moment I could not register where I was or why. Slowly, I began to gain wakefulness, and with it, a raging thirst and a blinding headache. From the scant promise of dim light at the edges of the window blinds, I figured it to be almost dawn. I reached to the nightstand and switched on the lamp. The fledgling raven feather fluttered up ever so slightly from where I had left it and then floated back down and settled again next to my keys.

33: MISTAKEN IDENTITY

With my head pounding, I went to the kitchen to make some coffee. I knew that the housekeeper would come and provide breakfast, but I was already up, and it would be another two hours before she would arrive. I started a pot brewing and went back to the guest room to take a shower. Mountain seemed as worn out as me, and hadn't moved to get up even when I had gone to the kitchen. Once I was dressed and ready, I knelt down on the bedroom floor beside him and rubbed his tummy. He was so warm and cuddly that I curled up on the rug behind him, spooning him against my chest, wishing I could just snuggle up and fall asleep, this time without dreaming. Finally, I made myself get up. "Come on, buddy," I said. "I know it's early, but we need to get going." I took him to the front door and opened it to go outside with him.

The fog that had begun to develop when I sent Rico home had metastasized overnight. In the dim light of early morning, the almost-viscous mass spread itself across the ground and clung there. The wolf disappeared from view as soon as he moved a few yards away from me and I had to rely on my ears to track him. He did his business, and then scurried back to my side, as if he, too, felt wary about this obscuring vapor.

I pushed the door shut and thought about stoking a fire in the lobby woodstove but decided against it. I had too much to do and needed to get going. But first, I needed some coffee, and I would give the wolf the rest of that ground meat. Mountain and I went to the kitchen and I pulled the half-full packet of hamburger out of the fridge and broke the remaining contents from it into bite-size lumps for the wolf's breakfast. I set Mountain's bowl down and was about to get myself a cup of java when I heard footsteps crossing the *Saltillo* tiles of the lobby floor. I tiptoed as lightly as I could to the edge of the pantry, reached into the holster on my right hip, and drew out the SigSauer pistol.

A man's head and upper torso leaned around the door frame and peered into the *cocina.* "Holy shit!" Coronel threw his hands up. "What is it with you drawing down on me all the time?"

"Damn, Coronel," I said in exasperation as I lowered the gun. "Don't you ever knock?"

Mountain, who had come up right behind me, wagged his tail and darted over to greet the agent and sniff his boots.

Coronel distractedly reached a hand down and patted the wolf, but looked directly at me as he said, "Well, I would have knocked, but I didn't see the point when the door was wide open!"

"I just closed that door. I made sure it was shut because it's cold in here."

"Take a look." He opened his palm and swept it in front of his body. "It was just like that when I got here."

I stepped through the kitchen archway and looked toward the entry, my gun still in my hand but down at my side. The front door yawned wide, nearly back against the wall behind it. Mountain trotted over to peer out into the fog.

Coronel said, "I wasn't about to close that until I figured out what was going on. The noise might have..."

"You know, I had that same thing happen to me the first time I came here. I had closed the door and was looking around in the house when I heard a sound. I went back in the lobby and it was like it is now. Freaked me out."

"Okay, then, we have three things that we need to do something about. One, we've established the door has a tendency to come open by itself, so we'll double-check that it's closed tightly from now on. Two, I'd really like to see you stop pulling your gun on me, I really would." He paused and rubbed his forehead.

"I'm sorry. I'll try not to do it again." I holstered my pistol. "And, three?"

"Three, like I said before, why don't you call me Hank? I figure I've survived you looking down a barrel at me—what is it, three or four times now? So we can probably do away with the Agent Coronel stuff and get on a first-name basis."

"You brought a gun to my door, too, you know, Hank." I said his name with emphasis.

"Well, like I said, let's try to end that tradition, too, what do you say? Now, is that coffee I smell?"

"I just made a pot. Come on in and join me." I went back to the counter and got a second mug out of the cupboard.

"I'll just close the front door first. Come on, Mountain. You don't want to go out in that pea soup, you'd lose your way. Stay in here with us." He went back to the lobby and I heard the big door slam and both paws and boots coming back across the floor toward the kitchen. "That should do it."

Sitting at the table and sipping from our cups, Coronel and I began exchanging notes while Mountain slipped off to the edge of the living room where he could lie on the rug. I started off by telling about the incident with Zeke Mitchell and that he was an investigator who was looking for Abasolo, too, but wouldn't reveal why. I was reluctant to share my hunch about Abasolo having lost a baby because all I had to go on was the poem, which could have been taken as metaphorical. And I wasn't about to go into the whole crazy story about Quintana, his coven, and the bones, because I didn't even know what that had to do with Abasolo. Maybe something to do with her using peyote, but I didn't know that for sure. Instead, I went over what little I had learned from Father Anthony about why Abasolo had bought the property next door and deeded it to the Mission. I was about to tell him about Rico stealing the peyote for her when Hank's phone rang.

The agent stepped out of the kitchen to take the call, but I could hear his end of it. "Okay, and when will that be? It's foggy as hell here, which isn't going to help at all. Well, I appreciate this. I owe you one. Call me after the pass and let me know if you got anything, okay?"

When he came back to the table, he turned his chair around, sitting in it backwards, with his arms folded over the top of the backrest. "Sorry to interrupt your briefing. In short, you've got nothing earthshaking, right?"

I shook my head.

"Well, I only have a little time here this morning, so let me tell you something. Adoria Abasolo is not Adoria Abasolo." He let that sink in, then went on: "Remember when I told you I thought something looked 'off' about her birth certificate? It turns out I was right. It was a fake."

"Well, if she's not Adoria Abasolo, then who is she?"

"Her real name is Inés Otero. And not only is she *not* who she said she was, she's not even Brazilian. She was born in Bogotá, Columbia about two-and-a-half years before the date on that phony birth certificate."

"That's just crazy." I tried for a few seconds to make sense of this. Everything I learned about the poet ranged from confusing to incredible. "Why did she change her identity?"

"We don't know that yet. But we're working on a couple ideas."

"But, how could she even pull that off? I mean, she went to three different universities. She had scholarships and grants. She won a Pulitzer and the Nobel Prize, for goodness' sake!"

"Like I said, we're pulling on the loose threads. I think we'll know more before the day is out. But one more thing I wanted to tell you is that we finally got her cellular records. Not the phone itself, it hasn't been active for several days; we tried pinging it for location and got nothing. But the number Abasolo…Otero was calling so frequently before she died? It's the direct line to one of the offices of the Archdiocese of Los Angeles. Do you have any idea why she might have been phoning them several times a week for the past couple months?"

"No." I shook my head and sighed. "But I can think of a couple of people who might be able to help me find out."

"It's getting late. By that, I mean that it's getting harder every minute to hold out hope that we will find her alive. You see that, don't you?"

"I do."

"I know you're doing everything you can, but I just want you to be prepared for that possibility." Harold Coronel got up from his chair and scooted it back under the table. "I gotta go. I just have one more thing for you," he said, pulling a folded piece of paper from his back pocket. "I know your phone was destroyed in the car fire. We've been monitoring your number, and you've had several attempted calls from the same origin. You got a text message from that number last night." He put the paper down on the table and slid it toward me.

I stood up. "You've been monitoring *my* phone?"

He grimaced. "I'm sorry. It's protocol."

"At least you could have shown me the courtesy of telling me that," I said.

He winced. "It kind of defeats the purpose to do that, in most cases," he said. "Really, I *am* sorry; it's not like I don't see you as being one of the team."

"Well, you can just take your team and…" I threw up my arms. "Let me just say this: I don't have anything to hide, but

I'm still completely chagrined. You and…*The Bartender*…and your *team,* whoever that is… you ask for my help and then you treat me with suspicion."

Mountain appeared in the entryway to the kitchen and looked at the two of us.

"Look," Hank said, "it wasn't me that did it. And I don't feel that way. I don't blame you for being upset. I'd be mad, too."

I picked up the piece of paper from the table.

"He's a lucky guy," Hank Coronel said, jutting his chin in the direction of the folded sheet in my hand. He turned and went out of the kitchen, stopping to squat down and give Mountain some rubs behind the ears and along the back of his neck before he went on toward the lobby. I heard his footsteps crossing the tile floor again, heard the door open, and heard it shut with another slam.

Mountain watched him leave and then looked at me.

I unfolded the paper and read Kerry's text message:

> *Was wondering why you didn't pick up when I called. Worried. Just got your email. Hope you have a phone again now and get this message. Need to hear your voice. God, I miss you so much. Please call. Love you.*

34: O, BROTHER

As I started down the cliff-edge road to the monastery, the cold miasma of blue-white mist restricted my view so severely that I worried that I might misgauge even a slight turn in the track and send the Jeep—with me and Mountain in it—off the side into the abyss. When I approached the big log archway a scarf of haze parted just enough to reveal the sign listing the times for mass and vespers. It reminded me of the cowl on a monk's habit, which only disclosed the identity of its inhabitant at close range.

I rang the bell in the covered alcove, and this time, Father Anthony answered the door himself. From the look on his face, he was less than overjoyed to see me. "Miss Wild. I wasn't expecting you."

"I know, Father, and I apologize. I wonder if we could talk? Just for a few minutes? It's very important."

He let out a heavy sigh. "Just for a few minutes. Come into the library."

I followed him and once he had taken a seat, I took one as well. "I have to ask you…"

"I already told you everything that I can." He crossed his arms over his chest. "I will not violate the priest-penitent privilege."

"Father, I just got reminded how crucial the element of time becomes when someone has disappeared. The more time passes, the less likely it is to find the missing person alive. I only ask in the desperate desire that we might still find your neighbor and benefactor, and hopefully before it's too late. The last time anyone seems to have seen her was more than a week ago. If you won't answer my questions, you might come to regret that, especially if it could have helped us locate her sooner. And, besides, if you won't tell me whatever you can, others will come to ask these same questions, and more."

"It doesn't matter who asks. The sanctity of the confessional is rooted in the imperative need for confidence and trust. Even the Supreme Court upholds that."

"What if I told you that your neighbor is not who you think she is, that the name Adoria Abasolo is an assumed identity?"

His eyes widened.

"She didn't confess that to you?"

"No, she did not."

"And did you know she was taking peyote, that she'd had a young boy steal some for her?"

He struggled to keep his face from revealing the answer, but I could tell that his response, if he would have agreed to give one, would have been affirmative.

"Just nod, if you feel like you can do that much."

He nodded.

"And did she tell you about a baby she lost when she was young?"

He squirmed a little in his chair, then raised his eyebrows.

"Or did she have an abortion?"

He turned his head slightly, frowning.

"Oh, I see. She gave a baby up for adoption, right? She told you about that."

The abbot made the slightest nod.

"It was in Los Angeles, right?"

Another almost imperceptible dip of his chin.

"And she was trying to find that child. That's why she had been calling the Archdiocese of Los Angeles. She must have given the child up through a Catholic charity service of some kind."

Father Anthony's face now changed from guarded to sad, but he didn't speak or make any sign of agreement or otherwise.

"When she called them, do you know if the Archdiocese of Los Angeles gave her any information about the child?"

There was no response to this from the abbot either.

"I believe Ms. Abasolo was taking the peyote to try to have a vision and connect with her child in that way. Am I right?"

The father's expression showed either confusion or concern now, and he was quiet for a moment while he considered what to say. Finally, he held up a finger and offered: "Let's say you asked me this as a hypothetical question about no one person or incident in particular. Generally speaking, the Church does not condone the use of drugs for non-medical purposes. If one of my charge was seeking my counsel about what you mentioned—hypothetically, as I said—I would urge them to stop."

"And yet, she told you she was going to the fireplace...the peyote ceremony...after she took confession with you."

Again, the abbot did not speak for a minute or so, pulling at his beard as he ruminated. "Again, theoretically, if there was some kind of a theft, if one of my parishioners happened to have something that was stolen by another person, of course I would urge them to do whatever was necessary to return the ill-gotten goods to their rightful owner, and to make reparations if they were involved."

"Do you know if Ms. Abasolo ever learned the identity of, or located her child?"

"I do not."

"Was it a son or a daughter?"

He shook his head.

"Okay, don't do anything if I'm getting warm, but would you please at least hold up a hand to stop me if I'm getting cold? Was it a daughter?"

He lowered his hands to his lap and raised his chin, looking directly at me.

I drew in a big breath. *Adoria Abasolo was looking for her long-lost daughter!* I was quiet a moment, taking this in. "But, now I'm wondering about something we discussed previously. If Abasolo knew that she had a child, if she was working to locate the child, why was she in such a hurry to deed the property she lived on to you? Wouldn't she want to bequeath this to her sole living relative?"

Father Anthony's brow furrowed. "There is a stipulation that allows for a living heir...the rights to the property would revert in that case."

"And that would mean the end of your beer brewing and perhaps of your status as a monastery, if that happened."

"It could. Unless something could be arranged with the heir about the water rights, it very well could."

"I have to ask: is that why you tried to dissuade me from finding all this out? To protect the plans for the monastery to have an economic future?"

"No. Heavens, no! Of course I want the monastery to continue our work, but I also trust in an almighty and powerful God Who determines the future of all of us, this mission included. I would have abided by His will, even if it meant we had to close the mission. When you came here the first time, I truly did not think there was any problem. I suppose I just wanted to believe that Ms. Abasolo had gone to visit someone and would return soon enough...so I tried to overlook some of this initially. But when you kept coming here asking questions..." His brow furrowed. "May God forgive me if I have betrayed Ador...what was her real name?"

"Inés Otero," I said.

He closed his eyes and clutched the large crucifix he wore. "I don't know which is worse—that I held off giving you information, or that I have likely violated the seal of the confessional with all I let on to you today."

"I know you must feel conflicted, but thank you, Father Anthony. I'm hoping this can help us find out where she is and what happened to her."

He stood, bringing his hands together and dropping his lips to the tips of his fingers, working through a thought before giving it voice. "I have to return to my preparations for the archbishop."

"I just have one more thing…"

"Miss Wild, please."

"Do you know anything about the author Videl Quintana?" I watched his face carefully.

He wrinkled his brow. "No. Why?"

"I didn't think so. Never mind."

We walked to the foyer and the abbot reached for the big iron handle and pulled the door open. "I am uncomfortable with how much I may have revealed in our discussion," he said.

"I already had a lot of the information. You really didn't tell me much that I hadn't guessed. You just confirmed a couple of hunches."

"I am willing to suffer whatever penance I must pay for what I have done if it means that you find her," he said. "But you must find her. None of this will have been worth it if you don't."

35: A CLEARER VIEW

As I prepared to make a left turn out of the Mission's drive onto the county road, a car rocketed around the curve and barreled toward me like a streak of lightning. I stomped on the brake to avoid being T-boned, and Mountain careened into the back of my seat. The oncoming torpedo swerved, tires squealing, and then accelerated again without so much as a pause, racing down the road at what must have been nearly twice the speed limit. I felt my heart pounding in my chest and at my temples, adrenaline surging through my veins. I backed up a few feet so the Jeep's nose was off the asphalt road and got out and opened the back door to check on the wolf. "Are you okay, Mountain?"

He sat up and wagged his tail.

I threw my arms around him and hugged his neck. With one hand, I felt along his sides and haunches for any sign of tenderness. I pressed my chest to his as he sat upright in the door opening, and then cupped my palm around his sternum to feel his heartbeat. Like mine, his pulse was rapid. "Let's get out for a minute and let me watch you move around, make sure you're okay." I held the door for him and he jumped out. "Come on, I want to walk a bit and make sure you're moving all right."

A few minutes later, I was behind the wheel again and headed toward Peñasco and the ranger station, still shaken and hypervigilant after the near-miss I had experienced. It had happened so fast that I couldn't be entirely sure, but I thought the car that almost rammed me had been a green Subaru. A Subaru was a common enough car in these parts because of its ease in driving on snow. The dense fog had prevented me from seeing the driver or how many people were in the car, or even the car itself until the last instant. But it looked like the same color and model as the vehicle that had been towed by the tribal police at Tanoah Pueblo the night before last, the one that belonged to the couple I had dubbed *the redcoats.* I wondered about that odd pair. The first time I'd spotted them, they were bending Dominic Gomez's ear in the Bear's Paw. Then the next evening, I'd seen them at Tanoah Pueblo. If that was their car and they were back on the High Road now— two days later—where were they headed in such a hurry? They could have killed Mountain and me at that speed in this pea soup of a fog! And if it was the redcoats in that car, what kind of a tourist trip were they on? In winter, there were few businesses open up here; a day would allow you to take it all in with time left to spare. The small number of off-season tourists who visited New Mexico in the dead-of-winter months came to get good lodging deals and avoid the crowds in Taos and Santa Fe, where there were shops, cafés, and artists' studios open, regardless of the weather. Here, on this sparsely-populated ridge along the shoulders of the Sangre de Cristo mountains, winter was always ready to steal back the roads and make them impassable, and there weren't but a few establishments open during the colder months as a result. Bed-and-breakfast owners from Chimayo to Taos closed up shop and took their vacations this time of year. Even the potters and painters in the lower and sunnier places along the Rio Grande around Pilar and Dixon opened late and closed early, or left a note on the door for weeks that read, "Be Right Back."

While my mind wandered over all this, somehow I had gotten to the ranger station without thinking at all about driving, and I was grateful that my anxiety meter wasn't pinging code-red any more. As I chose a parking space at the back of the lot, I noticed that I could just make out the horses at the water tank in the pasture behind the facility, which meant that the veil of vapor that had taken over the High Road was beginning to thin as the sun climbed higher in the winter sky. I put Mountain on a lead and walked him along the grass at the edge of the asphalt and then toward the door of the station with me, reminding him on the way to be on his best behavior so he would always be welcome there. Even though I didn't plan to be there long, I wanted to take him in so I could keep an eye on him in case he exhibited any signs of injury or soreness. I also wanted him near me for my own comfort. Before I opened the door to go inside, I squatted down and engaged my best friend in direct eye contact, something he would rarely do with anyone but me. "You know I love you, don't you, Mountain?"

He searched my face with rapt attention, his eyes clear and bright, his ears up, attentive. He pushed his nose between my arm and my chest and nuzzled his head against me, then stood up and wagged his tail, eager to get on with whatever we were going to do next.

To my surprise, Dominic Gomez occupied the chair behind the counter at the receptionists' desk. When he saw me, he smiled and reached down to retrieve something from the top of his lunch cooler, which sat on the floor beside him. He pushed a small box across the counter to me. "Roy had me bring this up for you. It's your replacement phone; same number as you had before. He wanted me to tell you that he's sorry, he can't get you a different vehicle right now. They have to get me a new one first."

"I'm sorry about your Blazer."

"I'm just glad you're okay. It could have been me. I heard it was tampered with."

"Did the fire investigator report that?"

"Not yet, but that's what I heard."

"Who would…?"

"You know we just had that whole thing with Ibanez over his cows, and he was over twelve hours later getting them out than he promised he would be. Then I leave the Blazer here, and first thing the next morning, you drive it a few miles and the car catches fire and the engine blows. That's my rig, the one I always used. I don't think anybody knew you would be taking it. Even I didn't know it, because I was off that day."

I was starting to feel an overload after not sleeping, the terrible dream, the close call with the speeding car. "So what will you do until they get you a new truck?"

"For the next couple days, I work here. They let me use an old beater from the maintenance facility, but that thing is on its last legs, so I'm not supposed to drive it unless I absolutely have to. Roy put me on one of those public lands resource sharing assignments like you're on. I'll be here for a day or two until they figure out a rig for me. I live closer to this station than I do to the Taos field office so I don't mind helping out here for a little bit."

I took the device out of the box and powered it on; it was fully charged. "Mind if I use that cubicle over there to make a couple calls?"

"No, go ahead. I think Miss Vicky likes having some company. She told me to make myself at home."

I noticed a red dot on the new phone's screen indicating a voicemail. Hank had said Kerry had tried to call me several times, so the message had to be from him. I decided to wait until I wasn't so pressed for time so I could savor hearing his voice and then hopefully hear it again when I had a chance to call him back. Right now, I had a few calls to make that were more imperative.

My first was to Carla at the library. I asked her if she would do a lightning search on Quintana and his coven of witches and then give me a brief summary.

"I pulled up some of this information when you asked about the peyote before," she said. "That's the crazy stuff I was telling you about from when Quintana died."

"So can you get as complete a picture as possible and then knock it down into a CliffsNotes version for me, maybe in a couple of pages?"

"Sure. Like I said, this story's intriguing. It will be fun."

"I really need this fast. Can you get back to me as soon as possible?"

"By that you mean today?"

"Even sooner," I said, meaning it.

I was rummaging in my pockets for the business card the private detective had given me when Buzz purred from inside my backpack. I glanced around the ranger station to see who might be looking, but neither Dominic nor Vicky was paying me any mind. I pulled the device out of the pack. "Wild, Resource Protection." I said. Habit, again.

"I've got something" It was Coronel. "It's not good news."

"You found her."

"Maybe. I found her car."

"Well, where is it? Maybe she's…"

"It's at the bottom of a ravine. It went off the side of the cliff on a road that serves as the northwest border of the reservation leading down into Picuris Canyon. Let's see, it's…" he paused a few seconds. "It's Indian Service Route 210. The rear of the car aims skyward, the front end buried in the ravine. It's not likely anyone in it would have survived."

"I'll come right now. What's your location?"

"I'm not with the vehicle. I received this information remotely."

"Remotely? What do you mean by that?"

"Satellite imagery. A friend of mine at NOAA obtained it from a weather satellite. We got an area scan three days ago, and then I asked for a closer view of a few targets that looked like possibilities. He captured a good photo of it during a recent pass."

"But how did you know..."

"Her car was missing. From day one, it's been a primary objective to find it. Her Mercedes wasn't new enough, and she hadn't paid to continue the tracking service that you get when you first buy them, so I couldn't use that. So I asked my guy to grab sat images within a twenty-mile-radius of her house. He got them, and then, like I said, we asked for a zoom on a couple specific areas, and we got a hit. With computer enhancement, we can read the numbers on the plate in the picture. It's her Mercedes."

"Well, maybe she's not...maybe she wasn't driving the car."

"That is still a possibility, but the odds aren't good at this point, given that we have no other leads to her whereabouts. But we'll know soon. We reported the wrecked vehicle to the local authorities, which in this case was the county sheriff's office. They're the ones who will investigate the crash scene and perform the recovery if there were any victims. In the meantime, you and I should proceed with whatever lines of inquiry we were pursuing until we have more news about the car and if there were any occupants."

I struggled not to feel hopeless after this update. As the past few days had unfolded without so much as one glimmer of good news, I had grown increasingly less able to ignore the nagging feeling in the back of my mind that we would not find Abasolo alive. But I hadn't faced it squarely until now. The woman for whom we were searching could well be dead at the bottom of a ravine in her smashed-up car, and there would be no good news for *The Bartender*.

I continued searching my pockets and finally found the private detective's card. It contained just three words: Zeke Mitchell, Investigator, and then a telephone number. I dialed that number.

"Hello, Miss Wild," Mitchell's voice said.

"How did you know it was me?"

"Caller ID says US Government, and it's a Taos area code. You're the only fed I know from Taos."

"I want to ask you something."

"I already told you, I don't share."

"Well, I'd like to change that."

"I'm listening."

"I would be willing to share some information I have recently learned, under the right circumstances, and if it is mutual, of course."

"I'm still listening."

Once again, I stuck my head around the corner of the divider and panned my eyes across the station office. Gomez had gone to the back in the direction of the restrooms before I began the call and had not returned to the front desk. Vicky was opening boxes of brochures in the entry area and positioning the leaflets in the information rack as fastidiously as a florist arranging blooms in a bridal bouquet. "First, tell me this. Abasolo had a neighbor who came to take writing lessons from her on Mondays. Her name was Susan Lacy. Do you know anything about her?"

"I might. And if I do?"

"If you do, I have some information on Abasolo that I could share."

"Like what?"

"Like..." I thought a moment about my instructions to keep my mission undercover but time was running out to find Adoria Abasolo alive—and perhaps had already passed. "Like about an alias, another name she used."

"You mean Lola Zorate?"

"Lola Zorate? Who is Lola Zorate?"

Mitchell went quiet for a few seconds. "I think I might be out ahead of you on this thing."

My mind was spinning. *Who was Lola Zorate?* "I had a different name in mind."

"A name that is neither Zorate nor Abasolo?"

I didn't respond.

"Okay. Then perhaps I could be persuaded to share a few notes."

I had been pursuing a weak hunch about Susan Lacy, but now the new name that Mitchell had thrown into the mix tipped me off-balance. "I can't really talk where I am right now. Is it possible we could meet and have a chat about some of this?"

"Sure. Where?"

"The closest good place for me might be the Bear's Paw in Peñasco. Can I buy you a cup of coffee in exchange for a few minutes of your time?"

"I'll be there in thirty minutes." He hung up.

36: WHERE THERE'S A WILL

Mountain had been snoozing on the carpet with his nose under the office chair, so I scooted carefully to one side to avoid running over him with the wheels. I reached down for the backpack and returned Buzz to the front pocket. Suddenly the phone I'd just been using, the replacement for the Screech Owl, sounded. This newer model with its sleek display and big glass screen had a much kinder voice than the old phone—a double chime—and I thought in a flash that it didn't deserve the same moniker as its predecessor. I answered: "Wild, Resource Protection."

It was Carla from the library. "Since you're in such a hurry, I reduced everything I had before down to a rough outline. Check your email."

"Wow, that was fast!"

"Like I said, I already looked up a lot of this stuff. If you want more, I can keep digging."

The document Carla sent contained two paragraphs, a short timeline, and two bullet-point lists. Although some of the information here had been touched on in the *Outside Magazine* article I had read at Abasolo's house, there was enough new data in this small amount of text to render me incredulous. The two paragraphs and the timeline were an overview of how Quintana went from being an unknown undergraduate sociology student at UCLA to a bestselling author, self-proclaimed sorcerer, cult mystic *cum* psychedelic guru, and patriarch of a polygamous clan that included at least three wives and a number of children, none of whom bore Quintana's name. The bullet points illuminated one or two significant details on each of the key figures in the family (or coven), with the caveat that each of these people in Quintana's bizarre circle had "erased their personal history" and so in many cases, their real names and backgrounds were unverifiable. One of these names practically flew off the page at me: *Lola Zorate.*

After scrolling through the document, I sent the file to the same printer I'd used previously, then stepped over Mountain and got up to go stand beside the output tray it and grab the pages as they emerged. The wolf woke up, stood and stretched, and watched me. As I walked back to him, I folded the newly printed pages and stuffed them in the back pocket of my jeans. "Come on, Mountain," I said, giving him a rub on the back of his neck. "We're going to see that guy we caught in our trap last night when we were driving home from Tecolote's." As I said the *bruja's* name, I felt a stir of concern. I had to find some time somewhere in this day to check on her and see how she was feeling.

It was just after ten in the morning when I got to the Bear's Paw. Mitchell's Humvee was already parked outside. Since the early-morning breakfast crowd had already come and gone, the tables inside were now empty except for the one where the P.I. sat sipping from a cup. I ordered a coffee at the counter and gestured to him to see if he needed a warmup, but he waved it off and went back to studying a page in the leather document folder that was open in front of him.

I took a chair and pulled the two printed sheets out of the back pocket of my jeans. I left them folded but set them down next to my cup. "Good morning."

"Same to you," he said. "What have you got there?"

"A little research stuff," I said. "I was hoping we could talk about Susan Lacy as an opener. Have you spoken with her? Do you know where she's staying?"

He jutted his jaw forward as if he were deciding what to say. "I have not spoken with her. I do know where she is staying. Now, you tell me: what's this about a third name for Abasolo?"

I shook my head. "I don't know whether it's a third name. I didn't even know anything about the other name you said until we spoke earlier, the *Lola* name."

"Lola Zorate. I kind of gathered that. Is that what your research here is about?" He flipped a hand toward my folded pages.

"No. Well, maybe partly. I want to talk about that, too, in a minute. But first: can we just team up on this thing? Abasolo's been missing more than a week. If we don't find her soon, we may not..."

"I'm a private investigator," he said. "I don't get involved at that level."

Hearing this, I felt deflated. "Okay, well how about you just help me with anything you can because I *am* involved at that level?"

"I don't know where she is. You probably know as much about what happened to her as I do. But it sounds like I know something about her past that you didn't."

"Yes. What's this Lola Zorate thing?"

"First tell me the alias you had for her. Then I'll tell you what I know about the Zorate name."

"Inés Otero. That's her real name. She wasn't born in Brazil, she was born in Bogotá, Columbia two and half years earlier than her fake Brazilian birth certificate says she was."

"You have this document? The real birth certificate?"

"I don't have it. But someone on my team does. Believe me, if he says it's real, it's real."

He twisted his lower lip between his fingers as he considered this new revelation. "I thought her real name was Lola Zorate. In fact, the way I first located Adoria Abasolo was when a couple of people saw a photo of her from when she was younger— when she was speaking at her graduation as the valedictorian of Stephens Women's College. The picture was in *The L.A. Times* after she was named U.S. Poet Laureate last fall, and they said right in the feature that they didn't have any current photos of her, so they pulled out a few from the past, and that was one of them. Some people recognized her as Lola Zorate from Los Angeles, and they hired me to verify this. That's how I got started on this case.

"And did you verify it? I mean, do you have a document that shows she's really Lola Zorate?"

"I think what I have already could make the case. That's why I'm still here, tying up the loose ends, but I think I could do it with what I have now if I had to."

"Make a case? Are you working for an attorney? Is there some kind of a case involving Abasolo? Did she change her name because of a crime?"

"We can talk some more about this when I see what else you have. But let me just say something about people who change their names: if you're a celebrity who wants one of those crazy one-word names, or you're trying to Americanize your name so you can succeed more easily, you go to court and you legally change your name. If you don't do that, it's a tell for a guy like me. I see that and I presume you're probably hiding something, and that's usually something that could jeopardize you legally or criminally. Abasolo was hiding something."

"Hiding what?"

"I believe it's your turn to share."

"Well, all I know is that Adoria Abasolo was born Inés Otero. And I'd like to get more information on the Lola Zorate part, too, but I'm really more concerned about finding her than I am about figuring out her past at the moment. I'm concerned that she's been missing for more than a week, and no one has seen or heard from her in that time. I feel like if we don't find her very soon, we may not find her alive. To be honest, it may already be too late. This woman Susan Lacy is somehow tied to Abasolo. She was taking writing lessons from her. She's not from around here, and Abasolo's basically a hermit, and yet this Lacy person gets the poet to give her private writing lessons. It's just too odd; it's been bothering me from the very beginning. I can't help but wonder what that's about. And I'm glad you know where she lives. Nobody else seems to know. I ran into her once at Abasolo's house and I haven't been able to find her since."

"I followed her home on that bike of hers. She's staying in a rented *casita,* a good way north of Abasolo's—almost to Ojito—then off on a dirt road that is barely wider than a hiking trail and up a steep dirt drive that hasn't been graded in years, a real mess. I did a little checking on the place; they had a listing on Air B&B, rent was really cheap by the month, probably because of the terrible road and how far it is from anything. Anyway, that listing must be how Lacy found it. She's been staying there for a couple months. She's from L.A."

"Hmm. From L.A. That's certainly a repeating theme here, isn't it? So have you tried to talk to Lacy?"

"I just followed her at first, to find out where she lived. I had my secretary do a background check on her. I wanted that before I talked to her so I could ask the right questions."

"Did you come up with anything?"

"She's 37, never married, no children. She has a doctorate in literature from Stanford. She taught at UCLA until last May, when she took a sabbatical. She has published two books, both of them used as textbooks—both feminist approaches to interpreting literature. That's all I have so far. I can't see another tie she might have to Abasolo except for the poetry thing. So I wasn't thinking she was a person of any real consequence, like you seem to."

"Hmmm," I said, taking a long drink of my coffee. "Do you know anything about Lacy's parents?"

"I haven't gotten that deep into the weeds on her yet. There's a lot of moving parts in this case."

I reached down and unfolded the two pages and spread them side by side on the table. "I just got this right before I came here, so I'm playing catch up. Since you think Abasolo used the name Lola Zorate, I think I need to get up to speed on that part of this mystery."

He tipped his chin up. "What do you have there?"

"It's a bare bones sketch of the Videl Quintana 'family.' The name Lola Zorate is one of five women listed here as 'witches' in his coven. The whole thing is unreal. Do you believe that Abasolo was the same person who called herself Lola Zorate, one of Quintana's witches?"

"I do. And that's precisely why I'm here. Because if Abasolo is, in fact, Lola Zorate, then she's Quintana's one and only legal wife. And that means she would be the primary heir to Quintana's fortune."

My mouth fell open. "What?"

He leafed through his document folder and opened it to a photo, then spun the notebook around to show me. "This is a picture of Lola Zorate with three of the other women in Quintana's harem. That one there is Zorate." He pointed to a beautiful, dark-haired, olive-skinned young woman in a faded color photograph, then twisted the notebook around and pulled out another page, placed it beside the first one, and spun the folder back to face me. He pointed at the photo on the second page. "And that is Adoria Abasolo four years later speaking at her graduation from Stephens College." The two images looked almost identical. "I have looked everywhere for evidence that Adoria Abasolo existed before she went to Stephens College.

The first time she appears in any public record is when she did her college entrance exams in Columbia, Missouri, at the university's testing center, as part of her application process, and her score was the highest overall in the state that year. That's why such an exclusive private college offered her a full scholarship. Her application papers for entrance show that while in high school, she took some advanced courses at the university in São Paulo, but I don't know if they are real—or if they are not, where she got them. I haven't been able to track that yet. But at the same time Abasolo was supposedly taking those advanced high school and pre-college classes in Brazil, Lola Zorate was studying at UCLA *as Lola Zarate* while married to Quintana. And now you're telling me that she wasn't even born in Brazil. I'm thinking those Brazilian transcripts were as phony as that birth certificate she gave them." He sat back from hovering over the documents and threw up his hands. "What do you make of all this?"

"I don't know. I'm baffled."

"Look, I gotta ask: is this exchange going to be fair? Do you have anything for me there?" He gestured toward the two folded sheets in front of me.

I pushed the papers toward him. "This is stuff that you've already figured out, however, I do have something else that might be a big deal. But before I get even more confused, can you just fill me in on this Quintana connection? Then, I'll take my turn."

"Okay, might as well. I think it's all going to come to light pretty soon anyway. First, there's this: Videl Quintana also did that 'erasing your personal history' thing he wanted everybody associated with him to do. He was born Xavier Benítez in Uruguay, four years before he claimed he was born in Argentina as Videl Quintana." He tapped his finger on the table for emphasis. "So do you see why, when you said you had another name for Abasolo, I didn't even question it?"

"What a mess! This blows my mind! Tell me about Quintana's will."

"It's just as complicated as the man was," he said, and he pulled his notebook back in front of his chest and thumbed to a page in it, then twisted it around for me to see. "First of all, these are the so-called witches." He showed me a printed list with details after each name.

"Witches of Quintana Coven":

- **Lola Zarate** *(Adoria Abasolo)* Became disciple to Quintana at age 16. Legally married to Videl Quintana 06/28/1968 in Las Vegas and never divorced. Disappeared from Quintana coven at age 18 in August, 1971 and changed identity.

- **Rachelle Helena** (a/k/a *The Nonbeing)* Quintana's second (not legal) wife (married with L.A. County license 07/16/1981) Bears a daughter (Nona Dodd — see offspring below) to Quintana. Kicked out of the coven by Qual but then welcomed back after a few years. Presumed deceased in suicide pact.

- **Qual** *(a/k/a The Wingless Bird—has had at least four different names, none of which are real)* Adopted by Quintana 08/31/1981 as an adult (age 19). Sexual partner to Quintana; married him in unlicensed ceremony after/while he was married to Rachelle Helena. Presumed deceased in suicide pact.

- **Salma Esteban** *(not her real name)* One of the witches in Quintana's coven; also the leader of the Sorcery School and appeared in public classes, workshops, retreats, etc., on behalf of the foundation and the Sorcery School. Presumed deceased in suicide pact.

- **Yini** *(not her real name)* One of the witches in Quintana's coven who published a book on learning to become a sorcerer. Presumed deceased in suicide pact.

Offspring of Videl Quintana:

- **Nona Dodd** Born 07/28/1981 daughter of Quintana and Rachelle Helena; raised by maternal grandparents in Iowa. Never associated with coven or Quintana after Helena left, even after Helena returned to the coven.
- **Possible offspring unverified: Twins** Born approximately 1982, mother unknown, father presumed to be Quintana but not certified, home birth, no birth certificate until they were enrolled in a middle school in Los Angeles at age ten, in 1992. Raised by coven without parentage specified.

Mitchell pointed to the name of Nona Dodd, Quintana's one acknowledged child. "That woman and her mother have both been specifically excluded, by name, from the will."

"So you believe that Abasolo, as the only living wife, or witch, or whatever, is first in line to inherit because this child has been excluded?"

"It's not that simple, but yes. It's a very strange, very complex will. There are five orders of succession. The first is his foundation, which gets ten percent of all royalties from his work so long as it remains in operation. The second order of succession is where it starts to get crazy. The will states that the remaining 90% of his estate, including all property (real and otherwise) goes in full to his 'true wife' and her heirs or assigns. But it does not name the true wife."

"And you think that's Adoria Abasolo."

"I do, yes."

"Well, it looks like all the other witches are presumed dead, so I wouldn't think any of them was claiming to be the true wife. So, whom are you working for?"

"I told you, the will gets complicated after the true wife and her heirs. There are five orders of succession, in total. I'm actually working for some folks who would inherit in the fifth order of succession. It's a big fortune, millions of dollars and still growing from his book royalties. It's been in probate for years now. My clients have come forward and wanted me to prove that none of the heirs in line before them are alive or have a valid claim to the will."

"Well, what about the third and fourth orders of succession? What happened to those beneficiaries?"

"After the true wife and her heirs or assigns, the third order is the witches, excluding Rachelle Helena, who for some reason is treated like an outcast, along with her daughter. So that's these three." He pointed at the names of Yini, Salma, and Qual on the list of witches. They divide equally, but if they don't inherit directly—which they won't because I believe they are all three dead—then the next order, the fourth order of succession is Quintana's children. And here, he specifically excludes the one child for whom he is named as the father on her birth certificate, Nona Dodd. She has gone to court three times, twice on appeal, to contest the will, and she's lost all three times because the language of the will so specifically excludes her under any order of succession. So, if Quintana had any other children...any other children that weren't born to the true wife, they would be the inheritants here at the fourth level of succession. And the fifth level, that's the heirs and assigns of the witches. And that's who I'm working for."

"But if these aren't the real names of these women," I said, pointing my own finger at the list of witches, "then how do you know the people you're working for are really the heirs and assigns?"

"Well, on a practical level, it doesn't matter to me. They hired me to find out if there was anyone out there ahead of them in line to inherit. That's led me here, and I think there is, and I think it's Adoria Abasolo, or Lola Zorate, or Inés Otero—whatever her real name turns out to be. But if I do not find that person, if she's not who I think she is—or if she *is* who I think she is but she's not still alive and doesn't have any heirs, any family that we know about—then I go on working to try to prove my clients' claim to the will, which could involve some DNA evidence."

I thought about this for a moment. "They found the bones of the one they think is that woman Qual; they did that with DNA evidence. Do you have DNA on the other ones?"

"I haven't gone down that road yet, but that would be something I would consider. My first order of business was to identify Lola Zorate, whom I believe was the 'true wife' referred to in the will. In any case, Zorate would inherit, and if anyone else tried to appeal, she could disprove any other claims because she was the only one legally married to Quintana. So I had to rule that out before I went any further, and I don't think I can rule it out. I think Adoria Abasolo is Lola Zorate." He took a big drink of coffee and then said, "Since all the witches changed their names time and again, it is not known for certain if any of them besides Rachelle had children. These two," he pointed to the text that said *The Twins*, "were raised in the compound, home-schooled, and no one claimed to be their parent. It's a bizarre situation. I have no idea if they are Quintana's or not. There were a lot of people living in the compound for decades, not just the witches, but other so-called 'disciples' of Quintana's. But if these twins wanted to go the DNA route, and they could prove it up, they might be able to make a claim under the fourth order of succession, as children of his. Quintana died of liver cancer, but before he did, he underwent DNA tests to try to find a match for a transplant. That DNA is in the custody of the court, and it could be accessed if there were a legitimate claimant. But, first of all, since Lola Zorate is Abasolo or Otero or whatever, she trumps them altogether. And I don't represent them, so for me, it's just a side note, and if I go any further on this case, I'll caution my clients about it as a possible challenge. Me, I'm working for the relatives of a couple of the witches, and right now, I'm thinking none of them...nobody else inherits if we find the poet."

"This is all too weird," I re-folded my sheets of paper, which now seemed wholly inadequate to explain this uncanny story.

He put both palms down on the table and gave me an intense stare. "Are you going to tell me who you are working for, and why you're being so secretive about your search for Abasolo?"

"I'm sorry. I can't. I would if I could, but...I can't tell you that yet."

He leaned back in his chair. "Okay, I've shown you my hand. Now, you show me yours. Or whatever you *can* show me, I guess."

"Well, I didn't know any of this before we sat down to talk. So I was looking at it without any of this background. I was starting to focus on Susan Lacy because I had another idea, but I could be off base."

"What's that?"

"I thought she might be Abasolo's daughter. You see, Abasolo gave up a baby for adoption in Los Angeles. I don't have the exact details or dates or anything, but I just keep intuitively going to that...and it feels like one of those gut things that I can't ignore. You know what I'm talking about?"

He nodded his head. "You have evidence of this adoption?"

"I don't have paper in hand. But I believe I can say for sure that Adoria, using whatever name she decided to use at the time, gave up a baby for adoption in L.A. And I was thinking that maybe Susan Lacy came here looking for her birth mother, and that either they both just figured it out for sure, or were about to do so when..."

"When Abasolo went missing. Where do you think she went?"

I bit my lower lip. "That's another piece of information that I have that you don't know yet. Her car has been found. It went off the cliff into a ravine."

His eyes widened. "So she's dead?"

"I don't know if she was in the car. The sheriff's department is investigating the crash right now. I don't have any more than that until we hear what they find."

"But she hasn't been seen in—what is it now? Seven, eight days?"

I nodded my head but didn't speak. "The only lead I have left is Susan Lacy. That's why I called you, to see if you knew where I could find her. If I'm wrong, and she's just someone who came here to study writing, then that's that. But if she's a woman who came here trying to determine if Adoria Abasolo is her long-lost birth mother…"

"And if Abasolo *is* her mother, then that could be a big development. She could be a suspect, you know, in the poet's disappearance. This Lacy gal could be angry about being abandoned by her mother at birth, or just care nothing for her since she never knew her. But she may have figured out that with Abasolo gone, she would inherit 90% of Quintana's fortune at the second level of succession, with only the foundation taking its 10% share before what she gets."

"Actually, I didn't know anything about the will until we talked today. And I could be wrong, but I just don't see Susan Lacy as a kidnapper or a murderer. I'll admit I only met her and talked to her for a few minutes, but she didn't seem like she had anything to hide. She acted genuinely surprised that her writing teacher wasn't home on Monday. So I'm not looking for her because I think she's a suspect. I want to find her because I'm hoping that she can give me some idea of how to find Abasolo."

"What do you say we go find out?"

"You'll take me to where she lives?"

"Why not? We could sit here and hash out a dozen other things, but if we can put this piece in perspective, it might shed some light on all the rest of it."

We stood and took our used coffee cups up to the counter. "I have my wolf with me," I said. "So you drive, and I'll follow you, okay?"

"Why don't I just ride with you?"

"Okay, if you don't mind getting wolf hair all over your clothes. It could take away from that sleek black tactical look you got going there." I grinned.

He smiled and went back to the table and put a five-dollar bill down and set the salt shaker on top of it.

"I already left a tip in the jar up here at the counter when I got my coffee." I said.

"People gotta eat," Zeke Mitchell said, and he winked as he walked past and then opened the door for me to go through.

37: GONE, GONE, GONE

The dense fog from earlier that morning had cleared completely now, but a cold, wet blanket of dew lingered on every surface. The rural road to the place outside of Ojito where Susan Lacy rented a *casita* was so muddy I had to put the Jeep in four-wheel drive to navigate it. Mountain and Mitchell bumped and jostled along in the car as I held tightly to the wheel. We got to the base of the narrow uphill drive and I opted to turn the Jeep around so it faced back toward the main road and leave it parked at the bottom of the hill while we walked up to Lacy's *casita*. I put Mountain on a lead, lest the property owner take him for a coyote and shoot him, as happened entirely too often with dogs that ran loose in northern New Mexico. We made our way up the muddy track, our boots squishing in the mud as Mountain nosed happily alongside.

When we got to the main house, a woman came out the front door and held a palm like a visor over her eyes, squinting against the sunlight as she studied us.

I looked at Zeke Mitchell. "You or me?"

"You're the fed."

"Yeah, but in some places, that's grounds for getting shot at." I forced a smile and called out, *"¡Hola! Estamos buscando a Susan Lacy."*

The landlady told us that she was sure that her renter was at home, because both her car and her bicycle were there at the *casita.* She pointed over the rise, where we could just make out one corner of a roof. We walked farther up the drive to the top, where a blue Toyota wearing a light coat of frost huddled in its parking spot in some low brush. It was fitted with a rack on the back holding the fancy tricked-out hybrid bike I had seen before. We rounded the stub of the ridge and walked down the sandstone step-path to the casita, which was set into the side of the hill. The steps led along the side of the structure and around it to the front, which overlooked a narrow valley dotted with a few small adobe homes. Thin plumes of smoke danced above them, and the incense of burning *piñon* wood drifted across the vale.

I stepped onto the *portal* and up to the door and saw that the door was ajar. "Miss Lacy?" I leaned my head to look into the narrow slot between door and frame. I glanced back at Zeke Mitchell, who stood behind me. Again, I called into the house, "Susan Lacy?" I held the flat of my palm in front of Mountain's face, signaling him to stay, and handed the end of his lead to Mitchell. Then I pushed lightly on the door, and stepped to the left, out of the opening it framed. Reaching behind me to unsnap the holster on my pistol, I drew out the P229 but kept it low and at my side. "Susan Lacy," I called louder and then raised the gun and leaned into the doorway to get a better look inside.

The *casita* was small, just three tiny rooms: a narrow, multi-function main room with a tiny kitchenette at one end, a bathroom no bigger than a closet, and a bedroom where the bed covers were rumpled and pulled to one side as if Susan Lacy had just gotten up and would be right back.

"She's not here," I said.

Mitchell stood just inside the front door, still holding Mountain's lead. "I see that. But where did she go without her bike or her car?"

I looked around the main room and went to the tiny stove in the kitchenette. Like the rest of the place, the kitchen area was clean, the counters spotless; there were no cups or dishes in the sink. She was obviously a fastidious person, and it seemed unlikely she would have left the kitchen and the rest of the house in perfect order but the bed unmade. I walked over to the woodstove, and held out a hand. It was barely warm; the fire from last night had almost gone out. "I don't know," I said, looking at Mitchell, "but she's gone."

The private detective and I were quiet as I maneuvered the Jeep back the way we had come, to the graded county road and then onto the asphalt and south again to Peñasco, where talking became impossible because of the Gatling-gun din of mud gobs being flung from the tires against the underside of the jeep once we got on the highway. When we got to the Bear's Paw, it was lunchtime, and the parking lot was full. I pulled into the only space I could find, a narrow spot far from the entrance at the southern edge of the lot, and Zeke opened the passenger door and got out. He leaned down and looked at me. "You have my number," he said. "And you called me, so I have yours."

"Right. I'll let you know if I learn anything."

"Likewise." He reached across the back of the seat and gave Mountain a scratch behind the ears. "See you, big guy," he said.

Moments after he closed the door, Buzz began to vibrate and drone. I had moved my backpack from the front to the cargo deck behind my seat so Mitchell could have the space—and as a result, now my pack and the device were out of easy reach. I got out and opened the side door and retrieved the phone from the front pocket of the pack. "Agent Wild," I said. I didn't get back in the car, instead preferring to move around a bit after the bumpy ride. I rolled the window down halfway so Mountain could have some fresh air, swung the door shut, and walked in front of the car.

Coronel's voice was almost lyrical. "I have good news. We still have a shot at finding Abasolo. There were no remains in the car."

I drew in a breath. "But, what happened? I mean how did the car...?"

"I don't have details yet because that Indian Service Route is all mud and ruts so they will have to send a crew on foot to look at the spot where it went over the side. But the way they got to the car itself was through a mine in the canyon below the cliff. The wreck wasn't too far from where the mine road ended, maybe a mile or so. Evidently the local fire department has some kind of super all-terrain vehicle with a winch on it, and they took a crew of guys in on that and a couple ATVs. They pored all over the crash site. No sign of any human remains."

I realized I had been holding that deep breath I took, and now I let it out with a huge sigh of relief. "So she might still be alive?"

"That's a *might*. But now we are no longer alone in looking for her. Now that they've found the car, the FBI has been called in and it's officially a missing person case. I got in touch with their agent to get the details, and I had to let her know that the Secret Service was also looking for Abasolo. I'm afraid that *The Bartender* is going to have to figure out how to message this, because it's bound to go public soon. I did get one bit of information from the FBI agent: they found a letter in the glove box of Abasolo's car. I haven't gotten a copy of it yet, but she told me it was from the Archdiocese of Los Angeles."

I grinned and started bouncing from foot to foot with excitement. "This could be a break! I was going to tell you this morning when you came by and we had coffee: I didn't have confirmation then, but I had begun to suspect that Abasolo had given a baby up for adoption in Los Angeles when she was younger."

"That's the idea you were going to check out when I told you she'd been calling the Archdiocese?"

"Yes. I had a hunch, but it was just an inkling, and you were in such a hurry..." I swallowed hard. "I have another hunch, too, that the neighbor I told you about, Susan Lacy, the one who came for writing lessons…that she is Abasolo's daughter."

"What? Do you have any…?"

"No, that's why I didn't say anything. But since we talked this morning, I did get confirmation that Abasolo gave up a child for adoption, a daughter. The part about Lacy is just a guess. But it still feels right to me. We have to get a copy of that letter," I said. "If it names Susan Lacy as the daughter…"

"It won't be a problem to get a copy. We coordinate with the FBI all the time; it just may have to go through a few switches and gears before someone okays it. In the meantime, why don't you find Lacy and ask her?"

"I just tried to do that. I have a feeling that they both—the poet and her daughter—may have just figured this out before Abasolo disappeared. But now Lacy is gone, too."

"What do you mean *gone?*"

"Her house is empty, but her car and her bike are there. Her bed looks like she just jumped up out of it and left it in a hurry. Her landlady didn't see anything, thought she was there at home. But she's gone."

My bladder was begging to offload all the coffee I had drunk that morning, so I pocketed Buzz and called out to Mountain, "Wait right here, Buddy, I'll be right back." I walked past the crowded row of cars and into the Bear's Paw to use the washroom. The restaurant was as noisy as it was busy. People stood in line at the front counter waiting for a table or to place carry-out orders, every chair was occupied, and a duo of waitresses shuttled food in and out of the kitchen at a rapid pace. Several women had gotten to the washroom before me, and we waited in line outside the door for a turn to use the single-seat accommodations.

When I finally got back outside, I spotted an older, oversized rusted red truck with a pipe gate across the back blocking the very end of the lot where I had parked. I felt a twinge of worry, realizing that I had been so preoccupied with the news from Coronel's call that I had left the doors unlocked and Mountain inside the Jeep. I picked up my pace and started to sprint toward the pickup, sensing a danger I couldn't yet see.

As I raced past car after car, I saw that the bed of the truck contained a huge cage, and an animal was slumped in the floor of it. "Mountain!" I cried out as I realized it was my beloved wolf companion, locked up in a big crate. A tall man climbed into the driver's seat and I was sure it was Lor Talgren, though I had only seen him from behind. There weren't that many long, lanky, fair-haired men in rural northern New Mexico, and only one who was out to do harm to my wolf. The truck started to nose out onto the highway and I still had several cars to get past before I was there. I accelerated my pace, yelling at the top of my voice, "Mountain! Mountain! Help! Somebody, help! That man is stealing Mountain!" As I grew closer, I could see the bright orange feathered trip of a tranquilizer dart lodged in the wolf's shoulder. He lay unconscious in the cage.

The truck's tires squealed as Talgren pulled onto the road, narrowly missing an approaching car. I ran faster, gaining on the truck, avoiding the oncoming vehicle as it swerved onto the shoulder. The tailgate was only a few feet ahead of me. I churned my legs up and down as fast as they would go. My chest felt like it was going to burst; the fear and the cold made my lungs burn like they were on fire. "Stop the truck! Mountain!" I screamed. "Stop! Help! Mountain!" I threw out my left arm and lunged, barely connecting with three fingers of my hand to the pipe gate across the rear of the truck bed. I clung on and kept running, but Talgren accelerated. My feet failed to keep up and I tripped, my legs were dragging, the road tearing at my jeans and boots, but I kept my fist grasped around the gate and reached with the other arm and hooked my right hand on the lower rung of it. Talgren yelled out the open window as he drove, "Goddamn whore! Let go!" He gunned the motor and I felt searing pain in my right calf as the asphalt tore at the skin and flesh of my dragging legs. I tried to twist and let the backs of my boots take more of it, but suddenly, the truck lurched to a stop in the middle of the road, and the side of my face rammed into the end of the truck bed. Before I could get my feet under me, Lor Talgren rushed around the side of the truck with a long black flashlight held high like a club. I was struggling to get my footing, my fingers still locked around the rails of the rear gate as if they were melted into the metal when Talgren drew back like a batter at the plate and drove the length of the flashlight into my side so violently that he knocked me to the ground. I felt my stomach contract and heave. My head spun. I couldn't get my breath, and then Talgren's boot came at my midsection so fast that I saw a blur of muddy brown leather and grit, and then nothing more as I was sucked into blackness.

When I came to, the ground was spinning and I felt such pain in my midsection that I rolled slightly to one side and a stream of bitter bile erupted from my throat and out of my mouth. I could not hold my head up and I felt warm acid run down the side of my face and onto the road.

"The ambulance is coming," someone said. "Here comes the sheriff. Hold on."

"Mountain," I gasped, then heaved again. "He took my Mountain."

☽

At the clinic in Embudo, the doctor used tweezers for what seemed like an hour to pick rocks, grit, and bits of my ripped up jeans from the wounds and then bandaged the contusions on my legs. My mid-section was starting to purple with bruising where the tip of Talgren's boot had struck. "Just to be sure there are no serious injuries we couldn't see on your ex-ray, I'd recommend a transport to the hospital in Albuquerque for observation—at least for a few hours," she said. "This clinic will be closed for the night soon, and if something comes up or you have too much pain and need something stronger, we won't be here for you until morning."

"I have to find Mountain," I said. "I'm not going to a hospital, or anywhere else, until I find my wolf."

"Well, I can give you some tablets for pain, but you shouldn't drive while taking them. Someone will have to get you home. The X-ray was negative for any new breaks, but you have one rib that looks like it's mended from a previous injury. Have you had a cracked rib before?"

I nodded. I'd taken a beating the previous winter and been kicked in the same place, which could be why it hurt so badly this time.

The doctor went on: "Those lacerations on your legs need to be kept clean and re-dressed daily; that kind of lesion is prone to infection. I can prescribe some oral antibiotics and an ointment. I used a numbing agent when I cleaned the wounds, and you already had some pain medication in your IV drip, but both of these areas—your mid-section and your legs—are going to start hurting again soon, and when they do, you're going to need that pain medication. So if you won't change your mind and let me arrange for a transport to the hospital, then call and get yourself a ride home and I'll go write you a scrip."

I sat upright and swung my legs over the side of the table, and felt tremendous pain in the center of my torso when I did. About the time I was considering how I would manage to stand, Deputy Sheriff Jerry Padilla came in the door of the exam room and said, "I need to talk to you before you get up."

It gave me a good reason to remain seated while I tried to get the room to stop whirling.

He told me that customers at the Bear's Paw had seen the confrontation between me and Lor Talgren and called 911. A sheriff's deputy and an ambulance were dispatched at once, and fortunately, one of the people lunching there had been an EMT, who tended to me with ice packs on my belly and dish towels around my bleeding legs until the paramedics arrived. She had insisted they not move me until the ambulance arrived, so volunteers directed traffic around me until it came. Several of the patrons of the café were locals who recognized Lor Talgren and his truck and gave this information to the deputy on the scene. A sheriff's car was dispatched to Talgren's place, but neither he nor the truck he'd been driving were there. They had put out a warrant and were searching for the man.

"Mountain?" I asked, "did they find him?"

Padilla shook his head. "We all know…everyone knows that wolf is your buddy. But he wasn't there. We'll keep looking. But we did find something at Talgren's place that's going to make sure he goes away for a long time when we do get him."

I was gripped with terror from the news that they didn't find Mountain. I didn't care what the deputies had found.

"He had a meth lab going in the vat room of that old winery. When we find Lor Talgren, he's going down bigtime, and not just on theft of your animal and assault and battery, but on federal drug charges of use, manufacture, and sale. Let's see," he pretended to count on his fingers. "That will mean he won't see daylight for decades."

I began to sob, and every time I drew in air, my midsection hurt more. "Mountain," I cried. "You have got to help me find Mountain!"

☽

Padilla must have talked with the doctor while I was getting dressed, because he only grudgingly agreed to give me a ride back to my Jeep, and he harped at me all the way about how they would find Talgren and I should check myself into the hospital and get better. When we got to the Bear's Paw, I thanked him for the ride and struggled to get out of the cruiser's passenger seat. Padilla came around to help me. "I don't feel right about this," he said, holding me by one arm as he escorted me to my Jeep. "You aren't in any shape to drive. And unless you moved from out there west of Taos, you got a long ways to go before you get home tonight."

"I'm staying up here...at a friend's. It's just right down the highway, before you get to the Mountain Mission. I'll be okay."

He held out my handgun in its holster. "The paramedics said one of the folks on the road gave this to them, that you'd been wearing it and it came off when...they turned it in to me. You put it in the glove box and lock it up, okay?"

"Okay." I bent down to swing sideways into the car and felt like I might pass out. So I backed into the seat using both my arms on the sides of the Jeep's door frame, wincing as I lifted my bandaged legs into the car. I set the gun in its holster on the passenger seat, but I wasn't about to lean sideways to reach across to the glove box.

"Tell me you'll go straight to where you're staying and no place else," Padilla said, bending down to look me right in the face.

I looked right back at him. "If that's what you need me to say."

"Goddamnit, Jamaica, I'll call Roy and have him order you directly to go home and get in bed."

"I'm not working for Roy this week. You want me to go rest, then find Mountain, Jerry. You find him. I mean it."

"We got every available deputy on it."

"Now push my door closed for me, will you? It hurts too much for me to lean over and pull."

I waited for Padilla to pull away in the Ford Explorer, working hard to stifle what I knew was inevitable. As soon as he was gone, I scrambled out of the Jeep again, crying out with the pain in my legs and my stomach, took two steps, then doubled over with nausea. I drew in a breath, bent over and heaved again, bringing up nothing but agony. The IV's pain medication was beginning to wear off. I had the bottle of pills to take home but I knew not to drive while taking them. Besides, I couldn't risk taking one now; I needed to keep my head clear. I knew who could help me with both the physical anguish and possibly even with finding Mountain, too, and as soon as I could muster the strength to get back behind the wheel, I intended to go see her.

☽

I arrived at the village of Agua Azuela at almost the same hour as when I had come the day before. As I always did, I parked my Jeep at the bottom of the hill, behind the wall of the compound that surrounded the village church, an ancient adobe structure that had been built by the conquerors from Spain who settled there in the 1500's, and whose descendants lived there still. Normally, the church—surrounded by its large wall-enclosed yard—sat empty between the services for mass on Sundays. Those were only sparsely attended by a handful of faithful; there was no priest to administer the sacrament. The rituals were instead presided over by members of the *Penitentes,* a dwindling secret brotherhood who practiced the ancient rituals of self-mortification and mock crucifixion and the procession of Christ dragging his cross to the *campo santo* during the season of Easter. But on this late Thursday afternoon in early January, the church yard was uncharacteristically bustling with villagers scurrying in and out of the big, thick-walled structure. Perhaps they were preparing for a wedding on Saturday. I worked my way out of the vehicle and then started up the goat path toward Esperanza's *casita,* clutching at my gut, where a dull pain throbbed with every step I took. It was nearing dusk and the sky was coloring up, clouds massing in the west reflecting a reddish cast to the light as the sun sank toward the horizon.

I had to stop several times before I made it to the top of the steep path. My mid-section ached, and my calf muscles burned. I felt woozy and off-balance, and I hoped Tecolote would have a salve or a tea that would heal my middle and the wounds on my legs, perhaps even something to help clear the fog in my head from the residue of the drugs I'd been given at the clinic.

When I finally rounded the top of the hill, I gasped, then shuddered, and my mind suddenly vitrified into a mix of fear and wonder at the scene before me. The vast rumpled cape of now-blood-red clouds had spread itself across the sky behind the *bruja's* casita, the sun an angry scarlet orb at the center, the air pulsing with rubescence. On the roof of the adobe hut, along the railing of the corral, on top of the outhouse, on the tall stems of choya, atop the soft feathery mounds of sage, on every bare spot in the yard, and on every brush and shrub surrounding her home, ravens—dozens and dozens of ravens—had convened. They waited in silence as I approached. In the eerie crimson glow, they all seemed to be watching me with great curiosity. I walked up the trail to the *portal,* and three of the birds fluttered off of the porch rail and into the yard. They did not cry out or bark in protest as ravens almost always do, but instead held a numinous, noiseless vigil. As I edged toward the open door of Esperanza's house, those in my path puffed their neck feathers and scuttled to either side, complaining with little soundless huffs, ticks and flits that I could see but not hear. I felt like I had wandered into a surreal silent film. At the doorway, I looked inside, and a gigantic raven stood on the table where I always shared tea, often a meal, and always curious conversations with the old *curandera.* This bird was as big as a great horned owl, and as black and shiny as tar.

Commanding my attention, the raven danced from one foot to the other on the table top, lifting its wings and puffing up the feathers of its chest to make itself seem even larger, as it would when challenged by a rival for some prize it had scavenged and had no intention to share.

"Tecolote?" I called loudly, stepping one foot through the doorway. The room was cold, semi-dark, empty of life, save the black feathered conqueror who had claimed it as his territory now.

"*Ka-ka!*" The big raven answered and spread its wings wide, but it did not lift off of the table. Before it, on the scarred wooden plane, lay the hand-stitched deerskin pillow I had made for Tecolote and given her one year for Christmas. Nesting in the center of it was a tied piece of cloth, no bigger than a tea bag. I reached forward to pick this up and measured my movements so as not to stimulate an attack from the big black bird. The raven watched me carefully, but did not move. I plucked up the pouch and held it high to look at it, then sniff it. As I inhaled its musky fragrance, I felt a slight lessening of my pain. I knew Tecolote had left this remedy expressly for me since she had placed it on the pillow I had made for her.

All at once, all the ravens began to cry: "*Ka-ka! Ka-ka! Ka-ka!*" The sound was almost deafening. They flew from the roof into the yard, from the yard up to the roof, from the fence into the brush and back down to the ground again, the air filled with a cloud of moving black objects screaming over and over again, "*ka-ka!*" They seemed to be saying: "*She's gone!*"

38: LOCKUP

As I pulled onto the High Road, I worked to crank the wheel with my left arm alone and spare my right side, because it hurt each time I tried to employ the arm or the muscles on that side of my torso. The new BLM phone chimed and I punched the hands-free button on the wheel to answer it. "Agent Wild," I croaked, unable to mask the agony in my voice.

"We got him," Jerry Padilla's voice said through the speakers. "We found Talgren."

A jolt of new energy streaked through me. "Is Mountain with him? Where are they?"

"Hold on there, now. Just hold on. The wolf wasn't with him. We pulled him over in his truck and we got him down in lockup."

"I'm coming. I'll be right there."

"No, wait. Just wait a second. I'll come get you. I'll come and pick you up where you're staying and I'll take you there."

"We have to make him tell us where Mountain is. There's no time..."

"I will get you there just as fast as you could go yourself, if not faster. I'll run hot with the lights flashing and we can take it over the speed limit as far as it's safe to go. I'm just north of the ranger station in Peñasco right now. So where did you say you're staying along the High Road?"

"Meet me at the Bear's Paw in ten minutes," I said, and I clicked the button to disconnect.

At the county lockup, Padilla walked me through the gate where Lor Talgren stood shaking in the corner of a cell. "He's got the DTs," Padilla said. "Tweaking bad for a fix."

As pathetic as the big man looked, I felt no sympathy or compassion for him, but I had promised myself to keep calm and try to get the information I so desperately needed, so I intended to be polite. "Lor?"

He looked up and across the cell at me, his teeth chattering. His eyes were red-rimmed and his lips fluttered uncontrollably.

"Please tell me what you've done with Mountain."

He looked at me and managed a wobbling sneer, but he could not hold his lips in place and so gave it up and looked down at his arms, which were crossed tightly over his chest. His right hand pulled at the skin around his left elbow as if there was something alien attached to it that needed to be removed.

"I'm sorry about your dog," I said. "I'm sorry the bat infected it with rabies. I'm so sorry you lost him. But my wolf shouldn't have to suffer for what the bat did. Please tell me where he is so I can go get him."

He looked up at me again, a crazed look in his eyes, his mouth still working, his chin now shifting from side to side as his teeth continued to clack and chatter. "You did it. Not some bat. You did it. You had them come get my dog and they put him down. Now you have to pay for what you did."

I felt tears well up and threaten to spill, but I somehow managed to keep my composure. "Okay, I've paid. You beat me with that big flashlight, you kicked me in the stomach and you drug me behind your truck. What else? It's not Mountain's fault your dog got rabies. Tell me where he is."

Lor flew across the cell at an astonishing speed and with such force that I jumped back, slamming my shoulder into Jerry Padilla's chest and stepping on the toe of his boot with my right heel. He caught me by the backs of my upper arms and set me right again. "Talgren, tell us what you did with the wolf and I'll consider speaking up for you at your trial."

But the big blonde man ignored him and grabbed the bars of the cell right in front of where I stood and gave me a seething glare. "You got my prize dog killed," he said. "So your wolf has to die." He worked his mouth for a second and then spat a huge glob of phlegm into my face.

I tried to raise my right arm to wipe my face with the sleeve of my jacket, but it hurt so much that I couldn't lift the arm all the way. I spun around and made to leave, not wanting to show any sign of weakness in front of Talgren, and Padilla followed close on my heels. Before he put his key in the gate to let me out of the cage area, he held his handkerchief up and gently blotted at my face, then pressed the soft cloth into my hand and unlocked the gate.

On the way back to the Bear's Paw, Padilla tried to reassure me. "He's jonesing right now, needs a fix bad, you see, and that makes a meth addict insane. You can't reason with him. He might talk when he gets a little more detoxed. I'll keep on it. I'll get him to tell me where he's got Mountain. I promise."

My lower lip quivered as I rode along in silence, trying hard to suppress another bout of sobbing.

"We'll keep looking for him," Padilla said. "He's gotta be someplace Talgren goes to regularly. We got guys on it. I promise we won't stop till we find your wolf."

Tears escaped in spite of my efforts and they felt hot and stinging as they made their way down my face. I had scrubbed my cheeks, nose, and chin with the harsh hand soap in the washroom at the lockup to try to make sure I got all of Talgren's foul fluids off of my skin. "I won't stop either," I said softly.

"Beg your pardon?" Padilla leaned over slightly in my direction.

"I won't stop until I find Mountain."

The deputy was ready to argue with me when the double-chime sounded from the new phone again and I pulled it out of my jacket pocket and pressed to answer.

"Jamaica, where the hell are you?" It was Roy.

I wanted to reply but, inside me, the dam that had constrained my sorrow broke, and a sob came out like the wail of a banshee and rivers of pent-up tears flooded from my eyes. My chest heaved and hurt and I sobbed and sobbed. I dropped the device on the seat and Padilla picked it up and held it to his ear.

After a minute of listening, he said, "Roy, this is Jerry Padilla. Your agent here is in bad shape. She's hurt pretty bad and she's all broken up about Mountain. So don't bark at her right now, okay?"

He was quiet for a few seconds, then responded, "I'm taking her back to where she's staying. She really needs to rest and try to heal. And we got to find that wolf for her. If you got anybody you can put on it to help, I know she'd appreciate it."

After Padilla helped me out of the county cruiser, he put a hand lightly on each of my shoulders and looked down into my face with a stern expression. "If I catch you out in that Jeep of yours before daylight, I will have you arrested for driving while impaired. Do you understand me? You're to go straight to bed and stay there and let yourself heal a little. It's dark now, we don't have any leads, we already searched Talgren's place, so we gotta work on getting him to talk to us when he comes down some. I promise I will get it out of him—beat it out of him if I have to. We *are* going to find out what he did with Mountain and go get your wolf for you, you got that?"

I tried to avoid his stare, but he kept twisting his head to engage my eyes until I looked back at him and held his gaze. I nodded my head and whispered, "I got that."

"I'll head back down to the county lockup and when I see him start to look almost human, I'll interrogate Talgren."

"Please do." And then I started to cry again, which vexed me because I was not normally much of a crier. "I just want Mountain. That's all. I would be willing to drop the assault and battery charges..."

Oh, no you don't," Padilla said, as he walked me toward the door of my Jeep. "You aren't going to do that, and even if you tried, he would still be going to the big house for a long time. He was operating a meth lab, and that's a fed rap. No matter what, he ain't going home, he ain't passing go, and he ain't collecting two hundred dollars. He is going to prison. But I will make him talk before that, if there is any way in hell to do it. I promise you that. Now get out of here. Did the doc give you anything for the pain?"

I nodded.

"Okay. Well take some of that stuff and go to bed. I'll call you tomorrow with an update."

I got in the Jeep with great difficulty. Padilla watched me from a few feet away, standing beside the open driver's door of the SUV, making sure I was going to be able to drive. I gave him a half-wince-half-smile and held my fist out with my thumb pointed skyward and started up the Jeep. I waited for Jerry to get in his vehicle and drive on from where he had parked behind me. He pulled onto the highway and the supercharged SUV sped off to the south, its taillights streaming bright ribbons of red lightning behind it as it vanished into the dark.

Before I could back up the Jeep and disappear into the night as Padilla had done, Buzz purred, danced, and lit up, so I shifted the transmission back into park, and answered. Hank's voice said, "You were right."

"I was going to call you," I said.

"Did you hear me? You were right. The letter from the Archdiocese identifies the girl child Abasolo gave up for adoption as Susan Lacy. It says that Lacy had given her permission for her identity to be revealed in correlation with her own inquiries. So she had been looking for her birth mother, and she had to have known that Abasolo was also looking for her, at least by the time this was written, which was a week before Christmas."

I barely registered all this. "Mountain. He's gone," I blurted. "He's been taken!"

"What? Where is he? Where are you? I'll come to you."

"I'm at the Bear's Paw in Peñasco. He's not with me. He's gone."

"I'll be there as soon as I can," the agent said, and he hung up.

I decided to call Kerry. I reached into my pocket to retrieve the BLM phone and again saw the red dot indicating I had a voicemail. I pressed to play it, thinking that hearing his voice would soothe me. But it wasn't Kerry's voice on the recording.

"Miss Jamaica?" It was Federico Yazza, young Rico. "I don't know who I should tell about this, but I figured since you got a badge and you work for the BLM, maybe you will know what to do. Someone has been coming and going to this place down below the rim of the canyon just outside the rez. It's an old ruin. I didn't think nobody knew about it but me. It used to be more covered up than it is now, but one time I went down on that ledge using a rope, and I could see that somebody's been in there and dug it out some. I think maybe they are in there now. I thought you ought to know. Don't call me back on this number, it's my uncle's phone, and I'm not supposed to use a phone right now because it's Quiet Time. Just come to the rez tomorrow and I'll watch for you and show you where I mean."

I looked at the date and time of the call and noted that he had called late last night, after he had left Abasolo's. So *tomorrow* meant today, and today was already over, or nearly so. I hadn't listened to the message in time, and now it was after dark and too late to go to the pueblo or to see anything in the canyon from the rim.

I was about to call Kerry when I recognized the growing clamor of a loud, hammering souped-up truck engine approaching. The same Darth dooly diesel that Ibanez had come in before had pulled into the now-empty parking lot, stopping right behind my Jeep. I looked toward the restaurant hoping someone might be there to come to my rescue again, but the place was dark and empty—even the sign wasn't lit— because the Bear's Paw was closed in the evenings in the winter, except on weekends. "Oh, no," I said. "Oh, no." I turned off the engine, pushed the door open and struggled out of the Jeep and to my feet. I was damned if I was going to let anybody intimidate me while I sat helplessly in my car.

The driver turned off his headlights, but not the engine, and the diesel pounded and clanged and rumbled in the otherwise-quiet night. Ibanez jumped out of the truck and came toward me, and as he got closer I could see his menacing scowl.

I did what I would have done if a bear or a mountain lion challenged me in the wild. I stood as tall as I could and threw both hands in the air, half-shouting, half-crying: "Eddiejoe Ibanez! You want to throw a sack of shit at me, go ahead! You want to insult me, try to intimidate me, you go right ahead! I got no backup, I'm barely able to walk upright just now, and my wolf has been stolen and we don't know where he is, so you do whatever it is you came to do, and get it over with!"

He came closer and pushed out his lower lip. "I came to help you."

I was going to protest more until I realized what he had said. "You came to help me?"

"I got an idea where that big goon took your wolf."

39: HAD A DOG IN THE FIGHT

If there truly were angels, I would never have guessed that one of them would look like Eddiejoe Ibanez. As I followed the black Vader-mobile down the High Road at top speed, I used the hands-free system in my Jeep to make a series of calls. First, to Jerry Padilla: "Send a car. I need backup. I'm pretty sure we're headed to the place where Talgren left Mountain." My next call was to Dominic Gomez, because he had told me he lived close by and I hoped he could get there quickly, maybe sooner than the sheriff's office could. I would have called Coronel, too, but I couldn't use Buzz with the hands-free unit and I couldn't switch phones—we were driving fast. Ibanez had told me that Talgren's dogs had all been raised and trained for fighting, and that illegal dogfights were held monthly at an old abandoned church on a little-used back road on the way to Vadito. When I relayed this to Gomez, he said he knew exactly where the *peleas de perros* were held. Padilla knew the abandoned church and was on his way.

Tears streamed from my eyes as I drove; my parched lips begged for a drink of water, my cheeks felt hot, but I kept both hands on the wheel and my eyes on the taillights of Ibanez's truck. Once I knew I had help coming, I called Roy. "We're going to get Mountain," I said. And I repeated what I had told the others.

He was already in action. "As soon as Padilla told me what happened, I staged a crew at the ranger station in Peñasco and they started a search and rescue—a few of them are up there right now, and more are out looking for Mountain. I'll let them know. The Forest Service keeps a large animal vet on call for the horses they keep there, and they got him on standby if we need him. Maybe I'll have him head on over to the ranger station so he's ready…you know, just in case." Roy said. "Anyway, right now, I'm about to turn and go through Dixon, so I might get to that church before you do. I'll lose my cell coverage any minute now, but don't worry; I'll see you there. You drive safe, don't do anything crazy. We're going to get Mountain, so just stay calm and be safe."

Ibanez set a terrifying pace, but I wasn't about to let the rear of that truck out of my sight, so I kept the pedal down on the Jeep and fought the ruts and washboards and cried out aloud as the jarring and bouncing tormented my midsection with bolts of anguish. My breath came and went in hot gulps and blasts, my heart felt like it was about to explode in my chest, my hands were so clammy that I kept taking one and then the other away from the wheel to wipe them on the legs of my jeans so I wouldn't lose my grip.

At one point, Ibanez veered wildly to the right, and I spotted an oncoming truck moving at a terrifying clip toward us. We both quickly pulled into the ditch and surrendered the road to the crazed driver, who never even slowed as he barreled by. We were lucky there wasn't a collision.

After the turnoff to Vadito, Ibanez suddenly killed his lights, but he kept going, and he eased around a bend that must have bordered a stream or a river. I saw the tall inky shadows of cottonwoods. There was no moon yet, so it was hard now to see the black truck without lights. Although I feared I might rear-end him, I dreaded more that I would lose him and not get to Mountain. The truck stopped and idled for a few moments at an old wrought iron gate on one side of the narrow road. Its design was simple but powerful: sharp-pointed spears mounted over black iron crossbeams, and in the center, where the two halves of the gate met, a huge, ornate iron cross—a symbol that once marked passage onto hallowed ground. But it was obvious that years had passed since it had been maintained by the parishioners. Now, the tips of some of the spears were either bent or missing, welds had broken leaving a few hanging and others tilting askew, and vandals had used the cross for target practice and the face of it was scarred with pockmarks. The gate had been left open, each half swung wide to the side. Ibanez idled through a few yards, pulled over into the field, parked the truck, and turned off its noisy engine. I parked behind him and cut the motor on the Jeep. He walked back to me as I was struggling to get out. Adrenalin masked my pain more and more now, and I found myself able to bring myself upright in half the time it had taken me when I'd gotten out to confront him at the Bear's Paw earlier.

"Someone's here," Eddiejoe said. "That gate is usually closed. That *loco idiota* that almost creamed us probably came out of here, but there's a couple more trucks up there by the church. We need to be careful."

I had already clipped my handgun to the back of my belt, and I was carefully opening the side door to get my rifle when a loud popping sound broke the silence; and then another pop followed. "Gunshots!" I rasped. "Mountain!"

Ibanez struck out running for the church, and I tried my best to go after him, but my legs were so swollen and stiff that I could barely hobble. I hadn't gone far when I heard tires crunching on the dirt drive behind me, but I didn't care, I was fixed on the old church ahead, desperately praying that someone hadn't shot Mountain. I stumped along without stopping to see who was coming, and then I heard Padilla's voice: "Get in the car, Jamaica."

I turned and looked at him, my rifle in my left hand. "Gunshots! Up there! There were two gunshots!"

"I heard 'em," he said. "Now get in the car. You'll get there faster than you can gimping like that."

I climbed into the passenger seat. Jerry proceeded slowly up the drive in the dark with his lights off. "I got another car coming," he said. "Wait! Isn't that Roy's truck?" Padilla rolled the SUV to a stop at the edge of what had once been a graded parking area.

I looked at the white Chevy Silverado and could just make out the BLM Taos emblem on the door. "Yes, that's Roy!" I opened the door on my side of the cruiser and heard shouting. Jerry, who had sprung out of the seat and drawn his weapon, disappeared toward the sounds. I strained to make out what the voices were saying as I got to my feet and started after him.

Then I heard: "We got him! We got him!"

I had only made it a couple yards past the sheriff's car when I saw Eddiejoe Ibanez coming fast through the gateway in the churchyard wall, then another, odd-shaped figure I couldn't make out right away. I stopped, my heart throbbing in my chest, the hair standing up on the back of my neck when I realized it was someone, a man walking fast, carrying a limp body in his arms...the body of a wolf. I screamed: "Mountain!"

In a flurry of action, Padilla dashed to his vehicle and yanked open the back door, and Ibanez ran toward me and grabbed me by the arms, as if he thought I might collapse. The men's voices were all talking at once; I heard Dominic Gomez saying, "Use my jacket! Here—use my jacket!" Roy cursed and muttered something I couldn't make out and then the deputy ran around the car to the other side and opened the rear passenger-side door and plunged in, coaching the others, "Hold his head...there...hold his head...get that front paw, it's caught...now ease him in here."

And then Roy was at my side, and he took my arm and Ibanez held the other as the Boss said, "Jamaica, he's hurt bad. We gotta go."

I turned gingerly in the front passenger seat, and looked at my beautiful wolf-boy lying across the length of the seat in the back. Jerry Padilla sped with lights flashing down the drive, then the dirt road, and then the highway behind me. "Please hold on," I whispered. "Mountain, please hold on!"

When we got to the ranger station, a crew of folks rushed out. They eased Mountain onto a sled and into the station before I got to the door. Buzz began vibrating in my pocket, but I ignored the device and hurried inside. Once again, Roy took my arm. "The vet's already working on him. You need to stay back and give him room."

"Let me see him," I cried. "Let me at least see him!"

Roy held onto my bicep and ushered me toward the makeshift surgery the rangers had created by pushing two desks together at one end of the offices, padding the desk tops with horse blankets and a sheet. A tall man in a plaid shirt leaned over my beautiful wolf, and I saw ripped flesh and deep gashes on Mountain's legs, his chest, his face, and his sides. One of his ears was torn at the tip and he had swollen mounds on his side and flank and blood oozing from numerous puncture wounds. "Mountain," I said, my voice too loud, shaking. "Hold on, buddy. I'm right here. I'm just right here."

The vet moved to the end of the table near the wolf's head, blocking my view, and Roy turned me back toward the other side of the offices. He steered me to a chair and helped me into it, then squatted down in front of me. I looked into his face as tears streamed from my eyes. "Is he going to die?"

"That ole' boy that's working on him is going to do everything he can," Roy said, "but I won't lie to you, Jamaica. Mountain got tore up pretty bad by those pit bulls in there. The guys that were there bugged out as soon as they saw us come in, but they let the dogs out of the pen to attack us while they got away. Those bulldogs both came after me and Gomez, and even when I fired my rifle in the air, they didn't stop. One of 'em grabbed onto Dominic's leg and was about to tear it off, so he drew his pistol and shot him. The other dog just went limp and laid down after that. It turned out that one was already hurt bad himself, and I managed to get him corralled into one of those steel cages they had there. Then we found Mountain over in a corner." Just then, Roy's phone started chiming and he moved away to take the call.

I dropped my chin to my chest, trying to think what to do.

Eddiejoe Ibanez's shadow fell over me and I looked up at him, his face still a sneer. "They give them dogs steroids to make them more violent in the fights. And other drugs so they won't feel the pain no matter how bad they are hurt. They just want to make sure they will keep fighting until one of them dies. Those guys raise them to do that, they train them to kill. That *pendejo* Talgren must have got those two dogs hopped up and then put them in with your wolf, knowing they would try to kill him."

I felt my face squeezing itself into a grimace of anguish, but I could do nothing to stop it. I would have cried, shed tears, made any sound, but I could not. In my misery, my grief and fear, I had lost the ability to do even that.

Ibanez reached out a hand and put it on my shoulder.

"Why did you...?" I tried to form words as I looked up at Ibanez.

"Enemigo de mi enemigo—enemy of my enemy," he said. "You and me, we maybe got into it over a *little* thing, but I got a really big thing with Talgren. He started cooking those drugs and peddling them all over this place more than a year ago. Everyone over here hates him. My little brother, he got hooked on that shit, and before Thanksgiving, he OD'd. It almost killed my mom to lose him, he was her baby. Ever since that

happened that *culo* wouldn't dare come anywhere around Peñasco because of me, he knew I would make him sorry if he did. But today, he must have decided he wanted to hurt you more than he was worried about me hurting him. When the people over here saw what he did to you, dragging you down the road and beating and kicking you, you know, word got around, they called me. I would have gotten that *cabrón* myself and drug him down the highway for everyone to see if the sheriff hadn't arrested him first. When they told me he stole your wolf, I figured he probably took him to that place where he fights his dogs. I was on my way there when I saw you pulled over in front of the café."

"Thank you," I said.

"*De nada.* I hope that wolf of yours is going to make it. I'll light a candle for him. I'll have *mi madre* say a prayer, too. Maybe sometime, if I need a grazing permit, you can help me out with that," he said, and the sneer turned into a smile.

I wanted to, but I could not smile back. I was almost numb with worry about Mountain, and with exhaustion and pain from the ordeals of the day.

Roy edged forward and said, "Sorry to interrupt, but I just got a call from dispatch and I have to get back to Taos right away, so I'm gonna have to head out now." He turned to face Ibanez. "I want to thank you, too. And if you ever need a grazing permit, or if there's anything else I can help with, you give me a call." He handed Eddiejoe a card. "Jamaica, I'm sorry I have to go, but I'll be back as quick as I can. And you call me if you need anything." He turned and left through the main entry door.

Ibanez looked down at the card as if it were a winning lottery ticket, then held it up and waved it, grinning at me as he, too, exited the ranger station.

Once again, my pocket vibrated and suddenly I remembered that I had told Coronel I would wait so he could meet up with me at the Bear's Paw—*when was that?*—well over an hour ago. I pulled out Buzz and held it up to answer.

"What happened to you?" Hank Coronel's voice was an equal mix of anger and worry. "Where are you?"

"I'm sorry. I'm at the ranger station. The vet is trying to save...he's working on Mountain."

Hank was quiet for several seconds. "Is he going to be all right?"

"I don't know," I whispered. "I don't think so."

"Are you all right?"

"Yes," I lied.

"Well, you stay there and take care of Mountain. And call me when you have news."

I had stiffened sitting in the chair so it was not easy to stand up again, and once I did, I felt like I might teeter and fall over before I managed to get my legs to move under me. I made my way closer to where the vet stood over Mountain, but Dominic Gomez interceded. He blocked my view and took me by both arms and said, "Now, Jamaica. Let the doctor work on your wolf. Give him room to do what he needs to do."

"I heard you got bitten trying to save Mountain. Are you okay?" I looked down at his bloodstained pant leg.

"I'll be all right. I just gotta go down to the clinic in Embudo tomorrow to get a tetanus shot. It's just a few little puncture wounds, but they're deep, they bled for a bit. They gave me first aid here, antibiotics and a bandage wrap. I'm going to stay here tonight and help watch over your wolf, and then I'll go get the shot first thing in the morning when the clinic opens."

"Thank you," I said. "For...Mountain."

He shook his head. "I don't know how long he had been there before we got to him. They got him pretty good, those two dogs. I had to shoot..."

"Roy told me. I'm so sorry."

"I tell you, that didn't bother me, having to shoot it, that dog was ruined. That kind of dog would attack a kid if he saw it running, or the UPS guy or anyone, that's the way it was, just completely ruined. And if I didn't shoot him, he would have torn me up like he did your wolf. I'm the one who's sorry—for you. I wish I could have gotten there sooner."

I saw that someone had made some coffee in the break room, so I went and got myself a cup. I reached into my jacket pocket and pulled out the *remedio de hierbas,* the aromatic remedy that Tecolote had made me. I held it firmly against my nostrils and the soft, gelatinous compound inside the cloth conformed to the underside of my nose. I inhaled deeply. Again, I felt the tiniest surge of relief. But it was not enough. I took out the bottle of pills the doctor in Embudo had given me for the pain. I bit a tiny piece off of one of the tablets and washed it down with some of the coffee, then topped off my cup with more of the black liquid. I was going to need to stay alert, but I couldn't keep hobbling around incapacitated, so now—like Talgren's pit bulls—I needed at least a little bit of the drug the doc had given me to mask the pain so I could go on fighting. I went back to my chair and pulled another in front of it. I sat down gingerly in one, and put my legs up in the seat of the other to ease the pain of the swelling. I drank the rest of the coffee, hoping it would offset any drowsiness the pain meds would cause. I sat there for a few minutes and tried to focus my mind away from the wolf and my fear and worry, because I couldn't do anything about that, but there might be something I could do about the mission I had been working on for the past few days. I pulled out the new BLM phone. First, I sent a short text to Kerry: *I need you. Call as soon as possible.* And then I got ready to make some calls.

Before I finished dialing the first number, a shadow fell over me, and I looked up and saw the veterinarian who had been working on Mountain standing in front of me.

I got up at once, and noticed that, already, the combination of Tecolote's herbs and the pain medicine was helping.

"I've done everything I can do for now," the vet said. "Your boy's sedated. He's on an IV to keep him hydrated and that's also got antibiotics and pain medicine in it so he gets a steady dose. I don't want him moved. I'm going to go home and get a few hours of sleep, and then I'll come back and check on him. You should do the same. The rangers here have divided up into two shifts, and they're going to watch him through the night and call me if they need to."

My lips started to tremble. "Is he...? Will he live?"

The wrinkles around his eyes deepened. "He might have a shot at it if he doesn't develop an infection. He's got a long way to go before he's out of the woods."

"Can I see him now? Is it all right if I touch him? Is he going to be able to walk again?"

He held up a palm. "One thing at a time. Yes, you can go see him. But I don't want you to touch him; keep a little distance and let him be. He's got wounds and scratches and scrapes everywhere, and the flesh was torn back in a few places. I cleaned them up the best I could, but you could contaminate him with your germs. Plus, he might rouse if he senses you, and he needs to sleep and not move so those sutures can set. As for what he's going to be like after tonight...well, I can't assess anything more until we get him a little further out of the woods. Then we can talk again."

As I crossed to the back of the office area, I saw a female ranger setting up cots in the break room. Two men in green Forest Service hoodies had drawn up chairs near Mountain to make sure he didn't try to move or somehow scoot off of the double-desk operating table they had created for him. When I approached, the men smiled at me. Painfully, I managed to maneuver myself down on one knee a few feet from my best friend and put my face at eye level with his. "I love you," I whispered. "I love you, Mountain. You can do this, buddy," I said. "I know you can."

I headed back to my pushed-together chairs to make my calls, and almost ran into Gomez coming out of the washroom. He had untucked his shirt and I could smell soap, as if he'd just washed up. He was headed for the break room, and likely one of the cots.

"Wait," I said, "Sorry. I know you need to get some rest. I have a question. I could look this up, but it could also be a colloquialism, so I thought it would be better just to ask you."

He shrugged. "Shoot."

"What does *los gemelos* mean?"

"*¿Gemelos?* It means twins."

40: LOS GEMELOS

I called Zeke Mitchell first. "When we were talking this morning, you mentioned a set of twins who might be able to inherit from Quintana's will."

"Yeah. I don't know that they could for sure, but they might be in line, maybe in the fourth succession if they prove to be Quintana's or the fifth if they could even just prove that they were born to one of the witches, which is where their heirs and assigns inherit. But like I said, I had to rule out Abasolo before I looked into any of that, because if we're right about her, none of that matters. She gets it all after the foundation's 10 percent. And maybe now her daughter…"

"The twins," I interrupted, "how old are they now?"

"Let's see…" I could hear him moving things around, papers shuffling. "They would be about a year younger than Nona Dodd—she's the only known child, the one I mentioned who got specifically excluded from the will. Let me see here, Dodd was twenty-seven in August. So they would be around twenty-five or twenty-six, I guess. Why?"

"Hmmm. Male or female twins?"

"One of each."

I drew in a breath. "Do you know their names?"

"Yeah, I do. I have them here someplace. My secretary just sent me a copy of the birth certificate that got created when they enrolled in middle school. It shows their mother as Ursula Lindstrom, and their names are…"

We said the names in unison: "Uma and Kyle."

"That's right," Zeke said, surprised. "How did you know?"

"I thought they were a couple, but they're twins!"

"No, I mean how did you know their names?"

"I met them, they're here!" I said. "They're here in northern New Mexico."

"Where? How did you know…?"

"In a minute. One more thing: Ursula Lindstrom, the mother named on their birth certificate. She's the one that was known as Qual, wasn't she? The one whose bones were found in Canyonlands?"

"You must have read that article in *Outside Magazine,* too. Yes, I think she is—she *was*, I mean. So, there's an avenue for the twins with Qual's DNA at the fifth level of succession, or like I said, if they're Quintana's they would be in line to inherit before my clients. But Abasolo is first. She and her daughter basically get everything, so none of that counts unless…"

As soon as I had finished that conversation, I called Coronel again. "When you were telling me about the satellite photos, you said you had a few possible targets in those specific areas you were searching. Any chance you also identified those other objects? Were they cars, too? And what made them stand out so much that you wanted a second-pass look at them?"

"You know, you're good at this, you're a natural. I'm only slightly ahead of you on that. Even though the area is only sparsely populated, we couldn't peg every car and enhance it, that would have taken forever. So I looked at cars that seemed out of place, not in front of a house, not where a car would normally be parked, and of course, the nearer to Abasolo's place, the more I wanted to see it. I did look closely at the other two potential targets and we did some enhancement on those images. One of them was not a fixed target, but it appeared in both sets of photos."

"Meaning it moved after the first pass?"

"Affirmative. But it was in the same general vicinity in both sets of photos, so I had the IT guy blow up the image of it, too. The angle doesn't give us a look at the plate. But it's a green SUV, maybe a Subaru."

"Holy shit."

"What?"

"Where was it?"

"On the first sat pass, it was parked in an area where there used to be a mine, north and west of the pueblo. On the second pass, it was down all the way at the end of the mine property, off-road, right near where the mine abuts public land at the mouth of Picuris Canyon. At first, I thought the car had to belong to someone from the mining company. They went bankrupt and closed up, but I guessed maybe it was someone who was overseeing the property. I didn't think any more about it once we located Abasolo's car. But then, when they didn't find her remains in the car, I began to think about that green SUV."

"Did you tell your FBI contact about the green car?"

"No. For one thing, those satellite images were done for me as a personal favor, and people could get in trouble…and for another, *The Bartender* has not given me the green light to fully read anyone else in. The car crash prompted the missing persons on Abasolo and the involvement of the FBI, I didn't. But it was easy enough for me to call the FBI—since the car was identified as Abasolo's and everyone knows she's the poet laureate—and say that *The Bartender* was worried and wanted to know anything they found out…get some information as a professional courtesy. But what you and I have been doing these past few days is not public, not with anyone, even the FBI."

"Well, I think you should call your FBI contact. Either you could do it and say it's a professional courtesy in return, or give me her name and number, and I'll do it. We need to convene a search party by dawn."

"You think someone's got Abasolo back in one of those mine caves?"

"I think two people have Abasolo, and I think they have her daughter, Susan Lacy, too."

41: THE DREAMERS

Roy called me before I could dial the phone again. "I'm on my way back to you. I'm bringing a couple people with me. They say they've got to see you at once, that it's a matter of life and death."

"Who are they?"

"Just stay right there at the station and we'll be there shortly."

When the glass door at the entry opened, I was standing over a set of quads showing every geographical detail of the ranger district, scrutinizing them with a magnifying glass. Roy stuck his head inside and saw me, then withdrew and held the door open while two people came through. First: Yohe, wrapped in a Pendleton blanket, her head covered with a bright-colored scarf tied under her chin. The second: a man wrapped in a chief's blanket, wearing long silver braids with a black strip of cloth tied across his forehead. I did not recognize him. Roy ushered them over to me.

I bowed my head to honor the elders, then spoke to Yohe with a smile. "Auntie Yohe, I am so happy to see you."

She held a hand in front of the tall man. "This Bernat Deherrera. Him chief Carry Water Clan."

I dipped my chin again and said, "I am so happy to meet you, Uncle. I know Paul Deherrera from Picuris."

The old man spoke with a hoarse, cracking voice, "My nephew."

I looked around, then pointed to the chairs where I'd been sitting earlier. "Please, sit down. Can I fix you some coffee or get you anything? Maybe some water?"

Yohe answered as they shuffled toward the chairs, "That be nice, maybe some coffee."

I tiptoed into the break room where Gomez and the woman ranger were sleeping and put an envelope of coffee grounds into the basket, then filled the pot with water and poured it into the well of the machine. I turned the switch to the *on* position, and rummaged around in the cupboards. All I could find was a box of crackers and a couple of packages of Twinkies. I grabbed these, two cups of water, and some paper towels and headed back to the entry lobby area where the Tanoan visitors sat in the chairs. Roy had gone across the length of the offices to talk to the guys watching over Mountain.

"I brought some things." I gave a cup of water to each of the Tanoans. "The coffee is brewing and it will be ready in a minute. Would you like something to munch on?"

Yohe's eyes lit up when she saw the Twinkies, so I set the box of crackers on an empty chair and gave them each a package of the sweet cakes and a paper towel. I went back to check on the coffee, and noticed that Roy had pulled up a chair next to Mountain and stretched out his long legs in front of him, one boot crossed over the other at the ankles. I watched him pull his cowboy hat over his face and cross his arms over his chest, prepared to take a nap.

I returned to the Puebloans with cups of coffee. "I am so honored that you came all this way to see me," I said, knowing better than to ask why they had come.

"This coffee good," Yohe said.

The clan chief nodded in agreement and took another bite of his second Twinkie.

"Bernat not talk good English. He want me help, come tell you what the dreamers see."

"The dreamers. The peyote dreamers?"

She grimaced, wiggling her head quickly back and forth as if Bernat Herrera might not see this small gesture.

I instantly regretted asking the question, and I gave her an apologetic look. But I dared not speak, not even to say as much, if I wanted to hear more of what they had come to tell me.

"You come see me that time, I tell that boy take the medicine." Yohe said. "This night, the dreamers not have that medicine. But some the people grow the medicine, that way we always have some coming up."

I nodded my head.

"You talk one these. Make offering. You ask Him."

Suddenly, I realized that she was talking about Momma Anna's peyote plant, and how she had told me to ask *Him* for help finding Abasolo. "I did," I agreed.

"That one some the medicine for ceremony tonight, you got answer now." She turned to look at her companion, then turned back to me.

After a few moments of silence, Bernat raised his chin and looked right into my face as he delivered a low, guttural, vowel-laden soliloquy in Tiwa. He went on for more than a minute, then stopped and stared at me even more intensely, his eyes bulging a little from their nests in the soft brown fleshy folds around his eyes. He seemed to be waiting for me to acknowledge the gravity of his message.

I looked at Yohe, then back at Bernat, then at Yohe again.

"The dreamers go next other time. They see that Spanish."

I gasped. "Is she alive?" I blurted it without catching myself. "I'm sorry. I just, I'm not feeling so well, I apologize. It's...I've been worried about her. I fear she is in danger. I pray that she's alive."

Yohe looked at Bernat. He gave the slightest nod. Then Yohe spoke again. "They see that Spanish you looking for. This woman need water, need help. She hurt, maybe fall. The dreamers see you fly, see birds. Ancestors make them shiny birds. The dreamers got blessing for you so you can fly."

"I need to know where she is." I turned to look at Barat and out of frustration, I reached both hands to my temples and grasped my head. "If you know where she is…" Realizing how this must have looked, I brushed my hands through my hair and then lowered them back into my lap. "If you know where she is, I need to find her."

Yohe spoke to Bernat in Tiwa and he looked down at his knees and closed his eyes, muttering.

"That cake coming up," Yohe said, as she sprang from the chair and grabbed a wastebasket next to a nearby table. She shoved it in front of the old man's face, and he gratefully took it in both hands and stuck his head into the plastic bucket and retched. Yohe turned to me. "More water."

I hurried to fill the cups again and brought water and a damp paper towel to the peyote chief. He drank both cups dry and blotted his mouth with the towel, then looked down into his lap again. Yohe was standing at the ready with the wastebasket but it appeared that his episode of vomiting was over for now. She set it down and then spoke to the chief in Tiwa again.

Bernat began rocking forward and back in his seat and singing softly under his breath. He went on like that for a minute or two, and then he circled his fingers over his head. I had seen Momma Anna do the same gesture before with cornmeal in her fingers when offering thanks and saying her ritual prayers. The circle over the head was to honor *the above,* one of the seven sacred directions. Deherrera finished his song and then looked at me. He sat silently studying my face for another long minute, then uttered a stream of words in Tiwa to Yohe.

"You know that place. They gather the clay to make the pot," she translated. "Many ancestor make pot, that clay. That way they shine."

"The micaceous clay. I know where they were mining the mica from the earth."

Yohe nodded. "He say you must fly where ancient ones make the birds. They there in morning, first light. He give spirit blessing you this time."

The peyote chief took hold of Yohe's wrist and said a few more words with some urgency in his voice.

Yohe cocked her head to one side to listen, then turned and looked at me with a grim face. "He say that Spanish a dreamer. She come village, dream with Carry Water Clan, that next time, full of life, lot of hope. They meet her this time in dreaming, she cry out to them. He say she might die today. That why we come right away. You must fly, save that one."

When Yohe finished speaking, Bernat Deherrera got up from his chair and looked around. He folded his blanket onto the seat and went toward the washrooms. Yohe looked at me and said, "The medicine make everything come out fast from here." She rubbed her belly. "Now that water, that cake coming back out, maybe next other way."

After excusing myself from my Tanoah visitors, I crossed the office area and went to be near Mountain to try to collect my thoughts. I wrapped my left arm protectively around my right side as I felt ready to cry. The poor wolf looked completely inanimate, as if he weren't even alive. He also looked smaller than usual, and I guessed that was from dehydration and loss of blood. He had been shaved in so many places, and long seams of railroad-tie stitches laced swaths of his flesh together. Where his fur remained, it clumped together, greasy and matted, probably from the drool of the fight dogs. A drip IV was taped to his shaved foreleg. He looked so fragile—not the strong, willful, life-loving companion he had been before Lor stole him from my Jeep just hours ago. My jaw trembled as a tear rolled down my cheek. Beyond the emotional angst, the physical pain was starting to overtake me again, and I knew I would have to inhale another dose of Esperanza's aroma remedy and perhaps also take another bite off of that tablet to take the edge off. I reached down and nudged Roy's shoulder. "Boss, I need to talk to you," I whispered.

42: THE RIGHT PLACE

Roy's face grew redder and the skin around his eyes tightened as I told him about the secret assignment I'd been working on and why I needed him to help me get a search party together before dawn. He twitched his head back and forth in an almost imperceptible little nay-saying move. Anyone who didn't know him might have seen this as a tic of some kind, but I could tell that he was angry. I wasn't sure if he was mad at me, at the situation, or something else, but regardless, I kept talking until I had told him almost everything.

"Now, that is one crazy story. Everything from dead authors to drugs to some screwed up will, and it's even got the next president of the United States involved in it. So how does all this connect up with Lor Talgren trying to kill your wolf?"

"It doesn't. That was…I had both things going on at once."

"How about Gomez's rig getting blown up? Was that Talgren, or this thing?"

"I don't know about that. I really don't think that was Talgren, but I'm not sure. No one but you and me knew that I would be driving that car."

"Do you mind letting me in on what the Indians there wanted with you?" He gestured in the direction of the two elders sitting in the chairs near the entry. "Is that yet another thing you got going on, or do they know all about this, too? Is that why they said it was a matter of life or death that they get here to talk to you?"

"They are peyote dreamers from the pueblo," I said. "They don't know any of the background I've told you, none of it. But they saw the poet in visions during their ceremony tonight. They said if we don't get to her soon, she's going to die, that she's hurt, maybe has fallen, needs water."

"Well, that just adds to the crazy. I know she's now officially a missing person. But you don't think she was just out hiking and took a fall? You think it was these twins from California that's got her back in one of the mines? And maybe her daughter, too?"

"You said earlier this week that you had a report that a bear had broken into one of the mine entrances, and we agreed that it wasn't likely that it was a bear this time of year."

Roy took off his cowboy hat and scratched his scalp vigorously, then put the hat back on his head. "I guess that doesn't sound any stranger than all the rest of this. Well, I sent all the folks who were searching for Mountain home. They already pulled a double shift. We still got Gomez here from our crew, and I can call the sheriff and request the SAR team. They're the ones trained for search and rescue, and they can bring some dogs. But you mentioned you told your—what is he, your handler?—to call the FBI. If they're going in, they'll want us to stay out of their way, unless they ask for support."

"I'll call the Secret Service agent right away—his name's Coronel. I'll find out if the FBI is on it. I just want to be ready in case..."

"Ready? You're not even ready to make a bed, the shape you're in. You're going to have to sit this one out, Jamaica. You can't go charging in now, like you always do."

I felt my nostrils flare. "So it's a good thing I asked you for some help, then, right?"

I called Hank, and he answered but told me he'd call me right back. In a matter of seconds, Buzz began vibrating. I took the phone to one of the cubicles and sat down to speak with Coronel. I kept my voice low and quiet, and as we talked, I pressed the malleable herb bundle to my nose and breathed deeply through it several times. I worked the bottle of pain pills out of my pocket and poured several tablets out onto the desk. Finding the one I'd already bitten into, I took another nip off of it, leaving a tiny piece remaining, which I slipped back into the bottle with the rest of the medicine. While I was doing this, Coronel told me that he had just gotten ahold of his FBI contact and told her about the green Subaru and the suspected disappearance of the second woman, Susan Lacy. He said, "She's already coordinating with local law enforcement, and it sounds like they are getting ready to send in a team to search the mines for Abasolo. You know I don't have any jurisdiction here, don't you? I am going to have to stay on the sidelines. But if there is anything more I can do, just call me."

As I stood up, I saw Roy coming across the office toward me, his phone at his ear. "Yes, ma'am. I'm the one who called the sheriff and requested a SAR team. Yes ma'am, we have a few personnel who can assist. Agent Wild is right here, I'll let you talk to her. Yes, that mine area is overseen by the BLM. Yes, ma'am we will. Here she is..." He thrust the phone at me and mouthed *FBI.*

☽

In the wee hours of the morning, a team consisting of Deputy Sheriff Jerry Padilla, six Taos County SWAT officers, two FBI agents, and a pair of New Mexico State SAR (search and rescue) dog handlers and their canines assembled at the ranger station. We circled around the map as Padilla laid out the plan. "I'll work command," Padilla said, "and Agent Wild here, because of her injuries, will remain at this station and relay any outside communications with dispatch. Now, we want to work under the cover of darkness for maximum stealth, so we'll move out immediately after this briefing. There's nine mine caves in the canyon there, and we don't know which one the targets are using. So, SAR will advance with SWAT protection until the objective is identified, and then FBI will take point once we know that. Command will stage here," he pointed at the road entering the mica mine property, "so everybody bump to this location in five, then ops will go in on foot from there. Jamaica, you arrange for an ambulance to stage here," he pointed to a spot on the road well back of the mine entrance, "and tell them to make sure they roll in silent and keep their rig out of sight, if they can. Any non-ops personnel will maintain radio silence unless contacted by command. There is a UHF radio repeater on the rim of the canyon approximately a mile from the mine, so we will use the SAR 2 UHF radio channel and hopefully we'll have coverage with that repeater. However this terrain is tricky, so if ops gets cut off from command, then FBI will take over comms at the scene. Otherwise, let me restate: radio silence. Understood?"

With all the hubbub in the ranger station, Gomez and the ranger had roused from the cots and joined the briefing, and a dozen or more first-responders from the Forest Service and law enforcement had arrived to provide additional resources if needed; they assembled around the map behind the core insertion team. Vicky Kasza, the ranger/receptionist who ran the station, had come in and taken over the facility. She ushered the two Tanoan elders into the break room and offered them the use of the cots. Yohe took advantage of this, but the peyote chief took a chair and remained upright with the wastebasket in his lap. He was still vomiting occasionally from the effects of the plant medicine that produced his vision of Abasolo in a cave with shining birds. Vicky offered them pillows and coffee and told them she would check back with them periodically. Kasza had also assigned a fresh duo to watch over Mountain. "Don't you worry, Jamaica," she told me, "I will personally keep an eye on him as well, and let you know the moment he wakes up or if there are any changes. You just focus on what you gotta do."

I only wished I had something I could do. It was three in the morning when the incident team left the ranger station. I went out into the parking lot and looked up at the sky. A weak winter half-moon had risen early, and now it trembled from behind a mask of clouds as it sunk toward the horizon in the west, leaving the landscape with almost no relief from the darkness. I raised my face to the stars and said a prayer that had many parts. Voicing my pleas to one twinkling light, I asked for my beloved Mountain to heal and come back to me alive and well from his own drugged dream state. To another, I asked for Abasolo's safe rescue from her captors. And to another, I sent blessings for her new-found daughter and hopes that she was alive and well and would be rescued along with her long-lost mother. And finally, I searched around the sky until I found the barely-visible Seven Sisters, the constellation Pleiades, and I asked for the safety of the team.

I thought I was through with my prayers and was about to go back inside when a night-flying creature—either a bird or a bat—startled me as it swooped past, so close above me, that I could hear its wings beating a fast, furious *shushing* sound and feel cold air rush across my cheeks. I remembered Esperanza telling me I would have to fly, perhaps many times, and suddenly a flashback of the old *bruja* overwhelmed me: Tecolote appeared just as I had last seen her, so weak and tired, struggling to kneel in front of her candles and her carved wooden saints, muttering a prayer. I turned to the sky once more and asked for her protection and healing, too.

As I started to go back inside the station, Dominic Gomez met me at the door, pulling on his jacket. "Vicky has taken over the wolf watch, and she has people on it," he said. "I'm going to go down to command and see if I can be of any help."

I wanted to go with him. I felt useless so far away from the action. After giving the instructions to dispatch for the ambulance, I had nothing to do, and couldn't foresee that I would need to do any more than that. The *curandera's* herbs and the additional bite of that pain pill I had taken were beginning to mask my injuries; plus, adrenalin was surging in my bloodstream now that we had a plan and were taking action. I wanted to go lead the search and rescue myself. But both Roy and Jerry Padilla had insisted that I stay at the ranger station. I held up a hand, delaying Gomez. "Dominic, I just thought of something I've been meaning to ask you. Do you remember Monday when you were in the Bear's Paw with your coffee, talking to the locals?"

Gomez nodded. "Yeah. My worst thing, small talk, although I guess it worked. Ibanez came out of the woodwork like Roy said he would."

"Remember when I came in the café, I interrupted a conversation between you and that tourist couple because you looked like you were trapped and they wouldn't shut up? You know, they are the ones we now think are the kidnappers."

"I more or less got that they were suspects from the briefing."

"You said those two were full of questions. Do you remember what they were asking you about?"

He wrinkled his nose, reached up and adjusted his ball cap on his head. "They wanted to know of any good outfitters who carried climbing gear. I didn't really know that much about it, so I told them they had to go to Taos. There's no shops up here anyway. Then they kept asking about some spirit cave or bird cave, something to do with birds in a cave. Now that I know more about it, I'm guessing they meant the mine."

Once the incident team had deployed, the ranger station morphed from a hub of noise, excitement, and activity to an oversized waiting room—sparsely populated, mostly quiet, empty-feeling—yet full of unseen currents of anxious energy left behind by those who had just departed, and barely contained in those who remained. The recessed lights in the ceiling bathed the walls inside with a harsh electronic glow while the blackness outside lurked hungrily at every window, eager to prevail and suck up the light. I went to sit near Mountain. He was still deeply sedated, but I could see his chest rising and falling ever so slightly with his breathing. With all his shaved patches, he looked half-grizzled and half-naked. Where the fur had been torn or shaved away, his blue-white skin looked lifeless, like the scaled flesh of a fish. I wanted to touch him, to pick up his big head and hold it against my chest, in my arms, to smooth his ruffled fur and soothe his hurting places. But I obeyed the vet's instructions and remained a few feet away. I closed my eyes and tried to will healing energy into his body.

I started when I felt a touch on my shoulder. It was the peyote chief, his face looking down at me with an expression of urgency. I jumped to my feet and followed him as he led me to the break room, where Yohe was asleep on one of the cots. He nudged her awake, and began muttering in Tiwa to her. The auntie sprang to her feet incredibly quickly for such a big woman, and an elder at that. She looked at me, then turned back to Deherrera and said something to him in their native tongue. Then they both turned toward me, and Yohe began to relay what the chief was telling her. "He say you got a message."

Deherrera mumbled to her again.

"That one, Indun message, that the right place."

The chief spoke a few more sentences in Tiwa.

"That place with the birds. You must fly. Before sun rise, you be there."

I stood looking at them, confused, and then suddenly I realized what the peyote chief was trying to tell me. The Indun message! I had forgotten about Rico's voicemail message, with all that had happened this night. "The team is looking in the wrong place! They're not in the mine caves, are they? They're at the ruin on the cliff ledge!"

Yohe spoke to Deherrera in Tiwa, who nodded vigorously. Then she looked at me and repeated what she had said earlier, "That one, that the right place. Must be there before sun rise."

I found Rico's message on my BLM phone and pressed the option to return the call. It rang and rang, but no one answered. I looked through my contacts and found the number for the BLM archaeologist, Prescott. I called him.

His voice was thick with sleep and slow when he answered.

"I need help locating that ruin just outside the Picuris rez," I said. "And I need it fast."

I tried the number Rico had called from again, and this time, I got an answer on the fourth ring. Paul Deherrera sounded angry. "There better be a good reason for this," he said, as a greeting.

"There is," I said, "I know it's Quiet Time, and I know it's after three in the morning, but your uncle is here at the ranger station, and—this is Jamaica Wild, by the way—and I...we...need your help."

Because of the order for radio silence, I tried to get ahold of Jerry Padilla but the call did not go through. The mine area was in a low area, no cell coverage. I tried phoning the county dispatcher to request that she try to hail him on the SAR channel which might work via the repeater on the canyon rim. "Deputy Padilla has requested radio silence for that scene," she said. "I am not able to relay a message by radio at this time."

"But they are looking in the wrong place," I argued. "They're wasting precious time. They need to go farther back into the canyon, beyond the mines. They need to hike back in and they'll need to climb from the bottom to a cliff ledge."

"Agent Wild, if you feel it is warranted, I can send another car to a second location."

"But you can't send a car into that canyon! Anyway, that team is already in as far as the mines; they could get there much faster than if you sent someone else. They need to keep going deeper into the gorge on foot, and then they are going to have to climb. They are wasting time searching through all the mines!"

"Agent Wild, all I can do is provide that information to Deputy Padilla when he breaks radio silence, or I can send additional personnel to a new location, if you are certain of one," the dispatcher said.

I got a similar response when I called Coronel to see if there were other FBI resources who could move on a new location: "I think we'd have to have real evidence that they are in this cliff ruin instead of the mine."

Prescott arrived, and he and I went to the map, where he pinpointed the location of the ruin. Not two minutes later, Paul Deherrera came in with young Rico hurrying behind him. While Paul spoke with Yohe and the elder Deherrera, Rico came over and looked at the map with us.

"We've got to re-direct that search team," I told Prescott. "If I could reach them on the radio, and I'm not even sure I could from here, I'd be breaking radio silence. And if it turned out that one or more of the suspects is in those caves at the mine, maybe as a lookout or whatever, that would ruin the element of surprise, and it could even be disastrous if the kidnappers took some sort of action in response."

"We could drive down to the command post and tell the sheriff," Prescott said.

I looked at the clock. "It's almost four a.m. Even if we drove there and waited until the team had searched the mine area so we could redirect them, that would take time. And then we'd still have to get to the ruin and get someone either up or down the cliff face before the sun came up. And that's if I can even persuade the team that I know they're in the wrong place because a peyote chief saw a vision in a drug-induced trance."

"And there's another problem," Prescott said. "From what I know of it, that cave has an unrestricted view of the canyon, and it faces east. There's no way to get in there without them seeing you coming after the sun comes up. Plus the team is going to need climbing gear. It's going to be a logistics nightmare. I don't see this happening fast."

Rico spoke up: "I can get you down into that cave at the ruin. You don't have to climb up to it. You can go down with a rope. I've done it a couple times."

I shook my head. "Thanks for offering, my man, but I don't want to put you in any danger. We think a couple of kidnappers are in there with two women."

"Is Auntie Adoria one of them?"

"I think so."

"Then I want to go. I'm telling you, I can get in there without anyone seeing me."

Prescott and I looked at one another. The archaeologist said, "What do you mean, son?"

"You go down to it from the top." He pointed to the map. "From up here. And there are two entrances to the cave. The big one looks out onto the canyon, like you said." He looked at Prescott. "You could probably stand up in that opening; it's real tall and it's also wide. But there is a small opening way in the back of the cave, just a little one. It comes in through a tiny tunnel that leads back into the mountain and comes out farther down the ledge. I don't think you could get through it, you're too big," he said to Prescott. He turned to me, "But you might be able to."

Prescott said: "That makes sense! It's probably an air shaft for ventilation for the ceremonial fires. Son, you said you've been in there. Show us how you get into the cave from that tunnel."

After we'd talked for a few minutes and Rico had done a crude drawing of the cave and its rear air-channel-entrance for us, I went to the break room and spoke to Paul Deherrera. "I know it's Quiet Time, but we need to get people to the east side of the reservation along the canyon rim. And right through the village is the fastest way."

I also called Vicky over to the map and put her to work. "I need you to wake up the fire chief with the Peñasco Volunteer Fire Department. We're going to need that Humvee that he drives, the one that's tricked out with the big winch on the front. And tell him I need rappelling gear. I know they gotta have that stuff for rescues around here; every mountain fire department does. Tell him I need at least two harnesses, preferably three, a rescue litter if they have one, and plenty of rope and cord, belay devices, and folks to man the anchors at the top and belay people up and down. I'm going to call someone in contact with the FBI and tell them we're going in here," I pointed to the map, "and you note that location so you can relay it to dispatch and then to command when they come out of radio silence, which I expect they'll do within an hour or so. In the meantime, we're going to go to the scene, and if we don't hear from the team, we're going to try to make it down to that cave before daylight breaks. If you get any news, use the fire channels to get word to us, okay?"

While the Deherrera men and Yohe were loading into Paul's car, and Prescott was throwing every piece of gear he could find in the lockers at the ranger station into the back of his truck, I went to Mountain's bedside and knelt down a foot or so from him. I watched him breathe, and while no one was watching me, I took the pill bottle out again and emptied the tablets into my hand, found the remnant piece of the one I'd been partitioning into smaller doses, and stuck it in my mouth. Although it was against the rules to take personal photos with BLM-issued phones, I snapped a picture of the wolf in his near-death state, and sent it to Kerry's phone with this message: *I won't be able to talk for a little while, but please try to get somewhere that I can call you in the morning. I need you.*

I turned my attention to the wolf once more, and I felt an agonizing aching sensation in my chest. I hated to leave him. For just an instant, I listened to the dogged drumbeat on the edge of my consciousness that had been chasing me for hours—the persistent chant of fear that whispered: *he might die.* If I left now, I might not be with him if he took leave of this life and left his pain and his broken body behind. "Oh, God," I said with a soft gasp. "Please hold on, Buddy. Please hold on. I have to go. But I'll be right back," I knew he wasn't aware of me, but I had to say it. "When you wake up, if I'm not here, just know that I will be right back. I love you, Mountain. I'll be right back."

43: LA CUEVA DEL CUERVO (THE CAVE OF THE RAVEN)

A freezing wind swept over the rim of Picuris Canyon as José Salas, the chief of the Peñasco Volunteer Fire Department helped strap me into the climbing harness. Two supports encircling my thighs connected to the thick belt surrounding my waist that was fitted with knotted lengths of rope, nylon straps, extra carabiners, and figure eights. As Salas cinched the harness tight, I flinched with pain. He stopped what he was doing and looked at me. "You okay?"

I exhaled hard—air that fogged into a cold cloud. "Yes, I got this. I'm just a little sore around my mid-section."

"Maybe someone else should go then," Chief Salas said. He took a second safety line made of triple cords looped and heavily-knotted to an ascender pulley and hooked this to the rappel rope and then to the belt at my waist. "You're going to need that part of your body to be strong. You have to lean back into that belt to rappel down the cliff, and if we have to lift you or if you fall, that's where you'll feel all the pressure."

"There's only a small opening into the back of that cave. I don't think anyone bigger than me could get through it; I'm about the thinnest person here. I wanted to rappel down instead of using the winch so I'd have control over the descent."

"I gotcha. Well, I'm the one who's going to belay you, so let's talk about how I'll know when you want to go down or come up," he said. "Usually if we can't hear one another, we use hand signals. But we can't see a thing in this darkness. So we're going to have to rely on rope tugs. It's not the best way to communicate, but it's all we got since you want radio silence. So let's talk one-two-three. One hard tug—give it a yank so I can tell you're not just taking a big step down or something—that means *on belay.* That tells me to let you take whatever rope you need, and I'll monitor it, keep it taut, but let you direct how the rope flows. Got that?"

"Yes."

"Echo, please."

"One good tug means *on belay.*"

"Okay, two: Two tugs, one right after the other but with a second or two in between—again, so I know you aren't just taking a big step and then a little one or whatever—two tugs means *off belay.* That tells me you've tied off to an anchor or reached the cliff ledge and aren't needing me for your sole support. You signal *off belay* when you get to that cliff ledge and need to go into the cave. Now echo one and two."

"One good tug means *on belay.* Two tugs, with a second in between means *off belay.*"

"Good," José Salas said. "Now, three good, hard tugs—and this is important, you tug three times, a second between each one so I can tell they are three distinct tugs—that means *give me more rope.* You got that? Then I let the rope play and you're in charge. Echo now: one, two, and three."

"One tug, *on belay.* Two tugs, *off belay.* Three tugs, *give me rope.*"

"You got it."

"I also want a second harness ready in case I need to send someone up."

"Right. I'm going to have your buddy Prescott here man the winch. It's hooked up to the spare harness, and you're going to attach the spare harness to your belt and take it down with you, and he's just going to let the line play until you stop. When you have someone strapped into the harness and you need it raised back up, you give it one hard tug, like *on belay.* He can test to make sure there's weight on the winch, and then raise it up. If he tests, and there's no weight, we'll just presume the wind or something else caused the tug, so he won't bring it up prematurely."

The fire chief grabbed a pulley attached to my belt and explained: "This here is an ascender pulley. I hooked it onto your safety, but it's not foolproof. We use it to haul gear up, mostly light loads, that's all we had. So just be aware that it's there if you need it, but try not to depend on it to come back up. Wait and come up on the winch line if you can. Also, I been thinking about this: with you going down there in the dark, it's going to be hard to see. Every time you come to a ledge, you're going to wonder if you're at the right one. So, you may need to flip your headlamp on just for a second and take a look. Since you'll be to one side of the main opening of the cave, I don't think there's any way they can see you but it's hard to tell how far a flash of light will travel. The moon set about a half-hour ago, so we got no moonlight at all. They might be able to make out a glimpse of light bouncing off the canyon walls without seeing it directly, and it could alert them. So if you need to use your light, make sure you direct your face into a recess, and don't turn outward or to either side. That way, the light won't bounce around."

I stood on the lip of the canyon while Salas briefed his small crew, including Prescott. As he spoke to them, I looked across the black robe of the night sky and saw the Milky Way as a wide highway of crystal-like stars, a glistening path that the Puebloan people called the Spirit Trail or the Ghost Road. Momma Anna had taught me that this ribbon of far-off lights was made up of the campfires of the spirits—who had left them burning to guide and comfort those of us ready to pass beyond the ridge.

Prescott finished his quick briefing, and as I was turning around to begin backing down the face of the cliff, Rico ran up to me and said, "Grandfather told me to tell you this: "He saw you fly from the nest of the *kòki'ína.*"

"What does *kòki'ína* mean?"

"I'm not sure. He still talks sometimes in the old language."

I leaned back into the harness, out over the cliff face, as José Salas held my belay line taut. I gave one good tug and said softly, "On belay." And then I began to walk backwards down the cliff face, the black embrace of night soon enveloping the small group above me until I could no longer see or hear them, and I was alone in the darkness with the vast, shadowy depths of the canyon below me, suspended beneath the Ghost Road by a thin rope.

Rico had estimated that the cave ruin, which was built into a natural cavity in the canyon wall, was less than a hundred feet down. It was only approachable by either climbing or descending the face of the cliff—except for the ventilation tunnel leading onto a narrow ledge to the north—but one still had to climb or descend to that, and also be small enough to go through it. We had set up so that I would rappel to the northern limit of the ledge so that I could approach the back entrance to the cavern with stealth. I had descended about eighty feet or so when I came to a fat twisted juniper that had rooted itself atop a protruding slab of rock, its arms stunted and thick, its roots gnarled, misshapen, and enlarged by its constant quest for water in this unlikely and inhospitable crag where it had somehow survived. I had to lower myself beyond this out-jutting lip with minimal contact with the cliff face. I perched one boot on the very top rim of the overhang and then reached with the other leg as far down as I could and heard and felt something crunch beneath the toe of my lower boot as it found purchase on flat stone. I lowered myself toward the rock base under the overhang and found myself balancing on the edge of what felt like a massive thicket. I reached up and flicked on my headlamp for just an instant so that I could see into the recess, and I quickly took in the beauty of an intricate construction. Sticks as much as three feet long and up to an inch thick had been interlaced carefully into a foundation at least five feet across and perhaps two feet high. Within it, smaller branches entwined to create an immense basket, and within this, there was yet another layer—a delicately woven inner lining made of fine twigs, pine needles, bits of fur, and even bones. Though the overhang created a ceiling no more than a few feet high above it, the nest-structure itself was so large that if I got on my knees, I could have crawled into it and had room to curl up in its center. It might have been an eagle's nest, or even a large hawk's. But the telltale signs that it belonged to one particular species of bird came from the décor, and these had sparkled back at me when I toggled the light quickly on and off. The female winged-one who had finished this dwelling had not only possessed a natural talent for engineering, but also an eye for beauty. She had decorated it with hundreds of bits of sparkling mica; and collecting shiny things was the purvey of this particular flier and its smaller relative who lived in the east. This was the home of a raven.

I pushed away from the mantle with the nest and continued to rappel down the cliff face. Within a few minutes, I reached another out-jutting section of flat stone. I rested both boots on the floor of this ledge and quickly toggled my headlamp. This was it. A narrow rim of rock made a path that widened as it went southward along the face of the canyon wall. Miraculously, another juniper had taken root and flourished here where the stone lip caught rain runoff and the morning sun warmed the backing wall. I looked for a place to tie off and chose a sturdy branch of the tree. I gave two tugs, waiting a second in between them. *Off belay.* I hooked my carabiner around the branch and two lifelines extended upward from it into the dark—one was the rope that I had used to lower myself down, and the other, the line from the winch with the spare climbing harness attached. I unscrewed the carabiner on the safety line, removed it from the rappel rope, and hooked the knotted line to my belt to take with me in case I needed it to secure myself to something or get around an obstacle on the ledge. But I removed every other piece of dangling gear from my harness. I didn't want to make a sound when I made my way into the cave, and besides, all that stuff added extra girth at my waist. When Rico had said the tunnel was small and that I *might* be able to make it through it, he probably wasn't considering that I would be wearing a big cumbersome belt with tons of stuff attached.

I felt my way down the widening shelf until it dead-ended at a round shoulder of rock. The night was so dark that I did not see the opening Rico had told me about. I stared for a minute or so, then ran my hands down the wall of stone in front of me until I felt an inlet near the base, against the edge of the canyon wall, and I stooped to run my fingers around the edges. This was the tunnel that led into the cave, and as the young man had said, it was, indeed, small and narrow. I lowered myself into a prone position and began to maneuver my way into the slot, belly-scooting with my arms doubled tightly on either side and my boots toe-walking behind me, inching forward little by little. My mid-section ached from the bruises, and my shins seared with pain from rubbing against the stone floor of this tiny tunnel. As soon as I had most of my body in the chute, I could feel warmth ahead of me and see light, but my belt harness snagged on the stone wall. I tried repeatedly to free myself. Using all the pressure my feet and hands together could create, I still couldn't move forward. I wiggled backward an inch or two, but the harness remained snared. I began to panic, feeling like there was almost no room for my lungs to expand when I breathed. Then I thought to twist onto my left side, and when I did, I felt the belt lift off its catch, and I was able to edge forward on my side, giving relief to my abdomen and the front of my legs. But I could not maneuver enough in this position, so again, I had to roll onto my tortured tummy so that I could use my feet and hands to push and pull. As I wormed forward, I smelled wood smoke, and just as I felt fresh, cold air enter my nostrils, I heard distant voices.

I emerged from the air shaft, which no doubt had been created by years of drainage when water trapped in the back of the cave found its way deep into the mountain and out onto the ledge where it fed the juniper that now held my lifeline, and perhaps that of Adoria Abasolo as well. The rear part of the cave was low-ceilinged and dark, while light from a flickering fire danced on the massive walls of the main chamber before me. I could not yet see the fire itself, because the cavity was large, and the ancient ones had built a wall of adobe bricks, now crumbled and half-decomposed, but still blocking much of this hindmost, compressed area. I surmised that the wall had been built so that this space could be used for food storage. Since it was barely tall enough for me to crawl in, it could not have been used for much else, especially not for sleeping, due to the draft caused by the opening I had just come through. I planned to crawl forward and examine more of the cave, but my pain from tunneling through the air chute was so severe that I stopped, rolled onto my bottom and sat as much as I could, head bent over, and knees folded. I delved a hand into my pocket and found the little cloth pouch that Tecolote had made for me and pressed it to my nose. I could not smell the fragrance any more. Had I used all its medicine up already? I managed to untie the bit of twine around the cloth. Inside the square of fabric was a gooey gob with bits of texture, as if dried herbs had been rolled into a marble-sized ball of soft cheese, or butter, or even grease. I sniffed this. It smelled acrid, no longer exuding the healing aroma. On impulse, I popped it in my mouth and had just swallowed it whole when I felt something nudge my right foot. A shiver ran through me. *What creature was huddling back here in the depths of this cave?* Again, I felt something press against my foot and then recede. I stopped breathing, my senses heightening, my pupils widening. I could not yet see the high opening at the cave's front that both Prescott and Rico had described, which was likely where the firelight was coming from. I could hear faint voices drifting along the current of air, but they were so muted that I could not tell whether they were male or female, much less what they were saying. I determined from all this that the mouth of the cave was some distance afar, and that was where the fire and the people who were talking were. I took my headlamp off of my forehead and held it in one hand, shielding it on the sides with the other, and aimed the light toward the farthest reaches at the back of the cave while I watched for it to illuminate the area directly in front of me. I toggled the switch as rapidly as I could. In the fast flash, I saw the source of contact I had felt through my boot. Susan Lacy lay bound, gagged, and curled into a fetal position on her side right at my feet.

I maneuvered onto my hands and knees and carefully pulled at the duct tape over Lacy's mouth. When I peeled it back, she frantically whispered, "Momma!"

I located the knife in my cargo pocket and began working on the tape around her wrists. "Where is she?"

"They are going to throw her into the canyon! They're just waiting for daylight so they can see well enough to make sure that she's dead!"

By now, I had begun sawing away at the layers of duct tape at Lacy's ankles. "We need to get you out of here. You'll have to go out the way I came in."

"I'm not leaving without Momma. She's hurt. They've had her taped up for over a week, they haven't been giving her much food or water. She broke her ankle yesterday when they were moving us up here from the mines, after those people found her car. She can't walk. She's in pain, dehydrated; they've been starving her. She's really weak."

Leaving Lacy's side for a moment, I crawled forward and took cover behind a section of the low, crumbling adobe wall. I still could not see the cave's opening. I made my way through a downed section of rubble and forward, keeping myself to the side wall of the passage. The ceiling here was higher, and a slight turn in its layout obscured the view of the outer chamber and the large main opening. I edged along the rock wall until I could see around a corner created by a massive shoulder of stone. The main chamber of this natural structure remained dark in spite of the flickering firelight, which failed to illuminate it, in part because the fire had been built at the very edge of the cliff at the mouth, rather than in the center of the main cavity. I could see the large opening well, though, and it was indeed tall enough that a man could stand easily in it. But the recess was shallow, not more than six feet deep before it took the turn and the ceiling dropped dramatically toward the rear of the cavern, from where I had just come. The cave's window onto the canyon was a perfect arch, and the floor was flattest at the very edge of the cliff. On one side of the fire, Kyle Lindstrom sat cross-legged, poking at the burning logs with a stick. On the other, Uma Lindstrom reclined with her left side toward the crackling embers, leaning back on her elbows, legs outstretched, her boots resting on something placed treacherously close to the edge of the cave mouth. Uma's footrest was Adoria Abasolo, huddled in a heap, bound and gagged as Lacy had been, curled on her side. "Once the sun is up, we'll get that tape off of her and throw her in first," Uma said, nudging with her boot, causing her captive's body to wobble precariously. "She's not going to give us any trouble, she's almost gone as it is. But the other one, if we try to take the tape off of her without knocking her out, she's strong enough to fight. We're going to have to hit her over the head first. No one will be able to tell because she's going to be all banged up when they find her anyway."

Kyle said, "Okay, but let's keep her conscious long enough so she can watch when her precious mommy takes a leap into the beyond, like she was supposed to do. That's what they all agreed! Our mother kept the pact. Now it's time for her to keep her part of the bargain. Then we'll take care of little Susie next."

Uma spoke again, "We want to make it look like mother and daughter jumped together."

"But how do we arrange to have them discovered? I don't want to make an anonymous call or anything like that. I'm worried they might be onto us, as it is. They nearly caught us back in the mine with this one when that big crew came through there and found her car. We should have brought her up here first thing, instead of waiting until we found the daughter."

Uma argued, "I didn't think they'd find the car with the Pueblo closed because no one could use that road. We would have been okay if that hadn't happened. Besides, it's too hard getting in and out of this cave, we couldn't have come and gone from here while we were still looking for the daughter."

I turned and edged my way back to Susan Lacy. "How are you? Are you okay?"

"I don't think so. I thought my leg was just numb, but now, I don't know. I think something's wrong with my right knee."

"Do you think you can put weight on it?"

"I don't know."

"Let me see you kneel."

Susan Lacy tried her best to put her weight on all fours, but when she did, she made a small cry.

At this, the murmur of voices from the main chamber stopped.

I grabbed Lacy's hips and helped her roll gently onto her side. We both waited, hushed. I could hear my own breath, my pulse at my temples.

A large *snap* broke the silence as a pocket of resin in one of the burning logs exploded, and then the twins resumed talking again, their voices growing louder as their disagreement grew more heated, alongside the fire.

I tried to think of a strategy. I had two injured hostages, and two kidnappers poised and ready to kill. If I pulled my gun and came from behind to confront them, I knew Uma would only need to press lightly to tip Adoria Abasolo over the edge and into the ravine below. I tried to calculate any way these two could be contained without someone dying. If I tried to lure them into the rear of the cave, I was sure their first response would be to dispose of Abasolo. If I tried to hold them at gunpoint, they could threaten to topple Adoria and turn the tables on me. If I shot Uma, even in an extremity, she would push Abasolo over the edge. Even if I shot her with deadly force, which I was loathe to do, she might accidentally do the same. If I shot Kyle to disable him, pushing Abasolo off the cliff still seemed like Uma's most likely response. I ran through scenarios in which I could possibly distract and separate them, but these all involved me and Lacy being trapped in the rear of the cave with no control over what happened at the entrance. There was nothing for it but for me to go in from the front.

I worked at my safety line until I lengthened it several feet, reconfiguring several redundant knots. I encircled Lacy's tiny waist with rope and ran it through the carabiner so that if it slipped, it would still catch under her arms. I took lead as we worked our way out of the tunnel and—knowing this time about the stone snag at approximately halfway through—I rolled to my side and managed to get through without incident. Lacy was smaller than me, so she didn't require this extra maneuver. Once I emerged and stood upright, I helped her get to her feet, but her right leg buckled. "I can't," she whispered. "I don't know what's wrong, but I can't stand on that leg."

The ledge wasn't wide enough for me to assist her, so I edged ahead and she half-crawled behind me, still tied to my belt via the safety line, dragging her injured leg. When we got to the juniper, I unhooked the spare harness. Susan had to lie on her back so I could get the leg supports on and then I cinched the belt tight once she sat up. "Tell them to send the litter down and be ready to bring your mother up."

"How are you going to get Momma out of there? They've got her right on the edge; they're just waiting for the sun to come up."

I looked around and saw that the darkness I had arrived in had begun to relent. Black night was fading to deep indigo blue, and daybreak was imminent. The east-facing cliff wall was hidden in obscuring shadow now, but in less than fifteen minutes, the sun would emerge over the far rim. I looked above me at the shelf where the raven's nest lay, and I looked to my left where the mouth of the cave would receive the first rays of morning light. "I'm going to fly," I said. And I gave the winch line a big, hard tug. In a matter of seconds, Susan Lacy began to lift and then to rise as Prescott ran the lift winch from above.

44: INTO THE MYSTIC

I calculated the distance between where I stood and the mouth of the cave. Once again, I reconfigured my safety line, undoing half the redundant knots and playing out the line until the triple cord was one solo length of about twenty-five feet. I kept one end of this hooked to my harness and then wound the rope repeatedly around me until I reached the other end and hooked that to the harness, too, along with the items I had removed from the belt before going through the tunnel. Then I tugged once hard on the belay rope: *On belay.* I worked my way up the rock face until I reached the raven's nest, then around one side of it to where I could reach the thick roots of the juniper that lived above it. I unwound the safety line from my waist until I had unfurled the entire length and it dangled below me in a loop again—one end of it hooked to my belt, and the other in my hand. I looped the free end of the rope through the ascender pulley, which I attached with my heaviest carabiner around the juniper root. I added a safety to the carabiner as well, by tying it to the root with a nylon strap for extra security, looping it over the root a few times, double-knotting it, and also passing the strap through the opening of the carabiner so that any resistance or freezing of the pulley would cause the strap above it to tighten its grip on the juniper root. As I worked at all this, the air around me grew softer and lighter with the promise of dawn. I could almost make out the interior of the nest. The rock face in front of me began to take shape. I drew in a breath and let it out in a whispered prayer: *Spirit, let me fly.* I tugged on the belay rope, waited a second, tugged again, let another second pass, and then tugged a third time: *Give me rope.* And then, I edged around to the right side of the roof of the *kòki'ína*'s nest and, doubling my legs up as springs, I pushed away from it with all my might.

And I flew...

At first, I swung wide away from the raven's nest even farther from the mouth of the cave than the north edge of the ledge, and I jackknifed my body, pulling back into the lift as my belay line grew longer, just as a child pulls back hard to gain momentum on a swing. When I reached the farthest point away on my pendulum ride, I pushed my chest forward, extended my legs into a straight line behind me with toes pointed, and I opened my arms as wide as I could. As I soared toward the cave opening, searing sunlight burst above the clifftop on the other side and flooded the rock walls around me with golden light. For an instant, I felt free, weightless, unbounded, and exhilarated, and just as I reached the cave opening, dazzling sparks—hundreds of tiny lights—nearly blinded me, as dozens and dozens of shapes on the cave walls shimmered in the sun's first precisely-directed rays, revealing the ravens carved with rough rock chisels and decorated with painstakingly applied flecks of mica and soot and tar paint. When my rappel line jerked at its zenith, a weight struck me in the middle of my body so hard that it took my breath away. Pain shot through me from the assault on my ribs and my bruised midsection, and I began to choke as if something had risen up from within me and was blocking my air pipe. Again, the rope seized and I dropped and swung wildly, now yards below the lip of the cave opening, the heavy weight upon me, threatening to break the line.

For an instant, I felt like I might pass out, and time seemed to stop as if I were suspended between the two possibilities of consciousness and escape. I felt a searing heat in my throat and I swallowed, after which came immediate relief, as if the lardy lump of *cura* had been lodged in my gullet all this time and had now suddenly melted and infused me with strength. I realized that Adoria Abasolo was clinging to me with both arms, half-tangled in both my lead and rappel lines and flailing one leg wildly. The rope lunged erratically back and forth as we swung, and I looked up and saw the faces of Kyle and Uma watching, their mouths open in disbelief as we passed out of their view, away from the mouth of the cave and back again toward the other end of the arc. I realized that my prayer had somehow been answered and my flight had put me right at the mouth of the cave at the exact moment they had pushed the poet off the ledge. "Shhhh," I said to Abasolo. "Hold on."

As I held tight to my belay line with my right hand, I managed to get hold of the safety with my left. At the top of the arc I yanked hard on the safety, and touched my boots to the lip of the ledge base of the *kòki'ína*'s nest, drawing line as fast as I could through the pulley to tighten it and hold us in place. A large black raven huddled in the center of the structure, it's head twisting rapidly on top of its neck to view us first from one eye and then the other. The bird did not leave its bed, and it thrust out both wings and began to flap them wildly. My feet slipped, Adoria grasped at me, pulling painfully on my shoulders, but I kept hold of the line and got the tips of my toes to light again on the stone shelf. "Get in here," I told the poet, and the raven stood up and moved off the center of the nest to one side of the ledge, surrendering the space to us. "It's okay. I know that raven. She's here to help. You'll be safe here. Go ahead and crawl in."

Abasolo managed to pull herself under the overhang and then fell backward into the nest and the bird watched all this with great interest, then stepped off the stone shelf and soared silently away, its wings catching a loft that lifted it toward the rising sun. I looked up and saw the litter high above me. A woman dressed all in black wearing a vest emblazoned with big white letters reading *FBI* was suspended alongside it, coming down to help with the rescue. Above her and to the south, a second FBI agent was rappelling down the cliff face, on the opposite side of the mouth of the cave. As soon as the litter reached the nest, I tugged hard once on my belay rope. *On belay.*

Leaning back into the harness, I walked myself down and over to the side, toward the cave entrance. Before I edged around the sidewall where I could be seen, I rested my boots against the stone and reached into the cargo carry pocket on the leg of my pants and pulled out my pistol. I sidestepped carefully, the rappel rope taut, until I could peek around the mouth of the cave. I pointed the gun into the opening. The Lindstrom twins stood on the edge, holding hands, their faces set with a grim determination. They both turned to look at me, and just as the witches who raised them had pledged to do, and as their own mother had no doubt done, they leapt into the beyond…and fell quickly and silently into the canyon below.

45: AFTERSHOCK

I stood over Mountain and looked down at him as he slept on the makeshift operating table in the ranger station where I'd left him hours before. The vet said, "He's been dreaming. He whimpers and his legs tremble and jerk, and he even opened his eyes for an instant, but I don't think he was conscious. This is all good news."

"How long do you think it will be before he wakes up?" I asked.

"I want to keep him lightly sedated for a while longer. He needs the time to heal. If he gets up and starts moving around, he could rip out some of his stitches. But I think your boy is going to make it. His temperature is fine, there's no sign of infection. He's got good pulse and respiration rates, his heartbeat is strong. And the dreaming eye movement and all the twitching in his extremities tell me that everything seems to be working so far. How are you doing? Did they give you something for your pain?"

"Me? Yes, I have some pills." I didn't mention the *curandera's* gift, which had no doubt given me the strength and energy to do what I had done that morning. I took out the bottle of prescribed medication and showed him.

"Don't drive while you're taking those things. And be careful to only take what you need. They can be surprisingly addictive. Take it easy with them."

I smiled. "I haven't taken any for a while. But just the same, I think I need to find a driver, because I have someplace I need to go and I'm too exhausted to drive. Will Mountain be okay if I leave for a couple hours?"

"I'm not going anywhere. I'll be right here with him."

Dominic Gomez drove me in my Jeep to Agua Azuela. I showed him where to park behind the wall of the churchyard. When we got out of the car, two elders from the village approached. I was ready to explain why we had parked there, but before I could speak, the woman held out her hand, reaching for mine.

"I know you are *una amiga de Tecolote.*"

"Yes, I came to see her."

The two villagers looked at one another, the woman still holding my hand in hers. *"Ella esta muerta.* I am so sorry to tell you."

"She's dead? No! When?"

"Ella falleció la noche en que vinieron los cuervos. Sabes, estuviste aquí esa noche."

I looked at Dominic for a translation.

"She passed away the night the ravens came," he said. "They say you know that, because you were here that night."

This time the male elder spoke: "The birds stayed until you came back again so they could tell you. That's why they were in her house."

I was stunned. I couldn't move or speak for several seconds. "But I didn't even get to say good-bye," I cried.

"Come. *En el sanctuario,"* the man said, taking my arm while the woman held onto my hand. They led me around the side of the church and through the front doors. I had been here before—several years ago, on the day I met Tecolote—and I remembered the ancient church's cold, thick adobe walls, its narrow nave with the hand-hewn pews lined up in rows along one side, and the garishly painted hand-carved wooden *santos,* depicting the saints and the savior just as folk artists of the fifteen-hundreds might have done. They shepherded me to a pew, and I noticed that others were gathered toward the front of the church, talking quietly.

I said, "Is she...? I want to see her."

The old gentleman gave me a sad smile. "I'm afraid you are too late. The undertaker just left."

Over the next hour, one after another of the villagers came to speak with me, and Dominic continued to serve as my translator, since nearly every one of them found English a challenge. One man told me that his father had been delivered by Esperanza, who had served as the village midwife at the time, and that his father was now 106 years old. When I voiced my incredulity about this, he ushered me forward to a thick book, a wood-and-leather-bound handwritten register of births, baptisms and deaths. He showed me the date his father had been born, and then introduced me to his papa, a stooped, leathery old man, who merely nodded and gave me a toothless smile.

"But that would mean Tecolote was well over one hundred years old," I said to the son. "Do you have a record of when she was born?"

The villagers shook their heads. "She was here before any of us can remember," one woman said. "She has always been here. Agua Azuela will never be the same now that she has chosen to leave us."

☽

News travels fast in tiny mountain towns like Peñasco. When we returned from Agua Azuela, Gomez and I discovered that Father Anthony, Brother Tobias, and several of the monks from the Mountain Mission had come to the ranger station when they learned that their neighbor and patron Adoria Abasolo had been found. And while the poet and her daughter had been rushed to a hospital in Albuquerque for treatment for exposure, dehydration and injuries, the brothers had brought big vats of soup and loaves of brown bread with cheese and soft butter from their own cows' milk, and they served a hot and hearty morning meal to all.

Not partaking nor present were the FBI, who—once they had failed to find the kidnappers in the mines and broken their radio silence—had redirected their tactical team to the cliff edge above the cave and had taken charge of the final minutes of the incident, helping with the hoisting of Susan Lacy and of Abasolo in the litter, and finally, of me. Then they had moved on to execute a recovery operation for the bodies of the twins.

Other than the FBI and the SAR team, the rest of the members of the crew who had gone to the mines had come to the ranger station for a mission debriefing. And so, the brothers' feast was delivered to a large crowd, including those who had remained at the station, the fire department volunteers, the members of Picuris and Tanoah Pueblo who had been a part of the adventure, sheriff's deputies, and the BLM gang, as well as a few locals who had stopped in to see what was going on and stayed for a free meal.

I was glad to have some nourishment, and I sat in a chair beside my wolf companion and consumed three bowls of the soup and at least a half a loaf of the bread, slathered with the delicious sweet butter and topped with slices of salty white cheese. Father Anthony came to where I sat, and although I knew it was improper, I was too tired to put my bowl, spoon, and bread aside and stand up. He didn't seem to take offence, and asked if he could join me. My mouth full, I gestured at a nearby chair, where one of the wolf watchers had taken leave of his post to go eat while I was there with Mountain.

"I wanted to see how you are doing," the abbot said.

"I'll be better when my wolf wakes up and we can go home," I said, swallowing the last bite of my breakfast. "I haven't been home in days. I just want to go there and sleep in my own bed for hours and hours. Maybe for days."

"I also wanted to apologize. I'm sorry I resisted...I wish I would have..."

I interrupted him. "When someone comes for confession, and they've done something they feel bad about, what do you do?"

"I usually suggest some form of penance. An amend. A good deed. Something like that. And if they need to ask for forgiveness...well, that's what I'm asking you. I hope you can forgive me for..."

I held up my hand. "I have something in mind that you could do that would also benefit someone else who needs to make an amend."

I led Father Anthony to the small group of native Puebloans who had gathered near the door, about to leave. Yohe was adjusting the peyote chief's blanket, while Paul spoke in a soft voice to Rico about something. "I'm sorry to interrupt," I said. "But I wonder if you might give Father Anthony and me a chance to talk with all of you a moment."

Yohe translated to the chief, and the elder Deherrera nodded his agreement.

"Young Federico has told me that he is eager to go home, but he recognizes that he needs to do something to show the tribe that he has learned his lesson. I think that he is looking for a way to do that." I paused.

The Indians all nodded, Rico most enthusiastically. His face lit up and he grinned at me.

"Father Anthony is also looking for a way to do something to offer service. Isn't that right, Father Anthony?"

The abbot raised an eyebrow at me but nodded ever so slightly.

"Then I suggest that Rico serve as a helper to the monastery on weekends for a time, but that you let him come home so he can resume school with his classmates next week when they come back after their holiday break. Father Anthony can send one of the brothers to pick him up on Fridays and he can stay and work at the monastery through the weekend and perhaps you..." I gestured in Paul Deherrera's direction, "could take him home and visit your uncle and your sister on Sunday evenings so he could be back in time to go to school on Monday mornings. If you are willing, perhaps Rico could keep to that schedule until you feel he has done enough penance to make up for his misdeed."

Yohe muttered for what seemed like a small eternity into the peyote chief's ear, Paul Deherrera looked at me and cocked his head slightly, smiling, and then clapped Rico on the back affectionately. All eyes turned to the elder in his blanket, who made a gesture with his palm parallel to the ground, crossing the space in front of him with a swipe of his arm, indicating the deal was good.

I looked at the abbot and he smiled, and Yohe giggled out loud. "White girl make good bargain," she said. Paul and the abbot shook hands and began discussing details, and Federico came up to me and started to give me a big hug.

"Careful!" I held up my hands and pulled away. "I'm hurting pretty bad right now."

"I promise, I'll be careful, Auntie Jamaica," he said. And he tenderly encircled me with his thin brown arms and then put his head against my shoulder. "Thank you," he whispered.

I felt a vibration in my pocket and realized it was Buzz, my Secret Service phone, which I had set on silent before I descended into Picuris Canyon on the rappel rope. I turned away from the group and pulled the device from my pocket. "Agent Wild," I said into it.

"Come outside," Hank's voice said.

"Outside where?"

"Outside the door," he said, and I looked through the glass windows in the front of the ranger station and saw him standing on the walk near the entry. I pressed to end the call and went out the door.

"I'm leaving, but I didn't want to go without saying good-bye," Hank Coronel said to me.

I handed him Buzz. "I guess I won't be needing this anymore."

He took the phone and tucked it into the pocket of his jacket. "Is Mountain going to be all right?"

"He's going to live," I said. "I don't know what it's going to look like, but I'm hoping he's going to recover completely. I'm going to take as much time off as I need, until we've both fully recuperated."

Coronel nodded his head, thinking about this. "Just to update you, I have this to report: Abasolo has a broken ankle, but no other major injuries. But she's very weak, mostly from dehydration, starvation, and exposure. They set the ankle, they're giving her IV fluids and nutrition, and it looks like she's going to be fine."

"And Susan Lacy?"

"Totally torn ACL. She's a little dehydrated, too, will have to have surgery and rehab for the knee, but she's otherwise good. I wanted to thank you, on behalf of *The Bartender.* It was requested specifically that I come tell you that in person. And *The Bartender* will be in touch with you directly soon."

I made a little saluting gesture. "Happy to serve," I said. "But I hope 'in touch' just means a thank you note or a box of chocolates or something. No offense, but I don't want to do this kind of thing again."

He looked at me for a long minute and said, "I enjoyed working with you, Jamaica Wild."

☾

It was a few hours later before it was quiet enough around the ranger station for me to go back to the break room and lie down on one of the cots. I was exhausted and eager for sleep. But before I allowed myself to rest, I had a call I had to make.

Kerry answered on the first ring. "Is Mountain going to be okay? Are you okay?"

I told him the story of the past several days, and he murmured sympathetic and comforting comments and asked a few questions as I unfolded the barest details. When I finished the brief recap he said, "Where are you now?"

"I'm at the ranger station in Peñasco. I'm not leaving Mountain again. I'm here until he wakes up, and then we're both going home together. I'm going to take as much time off as I need to until he's all better."

There was silence on the other end of the line.

"Kerry? Are you still there?"

"I'm going to lose you any minute now," he said. "You know how cell phone coverage is around here."

I sat bolt upright and cried out with pain as my abdominals exacted the price. I felt my arms tingle, the hair stand up at my temples and on the back of my neck. "Where are you?"

"A little over a half hour away. I'm glad you called when you did or it might have taken a lot longer because I was headed straight for Taos. But you were just in time. I'm about to turn onto the High Road down by Chimayo," he said.

"Really?" I swiveled my legs over the side of the cot so my feet were on the floor. I wasn't about to go to sleep now.

"Your message said you needed me but couldn't talk until morning. I got on a plane, got a rental car in Albuquerque. I'll be there before you know it."

46: FEMININE RISING

In the days that followed, Mountain and I did a lot of healing and a lot of sleeping, though my sleep was often troubled by dreams—and Mountain's was, too, evidenced by frequent whimpering and shaking in his sleep. Together with Kerry, we spent some time every day walking—limited distances at first, and then ever increasing ones. I enjoyed variations of Kerry's two signature dishes: Ranger Stew, and flapjacks with butter and warm maple syrup. And to entice the wolf to eat and gain strength, he made a rich broth from bison bones with plenty of meaty bits floating in it, and served it warm. Kerry did everything for us: kept toasty fires going in the woodstove, changed Mountain's dressings and gave him his antibiotics, tended the scrapes on my shins and calves, interpreted hilarious Rorschach meanings from the ever-changing patterns of bruising on my abdomen while tracing their outlines with his finger, massaged my shoulders, brought me books from the library and even read some of them aloud to me, told me stories of his recent adventures in the northwest, and when he went into town for groceries, he brought home newspapers to keep me up to date.

The FBI was given credit in the media for rescuing the poet laureate and her daughter, and I was relieved that I was never named personally in relation to the matter. Nor was the Secret Service. When the citizens of Peñasco learned that their town had been the focus of such a sensational crime, and the faces of the twins appeared in the papers and on television, a quartet of locals came forward with information that answered one of the unsolved questions in the case. Apparently the two couples had gone line dancing in Taos the night before the borrowed Blazer exploded. Late getting back to their village on the High Road, they spotted the red-coated couple tinkering with a car in the otherwise-empty parking lot of the Ranger Station. One of them had suggested they pull over to see if help was needed, but he was overruled by the others' desire to get home and get to bed before dawn. This aligned with the fire inspector's report that a gas-soaked rag had been stuffed into a crevice in the engine of Gomez's Blazer; the authorities surmised that the twins had done the deed to try to cover their tracks after asking Dominic so many questions about the local caves.

Abasolo, hounded by the press, finally agreed to do one exclusive interview, for a weekly in-depth television news show. It was filmed at a medical facility where the poet was recovering, and she appeared wearing a cast on her broken ankle and still notably weak from her ordeal. The details of this dialogue were recounted throughout the press for the next few days, and I read about it in the paper. In her candid conversation with the female journalist, the poet explained that she had come to this country at the tender age of sixteen to escape an abusive father. Soon after arriving and beginning classes at the university in Los Angeles, she met and fell in love with Videl Quintana, who insisted that she erase her personal history to liberate herself from her past, and taught her how to do so. When she later became pregnant, she had experienced enough of Quintana and his cult to know that she could not bring a child into that environment, and yet, she had no skills or economic power to raise the child herself. So, using what she had been taught, she once again erased her personal history so that Quintana could not find her, and she became Adoria Abasolo. Though it pained her, she did what she felt was best for the baby in giving her up for adoption, and then pursued an education so that she could live a better life and give something meaningful to the world. She said that, after decades of using the name Abasolo, she was going to keep it for as long as she lived, that it had become who she was. The fortune she was set to inherit from Quintana's estate would form a new foundation with the goal of educating, empowering, and supporting women to have better lives and serve larger roles in the world. Her daughter, Susan Lacy, was poised to become the managing director of the foundation, and together, they intended to do great things for women in the United States and around the world. And they had reached out to Lacy's half-sister, Quintana's other daughter Nona Dodd, and invited her to share in this endeavor. The poet laureate was not yet well enough at the time, (and I guessed the controversy over her past was great enough), that she did not travel to Washington to perform at the inauguration of her longtime friend, the first woman president of the United States.

The news media quickly moved on to that event—novel because not only was a female taking leadership in the White House for the first time, but a Latina, at that—and also for the first time, there would be no first spouse. After the initial sensation of Abasolo's interview, and a series of blips and blurbs for another week or so, the story of the poet's bizarre past and the events of the kidnapping rapidly began to fade in the media as more newsworthy events emerged in the country and around the world.

As for me, it was only one day after the inauguration when something happened that drew me once more into the matter. Kerry and I were just returning from walking Mountain on a long lead down the road. The idea was to give the wolf just enough exercise so he would continue to strengthen without taxing him too much as he recuperated. In fact, the lead was hardly necessary. Mountain limped and dawdled and seemed years older than he had been just weeks before, his energy low, his curiosity diminished, and his pain from the wounds still obvious. I was grateful he was alive, and I held out hope, but I feared my beloved Mountain would never be the same again.

As we approached my cabin, we saw an unmarked black Chevy Tahoe with dark-tinted windows parked in the drive. My heart fell in my chest. "Oh, no," I said, "not again."

A man walked toward me with a large envelope. "Miss Jamaica Wild?"

"Yes."

"I have a delivery for you. I'll need you to sign for it."

I used my pocket knife as an opener. Inside the thick outer envelope was a smaller one embossed with the seal of the President of the United States. I opened it and unfolded the delicate sheet of parchment-like paper within and stared at the message with disbelief. It read:

Dear Miss Wild,

I am happy to inform you that on the date listed below, you will be honored as the recipient of the National Intelligence Distinguished Service Medal. I will personally be presenting this award to you, however the ceremony will not be made public, and the guest list is restricted to members of the intelligence community and a select few others. You will be receiving more specifics shortly, but I wanted to be the one to tell you about the award and to send you this quick note to thank you personally. Strong women are the pillars of our country and it is my honor to know and to bestow this medal upon one of our nation's most courageous and dedicated heroes.

Sincerely, and with everlasting appreciation,
President Maria Clarisa Vargas

☽

Tecolote came to me in a dream that night. I heard a knock at the door, and before I could open it, the door flew back, banging against the wall behind it. The *curandera* stood on my front porch. "Aren't you going to invite me in? And perhaps you can offer me a cup of tea?"

We sat at my kitchen table over mugs of steaming *poléo* as if the events of the previous days had never occurred. "I came to wake you up again," the *bruja* said. "I am always trying to wake you up. You are not supposed to be the one who is a dreamer. You are a doer. You *do* things. It is I who am the dreamer now."

"I don't want you to be gone, Tecolote. I don't think I can bear it."

"Mirasol, this world is changing. It is making itself over. There is no longer a desire for the work I do. Even *los indios* are finding they cannot keep the old ways in this new world. *Esa magia está muriendo*—that magic is dying. It is the same for the wild things. Their way of life, the gifts they bring, this now is being squeezed away."

"But I don't want..." I was suddenly standing alone outside under the stars, looking over a vast, glistening blue-black landscape of rivers and canyons. Tecolote's voice was a loud whisper inside my head.

"Hush now, *Mirasol.* I told you I came to wake you up. You have been in a dream, but it is not you who has been dreaming. When you wake up this time, *debes hacer una elección.* You must choose."

"Choose what?"

"You can choose to wake up before the beginning of when *esos soñadores*—those dreamers—got ahold of you. Perhaps one minute or so before *ese hombre federal* breaks your door to wake you. If that is your choice, then this all will never have happened."

"And you will still be here? You'll still be alive?"

"No, *mi querida.*"

I felt a cold blast of wind rush past my body, chilling my arms and shoulders, my back, my legs.

"I am dreaming my own dream," the whispered voice said. "I am like the wind now. You will feel me, but I am no longer the same."

"What will happen to the poet and her daughter?" A host of stars began flickering all at once, as if the power that fed them was being interrupted and reconnected at a rapid rate.

"The dreamers have ahold of them too," Esperanza whispered, her voice now so soft I could barely hear it. *"La mujer poeta* became a dreamer to find what she was seeking. Everyone makes choices. If you go in that dream again, then you will save them; your choice will already be made. But if you choose to go again into the dream, you must choose to do it for you, not for them. That is what I came to tell you. Don't try to make someone else happy. You are always doing good things for others because you are a doer. *Pero* this time, think about what you want. Make yourself happy, *en esto y en todo*—in this, and in everything."

I did think about this, and the stars stopped pulsing and became brighter. *If I woke before all this happened, Kerry would still be in the northwest, gone back to his job there after our loving vacation together.* I felt aching loneliness, and I looked down and saw a large hole right through the center of my body, an empty wound, jagged at the edges. I looked through the hole and saw a deep canyon below me, its walls glowing red as I floated above it.

An echoed voice rang out against the cliff walls: "You can choose…"

My mind would not calm and frantically flashed through recent memories. The events involving the dreamers and the poet had returned Kerry to me…but Mountain and I had paid a terrible price.

"I don't want Mountain to suffer…" I called, hoping Esperanza would hear me.

The *curandera's* voice was so faint I could barely make out what she said. "You will think of a way to keep him safe."

I began to feel so tired, too tired to be aware any longer. I wanted nothing more than to sleep. And dream. As I drifted into slumber, I heard Tecolote whisper one more piece of advice: "If you choose to talk to *tu amigo la planta de peyote,* be sure to ask for something that will make you happy, too. *Los indios son buenos soñadores*—they are good dreamers. Perhaps they can help you."

OUROBOROS: INTRUDER

The door of my cabin crashed back against the wall and the silhouette of a man backlit by moonlight filled the opening. I roused instantly from my dream, rolled off my bed and crouched behind it as I grabbed the shotgun propped against the wall.

"Jamaica Wild?" the man shouted.

I cocked the pump-action with a hard pull, the sound a warning. "I'm a federal agent," I said. "Drop your weapon and put your hands up where I can see them."

The intruder raised his palms above his head, one of them holding an automatic. "Secret Service," he said, "don't shoot! I'll put it down right here." He squatted and I heard the *thunk* of the pistol on the wood floor. He stood again, palms raised. "Ma'am, I'm sorry to startle you. I knocked several times, but there was no answer. If you'll allow me to, I'll show you some identification." He lowered a hand, then raised it holding an ID folder over his shoulder and deftly flipped it open.

"Reach along the wall inside the door and flip that switch," I said.

In the newly illuminated scene, I saw Mountain poised in a low crouch in front of the man. He emitted a low growl.

The man saw him, too.

I said, "Toss the ID." I tipped my chin toward the mattress in front of me.

He flipped it onto my down comforter. I grabbed it and held it up, keeping my eyes on the trespasser. "Agent...Harold Coronel," I read. "What are you doing here?"

"I have orders to escort you to Kirtland Air Force Base. It's a matter of National Security."

"This must be some mistake."

"I assure you, there's no mistake. Could I ask you to put that gun down and call off your dog?"

"He's a wolf. And did you have to kick the door halfway off its jamb?"

"This matter is extremely time-sensitive. I couldn't tell if you were here, or if you were all right. Your dog didn't even bark."

I moved around the bed and went to Mountain, feeling exposed in my jammies. "It's okay, Buddy," I said to the wolf.

Agent Coronel said, "I'll make sure your door is all right while you get dressed and do whatever you need to secure the wolf."

"I'm not leaving him."

"I'm afraid you'll have to in this instance."

"Look, he goes with me."

"There's no place for an animal in the car."

"You'll figure it out," I said. Still clutching the shotgun, I went into my tiny bathroom with the wolf on my heels—and once Mountain and I were inside, I closed the door. Taped to the middle of the mirror was a note written in my own handwriting in red permanent marker. It read:

URGENT!!!
TAKE THIS NOTE, KEEP IT WITH YOU, AND DO THESE THINGS
WHETHER YOU UNDERSTAND THEM OR NOT:

- When you go to the pueblo later this morning, leave Mountain with Momma Anna for a few days—do this for his safety!

- When you talk to the peyote plant, you will have a request to make, but also ask for a way that you and Kerry can be together, and leave extra $$.

- When Roy calls about Lor Talgren, phone Deputy Padilla *right away* and tell him Talgren has a meth lab in the vat room of his winery (he does, so just do it). You'll be safe if you do this. You won't if you don't.

- Do NOT water the foxes, they will die if you do!

- Treasure every moment you get with Tecolote

A NOTE TO MY READERS

I celebrate my love for the WILD West in this series. I love to write, to explore, to adventure, to research, and to discover. I spend all my free time hiking mountains, deserts, and canyons, searching out new sources of wonder and amazement, new places of magic and enchantment to write about. I have traveled all over the globe, but I am most at home right here in the West—in the wild places, on the rivers, the cliff ledges and high mesas, in the ruins of the ancient ones, among the art panels left by the long-ago natives of this land. I love to visit my friends and adopted family at the pueblos. And I am hurrying to write about the west and the wild places as fast as I can, because these are vanishing, as are the cultural riches of my native family, who are slowly and not-so-subtly being modernized by the world that presses in around them.

So, my WILD Mystery Series is a love song to the WILD and to the West and to all the beings of all kinds who inhabit it now but may not for long . . . or may (if we are lucky) inhabit it forever.

I am lucky enough to share my life and my journeys with loving companions: a husband, a wolf, and a wildcat.

If you enjoyed this book, I hope you will tell your friends and family, and that you will look for my other works in publication. I invite you to visit me in my online home at:

WWW.SANDIAULT.COM

CPSIA information can be obtained
at www.ICGtesting.com
Printed in the USA
LVHW041206171119
637608LV00003B/94